say goodbye

PROLOGUE

'In the U.S., the dangerous spiders include the Widows and the Recluse Spiders.'

FROM *Spiders and Their Kin*, BY HERBERT W. AND LORNA R. LEVI,

A GOLDEN GUIDE FROM ST. MARTIN'S PRESS, 2002

He was moaning, a guttural sound in the back of his throat as his fingers tightened their grip in her hair. She curled her lips over her teeth, applying more pressure. His hips surged and he started with the usual stream of nonsense boys liked to murmur during a time like this:

'Sweet Jesus . . . oh God. Don't stop. You're so beautiful. OhmyGod, ohmyGod. You are the best! Oh, Ginny, Ginny, Ginny. Sweet Ginny . . .'

She wondered if he could hear himself speak, if he had any idea of what he said. That sometimes he compared her to saints. That he told her she was gorgeous, beautiful, a dark Georgian rose. That once, he'd even told her he loved her.

A guy would say anything at a time like this.

The gearshift was digging into her hip, starting to hurt. She moved her right hand to the top of his jeans and worked them lower on his thighs. Another small shift here, the boy now made a gurgling sound as if he were dying.

'Holy mother of God! Jesus, Ginny. Beautiful, beautiful, Ginny. Sweet . . . mother . . . pretty . . . lovely . . . are killing me! You are killing me! YOU ARE KILLING ME!'

Oh, for heaven's sake, she thought, *get on with it.* A bit

I

more maneuvering, a bit more pressure applied by her mouth, followed by a bit more pressure applied by her hand . . .

Tommy was a panting, happy boy.

And little Ginny would finally get a treat.

She retreated to the other side of the truck, turning her head slightly so he wouldn't see her wipe her mouth with the back of her hand. Bottle of Jim Beam was where they'd left it, rolling on the floor beneath her feet. She picked it up, took a swig, passed it to Tommy.

He still had his pants tangled around his legs and a dazed look on his captain-of-the-varsity-football-team face.

'Shit, Ginny, now you *are* trying to kill me.'

She laughed, took another swig herself, so big her eyes burned, and she told herself it was the whiskey and nothing else.

Tommy went to work on his clothing. Pulled up tighty-whities first, followed by his jeans, then buckled his belt. He did it matter-of-factly, with none of the awkwardness girls generally felt. It's why Ginny preferred front-seat blow jobs to backseat sex. Sex took longer and involved more logistics. Blow jobs, on the other hand, kept things simple and, with most boys, quick.

Tommy wanted the sour mash now. She handed him the bottle. Watched his Adam's apple bob above the collar of his letterman's jacket as he drank. He dragged his hand over his mouth, then handed the bottle back to her.

'Sex and whiskey. Doesn't get any better than this!' he said with a grin.

'Not bad for a Tuesday night,' she granted.

He reached over, stealing his hand beneath her shirt, cupping her breast. His fingers found her left nipple, squeezing experimentally.

'You're sure . . . ?'

She batted his hand away. 'Can't. Gotta get home. Mama said if I broke curfew one more time, she was locking me out.'

'Your mama? Isn't that the pot calling the kettle black?'

Ginny let that comment pass. ' 'Sides, don't you gotta catch up with your posse? Or maybe swing by *Darlene's*? She probably can't sleep without one last glimpse of Loverboy.'

She started the comment playfully, ended with an edge. Just because you knew your place in the world didn't mean you had to be happy about it.

Beside her, Tommy had grown quiet. He reached over, stroked her cheek with his thumb. It was a strange gesture coming from him. Almost tender.

'I got something for you,' he said abruptly, withdrawing his hand, going to work in his front denim pocket.

Ginny frowned at him. Of course he had something for her. That's how these things worked. White-trash girl fucks the brains out of rich, handsome quarterback, and in return he gives her pretty sparkling gifts. Because all boys had needs, but not all boys could get what they needed from their uptight girlfriends.

Tommy was staring at her. Ginny looked down belatedly at his offered hand and realized with genuine shock that he was holding out his class ring.

'What the hell is that?' she blurted out.

Tommy recoiled, but quickly caught himself. 'I know you're surprised . . .'

'Darlene will carve out your heart with a spoon if she sees me wearing that.'

'Darlene doesn't matter anymore.'

'Since when?'

'Since Saturday night, when I broke up with her.'

Ginny stared at him. 'Why the hell would you do such a stupidass move like that?'

Tommy's face darkened. He clearly hadn't anticipated this reaction, but once again he forged ahead. 'Ginny darlin', I don't think you understand . . .'

'Oh, I understand just fine. Darlene is beautiful. Darlene has pretty clothes and her daddy's money and perfect

3

lipstick, which naturally she doesn't want to smudge going down on her hunky boyfriend.'

'You don't need to put it that way,' Tommy said tightly.

'Put it what way? That precious little Darlene won't swallow? So now you've convinced yourself you're in love with Little Miss White Trash?'

'Don't say that—'

'Say what? The truth? I know who I am. Only one with shit for brains in this truck is you. Now, I wanted a gold necklace and you promised me!'

'So that's it? It's all about the necklace?'

' 'Course it is.'

He studied her, working his jaw. 'You know, Trace tried to warn me about you. He said you had a mean streak, the soul of a snake. I told him he was wrong. You're not your mother, Ginny. You could be . . . you are someone special. At least' – he squared his shoulders – 'to me.'

'*What the fuck is wrong with you!*' She couldn't stand it anymore. She popped open the door, hopped out of the truck. She heard him scrambling to get out the other side, maybe thinking he'd better stop her before she did something stupid.

They were parked off a logging road in the woods, the area deserted, the ground hard and uneven beneath her feet. For one impulsive moment, she wanted to run. She'd just take off, racing down the long blue tunnel spinning out between the tall Georgia pines.

She was young and strong. Girl like her could run a long time. God knows, she'd had the practice.

'Ginny, talk to me.'

Tommy's voice from behind her. Still earnest, but giving her space. Heaven help her, the boy had probably taken a poetry class, or started listening to Sarah McLachlan, or some such shit. Everyone wanted everyone to have depth these days. Didn't they realize that clichés were much easier to manage?

4

She took a deep breath, tilted her head up, stared at the stars. *When life gives you lemons,* she thought, *make lemonade.* The pure absurdity of the thought made her want to laugh, or maybe it was cry. So she did what she did best. She fisted her hands and worked the angles. Despite what people thought, a girl like her couldn't afford to be cheap.

'Well, Tommy,' she announced, 'I gotta be honest: You've taken me by surprise.'

'Well, yeah. Took myself by surprise, too. Wasn't like I *meant* this to happen.'

'This'll hurt you, you know. I wear that ring, kids at school, they'll say some awful things.'

'Let 'em.'

'Four more months, you graduate, you're done. Come on, Tommy, you don't need this shit.'

'Ginny—' he started urgently again.

She placed her finger over his lips. 'I'll take your ring, Tommy.'

'You will?' Hopeful now. Earnest. Goddamn Sarah McLachlan.

'Did you bring the necklace?'

'Well, I did, just in case, but—'

'Gimme the necklace. I'll wear the ring on it, beneath my shirt. It'll be our secret, something just the two of us know, at least until school is out. I don't need a big show to know you care. Already, this moment, what you've managed to do . . .' Her voice was growing edgy again. She forced herself to finish more brightly: 'It means so much that you thought to do this.'

Tommy's face lit up. He dug around in his pocket, finally producing a tiny ziplock bag containing the necklace. He'd probably bought it at Wal-Mart. Fourteen carat: It would turn the skin on her neck green.

Damn, all that for this?

She took the chain, looped it through the band of the ring, gave him a reassuring smile.

5

He grabbed her for a hard kiss. She let him. But then he started fondling her again, obviously intending to cement their new relationship with a rut in the woods.

Christ, she was tired.

With a bit of effort, she pushed him back, having to strain against one hundred and eighty pounds of testosterone. 'Tommy,' she admonished, panting. 'Curfew, remember? Let's not start our new relationship with me grounded.'

He grinned, his color high. 'Yeah, okay, guess not. But Lord, Ginny . . .'

'Yeah, yeah, yeah. Back in the truck, big boy. Let's see how fast you can drive.'

Tommy could drive fast. But they still didn't make it to her house until ten minutes after eleven. Front porch light was on, but nothing moved behind the shades.

With luck, her mother was out and would never know. After the night she'd had, Ginny felt she deserved a break.

Tommy wanted to watch until she was safe inside her house. She assured him that would make it worse, her mom might come out, make a scene. More coaxing. The cost of five valuable minutes, he finally drove off.

Her hero, she thought ironically, and turned toward her home.

It was small and gray, with no excuse for a lawn. Dull outside, even duller inside. But hey, as the saying went, it was home. At least it wasn't a trailer park. See, once Ginny'd had a dad. And he'd been tall and handsome, with this big booming laugh and thick strong arms he'd use to swing her up into the air as he walked through the door after a long day at work.

Her daddy had died one day. Coming home from a dry-walling job, catching his front tires on black ice. Insurance money had paid for the house.

Her mother had turned to other activities to pay for the rest.

Ginny tried the door. It was locked. She shrugged philosophically, headed round the back. It was locked, too. She tried the windows, but already knew they wouldn't budge. Her mom liked to lock up tight. Maybe their neighborhood had been blue collar once, but that had been about ten years and one economic class ago.

Ginny knocked on the door. Rang the doorbell. Not even a shade twitched.

Her mama had done it. Ginny had broken curfew, and her damn mama, who seemed convinced Ginny could do better if she'd just straighten up her act, had locked her out.

Fuck it. She'd go for a walk. Maybe in an hour or two, her mother would decide she'd made her point.

Ginny headed down her dark street, passing tiny home after tiny home. Folks who used to make a living. A lot who didn't anymore.

She'd just hit the intersection with the rural road when the black SUV zipped by. She saw the brake lights flare up, dragon eyes, as the SUV screeched to a halt twenty yards away. A head poked out the driver's side, too dark to see much other than the outline of a baseball cap. A heavy male baritone inquired, 'Need a lift?'

It took Ginny only a moment to decide. The vehicle looked expensive, the voice sounded deep. It appeared that her night was finally looking up.

Ginny realized her mistake five minutes later. After she'd climbed into the throaty SUV, running her hand over the soft, tanned leather. After she'd giggled and told the man, middle-aged, trim, that her car had run out of gas. After, with another giggle, she had suggested he could give her a ride around the block.

He didn't say much. Just took another left, another right, before abruptly pulling behind the giant self-storage warehouse and killing the engine.

Ginny felt the first shiver then. With a total stranger, there was always that initial moment when you were almost afraid. Before you remembered you didn't have to be scared anymore because there wasn't anything some asshole could take that you hadn't already given away.

But then he turned and she found herself staring into a flat, unsmiling face. Hard square jaw, tight lips, eyes oversized pools of unending black.

And then, almost as if he knew how she would react, as if he wanted to savor the moment the expression crossed her face, he slowly pushed up the brim of his baseball cap and showed her his forehead.

Inside the pocket of her denim jacket, Ginny's fingers wrapped tight around Tommy's ring. For she only needed one look at what the man had done to reach several realizations at once: Her mother wouldn't have to worry about curfew anymore. And young, lustful Tommy would never need to be embarrassed in front of his friends.

Because this man was never, ever letting her go home.

Some girls were smart. Some girls were fast. Some girls were strong. Ginny, poor Ginny Jones, had already learned four years ago, when her mother's boyfriend first appeared in her bedroom, that she had only one way of saving herself.

'All right,' she said briskly. 'Let's cut to the chase: Why don't you tell me exactly what you want me to do, and I'll start stripping off clothes.'

ONE

These are the things that no one tells you, that you must experience in order to learn:

It only hurts the first few times. You scream. You scream and you scream and you scream until your throat is raw and your eyes swollen and you taste a curious substance in the back of your throat that is like bile and vomit and tears all rolled into one. You cry for your mother. You beg for God. You don't understand what is happening. You can't believe it is happening.

And yet, it is happening.

And so, bit by bit, you fall silent.

Terror doesn't last forever. It can't. It takes too much energy to sustain. And in truth, terror occurs when you are confronted with the unknown. But once it has happened enough, you have been systematically violated, beaten, cowed, it's not unknown, is it? The same act that once shocked you, hurt you, shamed you with its perversity, becomes the norm. This is your day now. This is the life you lead. This is who you have become.

A specimen in the collection.

TWO

'Spiders are always on the lookout for prey, but predators are also on the lookout for spiders. Clever disguises and quick getaways help keep spiders out of trouble.'

FROM *Spiders and Their Kin*, BY HERBERT W. AND LORNA R. LEVI,

A GOLDEN GUIDE FROM ST. MARTIN'S PRESS, 2002

'We got a problem.'

'No kidding. Widespread production of metham-phetamines, a middle class that keeps falling further and further behind, not to mention all the ruckus over global warming . . .'

'No, no, no. A *real* problem.'

Kimberly sighed. They'd been working this crime scene for three days now. Long enough that she no longer noticed the smell of burning jet fuel and charcoaled bodies. She was cold, dehydrated, and had a stitch in her side. It would take a lot, in her opinion, to qualify as a real problem at this point.

She finished up the last swig of bottled water, then turned away from the tent city that currently comprised command central, and faced her teammate. 'All right, Harold. What's the problem?'

'Uh-uh. Gotta see it to believe it.'

Harold didn't wait for her answer, but set off at a half-jog, leaving Kimberly no choice but to follow. He trotted along the outside of the crime scene perimeter that surrounded what had once been a bucolic green field bordered by thick woodlands. Now half the treetops had been sheared off, while the pasture contained a deep, jagged scar of earth that ended in a blackened fuselage, crumpled John Deere tractor, and twisted right wing.

As crime scenes went, plane crashes were particularly messy. Sprawling in size, contaminated with biohazards, booby-trapped with jagged bits of metal and shattered glass. The kind of scene that threatened to overwhelm even the most seasoned evidence collector. Mid afternoon of day three, Kimberly's team had finally passed the holy-crap-where-to-begin stage and was now cruising into the job-well-done-be-home-tomorrow-night-for-dinner phase of the documenting process. Everyone was popping less Advil, enjoying longer lunch breaks.

None of which explained why Harold was currently leading Kimberly away from command central, the hum of the generator, the bustle of dozens of investigators simultaneously working a scene . . .

Harold continued to lope along a straight line. Fifty yards, a hundred yards. Half a mile down . . .

'Harold, what the hell?'

'Five more minutes. You can do it.'

Harold increased his pace. Kimberly, never one to cry uncle, gritted her teeth and followed. They hit the end of the crime scene perimeter, and Harold turned right into the small grove of trees that had started the whole mess, the taller ones forming jagged white spikes pricking the overcast winter sky.

'Better be good, Harold.'

'Yep.'

'If this is to show me some kind of rare moss or endangered grass species, I will kill you.'

'I don't doubt it.'

Harold dashed and ducked around shattered trees. Bobbed and weaved through the thick underbrush. When he finally stopped, Kimberly nearly ran into his back.

'Look up,' Harold ordered.

Kimberly looked up. 'Ah shit. We have a problem.'

*   *   *

FBI Special Agent Kimberly Quincy was the total package – beautiful, brainy, and pedigreed, right down to a legendary former FBI profiler father whose name was linked to the likes of Douglas and Ressler in Academy halls. She had shoulder-length dusky blond hair, bright blue eyes, and fine patrician features – a gift from her dead mother, who was the source of the second set of rumors that would follow Kimberly for the rest of her career.

At five foot six, with a thin, athletic build, Kimberly was known for her physical endurance, proficiency with firearms, and intense dislike of personal touch. She was not one of those teammates who inspired love at first sight, but she certainly commanded respect.

Now entering her fourth year at the Atlanta Field Office of the FBI, finally assigned to Violent Crimes (VC) and team leader to one of Atlanta's three Evidence Response Teams (ERTs), her career was firmly on track – or at least had been until five months ago. Though that wasn't entirely true, either. She no longer participated in firearms training, but other than that, it was business as usual. After all, today's Bureau considered itself to be an enlightened government organization. All about equity and fairness and gender rights. Or, as the agents liked to quip, it wasn't your father's FBI anymore.

At the moment, Kimberly had larger problems to consider. Starting with the severed leg dangling in a giant rhododendron bush ten feet *outside* their crime scene perimeter.

'How the hell did you even *see* that?' Kimberly asked now, as she and Harold Foster hustled back to command central.

'Birds,' Harold said. 'Kept seeing a flock of them startle from that grove. Which made me think a predator had to be around. Which made me think, what would attract a predator to such an area? And then . . .' He shrugged. 'You know how it goes.'

Kimberly nodded, though being a city girl herself, she didn't really know how it went. Harold, on the other hand, had grown up in a log cabin and used to work for the Forestry Service. He could track a bobcat, skin a deer, and forecast the weather based on the moss patterns on a tree. At six one and one hundred seventy pounds, he resembled a telephone pole more than a lumberjack, but he considered twenty miles a day hike, and when the Atlanta ERTs had worked the Rudolph crime scene – the Atlanta Olympic Park bomber – Harold had made it to the remote campsite an hour ahead of the rest of the crew, which had still been struggling up the densely wooded, forty-five-degree incline.

'You gonna tell Rachel?' Harold was asking now. 'Or do I have to?'

'Oh, I think you should take all the credit.'

'No, no, really, you're the team leader. Besides, she won't hurt you.'

He stressed the last sentence more than he needed to. Kimberly understood what he meant. And of course he was right.

She rubbed her side, and pretended she didn't resent it.

The problem had started on Saturday, when a 727 had taken off from the Charlotte, North Carolina, airport at 6:05 a.m. With three crew members and a belly full of mail, it was due to arrive in Atlanta at 7:20 a.m. Conditions were damp and foggy, with potential for ice.

What exactly had gone wrong was left for the NTSB to sort out. But shortly after 7:15 a.m., during the initial approach to the runway, the 727 had descended, clipped the right wing on the top of a dense grove of trees, and careened into a farmer's field, where it did an aviator's version of a cartwheel, nailing one combine, two trucks, and a tractor, while raining metallic debris down a half-mile-long skid that ended with the fuselage bursting into flame.

By the time emergency vehicles had arrived, the crew members had perished and all that was left was the minor detail of processing a mile-long debris field that involved three human remains, one plane, four pieces of farming equipment, and a blizzard's worth of U.S. mail. The NTSB moved in to manage the scene. And per the 'Memorandum of Understanding' between the NTSB and the FBI, Atlanta's three ERTs were mobilized to assist with evidence collection.

First thing FBI Senior Team Leader Rachel Childs had done was establish the perimeter. Rule of thumb for explosions and airline crashes – perimeter is set up fifty percent of the distance from the scene of the primary explosion to the farthest piece of evidence. So if the final piece of evidence is a hundred yards out, the perimeter is one hundred and fifty yards out. Or, in this case, the perimeter stretched two and a half miles long and half a mile wide. Not your normal the-butler-did-it-in-the-library-with-a-candlestick-leaving-behind-one-chalk-outline crime scene.

And absolutely perfect for the FBI's latest and greatest toy, the Total Station.

Modified from the standard surveyor's tool used by road crews, the Total Station was a laser-sighted gun, linked to special crime scene software. It turned data collection into literally a pull of a trigger, while spitting out up-to-the-minute 3-D models for death investigators to pore over at the end of each shift.

The process was relatively simple, but labor intensive. First, dozens of crime scene technicians worked the scene, flagging each piece of evidence, then classifying it – plane part, human remain, personal effect. Next, a designated 'rod man' placed a glass reflector on each piece of tagged evidence. Finally, the 'gun operator' homed in on the reflector and pulled the trigger, entering the evidence into the software's database from distances up to three miles away, while the 'spotter/recorder' oversaw the operation, detailing and numbering each item entered into evidence.

Everyone worked hard, and next thing you knew, a sprawling chaos of wreckage had been reduced into a neat computer model that almost made sense out of the vagaries of fate. It was enough to make any anal-retentive control freak happy, and Kimberly was guilty on both counts. She loved being rod man, though this time out, she'd had to content herself with recording duties instead.

The command center came into view. Kimberly spotted a cluster of white shirts and navy blue suits – the NTSB officials, poring over a huge blueprint of the original 727; then a pool of Windex blue – half a dozen crime scene techs, still wearing their hazmat gear; and finally, a pinprick of burnished copper. Rachel Childs, redhead, ERT senior team leader, and rabid perfectionist.

Kimberly and Harold ducked beneath the crime scene tape.

Harold whispered, 'Good luck.'

Supervisory Special Agent Childs had set out to become a famous Chicago architect. At the last minute, she'd decided to join the FBI instead. She ended up assisting one of Chicago's finest evidence gurus, and that was that, Rachel had found her calling in life. Her attention to detail, ability to sketch to scale, and obsession with paperwork had proven much more valuable to evidence documentation than it had to the further beautification of Chicago's skyline.

That had been fifteen years ago, and she'd never looked back. At five foot nothing, one hundred and four pounds, she was one small, dedicated, hell-on-wheels Nancy Drew. Who was about to commit her first murder.

'How the hell could you have missed something as major as *a human leg*?' she roared.

She, Kimberly, and Harold had stepped away from the gathered masses to the relative shelter of a noisy generator.

Rachel only dressed down her team members in private. Her team was her family. She could know they were fuckups. She could tell them they were fuckups. It was no one's business, however, but their own.

'Well, the leg's in a bush,' Harold ventured finally. 'Beneath a tree. It's not that easy to see.'

'It's February. Leaves are long gone. It should've been visible.'

'It's in a grove of pine,' Kimberly said. 'Harold led me straight to it. I still couldn't see anything until he pointed it out. Frankly, I'm impressed he saw it at all.'

Harold shot her a grateful look. Kimberly shrugged. He'd been right, Rachel wouldn't go too hard on Kimberly. She might as well spread the magic around.

'Crap,' Rachel grumbled. 'Day three, we should be wrapping up this mess, not restarting our efforts. Of all the stupid, amateurish . . .'

'It happens. Oklahoma City, the Nashville crash. These big scenes, it's amazing we can wrap our arms around them at all.' Kimberly again.

'Still . . .'

'We adjust the perimeter. We refocus our search on the western side. It'll cost us another day, but with any luck, one random leg is all we missed.'

Now, however, Rachel's frown had deepened. 'Wait a minute, you're sure it's a human leg?'

'I've seen legs before,' Harold said.

'Me, too,' Kimberly agreed.

But Rachel was suddenly holding her temples. 'Ah crap! We're not missing any body parts! We recovered three sets of human remains from the intact cockpit just this morning. And since I oversaw the effort, I know for a fact we had all six legs.'

Harold looked at both of them. 'Told you we had a problem.'

They took a camera, flashlights, gloves, a rake, and a tarp. A mini evidence kit. Rachel wanted to see the 'leg' for herself. Maybe they'd get lucky – it would turn out to be a scrap of fabric, or the torn arm from a life-size dummy, or better yet, the back hock of a deer some hunter had dressed up in clothing just to be funny. In Georgia, stranger things had happened.

With only two hours of daylight left, they moved quickly but efficiently through the copse of trees.

They combed the ground first to make sure they didn't step on anything obvious. Then, adjusting slightly, Harold and Kimberly caught the item in the combined beams of their flashlights, illuminating it within the shadows of the overgrown bushes. Rachel knocked out half a dozen digital photos. Next came the tape measure and compass, recording the approximate size of the bush, relationship to the nearest fixed point, distance from their current perimeter.

Finally, when they had documented everything but the hoot of a barn owl and the way the wind tickled the backs of their necks, like a shiver waiting to slide beneath their Tyvek coveralls, Harold reached up and carefully eased the item onto the cradling teeth of his rake. Rachel quickly unfolded the tarp. Harold lowered his find into the middle of a sea of blue plastic. They studied it.

'Crap,' Rachel said.

It was definitely a leg, sheared off above the knee with the top of the femur bone glinting white against the blue tarp. From the size of it, probably male, clad in blue denim.

'You're sure all three remains were intact?' Kimberly asked. She hadn't gotten to do any evidence collection this time out. She liked to think it didn't irk her, but it did. Especially now, when it seemed something obvious had been overlooked. 'I mean, the cockpit was badly burned, the condition of the bodies couldn't have been great.'

'Actually, the cockpit had separated from the main fuselage. It was scorched, but not annihilated; didn't get splashed with enough jet fuel to burn that hot.'

'It's not a pilot,' Harold said. 'Pilots don't wear blue jeans.'

'Farmer? Hired hand?' Kimberly asked. 'Maybe when the plane hit the tractor . . . ?' But she knew she was wrong the minute she said it. The farmer in question had already come by to study the wreckage and mourn his equipment. If he'd been missing a hired hand, they would've heard about it by now.

'I don't get it.' Rachel was backing up, studying the woods around them. 'We're in the trees where the plane first hit. Look there.' She pointed at the sharp white tips of shattered trees just twenty feet south of them. 'First impact with the wingtip. The right wing is yanked down, the plane bobbles, but the pilot corrects. In fact, he overcorrects because one hundred yards over there' – she swiveled, pointing at a target too far away to be seen – 'we have the deep gouge in the earth at the edges of the farmer's field from the left wingtip coming down, digging in . . .'

'Sending it into the fatal spin,' Kimberly finished for her. 'Meaning, at this moment, in this place . . .'

'Plane shouldn't be spinning yet, nor crew members' legs falling out of the air. Think about it: We're a mile from the cockpit. Even if the damn plane blew up – which we know it didn't – how'd we get a leg clear back here?'

Harold was walking a little circle, studying the ground. So Kimberly did the next logical thing: She moved back, angled up her head, and studied the trees.

As luck would have it, she found it first. Just fifteen feet away, nearly eye level, so she was proud of the fact that she didn't scream. The smell had warned her – rusty, pungent. Then she spotted the first bit of fluorescent orange. Then another, and another. Until finally . . .

The head was gone. So was the left arm and leg, leaving

behind a strange, hunched-over shape, still dangling from the limbs of a tree.

'I don't think we're going home tomorrow,' Kimberly said, as Rachel and Harold joined her.

'A hunter?' Rachel asked incredulously. 'But deer season ended months ago. . . .'

'Deer season ended beginning of January,' Harold supplied helpfully. 'But small game goes until the end of February. Then there are feral boars, bears, alligators. Hey, it's Georgia. You can always shoot something.'

'Poor son of a bitch,' Kimberly murmured. 'Can you imagine? Sitting up in a tree, looking out for . . .'

'Possum, grouse, quail, rabbit, squirrel,' Harold filled in.

'Only to lose his head to a seven-twenty-seven. What are the odds?'

'When your time comes, your time comes,' Harold agreed.

Rachel still looked seriously pissed off. One final sigh, however, and she pulled it together. 'All right, we got about an hour of daylight left. Let's not waste it.'

Turned out, the NTSB wasn't so interested in a leg in the woods. A dead hunter amounted to collateral damage in the aviation world; the FBI could have it.

Rachel made a few calls, ordering up a fresh crime scene van and enough experienced agents and law enforcement volunteers to conduct a line search. Fifteen minutes later, a crowd of county deputies and FBI agents were dutifully gathered in the woods. Harold passed out thin probes to each volunteer, then briefed them all on the importance of looking up and down. As the line monitor, he would do his best to keep everyone in a row, which often got tricky in this kind of terrain.

According to the local sheriff, one Ronald 'Ronnie' Danvers had been reported missing just this morning. Twenty years old, Ronnie had set out to go hunting three days ago. When he didn't return home, his girlfriend assumed he'd gone to visit some friends. This morning, when she called over to bawl him out, she finally realized her mistake.

'It took her three days to realize he was missing?' Fellow agent Tony Coble wanted to know. 'Feel that love.'

'Sounds like they'd been having some problems,' Harold reported. 'Girlfriend's pregnant and apparently moody.'

Harold absolutely did not look at Kimberly when he said that. So, of course, everyone else did.

'Hey, I am not moody,' Kimberly said. 'I've always been a bitch.' The cramp in her left side had finally eased, leaving behind an entirely different sensation, like a little hiccup beneath her lowest rib. The sensation was still new and miraculous to her. Her hand remained curved around her lower abdomen, a singularly motherly gesture, but she couldn't help herself.

The rest of her team was grinning at her. They'd already posted a stork on the wall above her desk. Last week, she'd returned from lunch to discover her in-box filled with pacifiers. G-men were supposed to be tough; lately, all she had to do was sigh heavily and someone was rushing to fetch her a glass of water, a chair, a dill pickle. Bunch of softies. Heaven help her, she loved each and every one of them, even know-it-all Harold.

'Here's the deal.' Rachel spoke up. 'We thought we'd have the luxury of going home tonight, or for those of us who never go home, at least visit the office to tend our current cases; that ain't gonna happen. We have one hour, maybe two. We gotta map this scene, then collect the evidence and get it back to command central, where we can document it under the outdoor floodlights. In other words, you can thank me once again for showing y'all a good time.'

The volunteers groaned.

Rachel simply smiled. 'All right, people. Find me Ronnie's head.'

THREE

'The brown recluse spins a medium-sized irregular web with a maze of threads extending in all directions without definite pattern or plan.'

FROM *Biology of the Brown Recluse Spider*, BY JULIA MAXINE HITE, WILLIAM J. GLADNEY, J. L. LANCASTER, JR., AND W. H. WHITCOMB, DEPARTMENT OF ENTOMOLOGY, DIVISION OF AGRICULTURE, UNIVERSITY OF ARKANSAS, FAYETTEVILLE, MAY 1966

Kimberly arrived home shortly after midnight. She moved through the darkened house with the ease of someone used to late hours and dim lighting. Bag, coat, and shoes deposited on the bench in the hall. Brief pause in the kitchen for a glass of water, glance at the answering machine.

Mac had left the lamp burning on the built-in desk. In the small pool of illumination he'd piled mail, topped with a purple Post-it bearing the hand-scrawled message: ☺

An empty pizza box indicated he'd been home for dinner. She checked the fridge for leftovers, found half a cheese pizza, and weighed her options. Lowfat vanilla yogurt, cold cheese pizza. It wasn't much of a debate.

She chewed the first slice of pizza while standing in the middle of the kitchen, going through the mail. She discovered the Pottery Barn Kids catalogue and ate the second slice while eyeballing all items made with pink gingham.

Kimberly was convinced she was going to have a girl. For one thing, she didn't know anything about little boys, so a baby girl made more sense. For another, she had lost her mother and older sister ten years ago to a psychopath. In her opinion, God owed her something, and clearly, it was a daughter.

Mac was holding out for a boy, of course, whom he was

planning on naming in honor of Dale Murphy of the Atlanta Braves and outfitting entirely in Major League Baseball uniforms.

Kimberly thought her little girl (*Abigail, Eva, Ella???*) could out-pitch Mac's little boy, no problem. And round and round they went. Winner to be determined sometime around June 22.

Kimberly and Mac had met nearly five years ago at the FBI Academy. She'd been in New Agent Training, he'd been attending the National Academy as a Special Agent with the GBI – Georgia Bureau of Investigation. First time they'd run into each other, she'd gone after him with a knife. He'd responded by trying to steal a kiss. That had pretty much summed up their relationship ever since.

They'd been married a year now. Long enough to have worked out the kinks in basic logistics – who was responsible for taking out the trash, bringing home the groceries, mowing the lawn – while still newlywed enough to forgive small faults and inevitable oversights.

Mac was the romantic. He brought her flowers, remembered her favorite song, kissed her on the back of her neck just because. She was the type-A workaholic. Every day an agenda, every hour a task that needed completing. She worked too hard, compartmentalized too little, and probably would have a nervous breakdown before the age of forty, except that Mac would never allow it. He was her rock; while, most likely, she was his ticket to sainthood.

No doubt about it: Mac would make an excellent mother.

Kimberly sighed, poured another glass of water. Her first trimester had gone well. Some tiredness, but nothing she couldn't push through. Some nausea, but nothing that couldn't be remedied by eating pudding. A normal woman would've gained thirty pounds; fortunately, with her athletic build and high-strung metabolism, Kimberly had barely gained ten, and was only now, at the twenty-two-week mark, beginning to show.

She was healthy, her baby was healthy, and her handsome, dark-haired husband was over the moon.

Which was probably why, on nights like tonight, Kimberly wondered what the hell they'd done.

They were hardly a traditional couple in a traditional marriage. They'd met over a crime scene and dated while trying to stop a serial killer. In the past few years, the most consecutive days they'd spent together was in Oregon working another case – the abduction of Kimberly's stepmother.

They didn't do Friday nights out. They rarely even had Sunday morning snuggles. Her pager would go off. His pager would go off. One of them would be gone, and the other simply understood it would be his or her turn next. They both loved their jobs, they both gave each other space, and that made things work.

Last Kimberly knew, however, babies definitely required Friday night caring and Sunday morning snuggles and lots and lots of time in between.

What would give? Her job? His job? Or maybe they could do it with help from Mac's mother? Then again, what was the point of having a child if you were only going to hand it over for someone else to raise?

Lately, Kimberly had started to have nightmares, terribly vivid dreams where Mac was killed in an auto accident, or shot on the job, or mowed down on his way to the Chick-fil-A for sandwiches. The dreams always ended with her holding the phone, *We're terribly sorry to inform you of your husband's death,* while down the hall came the high-pitched wail of a newborn.

She'd wake up, drenched in sweat and shaking from terror. She, a woman who'd once stood in a hotel room with a killer's gun pressed against her temple like a lover's kiss.

She was strong, she was intelligent, she was tough. And she absolutely, positively knew she could not do this alone.

On those nights, she would turn away from her

husband's warm, solid form. She would curl in a ball, her hand cradling her belly. She would stare at the dusky wall across the room, and she would miss her mother.

Kimberly finished the catalogue, set down her water glass, ducked into the guest bath, where she quietly brushed her teeth. Her hair still smelled like jet fuel, her clothes and skin reeked of an oily barbecue. She tossed her clothes into the laundry room, then padded naked down the hall to the master bedroom.

Mac had left the bedside lamp on. Used to each other's rhythms by now, he didn't stir as she started the shower, then rummaged the drawers for her pajamas.

When she finally slid clean and fresh beneath the sheets, Mac rolled toward her, raising one arm in groggy welcome.

'Okay?' he whispered.

'Found Ronnie's head.'

'Nice.'

She scooted into the warm spoon of his body, spreading his hand over her side, where the baby's kicks now registered like the flutter of butterfly wings, filling up the well of her heart.

Voices were talking:

'Come on, Sal. Surely you can do better than that. It's three in the morning, for God's sake. Chances are the girl has never even met Kimberly. She just wants a get-out-of-jail-free card. You know how these things are.'

At the sound of her name, Kimberly pulled herself further from the dregs of sleep. She opened her eyes to discover Mac standing across the bedroom, talking on his cell phone. The second he noticed her eyes were open, he flushed guiltily.

Then, very pointedly, he turned around, giving her his back as he continued to argue: 'What specific information has she given you to warrant an FBI agent's personal visit? Sure. Yeah. That and a quarter will buy you a cup of coffee. 'Sides, that'd be our ball game, not the FBI's.'

Now Kimberly was fully awake. And increasingly angry.

Mac was running his hand through his hair. 'Mano a mano, do you think she's for real or just some kid caught in a pinch? Well, I know that's not your call to make. Do it anyway!'

But apparently, Sal wasn't willing to play that game. Mac sighed. Mussed his hair again. Then reluctantly turned to face his wife, cell phone held against his shoulder, resigned expression on his face.

Before she could launch into her tirade, he went with a preemptive strike: 'It's GBI Special Agent Salvadore Martignetti. Couple of officers arrested a prostitute in Sandy Springs who claims she's your informant. She doesn't have your card or seem to know anything about you, but she's sticking to her story. The officers serve with Sal on VICMO, so they contacted him and he gave me a buzz.'

VICMO stood for the Violent Crimes and Major Offenders Program. Its goal was to bring together officers from all over the state in an attempt to identify larger patterns of crime. In reality, it was some bureaucrat's attempt at getting the dozens upon dozens of law enforcement agencies to play nice together.

'Hey, if Sal has information for me, he should be dialing me direct. Isn't that the point of all these cross-jurisdictional teams? We're all one big happy family, loading each other's numbers into our speed dials?'

Mac gave her a look. 'Don't start. The girl says her name is Delilah Rose. Mean anything?'

'Other than an obvious alias?'

'You don't have to go. For Christ's sake, you just got home three hours ago, and no doubt you're back at the crash scene by six.'

'What's she offering?'

'Won't give 'em any details. Says it's for your ears only.'

'But Sal has an opinion.'

Mac shrugged. 'Sounds like she's claiming to have information on another missing prostitute.'

Kimberly arched a brow. 'And that would be *GBI's ball game,* as you graciously put it?' she asked drily.

'Last time I read the statutes.'

'Not if the act involved crossing state lines.' Kimberly threw back the covers and climbed out of bed.

'Kimberly . . .'

'I'm gonna talk to a girl, Mac, not hoe the cotton fields. Trust me, even a pregnant woman can do this.'

After all these years, Mac knew when he'd lost the war. He returned to the cell phone. 'Sal? You heard? Yeah, she'll pay the girl a visit. Do me a favor? Make sure the station has plenty of bottled water.'

'Oh please,' Kimberly tossed over her shoulder, 'why don't you just ask him to stock pickles as well?'

Sal must have heard that, too. 'No, no, no,' Mac was already correcting. 'But if you want the inside skinny, she'll do anything you want for vanilla pudding. I keep snack packs stashed in my car. It's probably the only reason I'm still alive. Oh, and don't forget plastic spoons, otherwise it gets ugly. Yeah, thanks, buddy. Bye.'

By the time Kimberly exited the bathroom, she'd splashed cold water on her face and was fully awake. Mac had returned to their queen-size bed, but was sitting up, watching her with dark eyes. She pulled a fresh pair of slacks from the closet. He still didn't say a word.

The argument was already three months old, and not due to be resolved anytime soon. Kimberly pulled a tough caseload, even by FBI standards. In the post-9/11 world, the Criminal side of the house had been gutted to get National Security up and running. Atlanta's Violent Crimes unit went from sixteen agents to only nine, with fifty-hour workweeks becoming seventy-hour marathons. Days routinely started at nine a.m. and went to all hours of the night.

If that wasn't enough, Kimberly had joined the ERT as an 'extracurricular,' providing another forty to fifty call outs a year, for such high-stress situations as plane crashes, bank robberies, hostage situations, kidnappings, and the occasional cult leader showdown. Agents received free training for their extracurriculars, but no extra income. Agents served because they were called to serve, the work its own reward.

Kimberly had been only four weeks pregnant when Mac started to question why she needed quite so much work to provide her with a sense of reward. Perhaps she could rejoin White Collar Crimes or, better yet, transfer to Health Care Fraud with Rachel Childs. Rachel worked only five cases a year. True, they were document-intensive cases, but they also had a longer lead time, opening up flexibility for, in Rachel's case, managing the ERT, or in Kimberly's case, having a baby.

Health Care Fraud was valuable work. Indeed, as Mac liked to say when he really got going, fraud was the heart and soul of the Bureau.

Kimberly suggested that she join Counterterrorism and spend six months working in Afghanistan. That shut him up for a day or two.

In the FBI, everything boiled down to 'the needs of the Bureau.' Why weren't new agents allowed to pick their first field office, and in fact, the new agent from Chicago was most likely to be sent to Arkansas, even though the Chicago office needed the most recruits? Because from the beginning, the powers that be wanted to make sure everyone understood one simple mandate: The needs of the Bureau came first. You were serving the U.S. government, protecting the American people, and that was given as much weight and gravitas in the FBI as in any branch of the armed forces.

The Bureau needed Kimberly in Violent Crimes. She was good at the work, experienced in the field. Besides, to ask

27

for a transfer now would be insulting to her male teammates, most of whom had children, too.

She had on her shirt now, then a basic black jacket she could no longer button, but looked okay hanging open. She inspected her reflection in the mirror. Head-on, you'd never guess she was pregnant. But once she turned to the side . . .

Another flutter. Her palm pressed against the curve of her waist. Her own rueful smile, because as much as she loved her job, heaven help her, she already loved this, too.

She crossed to the bed and kissed Mac on the cheek.

'I'm right, you're wrong,' she informed him.

'You haven't heard a word I said.'

'Oh yes, I did.'

He cupped the back of her head, pulled her down for a more serious kiss. They both understood the importance of never leaving the house angry.

'Things are different now,' he said quietly.

'I know things are different, Mac. I'm the one wearing pants with an elastic waist.'

'I worry.'

'Well, you shouldn't. According to last week's exam, mommy and baby are doing great.' She sighed, relenting a fraction. 'Eight to twelve more weeks, Mac. That's all I'm asking for – this last little window before I become as big as a house, and then I have to obey your every command because I won't be able to put on my own shoes.'

She gave him a final kiss, feeling his resistance in the set of his jaw. She straightened and headed for the door.

She heard his last words, too. The line he never spoke, probably never would speak, but remained in the air between them.

Her father had also put the needs of the Bureau first. And it had destroyed her family.

FOUR

'The initial bite is usually painless.'

FROM *Brown Recluse Spider*, BY MICHAEL F. POTTER,
URBAN ENTOMOLOGIST, UNIVERSITY OF
KENTUCKY COLLEGE OF AGRICULTURE

Sandy Springs was located fifteen miles north of Atlanta, off Route 285 and Georgia 400. A major metro area, it boasted four hospitals, several Fortune 500 companies, and, of course, a freshwater spring. While Sandy Springs strove for a family-friendly reputation, it remained best known for its nightlife, with bars that stayed open until four a.m. and a plethora of 'massage parlors' always eager for new clients. Young, old, male, female, drunk, or sober, you could find a good time in Sandy Springs.

Which really started to annoy the locals. So in June 2005, they voted overwhelmingly to incorporate as a city, overnight becoming the seventh largest in the state. First order of business for the brand-new city council: form its own police department to crack down on the area's less desirable elements. Sandy Springs was jumping on the urban renewal bandwagon, by God, right down to a new collection of very trendy restaurants.

Kimberly hadn't worked with the new PD yet. She figured the officers would either be fresh-faced recruits or fifty-year-old state police retirees coasting into a second career in a middle-class metro area. She got a little of both.

Kid that met her at the door looked about three years

away from shaving. The night sergeant, on the other hand, with his thinning hair and growing middle, had clearly been around the block. He shook her hand warmly, angled his head at the kid and gave her a look that said, *Can you believe the puppy I got working for me?* In case that wasn't enough, he smiled and winked.

Kimberly didn't return the wink or the smile and after a moment Sergeant Trevor gave up.

'We picked up the girl shortly after one a.m.,' Trevor reported. 'She was working the MARTA station on—'

'She was working at the train station?' Kimberly couldn't help herself. Somehow, she'd assumed the girl had been pinched during a raid on a massage parlor. Streetwalkers were reserved for the red light districts such as Fulton Industrial Boulevard. In theory, Sandy Springs was too . . . hip . . . for that kind of obvious display.

'Happens,' Trevor said. 'Especially since we've started raiding more of the establishments. Some of the girls think they can blend in with the clubbers, you know, except the hookers show slightly *less* skin. Others . . . hell, they're too strung-out to care, or operating on orders to pick up more chicks, that sort of thing. Gotta replenish the henhouse, you know.'

Trevor puffed out his chest, clearly wanting to impress the fed. Before this job, he'd probably been a security officer, Kimberly decided. Any occupation that allowed him to wear a uniform.

The kid had disappeared. Kimberly suspected that was also due to Trevor's orders. He wanted this to be his show. She pinched the bridge of her nose and wished she were back at the plane crash.

She asked for Trevor's report on the arrest. He printed it out, she skimmed the particulars. Time, location, other activity. It seemed very straightforward. Girl had been found with an ounce of meth in her pocket, and was now looking at doing some time. So naturally Delilah Rose insisted she was an informant for the feds.

'I'll talk to her,' Kimberly said.

'Is it drugs?' Trevor blurted out. 'She gonna turn in a dealer, maybe a supply network? Meth, hell, it's taking over the entire state. Make her give you someone big. No penny-ante crap. The state's due for a major arrest.'

'I'll keep that in mind,' Kimberly assured him drily. 'Where is she?'

Trevor led her to an interrogation room, the other advantage of crying snitch. Rather than waiting in a holding cell, Delilah got her very own tiny square room and a can of Diet Coke. Not bad for a night's work.

Kimberly paused outside the door. Through the one-way glass, she had her first view of the 'informant.' She did her sizing up quickly and without giving anything away on her face.

Delilah Rose was white, a surprise in a state where the majority of prostitutes were African American or, especially in the massage parlors, Asian. She appeared to be early twenties, with the blotchy skin and dirty-blond hair of a woman living too hard, too fast.

As Kimberly stood there, the girl raised her face belligerently and stared at the mirror. Bright blue eyes, hard-set jaw. Tough. Sober.

Good.

'I'll take it from here,' Kimberly told Trevor. 'Thanks for giving me a call.'

'No problem. You'll let us know—'

'Thanks for giving me a call,' Kimberly said again, and shouldered her way past the hefty sergeant into the tiny room.

Kimberly took her time. Closed the door. Pulled out a hard plastic chair. Had a seat.

From inside her jacket pocket, she pulled a mini-recorder. Next, a small spiral notebook and two pens. Finally, she made a show of checking her watch and writing the time at the top of the pad.

Then she set down her pen, leaned back in her chair, and, folding her hands over her stomach, proceeded to stare at Delilah Rose. Minute passed, then two or three. Kimberly wondered if Sergeant Trevor was watching on the other side of the mirror. No doubt he was rapidly growing impatient with this lack of show.

The girl was good, but Kimberly better. Delilah broke first, picking up her Coke, then realizing the can was empty and returning it nervously to the table.

'Want another?' Kimberly asked quietly.

'No, thank you.'

Ah, manners. Most suspects, informants, addicts tried them on for law enforcement, maybe falling back on that childhood promise that if you just used the magic word . . . They were very polite. At least at first.

Kimberly returned to silence. The girl cleared her throat, then began rotating the empty can with her fingertips.

'You're trying to make me nervous,' the girl said at last, her tone sulky, faintly accusing.

'Are you high, Delilah Rose?'

'No!'

'Police said they found you with meth.'

'I don't do drugs! Ever. I was just holding the bag for a friend. How was I supposed to know it was meth?'

'Do you drink?'

'Sometimes – but not tonight.'

'I see. And what were you doing tonight?'

'Hell' – now the attitude was coming out – 'I wasn't doing *nothin'* tonight. Just visited a club for a little dancing. Then catching MARTA to fly home. Since when is needing public transport a crime?'

Kimberly merely eyed Delilah's outfit. Underneath a navy blue jacket that was too thin for this time of year, the girl was a walking advertisement for spandex. Short, shiny skirt the color of eggplant. Jet-black halter top, so tight her breasts spilled out the sides. Then there were the four-inch stiletto heels.

Kimberly caught a glimpse of what appeared to be a spiderweb, inked around the girl's navel, before Delilah self-consciously tugged her shirt down. A second tattoo peeked out from the back of the girl's neck, a spider climbing into the girl's hair.

'Who did the work?' Kimberly asked, pointing to Delilah's neck.

'Don't remember.'

'Nice web on your stomach. What's the ring in your navel? A spider for the web? Clever.'

The girl didn't say anything. Just stuck out her chin belligerently.

Kimberly gave her another minute, then decided she'd had enough. She started straightening up, grabbing her mini-recorder, the spiral notebook, the first pen.

'What the fuck?' Delilah cried.

'Excuse me?' Kimberly asked calmly, sticking the mini-recorder back in her pocket.

'Where the hell are you going? You haven't even asked me any questions yet. What kind of FBI agent are you?'

Kimberly shrugged. 'You said you weren't doing anything. You claim the drugs aren't yours. So okay. You're the Virgin Mary, and I'm going back to bed.'

Kimberly reached for her second pen. The girl grabbed her wrist. For a skinny, malnourished thing, Delilah Rose was strong. Kimberly understood that kind of strength. It was called desperation.

Very slowly, Kimberly met the girl's overbright gaze. 'I don't know you. We've never met. Meaning you're no informant of mine, and as far as I'm concerned, Sandy Springs can do with you whatever they'd like. Now let go of my wrist, or you will regret it very fast.'

'I need to talk to you.'

'I've been here six minutes. You've had nothing to say.'

'I don't want Sergeant Nimrod listening.' The girl had let go of Kimberly's wrist. Now her gaze flickered to the one-way mirror.

'Sergeant Trevor isn't your concern. I am your concern, and you've still not given me any reason to stay.' Kimberly picked up the pen, tucking it away.

'He'll kill me.'

'Sergeant Trevor?'

'No, no. The man . . . I don't know his name. I mean, not his real name. He calls himself Mr. Dinchara. The other girls, we call him Spideyman.'

'Mr. Dinchara?'

'You know, arachnid. It's a . . . what do you call it? An anagram.'

'Oh please.' Kimberly couldn't help herself. She eyed the girl's getup again, arching a brow skeptically.

'He's different.'

'Uh-huh.' Kimberly was already pushing back her chair, rising out of the hard plastic.

'He doesn't pay for sex. At least not in the beginning.' Delilah's voice was growing more urgent. 'Spideyman pays girls money to, like, play with his pets. You know, ten bucks if you'll touch the tarantula. Thirty if you'll let it crawl up your arm. Freaky kind of stuff like that.'

'Play with his pets?'

'Oh, the venom from a tarantula isn't strong enough to harm you, you know.' Delilah actually sounded earnest. 'They're really very shy and like . . . fragile. You have to handle 'em gently. Otherwise, you can hurt them.'

Kimberly didn't talk anymore, mostly because she couldn't think of anything to say.

Delilah, on the other hand, was finally on a roll: 'So at first, you know, the things he wanted involved his pets. But then he didn't want his spiders just walking across your

34

arm. He wanted to watch them walking across other areas. And, well, that got him pretty turned on. So then he wanted other activities, and yeah, maybe it's a little different and not all the girls were into it, but then again, he paid pretty good.'

'What's pretty good?'

'Hundred for a hand job, one fifty for oral. Two if you'd let the spider watch.'

'*Watch?*'

'From inside its cage, of course. I mean, you can't just have a tarantula wandering about when you're not paying attention. You might squish it.'

'Exactly what I feared,' Kimberly murmured. Just when you thought you'd heard it all, some pervert pushed the boundaries yet again. 'Okay, so you and Dinchara have a little thing going on.' Kimberly eyed the girl's tattoos again. 'I gotta be honest. Sounds like you two are a good fit, and as you said, he pays well. So why are you here?'

Delilah looked away. The chatty spell had ended, they had returned to the land of silence. 'Something went wrong,' the girl mumbled at last.

'No kidding. Come on, night's not getting any younger. Why did you ask to see me?'

The girl's lips trembled. 'Because of Ginny. Ginny Jones. She went away with him. And nobody's seen her since.'

Kimberly took a seat. She got out her notebook and pen, turned on the mini-recorder. The girl eyed the machine nervously, but didn't protest.

'I want protection,' she blurted out.

'You want protection? Like what?'

'A . . . a safe house. Police protection. Whatever it is you see on TV.'

'Delilah, that's TV. In the real world, it doesn't work like that. You gotta pay to play.'

'Pay to play? What's that mean?'

Kimberly was serious. 'That means you have to provide real information on a real crime. Something specific and detailed. If I can corroborate it, then we can talk options.'

'How specific?'

'Let's start with a name. Ginny Jones. Real or alias?'

'Virginia,' the girl whispered. 'Her real name was Virginia Jones, but everyone called her Ginny. She was nice. Not into drugs, some of the stuff you see. Just . . . I don't know. Something had happened somewhere.' The girl smiled wanly. 'Doesn't it always?'

'When did you last see her?'

'Three months ago. A Wednesday. Maybe a Thursday. I'm not sure anymore. She'd gone with the guy before. She's, umm, she's the one who told me about him. You know, when she saw my tats. Said there might be this guy, kind of freaky, but by the looks of things, nothing I couldn't handle, and hey, the money's good—'

'So Ginny knew Dinchara?'

'Yeah, I guess. I mean, okay.'

'And she was okay with the eight-legged audience?'

Delilah shrugged. 'Ginny said the spiders didn't bother her. She used to tell me she wasn't afraid of anything. At least not anymore.'

'So when did you last see her?'

'While back.'

'Delilah.'

'Ummm, several months ago, maybe one-thirty in the morning. Dinchara came by in his SUV.'

'Describe it.'

'Black. Silver trim. Fancy. A Toyota, I think, but a souped-up version. You know they sometimes upgrade them? This one has the fancier rims, the leather seats. Limited Edition.'

'License plate?'

'I don't know,' the girl said immediately.

Kimberly took a moment to study her again. The answer

was too quick, especially in this day and age, when the hookers also watched *CSI* and understood the value of information. 'Was it a Georgia plate?'

'Yeah, okay.'

'Starting letters?'

'I don't know. Honestly.' More defensive now. 'I try not to know too much, okay? The girls that get into that . . . It's like asking for trouble.'

'Describe him.'

Delilah's eyes fell. She worried her lower lip. 'Um, white. Middle-aged. Brown hair. Kind of wiry maybe, like a carpenter, someone who works with his hands. He has a smell to him, too. Some kind of chemical. I always figured he did some kind of trade, but I never asked.'

'Any distinguishing marks?'

'Like what?'

'Scar, tattoo, birthmark.'

'Well, you know, it's not like the guy takes the time to undress . . .'

'On his face then?'

But Delilah merely shrugged. 'I dunno. They all look alike to me.'

'They?'

'Men, johns, pervs, whatever you wanna call 'em. They're all the same.'

Kimberly gave her a dubious look.

Delilah finally perked up. 'Hey, there was one thing. His hat. He always wears a red baseball cap. I've never seen him without it. He doesn't even take it off, when, well, you know. So a red baseball cap. That's something, isn't it?'

'It's something,' Kimberly conceded and dutifully made a note. 'Other clothing?'

'Jeans,' Delilah supplied. 'Long-sleeved shirt. Kind of Eddie Bauerish, I guess. Outdoorsy, but preppy outdoorsy. I think he has money.'

'Why do you say that?'

37

'The car, the clothes, the hourly rate. Not just any shlub can afford that.'

'Describe his voice.'

'Ummm, a guy's voice?'

'Accent?'

Delilah considered the matter. 'Southern. A drawl, but not too deep.'

'Where are you from, Delilah?'

But the girl wouldn't answer.

'Accent? Vocabulary? Do you think he's educated?'

'He knows a lot about spiders.'

'So do you.'

Delilah flushed. 'My brother had one as a pet, long time ago. Named her Eve. I used to help him catch crickets for her. She was really pretty. Spideyman . . . he's not just a pet owner. He had this white spider, I once called it a tarantula and he got all mad at me: 'She's not just some tarantula, she's a *Grammostola rosea* . . .' – some Chilean kind of tarantula or something like that. He got pretty angry I didn't know the difference. He kind of . . .'

'He kind of what?'

'He scared me.'

'How?'

'Just, the look on his face. I don't know.' The girl shrugged. 'For a moment, I kind of thought . . . maybe I was a specimen, too. You know, *Slutto hookeroso*.' Delilah smiled wanly at her joke, but her eyes weren't in it.

'Did he threaten you?'

'No. He didn't have to. You could see it on his face. Some guys are like that, you know. They want you to see it coming.'

Kimberly didn't comment on that. She'd been involved in law enforcement long enough to know Delilah had a point. 'So how does he approach girls? In his car?'

'Not always. I mean, it's not exactly a street corner kind of game out there. It's more, you go to the right places, hang out, maybe you'll meet the right man.'

'You go to a club,' Kimberly filled in. 'You make a move, he makes a move. Then what happens?'

'You follow him. Maybe to a car, or someplace . . . quieter. You work out the details along the way. Get the money up front, do what you gotta do, then bada bing, bada boom, it's all done, and you're outta there.'

'And in the case of Mr. Dinchara, where did he lead you?'

'His SUV.'

'Did you ever have a problem getting back out?'

'No, but I make it quick. If you get the money up front, then you can make your exit while he's still . . . happy. Makes for a better getaway.'

Kimberly arched a brow. 'So basically, while the guy's pants are still down around his ankles, you're exiting stage right.'

'Works like a charm.'

'So you know Mr. Dinchara, and Ginny Jones knows Mr. Dinchara. Now why do you think Mr. Dinchara had something to do with Ginny going away?'

'Because the last time I saw her, she was with him. I saw them walking down the street, away from a club. I was actually a bit pissed, you know. I mean seriously, he paid half a night's work.'

'And?'

'And that's the last time I saw Ginny.'

Kimberly took a moment, organizing the information in her head, composing her next statement. 'Delilah, this is all very interesting, but I can't do anything with it.'

'Why not?'

'No evidence of a crime.'

The girl looked at her funny. 'Don't you believe me? I'm telling the truth. Ginny was my friend. He hurt her. He should pay!'

'In the last three months,' Kimberly asked bluntly, 'have you seen Spideyman again?'

Delilah's gaze slid away. 'Maybe.'

'Did you conduct any business with him?'

Barely a whisper now. 'Maybe.'

'Like you said,' Kimberly murmured, 'money's good. You're still willing to be alone with him, Delilah. How bad can he be?'

The girl didn't answer for a long time. When she finally did, Kimberly had to lean forward to catch her words. 'Last time I was with him, I was on my knees. Doing, you know. And right at the final moment, his hands suddenly wrapped around my neck, squeezed. I couldn't breathe. I was choking, hitting at him. And I heard him . . . I heard him whisper, *Ginny*. Then all of a sudden, he released my neck and I got the hell out of there.

'Thing is, I don't think he knows he said it. I think he was caught up in the moment. But I'm not sure. Maybe he realized it later. Maybe he knows that I know. I can't . . . I don't feel so good about things anymore. Because what if he did hurt Ginny? Choked her like that. And what if I'm the only one who can connect her to him? You gotta help me. It's not just about Ginny. It's me, too. I need police protection.'

Kimberly sighed, rubbed the bridge of her nose. 'You want my trust? Let's start with your real name.'

'Delilah Rose. You can look it up, the police did.'

'Name, date of birth.'

'Why is it always about me? I always gotta prove, prove, prove. I just gave you a pervert on a silver platter. Maybe you should prove yourself to *me* for a change.'

'Which brings me to my second question: Why'd you call me? How'd you even know my name?'

Delilah wasn't as quick to answer this time. If anything, Kimberly thought the girl suddenly appeared sly. 'You're the one who caught the Eco-Killer. I saw it on the news. The rookie agent, a girl, no less. I figure if Spideyman killed Ginny, you're the one who can make it right.'

'I can't make it right, Delilah. There's no evidence of a crime, and even if there was, it's not my party. You need to talk to the Sandy Springs PD.'

'No. It has to be you. You caught the Eco-Killer, you'll help Ginny.'

'Delilah—'

'I got something.'

Kimberly stilled, eyed the girl more warily. 'What is something?'

'That night, when he was choking me, I happened to notice it on the floor, beneath the seat. When he wasn't looking, I scooped it up.' Delilah looked around the room, as if to ensure they were really alone, then she reached down into her halter top, producing from her left bra cup a heavy gold ring.

'It's Ginny's,' she whispered, plopping it on the table with a metallic thud. 'She used to wear it on a chain around her neck. She never took it off. I mean *never*. So, see, this proves Ginny was in Spideyman's truck.'

Kimberly arched a brow, but moved the ring closer to her, using the tip of her pen and careful not to touch. It looked to her to be a class ring. The center stone was blue. Some kind of inscription appeared on the inside but was hard to read, given the layers of grime.

'Who else saw Ginny wearing this ring?'

Delilah shrugged. 'Dunno. Never asked.'

'Did she tell you how she got it?'

Another negative.

'Anyone else know you found it in Mr. Dinchara's truck?'

'Hell no! Now, see, this is the kind of business that can really get a girl hurt—'

'Yeah, yeah. Got that.' Kimberly frowned, studied the ring. Frowned again. Finally, she sat back. 'Can I take this?'

'Sure, yeah, that's why I brought it. You can open a case now, right?'

'Not quite.'

41

Delilah's turn to scowl. 'Hey, you asked for evidence, I gave you evidence!'

'Strictly speaking, Delilah, this ring is not evidence. No chain of custody, meaning it would never hold up in court. That it belongs to Ginny has not been corroborated. That it was found inside a subject's truck is equally murky. At the moment, it's merely a very dirty class ring.'

'I don't like your attitude,' Delilah said.

'Trust me, feeling's mutual.' Kimberly rapped the end of her pen on the table three times fast. 'Here's what we're gonna do, Delilah. Remember what I said? You gotta pay to play. We're going to consider this ring a down payment.' She took out a business card, circled the Bureau's main number on the front. 'Bring me more information. Times, places, even other people who can vouch that Ginny Jones used to work in this area, wearing this ring, and has now disappeared. Maybe, if you're lucky, you can find enough to build a case for the local PD. I'll help walk you through it, but I gotta be honest. As of this time, this is a case for the locals, not the FBI.'

She started gathering up her supplies again. This time, Delilah didn't try to stop her, just crossed her arms over her chest with a look of resigned hurt.

It wasn't until Kimberly stood that Delilah spoke again. 'How far along?'

'Pardon?'

The girl was staring at Kimberly's stomach. 'When're you due?'

For a moment, Kimberly was nonplussed. Then she caught herself. She was at that point now where other people were bound to notice. She said, 'Summer.'

'You feel okay?'

'I feel fine, thank you.'

'Smells bother me,' the girl said matter-of-factly. 'I get tired, too. But I keep away from the alcohol and the drugs.

Just because I hook for a living doesn't mean I don't want better for my baby.'

The girl let her jacket slide open, and for the first time, Kimberly saw it, the tight, rounded abdomen, not so different from her own. Delilah reached for Kimberly's mini-recorder, picked it up.

'Can I take this?'

'No. Government property. Gotta buy your own.'

Delilah put it back down. 'But if I can get more information from Spideyman, maybe get him saying something about Ginny on tape, then you'll help me?'

Kimberly was still staring at the girl's belly. She was suddenly sorry she had come down to the Sandy Springs PD. She didn't want to be handling a young, very vulnerable, pregnant hooker.

Her business card was still lying on the table. Finally, she picked it up and wrote her cell phone number on the back.

'If you get him on tape, call me at that number.' Then, not really as an afterthought: 'Delilah, be careful.'

FIVE

My older brother used to tell me, 'Do as I say, or the Burgerman will get you!'

'There is no such thing as a Burgerman,' I would shout back.

'Sure there is. He's big, seven feet tall, dressed all in black. He enters the rooms of all the naughty boys in the middle of the night, snatching them out of bed and taking them off to his factory, where he grinds them into burgers and sells the meat to grocery stores. All the cheap stuff that's turned brown in the meat market? That's naughty-boy burgers. You can ask anyone.'

I didn't believe him until one night I woke up, and the Burgerman was standing at the foot of my bed.

'Shhhh,' he said. 'Don't say a word, and maybe I'll let your family live.'

I couldn't talk. I couldn't scream. I couldn't move. I just stared at this large hulking form, nearly seven feet tall, all in black. I couldn't believe my brother had been right. Then I started to shake, and my heart started to pound, and I think I wet the bed.

'Move!' the Burgerman demanded harshly. 'You wanna save your family, boy, then get your scrawny ass outta bed.'

But I couldn't move. I could only shiver uncontrollably.

He tossed back the covers. He grabbed my arm and

yanked me to the floor, his fingers digging into my upper arm. He twisted my shoulder and it hurt.

My legs followed him on their own, I swear that's how it happened, because surely there was no way I wanted to go with a man like him.

In the hallway, he paused as if to get his bearings. I could see the cracked door of my brother's room, just two feet away. I could hear the sound of my father snoring one room beyond that.

Scream, I thought. This is it. Do something.

In the dark, I could feel the Burgerman appraising me. He didn't seem panicked or even alarmed.

Instead, he smiled, a flash of white in the dark.

'See, boy. See how much they care about you? I'm about to ruin your goddamn life, and your family can't even be bothered to wake up for the event. Remember this, boy. You mean nothing to them. As of this moment, they no longer exist.

'You belong to me.'

He took away my clothes. Tossed me facedown on the bed. I fought as much as a nine-year-old boy can fight, my face pressed into the mattress, my lungs screaming for air. I thought he would kill me. Maybe I prayed he would once he was done.

But he rolled over. Smoked a cigarette.

I didn't know what to do, lying facedown, wetness everywhere.

I fell asleep.

He woke me up, beat me, yelled at me until I did what he wanted me to do. Afterward, more cigarettes and then it all started again.

I lost track of time. I lived in a hazy, naked state, my insides too hot, my outside too cold. He wouldn't allow me to even have a blanket.

Sometimes he brought me food. Burgers, pizza. First time I ate, I threw up. He laughed and told me I'd get used to it. Then he handed me a spoon, pointed to the pile, and said if I wanted to eat again, I'd better get busy.

On and on and on. Life with the Burgerman, grinding the naughty boy into dust.

One day, he opened the door of the hotel room. The sunlight blinded me. I had to shield my eyes. The air smelled like rain and, unconsciously, I drew in a deep breath. The rain was the first thing I tasted that wasn't like ashes on my tongue.

Burgerman laughed. 'See, boy, even after all that, you still want to live. Guess you must have liked it some after all.'

He tossed me clothes. Not my old ones, but new ones he'd purchased somewhere. Barked at me to get dressed. 'Goddammit, show some pride, boy, and stop running around so naked. What're you trying to do, tempt me again?'

I scrambled to get dressed, but wasn't fast enough.

This time when he heaved off, he grunted, 'See, boy, told you you liked it.'

He drove me to another hotel. He wore a suit. I was in a stiff, navy blue sweat suit, two sizes too big. I felt thin and small and ghostlike. I must have looked like a refugee from a foreign war, exhausted, glassy-eyed, hollow.

The receptionist regarded me with concern.

Burgerman leaned close. 'I'm with Social Services,' he confided in a low voice. 'Just removed the boy from his family. Hard, hard case. The stuff his parents did . . . He's had a rough start, but God willing, I'll take him to a good home now and his real life will begin.'

'Oh, you poor thing,' the girl said.

Then, out of nowhere, I screamed. Screamed and screamed and screamed, told the world of my horror in each heart-stopping wail. I felt as if my lungs were going to burst out of my chest, my head explode with the terrible pressure.

46

'Told you his parents were monsters,' Burgerman said.

'Oh, you poor thing,' the girl said again.

Eventually he took me to a small apartment. There was a phone, but it only worked with a credit card. The outside door he rigged with a key in, key out lock, with him palming the only key.

At least he finally left me alone, sometimes for hours at a time. I would watch Bugs Bunny until I started to hate the rascally rabbit, so I turned off the TV and watched nothing at all. Just stared at the dingy gray wall. Stared and stared and stared and felt myself grow very tiny.

That was the first time I noticed a spider. I caught it. Put it in a cup, watched its desperate scramble to escape.

I guess the Burgerman was right in the end.

I must have liked it after all.

SIX

'*Brown Recluse Spiders are challenging to control, largely because of their secretive habits.*'

FROM B*rown Recluse Spider*, BY MICHAEL F. POTTER,

URBAN ENTOMOLOGIST, UNIVERSITY OF

KENTUCKY COLLEGE OF AGRICULTURE

Rita couldn't sleep. It was one of life's little ironies; now that she finally had the time to rest, she had lost the ability. Seemed like every night followed the same long gray arc. She would watch the glow of the moon sweep across the far wall. Catch the ripple of the curtains as the cold wind seeped through the edges of the aged windows. Listen to her tiny old house creak and pop as winter treated its wooden joints as poorly as it treated her flesh-and-blood ones.

By the time the sun finally peeked over the mountains, she would wonder for the fiftieth time why she didn't head to Florida like so many of her friends had done. Or maybe Arizona. Less humidity. More heat. She thought she would like Arizona.

She wasn't going anywhere and she knew it. She had been born in this house, back in the days when the midwife came to you and labor was no reason to see a doctor. She and her four sisters and three brothers had run through these hills, climbed these trees, trampled the flowers in her mother's beloved garden.

She was the only one left now. The wizened old woman everyone expected to disappear into a nursing home, much as her mother had done. But Rita was made of sterner stuff. She avoided the diabetes, high cholesterol,

48

and brain cancer that had stolen so many members of her family. She held on, whipcord lean, barely a pound above bird weight, but still capable of splitting a cord of wood every fall in preparation for winter. She hoed her own garden. Shelled her own beans, swept her own porch, and beat her own rugs.

She kept on keeping on, waiting for something not even she understood. Maybe because at her age, waiting was about all she had left.

Once upon a time, her high school sweetheart had whisked her away to the big city of Atlanta. Donny had wanted to see the world. Mostly, he'd seen the airspace above Germany before some Nazi had shot him down, and Rita went from being a young bride to a young widow in less than two years. She'd hardly been alone in her fate. Plenty of other pretty young things crying in their coffee or, more like it, their mid-afternoon brandy. But then the war ended, a stream of handsome men returning and scooping up most of those girls in a whirlwind of thank-God-we're-alive sex.

Rita had considered her options. Twenty was too young to be sitting home every night, and while she enjoyed her secretarial job, maybe some of Donny's wanderlust had rubbed off on her. She'd already cut the umbilical cord once. Might as well go out and see what there was to see. Find a strapping young man. Have an adventure.

It didn't work. In the end, she was not giddy or euphoric or, truth be told, that interested in clumsy, back-of-the-seat sex. Rita just wanted to be Rita. So she settled into the little house she bought with Donny's death benefit. She grew a garden. She built a front patio. And when the loneliness grew too much, she did the last thing in the world anyone expected her to do: She became a foster mom.

She took in kids for nearly twenty years, from squalling infants to sullen ten-year-olds. She would pick them up at the local Chick-fil-A, their worldly possessions filling a single black Hefty bag, easily tossed in the backseat. She would buy them lemonade, then take them home and give them the lay of the land.

She adhered to basic rules. Follow them, and things ran relatively smooth. Disobey and be punished. Some kids took to the system easily. Others learned the hard way.

Couple of kids scared her, though she liked to believe they never knew. Couple of the kids, she genuinely loved. Though again, she liked to believe they never knew. Life was tough enough without believing a single foster mom could make a difference.

She gave the kids a roof over their heads, three solid meals a day, a place to feel secure, and, hopefully, a foundation for someday, when they finally escaped the system and managed their own lives. She liked to think there were people scattered across Atlanta who still smiled when recalling the time they lived with a woman who ironed even the doilies and made them say prayers every night, and while they resented her at the time, they understood her now. And, maybe, they even loved her a little, though of course, it was only proper that she would never know.

Thinking you could change a life by becoming a foster parent was nothing but romantic claptrap, of course. Of the nearly thirty children Rita had seen in her day, at least five were dead. Drugs, violence, suicide, risky behavior. Did it matter?

Donny died. Her children died. And then one by one, her father, her mother, her brothers, her sisters, until here she was, back in the home of her childhood, one week from her ninetieth birthday, acutely conscious of the slow passage of time and the very real presence of ghosts.

She got out of bed, the sky barely a paler shade of gray, but close enough to call morning. She shuffled her feet into fat blue slippers, grabbed her thick terry cloth robe and shrugged it on over her long flannel pajamas. She wore a sleeping cap, not at all fashionable, but very helpful when your skin was thinner than paper and the old circulation system was moving so slowly she sometimes caught a chill while standing in front of the heated radiator in the parlor.

She made it downstairs, moving at an unhurried pace. In the kitchen, she got the water boiling for a cup of tea. Then it was over to the refrigerator for eggs. She ate two scrambled every morning with one piece of toast. The protein kept her strong, and the breakfast never failed to bring back memories of her youth.

Even now, she heard the floorboard creak behind her; her brother Joseph, in one of his moods again. Joseph had always been a trickster, liking to pull out her chair right before she took a seat.

'Now, now, Joseph,' she chided, without turning around. 'I'm getting too old for these games. Last time, you nearly cost me a hip!'

Another creak. She caught a glimpse of a shadow, dashing across the wall. She thought it was Michael, or maybe Jacob. They visited often, no doubt enjoying the familiarity of their childhood kitchen as much as she did.

She saw her parents less often, her mother mostly, hunched over the kitchen sink, humming a mindless tune as she washed vegetables or tended to dinner. Once, she'd encountered her father, standing in the middle of the parlor smoking his pipe. The moment she entered, however, he disappeared, seeming almost embarrassed.

Locals said it was the gold and crystals lining the hills that kept the ghosts so busy. An Indian shaman had explained in the paper that gold was the highest vibrating substance on earth, activating things, concentrating energy. Anywhere there was a large quantity of gold and crystals, he said, you had the perfect recipe for spirits.

Rita accepted that explanation at face value. Her house was nearly one hundred and fifty years old and had sheltered five generations of her family. Of course it was haunted.

As to why her mother would want to spend eternity cooking in the kitchen . . . well, Rita figured that she'd get to find out for herself soon enough.

She had her eggs done. Her wheat toast. Her Earl Grey tea. She set everything down on the small wooden table, one by one. Then, after a last glance to ensure that Joseph had left her chair alone, she took a seat.

Sun had spread out over the glorious expanse of the Blue Ridge Mountains, staining everything it touched a bright rosy pink. She thought it was a beautiful morning.

Meaning it was time to do what must be done. She got up, shuffled her way to the back door. It took her two or three hard yanks to get it to budge. When it was finally open, she stuck her head out and said firmly, in a voice that thirty foster children had learned never to argue with: 'Son, you can come out now.'

Nothing.

'I know you're there, child. No need to be afraid. If you want to talk, just be polite about it and say hello.'

After all these years of living with ghosts, Rita was nearly as surprised as anyone when a flesh-and-blood child materialized on her back porch. He couldn't have been more than eight or nine, scrawny shoulders hunched against the morning frost, sandy head down, expression clearly uncertain. Two weeks ago, he'd started appearing in her backyard. Every time she'd made eye contact, however, he'd bolted. This time, at least, he stayed put.

'Hello,' he whispered.

'Heavens, child, you're gonna catch your death of cold. Come on in. Shut the door. I'm not paying to heat the world.'

He hesitated again, but then his gaze went to her breakfast and she saw his hunger like a spasm across his face. He stepped inside, carefully shutting the door behind him. The motion showed off shoulder blades sharp as razor blades.

'What's your name, child?'

'I don't—'

'What's your name, child?'

'They call me Scott.'

'Well, Scott, this is your lucky morning. My name's Rita, and I was just fixin' to make more eggs.'

He didn't argue, but took a seat in the nice warm kitchen that smelled of scrambled eggs and fresh toasted bread.

Rita cooked. She fed. She cooked some more. Finally, when his stomach was a tight, round drum beneath the faded expanse of his yellow-striped shirt, he pushed his empty plate away.

'Rita,' he said at last. 'What do you think of spiders?'

SEVEN

'When the spider first spins the silk, it is liquid, but it soon hardens into thread that can be stronger than steel.'

FROM *Freaky Facts About Spiders,*

BY CHRISTINE MORLEY, 2007

Special Agent Sal Martigetti was waiting for Kimberly outside the station. Minute she exited, he flashed his lights. She glanced at his unmarked car, then pointedly looked at her watch. She was tired, hungry, and not in the mood.

In the end, however, she crossed over. Mostly because he'd taken Mac's advice and was holding up vanilla pudding.

He had the heat blasting, a welcome change from the early morning chill that stung, even in Atlanta. She took the six-pack of pudding, the offered bottle of water, and a plastic spoon. After an internal debate, she grudgingly offered him one pudding back, but he waved her off.

'No, no, all for you. The least I can do.'

He'd been listening to the radio. Some conservative talk-show host ranting about how the ACLU was ruining the world. As Kimberly settled in, however, Sal snapped it off.

'Been waiting long?' she asked, digging into the first pudding. She knew Sal only in passing. Had bumped into him at a barbecue, some police function somewhere. Both the GBI and the FBI were large organizations, meaning more of the agents were names she'd heard rather than faces she knew, and Sal was no exception.

Small, dark, and wiry, he possessed the sinewy build of someone who grew up hard, probably not far from the streets he now patrolled. He wore a light gray suit this morning, but still managed to look more like an up-and-coming hoodlum than a state investigator.

'Been here twenty minutes,' he commented, held up a greasy fast-food bag. 'Had my breakfast.'

'More comfortable inside the station,' Kimberly said.

'Not sure what I think of 'em yet,' Sal stated, jerking his head toward the Sandy Springs PD, which was an icebreaker of sorts coming from a GBI special agent.

Kimberly finished the first pudding, opened a second. Something about this felt all wrong. A GBI agent's insistent middle-of-the-night phone call that she needed to talk to some pinched prostitute. Then the same special agent waiting for her afterward. Kimberly tried working the angles in her mind, but came up empty.

'Sal,' she said at last, 'much as I appreciate the pudding, I'm not giving away the keys to the kingdom for snack packs. So if you want something, start talking. I have another appointment in thirty minutes.'

Sal laughed. It brought a spark to his eyes, eased the tightness around his jaw. He should laugh more. Then again, so should she.

'Okay, here's the deal: You know I'm on VICMO?'

Kimberly nodded.

'One of the whole points of VICMO being to bring law enforcement agents together from all across the state to look for larger patterns of crime.'

'I'm an FBI agent, Sal. I know my acronyms. We're tested every Friday.'

'Really?'

'No.'

He laughed again, dark eyes flashing bright. 'Okay, well, I have a theory on a larger pattern of crime: I believe someone's picking off prostitutes.'

Kimberly frowned, dug into her pudding. 'What do you mean you have a theory? The girls are declared missing or they're not. Missing stats go up, or they don't.'

'Not these girls. Runaways, hookers, addicts. Who cares enough to file a claim? They disappear and no one's the wiser.'

'They're also transient,' Kimberly countered. 'If they go missing, maybe it's because they hopped on a bus.'

'Absolutely. You're not talking about one of the population groups most likely to fill out the U.S. Census Bureau questionnaire. On the other hand, get a lot of officers in a room, and they each have a story of some girl or addict or whomever, who was pinched lately, and first question she asked them is have you seen so-and-so? She's looking for a lost friend, roommate, partner in crime. 'Course, no one knows what she's talking about, so end of story. You're right, these girls *don't* file missing persons reports. But one by one, they're raising the exact same question: Where have all the hookers gone?'

'Very poetic of you, Sal.'

'I play an open mic night, every Thursday at the Wildcat . . .'

Kimberly stared at him.

'Oh, you weren't serious.'

'I'm going to eat another pudding,' Kimberly said, and opened a third, not because she was hungry, but because she needed something to do.

'I don't get it,' she said at last. 'So girls are whispering about missing girls. Okay, but where *have* the missing hookers gone? If someone is 'picking them off' as you say, where's the evidence? Shouldn't missing Girl A, last seen here, correlate with unidentified Body B, now found there?'

'Tried that. No unidentified female bodies have been found lately.'

She gave him a look. 'Seems to shoot down your theory right there. If a predator was preying on prostitutes, he'd be disposing of the bodies somewhere. In Dumpsters, back alleys, along the interstate. Something would've turned up.'

Sal shrugged. 'How many of Ted Bundy's victims are

still undiscovered? He favored rolling them down ravines. Let's face it, this state has a lot of ravines. And chicken farms, and marshlands, and miles and miles of nothing at all. You wanna hide a body, Georgia is the place to do it. Or,' he conceded, 'maybe the guy crosses state lines. It's always a possibility, but you'd know better than me.'

Kimberly could already hear the skepticism in his voice. After all, if a subject was picking up prostitutes in Georgia and killing them in Louisiana, then it definitely would be a federal case and Sal didn't think this was a feebie case. He thought it was *his* case, so for that reason alone, the subject could only be operating inside Georgia lines.

Kimberly studied him. She was doing some math in her head and it wasn't working out in his favor. 'Trevor said they picked up Delilah shortly after one. But I didn't get called until after three. Anything you want to add to that timeline, Special Agent?'

Sal didn't bother to appear repentant. He simply shot her a grin. 'Heard you were smart.'

'Violent, too. Don't let the belly fool you.'

His grin broadened. 'Okay, sure, so maybe I took a shot at her.'

'Mmmm-hmmm.'

'If it's any consolation, little Miss Muffet wouldn't bite. Was adamant from the moment the police picked her up that she would speak with you and only you.'

'Liked her tattoos, did you?'

'How do you know her?' he asked curiously. 'Drug activity? Meth? Seems kind of low level to be narc'ing for a fed.'

'You never know where the good information might come from.' She narrowed her eyes at him. 'Why this level of intensity, Sal? Poaching an informant, rousing a fed in the middle of the night. From the sound of it, you don't even have a case, yet you're jumping through a lot of hoops to talk to one inked-up hooker.'

Sal didn't answer her. His gaze had gone out the window. He wasn't smiling anymore, and the dark look on his face had probably scared an informant or two.

'I got a package,' he said curtly. 'Fourteen months ago. No name on it, no note in it. Just three Georgia-issued driver's licenses stuffed in a plain white envelope and placed beneath the windshield wiper of my car. Nothing more, nothing less.'

'Driver's licenses? You talking forgeries or the real deal?'

'Real deal. I have valid photo IDs for Bonita Breen, Mary Back, and Etta Mae Reynolds. White females, roughly twenty years of age, addresses from the greater Atlanta area. I did some digging and guess what?'

'They're all missing hookers.'

'They're all working girls,' he fine-tuned, 'who haven't been spotted in months. Now, according to the grapevine, Mary headed for Texas, while Etta Mae ran off with some bartender. I've issued BOLOs for both, without any hits. So in my world, that makes them missing, though it's possible my supe has other ideas on the subject.'

Kimberly had to smile. She might know something about disagreeing with a superior. These things happened.

'Then,' Sal continued, 'three months ago, same thing. I come out to my car and discover a new envelope, with three new licenses: Beth Hunnicutt, Nicole Evans, and Cyndie Rodriguez. Except this time I get lucky. Beth Hunnicutt *has* been declared missing, by her roommate, *Nicole Evans*.'

'Wait a minute, wait a minute, wait a minute. The same Nicole Evans whose driver's license is in the envelope?'

'The very same. According to the missing persons file, Hunnicutt was last seen heading out for a 'big job,' by her roommate Evans. Furthermore, Evans asserted that Hunnicutt never would have taken off without grabbing her stereo equipment and collection of CDs from their apartment. Of course, when I tried to follow up with Evans, I discovered that she also hadn't been seen in months, and in fact, the third roommate, Cyndie Rodriguez, had disappeared, as well. Three more IDs, three more missing girls.'

'That doesn't sound good.'

'So says you, so says me. Brass, on the other hand . . .'

'Six missing girls and you can't make a case?' she asked in shock.

'No evidence of foul play. And technically speaking, of my six names, only one has been declared missing. The others are simply 'unaccounted for.' According to the bureaucrats we got bigger fish to fry – you know, the growing meth problem, gangland shootings, new requirements for Homeland Security, yada, yada, yada.'

Kimberly sighed. She'd like to say she'd never heard of such garbage, but she would be lying. Bureaucrats ran the world, even in law enforcement.

'Back to the envelope,' she mused. 'Someone is making the effort to outreach not once, but twice, to the police. That's something.'

'Envelope was unsealed and yielded no physical evidence. So for kicks, I ran it by a shrink friend who sometimes consults for the department on cold cases. His first thought was sure – a lot of killers like the spotlight just as much as celebrities, and are driven to reach out to local cops or press. The fact the package contained driver's licenses interested him, as the BTK guy out of Kansas liked to mail in driver's licenses of his victims to the press. So maybe a classic copycat element – hey, look how famous that schmuck is, I can do that!

'Problem is, the predators who make the effort generally crave recognition. It's about bragging, gamesmanship, and arrogance. Meaning there should be a note, poem, follow-up phone call, something. This . . . In Jimmy's own words, it's like mailing out a party invite without any directions on where or how to play. His best guess: The stash came from a third party.'

'*Third party?*' Kimberly asked incredulously. 'Like who, the guy's cleaning lady?'

'Think of it this way: A wife cleans out her husband's sock drawer. Comes across a stack of photo IDs. Now, there can't be any *good* reason for her husband to have the driver's licenses of three young women. Then again, she's afraid to confront him with it. So she sticks the plastic in an envelope, and discreetly passes it to the first cop she sees. Eases her conscience while keeping her distance.'

'Until she comes across three more driver's licenses,' Kimberly said drily.

'Hey, maybe the guy needed his underwear drawer organized as well.'

Kimberly arched a brow, turning the matter over in her head. The whole scenario bothered her on so many levels she didn't know where to begin. Six missing girls, only one of whom could be considered missing. No bodies or other evidence of foul play, but two care packages that could be considered to contain 'trophies' from a serial predator. Except maybe the envelopes didn't come from the unidentified subject, but a companion of the UNSUB who was too scared to contact police directly but savvy enough to deliver the licenses in a manner that left behind absolutely, positively no physical evidence.

Which, she supposed, brought them to Delilah Rose, a young prostitute pinched just this evening, claiming to have evidence about another missing hooker and adamant about speaking only with Kimberly.

Delilah troubled her. Kimberly didn't like the impression that the girl had homed in on her, all because of something she'd once seen on TV. The Eco-Killer had been a long time ago. And while the press had made out Kimberly to be a hero, she hadn't gotten to all the girls in time.

Sal turned to her now. 'Did Delilah give you something good? Mention any of these names? Because depending on what she said, maybe we could make it a multijurisdictional task force. My supervisor might finally green-light me if the case came from the feds.'

'Sorry, neither of us is that lucky. Story I got from Delilah Rose reads more like a Mad Lib than a three-oh-two. She was vague on all relevant details, including her own name.'

'Gosh darn, she's not really Delilah? Didn't Sandy Springs at least run her prints?'

'Oh, I'm sure they'll call me with the results. Maybe in five to six weeks.'

'So what'd she say? You were there an hour. I gotta assume you discussed more than just the weather.'

Kimberly considered the GBI special agent again, hand in her pocket now, feeling the weight of Ginny Jones's ring. Information was a game. With informants. With fellow law enforcement officers. Even with husbands and wives. For all his talk of cooperation, Sal clearly felt he owned this case. And if Delilah had opened up to him earlier this evening, like hell Kimberly would've been called.

'Delilah didn't mention any of the names from your photo IDs,' Kimberly told him honestly. 'She didn't mention a pattern of multiple girls disappearing, or anything like that. She does, however, fall into your first category of one working girl looking for a friend. Virginia 'Ginny' Jones. Went missing about three months ago. Name ring any bells?'

Sal shook his head, taking out a piece of paper, jotting the name down. 'No, hasn't come up yet. But I've found three more names of missing girls that don't match the known driver's licenses. Can't decide what that means yet. Maybe these girls simply left town, or maybe the wife hasn't cleaned out the T-shirt drawer, you know.'

'How long have you been working this, Sal?'

'Year,' he said absently. 'More since getting the second envelope.'

'Your supe must love that.'

'Hey, guy's gotta have a hobby.'

'Tracking missing hookers?'

'Tracking missing girls,' he said sharply. 'Sisters, daughters, mothers. You know what it's like for their families to go to bed every night not knowing if their loved one is alive or dead. Everyone, anyone, deserves better than that.'

Kimberly didn't have anything to add to that, which was just as well, since she'd noticed the time. She swung open the door, hand still clutching the ring. 'Gotta go!'

'Hey, where was this Virginia last seen?'

'Club scene, Sandy Springs.'

'Name of the club? Description of Ginny?'

'Told you Delilah was vague.'

'You gonna call Delilah?'

'In theory, she'll call me. Thanks for the pudding, Sal. Bye.'

EIGHT

'Spiders are exclusively carnivorous.'

FROM *How to Know the Spiders*, THIRD EDITION,

BY B. J. KASTON, 1978

Henrietta was not doing well. She had been on her back for nearly three days, but wasn't showing any sign of progress. He was careful not to touch her, understanding that even the most delicate examination could lead to disaster at a time like this.

She was old, nearly fifteen, which of course exacerbated the situation. At the first signs of pre-molt, he'd taken preemptive action, moving her to the ICU, where she could rest in dark, humid conditions. Using a small artist's brush, he'd even dabbed her legs with glycerin, paying special attention to the femur-patellar and the patella-tibial joints. In theory, the glycerin would help soften the rings of the exoskeleton, making it easier for Henrietta to pull free.

Unfortunately, it didn't do the trick. Now he stood in front of her, contemplating more drastic action. Perhaps it was time to sacrifice a leg.

Molting was an extremely dangerous time for a tarantula. Once a year, in order for the tarantula to grow, the old exoskeleton had to be shed, the tarantula climbing free from its outgrown exuvium with a fresh, larger suit of armor ready to go. For most of the year, in fact, the tarantula was in a state of inter-molt, slowly growing a new exoskeleton beneath the old. At around the twelve-month mark, in preparation for the transition, the spider entered pre-molt, excreting exuvium fluid between the old and new exoskeletons. This digestive juice began dissolving one layer of the old exoskeleton, the endocuticle, while bristles grown on the new exoskeleton started pushing the old covering away.

The bald patch on the tarantula changed from tan to black, signaling the pre-molt state. Shortly thereafter, the tarantula would roll over on her back to begin the molting process. And anywhere from twenty minutes to two or three days later, the molting process would be complete.

Unless the spider died.

Already he could see signs of distress. In Henrietta's age-weakened condition, she hadn't the strength to pull her legs free. As hours passed, her new exoskeleton started hardening inside her old exuvium, making it impossible for her to pull free from her shedding skin.

He either did something soon, or she would die trapped inside a prison of her own making.

He could amputate a leg or two. Quick tug and twist of the femur, and that would be that. It didn't sound pleasant, but a spider could lose a leg with relatively little harm.

Or, he could operate.

He'd never done it before, just read about it in various collectors' chat rooms. Little was understood about medical care for tarantulas. After all, dead spiders were rarely autopsied or studied for cause of death. A true enthusiast buried or mounted his or her pet. The vast majority of collectors, however, tossed the carcass away.

Some basics had been established over the years. For the ICU, he used a plastic yogurt container he'd thoroughly cleaned with a bleach solution, then lined with a paper towel he had sterilized in the oven, then soaked in cooled boiled water. He let both container and wet paper towel achieve room temperature before placing Henrietta on the paper towel and sealing the ICU with the original yogurt lid, now punched with three airholes.

He hated the plastic containers, preferring to watch his pets, but tarantulas – like most spiders – were shy by nature. They preferred the dark, particularly when in distress.

Even now, he worked upstairs in the gloomy master bath, room-darkening shades pulled, the air musty with the scent of fresh earth and faint decay. A nightlight offered a subdued glow, just enough for him to see Henrietta, without further traumatizing her system.

She wasn't moving anymore. Not even trying to pull her legs free. Dead?

He didn't think so. Not yet. But it was coming and the thought of losing her was nearly unbearable. She was his very first pet and while he had collected many more specimens in the years since – rarer spiders, more exotic colors – she would always be special. After all, once, a long time ago, she had set him free.

No doubt about it, he would operate.

He started by gathering supplies. A stiff piece of cardboard to serve as the operating table. Tweezers, magnifying glass, eyedropper, Q-tip. He returned downstairs to boil the tweezers and soak another piece of sterilized paper towel.

Boy was on the couch. He didn't make eye contact when the man appeared, but kept his eyes resolutely fixed on the TV. Smart boy.

While the tweezers cooled, the man set another damp paper towel on top of the back panel of a Cheerios box. Next, he dissolved two drops of Ivory dish soap in one cup of boiled water, cooled to room temperature.

He headed back upstairs, once more passing by the living room. This time, at the sound of his approaching footsteps, the boy flinched.

The man smiled.

Upstairs, he had to extract Henrietta from the ICU, careful not to jog her, given her delicate state. Once he'd slid her onto the hospital bed/piece of cardboard, he moved her closer to the nightlight and pulled out the magnifying glass.

Upon closer inspection, she appeared hopelessly stuck, her old exoskeleton barely cracked, not a single leg peeking through. It was much worse than he thought and he took a moment to draw in a ragged, pained breath.

Then he steadied himself. With the Q-tip, he dabbed the soap solution on the exuvium, careful to not drip any fluid that might get into Henrietta's book lungs and drown her.

While he waited thirty minutes for the solution to soften the exoskeleton, he decided to take his intervention a step further and fully remove the sternum piece of the old, molting shell. The plates were connected by a thin membrane, and were very easy to extract using the sterilized tweezers.

This process went smoother than anticipated and soon he'd removed most of the carapace and sternum plates.

Henrietta's legs remained trapped, however. Long, delicate new legs held prisoner by the hard rings of her old skin. Without use of her legs to work herself out of her old exoskeleton, she still wasn't going anyplace.

He got back out his magnifiying glass and considered his options.

Downstairs came the sound of the front door opening and closing. Hushed voices murmuring. Debating, no doubt. To disturb or not to disturb. Upstairs was his sanctuary, filled with his own special guests. None of them liked to come up here. At least, not any more than they had to.

Finally, however, the sound of footsteps, creaking up the old stairs, hitting the landing, approaching his room.

The door opened, flooding the room with unexpected daylight.

'Close it!' he snarled.

The door closed.

'Stand. Don't say a word.'

The intruder stood, didn't say a word.

Better.

He would have to break the heavy rings articulating each leg. If he could chip away that part of the hardened exoskeleton without damaging the soft, unprotected leg beneath, Henrietta might have a chance. Four joints each leg. Eight legs.

He settled in for the painstaking work, still aware of the presence behind him, the girl who did not move, would not move, until he spoke again.

Five minutes rolled into ten, thirty, forty-five minutes. An hour. He chipped away at the hardened exoskeleton on each leg, slowly, carefully, ring by ring.

When he finally looked up, he was surprised to find that perspiration stuck his shirt to his skin and he was breathing hard, as if he'd been hiking for hours, and not just hunched over a table in a pool of dim light.

He had all eight legs free, though several were bent awkwardly, clearly damaged. As he watched, however, one leg moved, then another. Henrietta was still with him, fighting to pull through.

'You are so beautiful,' he crooned to his favorite pet. 'That's my girl. That's my girl.'

'Is . . . is she all right?' a tentative voice finally came behind him.

He didn't turn around, his voice clipped as he set aside the tweezers. 'I don't know. Molt this bad, she probably has trouble with her mouth, pharynx, and stomach. Odds are she'll be dead by morning.'

'Oh.'

'But at least this gives her a chance.' He took grim satisfaction in that, snapping off the light, leaving Henrietta to fight her own war the way she would prefer – alone in the dark.

He finally turned, his eyes adjusting rapidly to the gloom and taking in the girl standing in the doorway. She had her chin up, a small show of defiance that showed off the spider tattoo on her neck, but didn't fool either one of them.

'Did you get it?' he asked without preamble.

Wordlessly, she held out the business card.

He snatched it up, turned it over, read the cell phone number scrawled on the back. For the first time all morning, the man smiled.

'Tell me exactly what you did.'

And the girl, being well-trained by now, did.

NINE

*'For laypersons, the most distinguishing feature of a brown
recluse is a dark violin-shaped mark on its back, with the neck
of the violin pointing toward the rear (abdomen) of the spider.'*

FROM *Brown Recluse Spider*, BY MICHAEL F. POTTER,
URBAN ENTOMOLOGIST, UNIVERSITY OF KENTUCKY
COLLEGE OF AGRICULTURE

The call came three nights later. Kimberly's team had finally wrapped up the crash scene and she and Mac were celebrating by eating dinner together. He'd brought home a honey-baked ham, accompanied with coleslaw and biscuits.

He ate the ham, she ate the biscuits.

'So once I had the ring all cleaned up,' she was reporting excitedly, 'you wouldn't believe the level of detail. Alpharetta High School is engraved around the center stone. Then on the right side, the word 'Raiders'—their mascot—with a picture of a football, engraved with a number eighty-six and beneath that the initials QB.'

'Really?' Mac said, helping himself to a fresh beer. 'You have the name of the kid's high school, plus the fact that he's the quarterback with jersey number eighty-six?'

'Oh, it gets even better. On the other side of the ring is a name: Tommy, with an emblem, Class of 2006.'

'I don't have any of that on my class ring,' Mac said.

'You have a high school ring?'

'Sure.'

'I've never seen you wear it.'

'Well, if my ring were as cool as Tommy's, maybe you would.'

Kimberly rolled her eyes at him, decided a fourth biscuit probably wasn't healthy for her or the baby, and went with some coleslaw. 'So now I have a first name, high school, and graduating class. I figure, okay, some afternoon when I'm in the area, I'll swing by Alpharetta High School, talk to a guidance counselor, and, ding, ding, ding, mystery will be solved. But then I have a better idea.'

'Of course.'

'I log on to the Internet. Figure I'll see what I can learn about Alpharetta High School.'

'And what did you learn about Alpharetta High School, my dear?'

'Hey, sarcasm is only going to earn you more middle-of-the-night diaper changes.'

'Point taken.'

She gave him a look.

He shrugged. 'Honestly, I'm interested. I spent the whole day sitting in a van, listening to two alleged drug dealers carry on a highly serious discussion of how Keanu Reeves is the most underappreciated actor of our time.'

'Was it his performance in *Speed*?'

'More like his decision not to make *Speed 2*.'

'So true.'

'All right, all right. Back to the ring . . .'

'Well,' she started again, mollified, 'Alpharetta High School is frighteningly large.'

'Alpharetta is frighteningly large.' They had originally looked at buying a home there. It was a booming, upwardly mobile, decidedly professional community just south of them. In the end, it was the booming that concerned them. From three thousand residents in 1980 to over fifty thousand now, the town was bursting at the seams, with all the public resource strains and traffic woes that generally came of such things.

'Nearly two thousand kids,' Kimberly reported. 'That worried me a little. School of that size, one kid could be hard to find. But then it occurred to me, check the sports page. And you'll never believe what I found.'

'Delilah Rose?' he guessed helpfully.

'No. Tommy Mark Evans. Varsity QB of 2006. His photo, game stats, everything, right there on the information superhighway. For that matter, I found pictures and names of all the cheerleaders, JV sports teams, drama club, chess club – you name the kid, his or her information is all there online. I tell you, it's not enough to monitor MySpace or YouTube anymore. Every public organization has a website that is freely giving away information and photos of America's kids. Think about it: I didn't even leave my desk and from one class ring, I surfed the Internet straight to Tommy Mark Evans's front step.'

'Our son will never be allowed a computer in his room,' Mac announced. 'Any portal out is a portal in, and I want to know what or who is coming into our home at all times.'

'Our daughter will probably never use a computer,' Kimberly countered. 'By the time she can type, it'll all be done on a cell phone and how the hell are we supposed to control that?'

'No phone privileges works for me.'

'So you're gonna be the Draconian daddy with a curfew and a shotgun?'

'Absolutely. But I'll also buy her a pony. I mean, er, I'll buy him a baseball bat.'

But Kimberly had caught the slip and was already grinning at him. 'I heard that. You're thinking about a little girl . . .'

'Any healthy, happy baby will be fine—'

'You want to buy pretty pink dresses . . .'

'Hey, can I help it if the clothes in the baby girls' section are much cuter?'

Kimberly was laughing now, mostly at the thought of her tall, dark, manly man husband going through the girls' clothing rack. But he probably did like the little pink dresses. And he probably would buy their child a pony. As well as a handgun with basic firearms safety lessons.

'Well, if you're done mocking me,' he said, making a show of hurt dignity as he stood and started clearing paper plates, 'what are you going to do now?'

'You mean because so far I've processed evidence and pursued a lead in a case where I don't actually have a case?'

'That was my thought.'

Kimberly didn't have a good answer for that one. 'What do you think of Sal?'

'Good guy. Reputation for digging his heels in and getting the job done.'

'Is he a renegade, works best by himself, alienates those in authority?'

'Actually, that would be you, dear.'

Kimberly nodded. 'True.'

Cell phone rang.

Mac glanced up. 'Yours, not mine.'

She got to her feet, sighing. 'Knew talking about work was a bad idea. It's like conjuring the beast into your presence.'

Second ring.

Her stomach felt a little too full. She rubbed it absently, asking Baby McCormack to please stop kicking the daylights out of the biscuits, as she crossed to her leather bag, dug around in the depths.

Third ring.

She finally found it, glancing at the screen: It was the 1-800 number for the Atlanta Field Office, which, at first blush, didn't make sense. She received calls from her supervisor or from her fellow agents, not the duty desk. She shrugged, flipped it open. 'Special Agent Quincy.'

And then . . .

Far away, very quiet, like a whisper in the dark, 'Help me.'

'Who is this, please?'

'Help . . . me . . .'

Kimberly glanced sharply at Mac, made an urgent motion for paper and pen. He scrambled at the kitchen desk.

'You have reached a federal agent. Please state your name and I'll do my best to assist you.'

'I don't remember . . . He took it from me. Maybe . . . if I could just find it again . . .'

'Who took it from you? Talk to me.'

Mac, paper and pen in hand, arriving at her side, regarding her questioningly.

The whisper again: 'Soon you will understand.'

The connection broke. Kimberly attempted dialing back, but the number was blocked.

She set down her cell phone, deeply perplexed. Mac still stood there, waiting to write up notes on a caller who hadn't provided any information.

'Delilah Rose?' he asked at last.

'Don't think so,' she said. 'It sounded like a boy.'

The phone rang again shortly after two a.m. Kimberly wasn't sleeping well, as if some part of her was expecting this moment. Beside her, she felt Mac tense at the first shrill note, and knew he'd been waiting, too.

She sat up and flipped on a lamp. On the bedside table, she had positioned her cell phone, notepad, pen, and mini-recorder. Once again the display screen registered the toll-free number for the Atlanta FBI. This time, Kimberly wasn't fooled.

She gave Mac a slow nod of acknowledgment, then snapped on the mini-recorder. She answered her phone in the hands-free mode, so they could both hear.

'Special Agent Quincy.'

Nothing at first. No greeting, or crackle of a bad connection. Then, somewhere distant, as if in the background, that faint whisper again: 'Shhhh . . .'

Kimberly glanced at Mac. She brought the phone up

73

between them, and with her ear closer, suddenly she could hear.

Moaning. Panting. The slapping sound of flesh hitting flesh. A muffled cry of distress.

'*Do you like that? Is that good for you? Answer me!*'

A small, whimpered plea.

'*That's what I thought.*'

Kimberly put her hand over her mouth to stifle her automatic cry of protest. Beside her, Mac had gone still. He'd heard it, too, and understood what it meant. They were eavesdropping on a sexual assault. Kimberly knew, because she had heard such tapes before, part of the work her father used to bring home before he realized his young daughters had taken to sneaking into his office and going through his things.

Recorded? Live? She didn't know, but she had seen the visuals that went with such sounds and already her stomach roiled. . . .

The whisper again, closer to the phone: '*Shhhh . . .*'

Banging now. Hard, metallic. Handcuffs, pounding brutally against a metal headboard, as someone struggled to escape. Then, a low, unmistakable rasp. The sound of a blade, slowly sliding across a sharpening stone.

All of a sudden, Kimberly understood this call was going to get much worse.

Frantically, her shaking hand trying to scrawl the words across the page: TRACE IT!!!

Mac throwing back the covers, leaping out of bed, grabbing for their landline.

'*You know what I want.*'

'*Mmm, mmm, mmm.*'

'*A name. Is one name really so hard? You just have to love her, that's all. Give me someone you trust, call a friend, adore. That's all I require of you. One single name. Then I promise your death will be quick.*'

'This is Special Agent Michael McCormack, requesting

Special Agent Lynn Stoudt. I require immediate assistance—'

A quick, short rip. Duct tape torn from the mouth.

A wail. A long, thin, horrified scream that went on and on until Kimberly had her hand stuffed into her mouth and even then could feel that poor, exhausted cry reverberating down her spine.

The voice, even closer now: 'Shhhh . . .'

'*Tell me!*'

'*Please . . .*'

The *wick wick* of metal slicing. A fresh, throaty scream.

'*I can skin you alive. Do you want to watch?*'

'*Dear God, dear God, dear God . . .*'

'*Darling, didn't your mama ever tell you? There is no God! Just me. I am your savior and I am your damnation and you had better make me happy or I will flay the cheeks from your skinny white face. GIVE ME A NAME!*'

'*I don't kno—AAAGGH!*'

'*ONE NAME!*'

'*Please no, dear God no, please, please . . .*'

The girl was screaming. Wailing hysterically, and now the man was yelling, too, demanding a name over and over again while in between came terrible wet noises and a violent banging.

Kimberly could feel herself start to disconnect. To disappear inside her skin, to spiral away from this moment, where a young girl begged for her life and a madman worked his knife.

The voice in her ear: 'Shhh . . .'

Mac across the room: 'Lynn, I need to be able to trace a phone call immediately. On my wife's cell. Number—'

'*How does that feel? How does that fucking feel? It's gonna get worse. I'm just going on and on and on, until you tell me a name. . . .*'

'*God, God, God.*'

'*Didn't you hear me? There is no GOD!*'

'AAAAAGH.'

'Name, name, name. Tell me a—'

'Karen. K-K-K-Karen.'

'Karen who? What is her last name? How do you know her?'

'I don't know, I don't know, I don't know.'

A fresh sharp scream as he did something terrible.

'Liar! If you cared about her, you would know her full name. If she mattered, you could remember her fucking details.'

'Please, please, please . . .'

'One last chance. Make me happy. Or I swear to you, next cut will be someplace you really value. I'm counting. One . . . two . . .'

'Virginia!' the female gasped. 'Her name is Virginia. Ginny Jones.'

'And why do you love her?!'

'She is my daughter.'

A pause.

'Excellent,' the man said.

And the next sound needed no explanation at all.

Mac was shaking her. Had she blacked out? Kimberly didn't want to think so. She had never fainted before in her life. She glanced down in bewilderment at the bed. Her cell phone was there, the screen blank.

Had it all been a bad dream?

And then she looked up, saw the somber expression on Mac's face, the worry bracketing his eyes.

'The caller hung up,' he said quietly. 'It's over now.'

But she shook her head. 'No, Mac. It's just begun.'

TEN

'Most [spider] species are not particular as to the insects
eaten but will take whatever happens to come their way.'

FROM *How to Know the Spiders*, THIRD EDITION,

BY B. J. KASTON, 1978

In preparation for her morning guest, Rita was fixin' to buy
some food. It was a slow process. First she climbed into the
old, claw-foot tub. Ran a trickle of lukewarm water – waste
not, want not – scrubbing what needed to be scrubbed with
an emaciated bar of Ivory soap.

She used to have a nice young girl in town set her hair.
The cost had become a bit much. The drive into town as
well. So she'd been letting her hair grow, a long, thin veil
that shadowed her shoulders like brittle lace.

She rolled on long johns. Flannel pajamas. One of her
mother's old pairs of black pants, belted tight at the
bunched-up waist. Her father's red plaid shirt nearly fell to
her knees, but it was warm, in good shape. Still smelled
faintly of his tobacco pipe even after all these years.

She wore his socks, too, the woolen ones that could
make your toes feel nice and warm even when it was thirty
out and the wind blew like a son of a bitch.

Then came the heavy peacoat, a hat, a scarf, a pair of
her brother's gloves. She nearly staggered under the weight
of the clothing by the time she made it to the kitchen,
finding the cookie jar and counting out its precious
contents. Social Security paid her $114.52 every month, not
bad in the summer when she grew her own vegetables and
picked berries in the brambles along the road. Winter,

however, was tough. She bought the day-old pastries, the expired meat, the long-gone vegetables. She figured if you cooked anything long enough in a stewpot, then it was safe enough to eat.

She allowed eleven dollars and forty-five cents. That oughtta get the job done.

More shuffling, then she was at the front door.

'Now, Joseph,' she said before departing. 'No funny stuff just because I went out. I know exactly where I left my hairbrushes and the silverware. You want trouble, go play next door. Mrs. Bradford was always colder than a witch's tit, anyway.'

Rita cackled at her own joke, opening the door and working her way slowly down the front steps, clinging tight to the wooden rail.

She and her brothers had never liked Mrs. Bradford. The neighbor woman had once told on them after discovering them eating apples from her tree. Well, if she hadn't wanted the kids to eat them, then she should've picked 'em herself. Whoever heard of a neighbor who couldn't spare an apple or two?

Mrs. Bradford had died ten years ago. Maybe Joseph could look her up, dial direct, do whatever it was ghosts do for fun in the hereafter.

Rita found her pace, a steady rocking shuffle, and set out down the road.

She lived on a side street not far from town. Once, this area had been large lots with small but grand summer homes. Her great-great-grandfather had built the quaint Victorian that belonged to her family, looking for a respite from Atlanta's heat. Times changed. Properties were sold and subdivided. Bit by bit, the old summer homes disappeared. Now she lived amid an odd patchwork quilt of prefab Colonials, double-wides, and low-slung ranches.

She supposed her neighbors were young couples. Folks that worked the restaurants and staffed the hotels for the summer and autumn seasons when the tourists outnumbered the locals ten to one and even buying a loaf of bread became a major inconvenience.

Rita didn't know. She didn't leave her house much or socialize with her neighbors. She was too busy with the dead.

She thought she knew where the boy came from, however. The house was tucked farther up the street from her, looking down over the rest. One of the last grand homes, it now featured peeling paint, skewed windows, a cockeyed front porch. Sometimes she saw lights on up in that house, in the middle of the night when God-fearing people should be asleep, not lying wide-eyed in their beds as she so often did. People in that house kept strange hours.

House fit her idea of who would have a half-starved boy who spent his time catching spiders.

She finally arrived at the store, weaving around the muddy, snow-rimmed trucks, past the gas pumps, into the little shop that always smelled of diesel and cigarettes.

She walked the aisles first, making a careful inventory. Bread, eggs, milk. She eyed bacon, it had been a long time since she'd had bacon. But the price put it out of the picture. Boys liked cereal. Heavens, the number of boxes she used to go through, when she had boys in the house. Not those sugarcoated cereals. She didn't hold for that. But the other brands, the basics.

She read the shelf label carefully. She had no idea puffed wheat could cost so much. Why, in her day . . .

In the end, she stuck with her original three choices. It would have to do.

Mel worked the register. She saw him most of the times she came in, which was to say she saw him every two weeks. He nodded at her, smiling at her odd getup.

'Cold walk, Rita?'

'Not once I got movin'.'

'Fixin' to make some breakfast, I see.'

'Yup.'

'Looks good. All you're missing is some sausage. I'm running a special, if you'd like. Two for one.'

She paused, contemplating. More protein would be good for the boy. And oh, the smell of hot sausage patties, browning up in her mother's cast-iron frying pan . . .

She sighed, counted out her money. 'I'm fine, thank you much, Mel.'

'Not a problem, Rita.'

He wrapped up her groceries for her, then looked concerned. 'Not sure about that bag, Rita. Especially if you're afixin' to walk home.'

'Yes, sir.'

'I could give you a ride.'

'Nothin' wrong with the legs God gave me.'

'Well, if you're set on it, maybe I can go in the back, get you a box instead. I'd hate for you to drop those eggs.'

'As you wish.'

Mel returned a short time later with a small box, set inside a plastic bag. He fixed it so she could hold the handles, then she was on her way. She gave him one last nod in parting.

Halfway home, having a resting moment, she checked her bag. He'd added two packages of sausage, plus a box of Earl Grey. For a moment, she was almost overwhelmed at the prospect of a brand-new tea bag, instead of a limp, tired one, three or four steepings gone.

One day, she should thank Mel, but thanking him would mean acknowledging what he had done, and so far, both of them had preferred this system.

It took her a long time to get home. She was starting to feel a little unsteady, swaying more and more with each step.

It would be good to get inside, have a cup of Earl Grey, hot, black, and strong. She would put her feet up in the front parlor as her daddy used to do. Maybe take a little nap.

But when she opened her front door, she discovered she had a guest. The boy had already returned, except this time, he was not waiting on the back porch. He was standing in her parlor, holding a framed portrait of her family.

For a long time, they simply regarded each other. Then Rita stepped firmly into her house, closing the door behind her, unwrapping the scarf from her neck.

'Son, the proper way of entering someone's home is to knock on the door and ask permission. Did you knock on my door, did you ask permission?'

'No, ma'am.'

'Then this was not the proper way of entering my home. Do not do it again.'

'Yes, ma'am.'

That settled, Rita shrugged out of her coat, discarded her hat. 'I was going to have some tea, but I suppose I could make hot cocoa instead.'

His eyes lit up.

'I don't have marshmallows,' she warned. 'Too expensive, that kind of nonsense.'

He nodded his head.

She shuffled past him into the kitchen, pretending not to see the way he watched her through half-slit eyes, nor the slim blade protruding from the back pocket of his jeans.

When your time comes, your time comes, Rita knew. But she was a tough old bird, and she figured the boy would discover soon enough that she had plenty of time left.

ELEVEN

'There are two ways in which spiders ingest food. Those with weak jaws puncture the body of the insect with their fangs and then slowly alternate between injecting digestive fluid through this hole and sucking back the liquefied tissues, until there remains but an empty shell . . . others with strong jaws mash the insect to a pulp between the jaws, as the digestive fluid is regurgitated over it.'

FROM *How to Know the Spiders*, THIRD EDITION, BY B. J. KASTON, 1978

'So to recap, you have met with a potential informant, processed a potential piece of evidence, and received two disturbing phone calls on your cell phone, both of which appear to have originated from our own call desk.'

'According to GBI Special Agent Lynn Stoudt,' Kimberly interjected, 'caller ID on a cell phone is meaningless, thanks to 'spoofing.' You go to the right website, and for a ten-dollar fee, have access to a toll-free number where you supply the destination phone number *and* the caller ID number of your choice. It's cheap, it's easy, and any seven-year-old with a laptop can do it.'

'Hardly an encouraging thought.'

'Now that we know what's going on, our own tech services department can probably set up a system for tracing the original call—'

'More resources,' Supervisory Special Agent Larry Baima countered, 'for a case that isn't a case.'

'Well it's *something*!'

'Yes. It's a mess. For God's sake, Kimberly, how do you manage to get yourself into these situations?'

Baima sighed heavily. Given that it was a rhetorical

question, Kimberly did the smart thing and shut up. In truth, she and Baima respected each other enormously. Which was good, because another supe probably would've written her up by now.

'One more time,' Baima said. 'What precisely do you know?'

'GBI Special Agent Martignetti believes an unknown predator has been picking off high-risk victims – prostitutes, drug addicts, runaways, the like. He has a list of nine girls 'unaccounted for,' plus he has received, from an unknown source, the driver's licenses for six of the girls. Enter Delilah Rose and her story of a fellow hooker, Ginny Jones, last seen three months ago in the company of a john named Dinchara with a fetish for arachnids. Delilah claims to have recovered a ring belonging to Ginny on the floor of Dinchara's SUV. I have traced the ring to Tommy Mark Evans, who graduated in oh-six from Alpharetta High School. Also listed as a classmate: Virginia Jones.

'Adding to the puzzle, we have two phone calls, both placed to my cell phone from an unknown number. First call, I personally believe, was the caller testing out the system, to ensure it would work for the middle-of-the-night main event. At this time, however, I cannot substantiate that claim.'

'But the caller was a male? Not Delilah Rose?'

She hesitated. 'According to Special Agent Stoudt, the same websites that provide caller ID spoofing also provide optional voice scrambling to make the caller sound like a member of the opposite sex. Sort of an upgrade feature. Given that . . . Hell, I'm not sure what to be sure of anymore.'

Baima pinched the bridge of his nose. 'I hate the Internet.'

'Yet it brought us eBay and Amazon.com.'

'I still hate the Internet.'

Kimberly didn't argue with him. 'At the end of the

day,' she ventured, 'I'm guessing the caller was Delilah Rose simply because I gave her my phone number at our last meeting. Maybe this was her way of trying to prove her case.'

'You could say that.' Baima had listened to the tape of the phone call twice already this morning, when Kimberly had brought it straight to his attention. Needless to say, it wasn't a great way to start the day.

'So,' Baima said briskly, 'we have a man – an unidentified subject – sexually assaulting, then torturing a female until she fulfills the UNSUB's demand for a name, at which point she is killed. The woman provides Ginny Jones's name, claiming to be Ginny's mother. Can you substantiate that claim?'

'Just submitted a request to Missing Persons,' Kimberly assured him. She hesitated again, then confessed, 'But I didn't have a first name, just a general description and the last name Jones. That's going to take some processing.'

Another dubious look from her supervisor. 'Moving right along then, your impression of the audio,' he pressed. 'Genuine, fake, real-time, taped? There are numerous possibilities. Give it your best shot.'

Kimberly tried to sound more certain this time. 'I think it was genuine. Not sure of timeline.'

'Explain.'

'The sounds over the phone . . . If this is a tape, then whoever made it knew exactly what violence and murder sound like. It's too real to be a script.'

Baima granted her a short nod of acknowledgment, a supervisory agent's way of giving a special agent just enough rope to hang herself with.

'Timeline?' he prodded.

'Last night, it felt live. This morning, however . . . I'm thinking recorded.'

Kimberly leaned forward, trying to explain herself. 'The second batch of IDs Sal received belong to three

84

roommates who all disappeared, one by one. Coupled with what I heard on the phone, I think that may be how this subject operates – part of his MO is to have each victim choose the next victim, someone close to her. Given the fact that Ginny Jones disappeared three months ago, then what we heard must have occurred prior to December.'

'Ginny's mother was abducted first. She gives up her daughter, who is taken second,' Baima stated.

'It's a theory.'

'Well, theories are fun, Special Agent Quincy, but in case you haven't noticed, we're pretty busy these days. To open a case, federal agents require evidence and – here's a thought – jurisdiction.'

'I have a recording of the phone call—' Kimberly started.

'Not admissible as evidence, as you cannot substantiate the source, nor establish chain of custody if it is a tape, which you believe it may be.'

'The ring—'

'Also issues with chain of custody.'

'The information provided by Delilah Rose—'

'Saddest excuse for a three-oh-two I've ever read in my life,' Baima intoned. 'Strike three, you're out.'

Kimberly scowled. 'Come on, you *heard* that call. We can't walk away. A woman died begging for her life. How can you—'

'We're not.'

Kimberly eyed her supervisor skeptically. 'We're not?'

'No, we're kicking it to GBI, where a case like this belongs. You said Special Agent Martignetti started things. Let Martignetti work missing persons and track down hookers. Better yet, maybe he can come up with a crime scene, or, heaven forbid, a body. One way or another, this is more GBI's jurisdiction than ours.'

'But Delilah won't talk to Martignetti—'

'Maybe no one has asked her nicely enough. Until we have evidence of crossing state lines, this isn't an FBI case.

Period. You have eighteen open files on your desk right now. Here's a thought: Pick one and close it.'

Kimberly scowled, chewing her lower lip. 'And if GBI wants to set up a tap on my cell phone?'

Baima gave her a look. 'Think hard about all the calls you get and from what sources. You're opening the door on each and every one. I'd find a better way to cooperate.'

'Point taken.'

Kimberly rose briskly, careful not to let the triumph show on her face.

At the last minute, her supervisor stopped her. 'How you feelin'?'

'Fine.'

'Your workload is pretty high, Kimberly. While you're still feeling so well, it might be the time to start planning ahead.'

'Is that an order?'

'Call it a friendly suggestion.'

'Once again, I live to serve.'

Now Baima did roll his eyes. Kimberly took that as her cue to leave. Her supervisor had granted her permission to find a better way to cooperate with the state. Surely that included delivering Tommy Mark Evans.

Kimberly's father had entered the Bureau after a brief stint with the Chicago PD. He'd been old-school FBI, in the days when G-men wore dark suits, obeyed all things Hoover, and lived by the mandate Never Embarrass the Bureau.

Truthfully, Kimberly had been too young to remember her father's time in the field, but she liked to picture him in a somber black suit, his dark eyes unreadable as he stood across from some petty gangster, breaking the suspect's alibi with a mere arch of his eyebrow.

After his workaholic ways imploded his marriage, Quincy had gotten into profiling, transferring to what was then called the Behavorial Science Unit at Quantico. In theory, he'd moved into the field of research in order to spend more time with his daughters. In reality, he had traveled more than ever, working over a hundred cases a year, each one more shockingly violent and twisted than the last.

He never talked about his work. Not when he'd been with a field office and certainly not once he started profiling. Instead, Kimberly had taken it upon herself to become immersed in her father's world, sneaking into his study late at night, flipping through his homicide textbooks, glancing at manila folders filled with crime scene photographs, diagrams of blood spatter, reports from coroners' offices filled with phrases like 'petechial hemorrhages,' 'defensive wounds,' and 'postmortem mutilation.'

Kimberly had been an FBI agent for only four years, but in many ways she had been studying violent crime her whole life. First, under the mistaken impression that if she could understand her father's work, then she could understand the man. Second, as a victim herself, trying to wade through the emotional morass that came with knowing her mother died a long, brutal death, fighting for her life inch by inch, as she crawled across the hardwood floors of her elegant Philadelphia town house.

Had Bethie died in a state of terror, feeling caught, helpless, trapped? Or had she felt outraged to have fought so hard and still lost the war? Or perhaps by then her pain had been so great, she'd been merely grateful. Mandy had died the year before. Maybe in those final moments, Bethie was thinking how nice it would be to see her daughter again.

Kimberly didn't know. Kimberly would never know.

And in the hours after midnight, her thoughts often took her to dark places where other people, normal people, God willing, never had to go.

In the end, she and her father rarely spoke of their jobs,

because it wasn't their jobs they had in common. Kimberly worked for the post-9/11 Bureau, operating out of a beautiful office compound in the middle of a serenely landscaped industrial park. Average age was thirty-five. Females comprised a quarter of the workforce. Men thought nothing of wearing pastel shirts.

Instead, Kimberly and her father shared something deeper, more poignant. They understood what it was like to strive so hard to save a stranger's life while living each day knowing they had failed the ones they loved.

Mostly, they understood the importance of always moving forward, because if you stood in one place too long, you risked getting crushed by the boulder weight of regret.

A little after eleven a.m., Kimberly headed to her car. She'd already checked the Georgia Navigator for latest traffic news, and according to the website, GA 400 was clear. Alpharetta lay just twenty-five miles north of the Atlanta Field Office, and Kimberly made good time.

This late in the season, football was done. Instead, Coach Urey was teaching gym class to a bunch of gawky ninth graders who were a mess of arms, legs, and interesting body piercings. When Kimberly finally found the gym, Urey didn't need to see her creds to talk. Her mere presence was enough for him to take a much-needed break.

She warmed him up with the usual prattle – how was football season, what did he think of the new high school, seemed to be a great group of kids.

Urey, who was about as wide as he was tall, with the requisite buzz cut and beer gut, took it all in stride. Should've made it to state this year. Kids really had the heart. But it was a young team, made some mistakes. By gawd they'd get 'em next year.

They walked down a hallway as they spoke. Urey offered her water. She declined. His gaze fell to her stomach, and she could see him mentally wrestling—was the woman pregnant, not pregnant, were FBI agents even *allowed* to be pregnant. Finally, he did the sensible thing and said nothing at all.

'So I'm trying to track down one of your former players,' she started out casually as they turned a corner in the vast hallway of lockers. 'Nothing alarming. I'm just cleaning up odds and ends from another case and have some property to return to him.'

'Property?'

'Class ring. It has the football emblem on it with his jersey number. That's how I knew to come here.'

'Oh sure, the kids load up their rings with everything. Hell, if I'd had all those choices in my day . . .'

Kimberly nodded her head in sympathy, as Urey re-trod the same ground Mac had already walked down. Apparently, men did take their class rings seriously. War medals, and all that.

'Do you know his name?' Urey asked now. 'Or tell me his jersey number. I can probably fill in the rest. Not that I spend too much time with these kids.'

'Ring owner graduated in oh-six,' Kimberly supplied. 'If I understand the symbols correctly, he played quarterback. Jersey number eighty-six.'

Urey stopped walking. For one moment, under the fluorescent lights, his face appeared gray. Then he collected himself, squaring his shoulders resiliently.

'I'm sorry, Special Agent Quincy. If you'd phoned ahead, I coulda saved you a trip. Ring belonged to Tommy Mark Evans. Fine kid. One of the best QBs I ever had. Great arm, but also solid. Held up under pressure. He graduated magna cum laude and got himself a football scholarship to Penn State.'

'He's out of town?' Kimberly asked in confusion. 'Going to college in Pennsylvania?'

But Urey shook his head. 'Not anymore. Tommy came

home for Christmas last year. Guess he went for a drive. Nobody really knows. But apparently he was in the wrong place at the wrong time. Took two bullets to the brain, *tap, tap* on the forehead. Parents still haven't recovered. You just don't expect a strong, handsome kid like that to suddenly wind up dead.'

TWELVE

Burgerman took me to the park.

Younger kids were on the swings, teeter-totter, merry-go-round. Some older kids, closer to my age, were flying around the beat-up court in a pickup game of hoops.

Burgerman nudged me. 'Go ahead. Join 'em. It's all right. Get some color on your face. Christ, you look like shit, you know?'

For a moment, I didn't believe he really meant that I could go. He nudged me harder, nearly knocking me to the ground, so I took the hint and went. I joined the team with shirts. Going skins would've invited too many questions.

In the beginning, I held back. It felt strange to be on a playground, to be around other kids, to hear them laughing and dribbling and swearing a little when a boy missed a shot or took an elbow to the gut. I kept waiting for everyone to stop and stare. I wanted them to ask, What the hell happened to you? *I wanted someone to say,* Hey, buddy, wake up, it's all been a bad dream, but it's over now and life is good.

But no one said anything. They played basketball.

And, eventually, so did I.

I could smell fresh-mowed grass. Hear happy sounds, kids goofing off in these last few days before summer became mercilessly hot and everyone headed straight to the swimming pools. There were birds. And flowers. And a vast blue sky and so much . . . everything.

The world, going on spinning. Round and round and round.

I went up for a shot. Made it. A kid slapped me on the shoulder.

'Nice hook.'

I beamed, went back for more.

I don't know time anymore. Time belongs to other kids, boys not caught in the Burgerman's grinding embrace. I just am, until I'm told otherwise, then I am not.

So I played until the Burgerman told me to stop. And then I didn't play anymore.

Burgerman led me to the side. Sun was starting to go down. Some of the other boys wandered off. Moms and older girls collected the little ones like ducks in a row, waddling them down the street.

I noticed one little boy off on his own, digging in the sandbox.

Burgerman noticed him, too.

He looked at me. 'Boy, fetch me that kid.'

Screaming. It went on and on and on. High-pitched and thin, a babble. I tried to cover my ears. Burgerman stopped long enough to slap me upside the head, knocking me into the wall. He socked me in the gut and when I doubled over, caught me again beneath the chin.

'ARE YOU LOOKING, BOY! BETTER PAY ATTENTION.'

And then the screaming again, on and on and on. Until finally, the Burgerman collapsed, rolled off, started digging around for his customary cigarette.

I could taste blood. I'd bitten my tongue, had a gash along my cheek from the Burgerman's ring. I didn't feel too steady. Thought I'd be sick.

92

The little boy had stopped struggling. He just lay on the bed, eyes glassed over, face stupefied.

I wondered if that's how I must have once looked.

Then he noticed me looking. His eyes found mine. He stared at me. Stared so long, so hard. Pleeeease.

I careened out of the room, made it down the hall, got to the bathroom just in time. Once I started, I couldn't stop. I vomited and vomited and still it wasn't enough. I couldn't get the horror out of my belly. It had seeped into my blood. I couldn't get it out. I couldn't get it off. So I threw up water and bile until I dry-heaved and collapsed onto the floor.

I blacked out then. It's as close to mercy as I ever got.

When I came back around, I could hear sounds again. Snoring, this time. Wouldn't last, though. An hour, maybe two.

The Burgerman always woke up hungry.

I crawled back down the hall. Peered inside the room. I couldn't help myself. I had to see, even if I knew I would be sorry.

The boy had curled up into a ball. He wasn't moving, but he wasn't asleep. He was staring at the far wall. I knew what he was doing. He was practicing being small. Because if he could be small enough, maybe the Burgerman wouldn't notice him anymore.

I knew what I must do.

Burgerman left his pants on the floor. I wriggled over to them, gingerly putting my hand into the pocket, until I found the key. It felt heavy and sharp in my hand. I didn't think about it. Just kept moving.

Over to the side of the bed, in front of the boy. Finger to my lips, shhhh.

I held up his clothes. The boy, maybe five or six, just lay there.

I thought I should tell him something. I didn't know what. He wasn't ready for the great truths of life. None of us were.

Finally, I patted his shoulder and dressed him as if he were a baby.

I left him one moment. Had to unlock the door. It squeaked a little upon opening and I stilled. Snuffling snore from the bedroom. So far so good. I peered out into the long gray length of the hall. No one was about. Seemed to me in this apartment complex no one was ever about.

Now or never, I decided.

And for some reason, I don't know why, I remembered that first night, the night I woke up to find the Burgerman standing at the foot of my bed. I remembered the sound of my father snoring down the hall. And, remembering, I started to cry, though at this stage of the game, tears were too little too late.

I crept back to the bedroom, blubbering. Grabbed the boy's shoulder, shook him hard.

His dark eyes slowly came up to mine. A faint hint of consciousness swam beneath the surface. Then he zoned out again. I slapped him hard, grabbed his shoulder, and yanked him to the floor.

Snoring stopped. Bed squeaked as the Burgerman finally moved.

Now I clasped my hand over the boy's mouth, pressed him against me, willed him to not make a sound.

Did I pray? Did I have any prayers left? None came to mind.

Bed creaked again, Burgerman tossing back and forth. Then . . . silence.

Not much time anymore. The beast was starting to stir.

I grabbed the little boy beneath the armpits and dragged him toward the door. Ten steps. Eight. Seven. Six. Five.

The boy wouldn't walk. Why the hell wouldn't he walk? I needed him to get his feet beneath him. Wake up. Stop shaking. Run, dammit, run. What was wrong with him anyway?

What kind of stupid shit didn't fight back? What kind

of miserable, stupid, pathetic boy let a man do this to him time after time, and couldn't even run for the goddamn door!

And suddenly I was yelling at the boy. I don't know how it happened. I was standing over him, looming over him, screaming so hard that spittle sprayed from my mouth: 'MOVE YOUR FUCKING ASS! DO YOU THINK HE'S GONNA SLEEP FOREVER? YOU STUPID, NAUGHTY BOY. GET UP. RUN, DAMN YOU, RUN. I'M NOT YOUR FUCKING DADDY!'

The five-year-old boy curled up in a ball, put his hands over his head, and whimpered.

And then, I realized what I didn't hear anymore.

Snoring.

I turned. I was helpless not to. Standing in front of the open door, so close, but so far away. The man's latest plaything curled at my feet.

The Burgerman stood behind me.

He smiled in the dark.

And in that smile, I knew what was about to happen next.

Time belongs to other boys. Boys that have not been beaten and starved and raped. Boys that have not stood there and watched a grown man kill a kid with his bare hands.

Boys that were not then handed a shovel and made to go out and help dig the grave.

'You want to die, son?' the Burgerman asked casually, standing back from the hole, leaning on his spade.

The body was wrapped in an old towel, lying beneath an azalea bush. I didn't look at it.

'It's not hard,' the Burgerman continued on. 'Hell, climb into the hole. Lie down next to your little friend. I won't stop you.'

I didn't move. After a moment, the Burgerman laughed.

'See, you still want to live, boy. No shame in that.'

He gave me an almost affectionate pat on the head. 'Pick up the shovel, son. I'll show you a trick to save your back. That's it, put your legs into it. See? Now repeat.'

Burgerman taught me how to dig a perfect grave. Then we returned to the apartment, packed up our clothes, and vanished.

THIRTEEN

'The spider's appetite may often appear insatiable, the abdomen swelling to accommodate added food.'

FROM *How to Know the Spiders*,
THIRD EDITION, BY B. J. KASTON, 1978

Kimberly found Sal at the Atlanta Bread Company. He was munching on a sandwich, a smear of mayo dotting his right cheek. Though he'd agreed to the rendezvous, he still appeared wary as she approached.

'Sprouts?' she asked, inspecting his lunch. 'Funny, you didn't strike me as a sprouts man.'

'Hey, I like veggies. Besides, after Sausage McMuffins for breakfast . . .'

'You ever cook, Sal?'

'As little as possible.'

'Me, too.'

She took a seat, sliding her brown leather saddlebag from her shoulder and digging around for her lunch.

'Are you eatin' pudding again?' Sal wanted to know.

'Cottage cheese with blueberries. Gotta get protein somehow.'

'How far along?'

'Nearly twenty-two weeks.'

'Don't look it.'

'It's the pudding,' she assured him. 'Have kids?'

He shook his head. 'Don't even have a wife.'

'Hasn't stopped other guys from procreating.'

'True, but I'm a traditionalist. Or a procrastinator. Haven't decided which. Does it move?'

'What, the baby?'

'Yes, the baby. It's not like I care about cottage cheese.'

'Yeah, she's starting to. Lots of little movements that get progressively worse if I'm trying to eat or sleep. If I'm doing nothing, of course, she's perfectly quiet.'

'She?'

'That's my guess. Mac wants a boy. Major league pitcher, I think. What's with you guys?'

'Sports matter,' Sal said seriously. 'What else would we do on Monday nights?'

Kimberly dug into her cottage cheese. She had a lot to report, but figured it was only fair to let Sal call the shots. He probably had some aggression to work out. Sure enough, he got straight into it.

'Nice, Quincy. Tossing me a name like that. Just enough information to make me feel like you cared without actually putting out. I have to say, at least when I got screwed, it was by a class act.'

'Think I shoulda told you 'bout the ring, huh?'

'It crossed my mind.'

Kimberly spread her hands. She'd given this some thought, and this was the best she could offer. 'Look: We can spend the next fifteen minutes with you feeling pissy because I didn't share the ring, and me feeling pissy because you tried to muscle in on an informant who'd already asked for me, or we can agree that we're both aggressive investigators, and get on with the matters at hand.'

'I don't trust you, you don't trust me, but because we're both untrustworthy, we oughtta get along fine?'

'Exactly.'

Sal considered the matter. 'Fair enough,' he conceded. 'Proceed.'

He finished his sandwich, dabbing at his face. He missed the mayo on his cheek, and without thinking, she reached across the table and got it with her finger. The intimacy of the gesture struck her after the fact, and she sat back, embarrassed.

'So, ummm' – she dug around in her cottage cheese, fishing for a blueberry – 'Delilah Rose gave me a class ring that allegedly belonged to Ginny Jones. I traced the ring to Tommy Mark Evans, who graduated from Alpharetta High School in oh-six. Ginny Jones was one of his classmates.'

'They were an item?'

'Coach Urey didn't think so. His memory was that Tommy had been dating a girl named Darlene Angler for most of the season, but maybe broke up before graduation. He wasn't clear on that detail. I spoke to the school secretary, however, and she's getting her hands on a yearbook for us. Hopefully that'll arrive by end of week. She looked up Virginia Jones for me—'

'Without a warrant?' Sal asked in surprise.

'I was using my nice voice. Besides, that's why you ask the secretary. They're preprogrammed to look up files for everyone at any time. They don't stop to ask why.'

'Good point.'

'So, Ginny attended Alpharetta for four years, but didn't graduate. Dropped out in February. Never returned. According to her files, calls were made to her home, but never answered. Finally, there's a yellow sticky with a handwritten note – 'family appears to have left town.' Guess that was the end of matters.

'Ginny had one parent listed as guardian. A mother, Veronica L. Jones. I made a couple of quick phone calls: Veronica L. Jones used to work as a waitress at the Hungryman Diner, but according to the manager, she no-showed her shifts and they never heard from her again. They do, however, have a last paycheck for her to pick up, should I locate her current whereabouts.'

Sal's eyes widened. 'She left behind a paycheck? That doesn't sound good.'

'Don't think it is. The Joneses owned a house in

Alpharetta. The town filed a lien against it in the spring of oh-seven to collect back property taxes. House is now in foreclosure. I couldn't find any trace of a missing persons report filed for either Veronica or Virginia Jones, and yet both of them are clearly gone.'

'As of February oh-six?' Sal asked with a frown.

Kimberly shrugged. 'February is when Ginny stopped attending school, so I would assume somewhere in that time frame.'

'But according to your friend Delilah Rose, Ginny didn't disappear until three months ago, November oh-seven. So color me confused.'

'Ah, but this is where the phone call gets interesting. Assume for a moment that the woman on the tape is Ginny's mother, Veronica Jones.'

'She says she is, so good assumption.'

'Well, let's say she was kidnapped in February oh-six. Now, Ginny comes home, but it's an empty house. And night after night, it remains an empty house. Ginny could do the sensible thing and contact the authorities, but what kind of teenager does that? Instead, she splits. Maybe she has friends in Sandy Springs, or thinks it'll be great to go clubbing for a bit, live on the wild side, never have a curfew . . .'

'Takes off to party, gets sucked into the scene, never gets back out.'

'Yeah. So mom's victim number one.'

'And nearly two years later,' Sal filled in skeptically, 'Ginny is victim number two?'

'Actually,' Kimberly said, 'Ginny is victim number three.'

'Tommy Mark Evans graduated from Alpharetta in June oh-six. Star quarterback, magna cum laude, all-round hometown hero. Got a full scholarship to Penn State and took off for college in the fall. He returned for Christmas break. December twenty-seventh, he told his parents he was going out for a drive. Never came home.

'They found his truck three days later, tucked back on an old dirt road. Tommy was slumped over the wheel, dead from a double-tap to the forehead.'

Sal arched a brow. 'Someone's been watching *The Sopranos*. Any evidence the kid was into drugs? Using, dealing? Maybe the landscape changed while he was outta town, and the new kingpin didn't like him coming back.'

'Coach Urey didn't think so, but he believes the sun rose and set on Tommy's shoulders, so I'd take his opinion with a grain of salt. Alpharetta PD handled the investigation. According to Urey, they never developed any major leads or made an arrest. The parents are still pretty torn up about it, losing their son at Christmas like that.'

'So now we got one missing parent and one dead classmate, both linked to Ginny Jones. Any other tragedies at Alpharetta I should know about?'

Kimberly shrugged. 'Hell, it's a big town. We're probably only beginning. That's why you should talk to the Alpharetta police.'

'Me?'

'They'll take your call before mine. Besides, technically speaking, I'm not even on the case. I did all this out of the kindness of my heart.'

Sal appeared wary again. Kimberly didn't blame him. What overworked fed ever did anything out of the kindness of her heart? Still, she thought a thank-you would be nice.

No such luck.

'I want the ring,' Sal declared. 'My case, my evidence.'

'It's secured in the evidence vault,' she assured him. 'I'll arrange for the transfer.'

'Anything else you haven't told me?'

Kimberly started to say no, then realized she'd left out one other rather salient fact, and sighed. 'Ummm, possibly

Delilah Rose mentioned that Ginny Jones was last seen with a customer going by the alias Mr. Dinchara.'

'Mr. Dinchara?'

'An anagram for 'arachnid.' Apparently, Dinchara likes to bring his pets along. You know, nothing like a night out with your favorite tarantula.'

Sal appeared positively mesmerized. 'No shit?'

'Not in the least. Guess no one else has mentioned him yet?'

'I think I would remember a story like that. What does he do with his spiders?'

'Oh, have them roam various body parts of the girls. Or, if he paid extra, watch.'

'*Watch?*'

'Ever get the feeling the world is becoming a freakier and freakier place?'

'Only every time I watch a reality TV show. So, a Mr. Dinchara with a pet tarantula. Hell, shouldn't be too hard to get a bead on a customer that unique. What was his involvement with Jones?'

'He was a client. Guess the spiders didn't bother Ginny; as you can guess they didn't worry Ms. Rose – apparently she has a soft spot for all things with eight legs. However, in addition to last seeing Ginny with Mr. Dinchara, Delilah claims she found Tommy's class ring on the floor of Dinchara's SUV. Ginny used to wear the ring around her neck on a chain, like a talisman. Delilah implied there was no way Ginny would've willingly left the ring behind.'

Sal was back to frowning. 'If Ginny wore Tommy's ring around her neck, wouldn't that imply to you that they were more than classmates?'

'Generally, the wearing of a fellow's ring is a sign of more than friends.'

'So clearly there is more to Tommy Mark Evans than Coach Urey suspects.'

'There always is. But if Ginny and Tommy were so tight,

why did Ginny take off? Last I knew, landing a hunky, varsity quarterback boyfriend would give any teenage girl reason to stay. I mean, the bragging rights alone . . .'

'We're talking ourselves in circles,' Sal said with a sigh.

'Lack of information will do that to you.'

'Bottom line, we now have ten missing females, one dead high school quarterback, one class ring connecting Missing Female A with Dead Male B, and one creepy-crawly mystery man. Anything I missed?'

'Ten dead bodies.'

He scowled. 'Anything else?'

She shrugged, more serious this time. 'The only real lead we have.'

'Which is?'

'Delilah Rose.'

FOURTEEN

'. . . the venom was used primarily as a paralyzing agent to inactivate the prey, which may actually remain alive for four to five days. The spider then feeds at its convenience.'

FROM *Biology of the Brown Recluse Spider*, BY JULIA MAXINE HITE, WILLIAM J. GLADNEY, J. L. LANCASTER, JR., AND W. H. WHITCOMB, DEPARTMENT OF ENTOMOLOGY, DIVISION OF AGRICULTURE, UNIVERSITY OF ARKANSAS, FAYETTEVILLE, MAY 1966

It was after six when Kimberly left the office. Traffic was piling up, the highway one long tangled snarl. She thought of heading back to work, waiting out the worst of the congestion. God knew she had a million calls she could make, 302s to process, reports to review. She didn't, though.

She drove to Alpharetta.

She didn't know the area well. Atlanta was so large she could spend decades here and still not make a dent in the explosion of sprawling townships that marked the city's phenomenal rate of growth. The city felt like a web to her, one that was constantly being spun larger and larger, gobbling up chicken farms and country lanes until a scenic drive one year became the location of the latest mall the next. And yet the state absorbed the booming developments relatively easily, peace still two hours away in the northern mountains, or three hours away on the southern beaches. Mac claimed there was no place else on earth he'd rather live.

She was still considering the matter herself.

She was armed with a map, a cell phone, and a nearly photographic memory. How lost could she get?

The drive to Ginny Jones's house wasn't bad. The

abandoned residence formed a small, gray mound against the darkening sky. Windows boarded up. Yard desperately overgrown. Yet it wasn't the most neglected-looking property on the block.

Kimberly worked her way through side streets, as lots became larger, houses more sprawling, lawns more perfectly manicured. It took her half a dozen wrong turns and about twenty minutes, then she found the next address on her list: Tommy Mark Evans's home.

It was a stately brick Colonial situated atop half an acre of emerald-green lawn. A silver BMW SUV was parked in the driveway. Expertly shaped corkscrew hedges lined the drive. That told her enough.

So Ginny was the poor, fatherless girl; Tommy the rich football hero. Now, was the situation more like Cinderella meets Prince Charming, or Lady and the Tramp, with the genders reversed?

Kimberly started to see the possibilities. Such as Tommy dating Ginny Jones, but feeling pressure from his peer group/parents to keep it quiet. Perhaps Ginny was feeling a little tender on the subject. All the more reason to run, once Mommy stopped coming home at night?

Kimberly had a final stop to make. It was now completely dark, making it difficult for her to read the map and drive her car. She took it in half-mile batches, looping through a maze of side streets, office parks, and residential areas until she nearly lost herself. She thought she was closer to Ginny's neighborhood than Tommy's, but could no longer be certain. A left at the oak tree, a right by the large birch.

Tires left pavement. She bumped along on the dirt. One of the last few rural roads in the area. Probably be developed by this time next year. Then there'd be nothing left to indicate where a young man had died.

She found the exact spot without difficulty. A white cross stood gleaming in the dark, a Christmas wreath drying out at the base, red bow flapping lightly in the wind.

Kimberly pulled over twenty yards back. She grabbed her jacket and walked the final distance to the memorial.

It was past seven-thirty now. She was not far from civilization, but the trees formed an effective buffer, and standing in this spot, she couldn't hear the sound of passing cars or make out the distant lights of a bustling community. With the new moon floating dark and hidden overhead, the only illumination came from her vehicle's twin headlights. It was quiet, still.

In spite of herself, she shivered.

Tommy Mark Evans, it said down the cross. Then, along the arms: *Beloved son.*

Kimberly looked around: at the thick cluster of rhododendrons, nearly higher than her head; the thin, scratchy outline of straggly pine trees, clutching at the night sky. She felt the deep ruts of the dirt road beneath her feet. Used her flashlight to illuminate the grooves of tire marks tracking in and out.

She could picture a young man joyriding down this lane, pedal to the metal, shrieking each time his monster tires hit a rut and sent him airborne. She could picture a young man and a female friend tucked alongside the road, necking hard and heavy, steaming up the windshield.

She could not picture a college kid coming out here alone, pulling over for no reason, and winding up shot two times to the forehead.

Tommy Mark Evans knew his attacker. She had no doubt in her mind.

An owl hooted. A squirrel burst out, making a mad dash across the lane. Kimberly watched the grass rustle on the other side of the road long after the squirrel disappeared into the brush, and the owl swooped by overhead.

She felt a fluttering kick in her side, her own child waking up. She pressed her hand against her lower abdomen, and for a moment, the powerful feeling of life while standing before a scene of such tragedy left her unutterably sad. She wondered how Tommy's parents had made it through the holidays. Did they surround themselves with photos of their son? Or did they find it easiest to pretend his life had never happened?

How had Kimberly's father done it? Looking at all those photos, visiting all those crime scenes of young girls and boys so viciously murdered, then coming home to his own family each night? How did you comfort your child's tears over a scratched knee when you could picture another child missing all of her fingers? How could you tell your child there was no such thing as monsters when you witnessed their handiwork each and every day?

And how had he borne it, when the call finally came in the middle of the night: *Sir, we regret to inform you about your daughter* . . .

Kimberly herself rarely thought about her sister. Her mother, yes. But Mandy . . . That loss was more insidious in ways she couldn't explain. A child expected to one day lose her parents. Her sibling, on the other hand . . . A sister was a companion, a peer. They were supposed to grow old together, standing up at each other's weddings, swapping advice on child-rearing, while one day trying to determine how to best take care of Dad.

Once, Kimberly had been the younger half of a paired set. Now she was an only child.

You'd think she'd get used to it, but she didn't.

Kimberly turned, started for her car, arms wrapped around her torso for warmth.

She had only taken two steps before her cell rang.

It was too dark, she thought. She was too alone, her mind filled with too many unsettling thoughts. Veronica Jones's last desperate screams. Her sister, head wrapped in white gauze on the hospital bed as the doctor flipped the proverbial switch and they stood together, she and her parents, to watch Mandy die. And then, just a year later, the House of Horrors that became her mother's last stand.

Mandy had been lucky. She had not lived long enough to know that, with her death, she had sealed their mother's fate. Had Veronica Jones understood? Had she truly realized what her anguished confession would mean for her daughter?

Her phone rang again. Kimberly wanted to walk away. But she was her father's daughter, helpless to say no, even when she of all people knew better.

'Special Agent Quincy,' she answered.

Nothing.

She waited for someone to tell her hush, for another macabre scene to start playing out in the background. But second passed into second. She heard nothing at all.

She checked signal strength, tried again. 'Special Agent Quincy.'

Still no words, but now, as she concentrated, she thought she caught the sound of breathing, low and even. She let the silence roll out again. The strategy didn't work.

'I would like to help you,' she said presently. 'It's okay if you need to talk.'

Nothing.

'Is someone there? Are you afraid of being overheard? Just make a sound, like you're clearing your throat. I'll take that as an affirmative.'

But the caller remained silent.

She started to feel frustrated now, walking in a small circle.

'Are you in danger?'

Nothing.

'If you talk to me, provide information, I may be able to offer protection. You can't just dial my number, however. You have to be willing to talk.'

Then, finally, that small voice again, high-strung, but hushed, like a child's: 'Shhhh.'

'Please, I want to help . . .'

'He knows what you're doing.'

'Who knows—'

'He knows everything.'

'Can you give me a name?'

'It's only a matter of time.'

'Listen to me—'

'You will be the next specimen in the collection.'

'Can you meet? Name the time and place, I'll be there.'

'Shhh. Remember to look up.'

The call disconnected. Kimberly stood there a moment longer, clutching her phone, totally bewildered. And then, mostly because she could not help herself, she glanced up.

The night sky yawned above her. A pinprick of stars. The more distant glow of the city. She forced herself to take in the shadowed outline of the trees, the bushes, the distant horizon. Nothing loomed in the dark unknown. No boogeyman leapt out to get her.

Then, to her right, a tree limb cracked. She forgot about decorum and bolted for her car. Running hard, fumbling with the key. She yanked open the heavy door and leapt inside. Door shut, locks engaged, engine cranked.

At the last minute, she caught herself before she tore down the dirt road like the half-dressed heroine of a teen slasher film. She was a professional, for God's sake. And heavily armed.

She got her breathing to steady, and safe inside the confines of her automobile, took final inventory. Nothing moved in the woods around her. No headless horseman came careening her way.

Just a solitary white cross, picked up in the crosshairs of her headlights.

She drove home slowly, trying to make sense of the caller's latest warning and wishing that everything about this case didn't fill her with dread.

Mac was home when she arrived. She pulled in next to his truck, shutting off the engine. She pasted a smile on her face, then braved the house.

Hallway light was on. Kitchen, too. She tossed down her shoulder bag, shrugged out of her jacket, wandering down the hall. No sign of Mac. She tried the family room with the large-screen TV and Mac's favorite black leather recliner. Still no husband.

She returned to the kitchen, looking for a note and starting to feel herself panicking again for no good reason. He could be in the shower, or out back, or have gone next door. There were a million logical explanations.

Except now she was wondering. The caller had her cell phone number. How much else did he know about her?

'Kimberly.'

She jumped and twirled, her hand automatically going to her chest. Mac stood in the doorway of the kitchen, leather bomber jacket on, dark hair windblown, as if just returning from a walk.

'Heavens, you scared me,' she said, hand coming down, feeling foolish.

Mac continued to regard her somberly, making no move to cross the kitchen, kiss her on the cheek, welcome her home.

'It's late,' he said at last.

'Sorry, got stuck at work.'

'I called the office.'

'I was out.' She frowned at him, not liking his tone. 'Is something up? If you wanted to reach me so badly, you could've called my cell.'

'I didn't want to use it,' he said flatly.

Her frown deepened. 'What the hell is going on, Mac? I work late all the time. So do you. Since when do either one of us bring on the inquisition?'

'You're working the case.'

'What case?'

Now he did take a step forward, his face intent. 'You know what I mean, Kimberly. Delilah Rose. This arachnid guy. You're getting involved. Five months pregnant. Five months *pregnant*, for God's sake, and you're wading knee-deep into this shit.'

'Of course I am. I'm a federal agent. Wading into shit is my job.'

'No, wading into shit is the Bureau's job. And GBI's job. As in, this state is swarming with hundreds of perfectly qualified investigators who could all handle this case. Like Sal, or your buddy Harold, or Mike, or John, or Gina. Each of them skilled and dedicated and just as tough as you are. But they can't work this case, can they, Kimberly? It always has to be you.'

'Hey, I'll have you know I kicked the case to Sal Martignetti first thing this morning. Even arranged to transfer the ring to state custody. You got your wish, Mac, it is GBI's ball game.'

'Then where have you been?' He asked the question quietly, which is how she knew she was in trouble.

And heaven help her, she dug in her heels, preparing for a fight they'd both probably regret later. But that was then, and this was now, and she never could stand to be wrong.

'Since when do I have to account for my time to you?' she asked.

'*Goddammit*,' Mac exploded. 'You think I don't know? I've already been on the phone with Sal. Who, by the way, wants to talk to you about his visit to Tommy Mark Evans's parents. You went to check things out, didn't you, Kimberly? Couldn't trust Sal to do the work. No, he's only investigated fifty or sixty homicides in the past ten years, what the hell could he know about this kind of thing? Did you hit the bar scene? Go hooker shopping? Or did you stand on a street corner and call, 'Here Mr. Freaky Scary Man. Come find fresh bait.' '

'I did no such thing! I drove around Alpharetta, checking out Ginny's and Tommy's respective homes. Nothing dangerous. Just sightseeing.'

'And your phone? Did it stay quiet?'

She thinned her lips mutinously, which was answer enough.

This time, Mac pounded the counter. 'That's it. As your husband, I have never laid down the law. But enough is enough. If you don't have the good sense to see it, I certainly do. You're off this case. *Fini*. Done. Let Sal handle it!'

'Please, it was just heavy breathing, obscene phone call one-oh-one. I'm not going to be chased off by a kid playing games, and you should be ashamed of yourself for even suggesting such a thing.'

'Kimberly, *don't you get it?*'

'Get what?' she shouted back, honestly bewildered.

'It's not about you anymore. It's about our baby, the unborn child growing in your stomach. Who is already growing and experiencing the world, even from the womb. Our child has ears, you know. I checked that damn book you gave me. At the twenty-week mark, babies can hear. And what the hell did our baby get to listen to last night?'

It took her a second. Then the dots connected, and her hands went reflexively to her belly, cradling the gently rounded curve in a belated act of protection. She hadn't thought, hadn't realized . . .

But yes, she was past the twenty-week mark. When the fetus had ears and the really dedicated mothers started playing Mozart and Beethoven in order to develop neonatal geniuses. Except Kimberly didn't have the time or patience for that nonsense. No, she just had her unborn child listen to the sound of a woman dying.

'I'm sure . . .' she started, then stopped, unable to continue.

Mac's shoulders finally came down. Across the kitchen,

his rage appeared to drain from him. He looked simply haunted instead. She should cross to him, she thought, slip her arms around his waist, rest her head upon his chest. Maybe if he felt the baby move the way she felt the baby move, he would understand that their child was doing fine, babies were resilient, blah, blah, blah.

But she couldn't move.

She stood there. Her baby could hear. And what had she made her baby listen to last night?

Mac was right. Life had changed.

'Kimberly,' Mac ventured, softer this time, tired. 'We're going to get through this.'

'If I quit my job?' she asked quietly. 'Stop being an agent, stop being a workaholic, stop being me?'

'You know I would never ask that of you.'

'But you are.'

'No, I'm not,' he insisted, voice rising again. 'There's a difference between not working at all and not working violent crimes. There's a difference between asking you to stay home and asking you to reduce your hours to forty a week. There's a difference between saying, hey, bail on all your assignments, and saying, Kimberly, please don't take on a new case that's not even FBI jurisdiction. I'm not asking for the sun, the moon, the stars at night. I'm just asking for common sense.'

'*Common sense?*'

'Maybe I could've said that better.'

'What's different right now, Mac? You tell me, what's really different?'

His turn to be confused. 'The baby?'

'The pregnancy! We're not dealing with a baby yet, we're talking about my body. The exact same body I've taken to work the past four years and brought home safe again.'

'That's not entirely true—'

'The hell it is! You want to talk trust? Common sense?

Then trust me to take care of myself, and this body, the way I have for the past four years. I'm not walking into shoot-outs. I'm not serving high-risk warrants. I don't even go to the firing range anymore, to avoid exposure to lead. Hell, I just spent six days at a crime scene and never even crossed over the yellow tape, just to be on the safe side. I'm taking my prenatals, avoiding alcohol, and watching my intake of fresh fish. Frankly, I'm doing a damn good job of tending myself and the baby, and yet the first time the phone rings, you're ready to pull rank. 'Hey, little lady, this is too tough for you, time to sit it out.' '

'I did not say that!'

'You might as well have!'

'What is wrong with you?' He was back to shouting now. 'How can you be so damn stubborn? This is our baby. How can you not love it as much as I do?'

The second he said the words, she could tell he wanted them back. But of course, it was too late. He had gone and said it, the statement that had hung in the air between them from the moment she had first discovered her pregnancy. His fear. Her fear. She had thought it would hurt. It did.

'Kimberly—'

'I think we should call it a night.'

'You know I don't mean that.'

'But you do, Mac. You do. Your mom stayed home with you. Your sisters are at home with their kids. For all of your talk, you're still a traditionalist at heart. The husband works. The wife stays at home. And she should be happy to do it, assuming she loves her family.'

'You're right, we should call it a night.'

'I already did.'

She turned, stomping down the hall toward their bedroom.

She expected him to follow. That was their pattern. She was hardheaded, proud, stubborn to a fault. But in the end, he could always talk her down, finagle a kiss, make her smile.

She needed him to talk her down. She needed him to put his arms around her and tell her she would be a good mother and she wasn't as awful and selfish and self-destructive as she suddenly felt.

But Mac didn't follow her down the hall. After a moment, she heard the front door open, shut, and then she was all alone.

FIFTEEN

Burgerman took away my Birthday. Said I didn't need it anymore. We celebrated a new day, homecoming. The day I belonged to him.

On my fourth homecoming, he brought me a case of beer and a hooker.

'I don't know,' the prostitute said. 'He looks pretty young.'

'What the fuck do you care?' Burgerman asked. 'I'm his father, and if I want to show my kid a good time, what's it to you? You should be grateful to finally have some fresh cock, instead of the usual limp dick. Go on, fine-looking kid like that. Knock yourself out.'

Funny thing was, I was a decent-looking kid. My life had ended, but my body didn't seem to know it. I grew. My shoulders broadened. My arms gained thin ropes of muscle. I even had the beginnings of facial hair.

I was getting old. Old enough that the Burgerman didn't touch me so often anymore.

He had other uses for me now.

The girl stepped obediently forward. Burgerman got out the camera.

'Don't be nervous, now,' the girl said. She touched my cheek. I flinched.

'Tell you what, honey, just block him from your mind.

Just pretend he's not even there. It's just you and me. A good-looking boy, a pretty young girl.' She giggled, revealing two missing teeth. 'Fine couple like us oughtta be able to have some fun.'

She took my hand, tucked it under her shirt, on top of her breasts. 'How does that feel, honey? Nice, huh? Gotta say, T-n-A guys love me. I got all the right curves.'

I thought she felt soft, flabby. I didn't know what to do with my fingers. My face was burning crimson. I looked away, but still couldn't stop the blush.

She moved closer to me now, her tongue licking her lips, her hands pressing my palm against her squishy breast. 'Come on, baby, flick your fingers over my nipple. Knead it, work it, you can't hurt me. Yeah, baby, that's what it's there for. Pretend I'm your mama, and you just wanna take a drink.'

I yanked my hand back, horrified. She was still licking her lips, her hips jutting out in a short black leather skirt, rolls of fat spilling over the waist.

Don't make me, I wanted to yell. Oh God, get away from me.

'Fuck it,' Burgerman said. 'You're scaring the damn kid. Just get it done.'

Girl shrugged, got on her knees, and went to work on my pants. Before I had time to protest, she had yanked out my penis and plopped it into her mouth.

I recoiled, but she had both hands gripping my hips, holding on tight. Burgerman had moved closer, zooming in.

He reached over casually and smacked me upside of the head.

'Moan, you dipshit. Camera's rolling. Make it look good.'

And finally, in that instant, his handprint red on my cheek, I could moan. I could make it look good. Those were my instructions and I knew how to function when doing what I was told. My body insisted on growing live flesh and blood, when in reality, I was nothing more than a robot. Obedient. Passive. Programmable.

The Burgerman seemed to realize this, too. He barked out more instructions and that speeded things along.

When it was done, the Burgerman was obviously fired up. I wondered if he would make me perform again, with the girl watching. I had been shamed in so many ways, it should hardly matter, and yet it bothered me. Maybe because she had been my first, and I wanted to seem like a man to her, even if she was nothing but a whore.

Burgerman didn't touch me, though. He went after the hooker instead.

She protested. He hadn't paid her enough, this wasn't the deal. So he beat her on the head with the camera till she shut up. Then he did what he'd wanted to do all along while her eyes swelled up and her lip bled.

Later, he tossed some money at her, and I could tell she realized she was lucky to get that much. She grabbed her clothes and fled.

Even hookers are smarter than me.

Burgerman cracked open the first beer, handed it to me. Took a second for himself, and offered a toast.

'Nice fucking, son. Knew I'd done good choosing you. You're gonna make me rich.'

He popped the tape out of the camera and, whistling, went into the closet, where he placed it in the safe with all the other dirty movies and home photos he'd started selling for boatloads of cash.

We smoked some joints. Drank more beers. Eventually, I passed out.

When I woke up, Burgerman was asleep on the sofa, snoring loudly.

The door was unlocked. I didn't even think about it anymore.

I got up and went to bed.

I dreamed of my mother, but when I woke up, I couldn't recall her face.

Dark hair, light hair, brown eyes like me?

I remember she liked to test spaghetti noodles by tossing them against the refrigerator. It made my brother and me giggle. I remember in the summertime, she would make pitchers of sangria and hang out by the pool.

I remember a long time ago, a lifetime ago, I sat on her lap with her arms around me and felt safe.

I can't remember my mother's face.

I haven't decided yet if I will try again tomorrow.

SIXTEEN

'In most species, the egg sac is closely guarded by the female.'

FROM 'SPIDER REARING,'
WWW.INSECTED.ARIZONA.EDU/SPIDERREAR.HTM

'Tommy's parents are convinced he was killed by someone he knew,' Sal was saying. 'Better yet, they think it might have been a lovers' quarrel.'

'Tapped two times in the forehead by an ex-girlfriend? Cold.'

'They aren't sure, but Tommy definitely had someone on the side his senior year. He started going out a lot, claiming to be catching up with the guys, but then the guys would call, looking for him. His mother questioned him once or twice, but he always finessed his way out of it. Oh, Otis called? Well, he wasn't with Otis, he was with Kevin. Kevin called? Well sure, that's because he was with Perrish. She didn't worry about it much at the time. Everything else seemed on track – his grades, football, school. She figured when he was ready, he'd tell them what was going on. Of course, now she wishes she'd pressed him harder on the subject.'

Kimberly merely grunted in reply. She was sitting in Sal's car, outside the Foxy Lady nightclub. The neon sign buzzed hot pink scrawl over Sal's face every other second, flashing the emblem of a half-dressed woman doing the cancan on Sal's nose.

'I don't get it,' she said finally. 'How do they go from Tommy had a mystery girlfriend to Tommy was shot dead by this same femme fatale?'

'Desperation. Lack of other answers. Something happened at the end of Tommy's senior year. They don't know what. He grew moody, withdrawn, stopped going out. The father thought his son might be getting nervous about graduation, the transition to Penn State, playing college football. His mom thought there'd been a girlfriend, and she and Tommy had broken up, not by Tommy's choice. Part of this conjecture was that Tommy was definitely *not* dating his yearlong steady Darlene, and according to Mrs. Evans, it wasn't like Tommy to go too long between girlfriends.'

'So maybe he was with Ginny Jones,' Kimberly mused. 'Then in February, she vanished, leaving him crying in his coffee.'

'Possible. Something went down. Tommy sulked, then went away to college. He seemed better by the time he returned for Christmas. Had to sit out the season, his father confessed to me, but Tommy took it like a man. Father's a bit crazy about football, let me tell you. Not sure Tommy would've led such a charmed life had he been, say, a chess champion.'

'Or then his father would've been into chess.'

Sal's droll look told her what he thought of that idea. Four more girls were coming down the street now. Kimberly had never seen so many thigh-high black leather boots and fishnet stockings in one place. She felt like she was trapped in the beginning of the *Pretty Woman* movie. Now all they needed was Richard Gere pulling up in a Lotus Esprit. Which wouldn't be out of the question. They'd already spotted three Porsches and a Noble.

So far, however, no sign of Delilah Rose.

'Night of the twenty-seventh,' Sal was saying, 'Tommy got a call on his cell phone. Took it in his room, very hush-hush. When he came out, he announced he was off to meet a friend. He was practically bouncing, his mother said, grinning and rushing his way out the door. Her gut reaction at the time – definitely the friend was female and definitely he was excited to see her. Now, understand Tommy hadn't been in town for four months. So if it was a female friend, most likely it would have to be a former acquaintance. Which made her wonder . . .'

'If it wasn't the mystery girl from his senior year.'

'And,' Sal finished with gusto, 'locals confirmed that the dirt road where Tommy died was Alpharetta's version of lovers' lane. Heavily wooded, lightly traveled. Perfect place for Tommy to rendezvous with la femme fatale.'

'Who then turned around and shot him?'

'Maybe absence had made her heart grow fonder. She was making a late quarter play. Tommy, on the other hand . . . Hey, a good-looking kid like that going off to college. I doubt he spent the fall sleeping alone.'

'So first our mystery chick dumps him, then when she can't have him back, she kills him?'

'I agree,' Sal said. 'Women don't make any sense.'

'Oh please. Like men are such a walk in the park.' Kimberly finished the comment more bitterly than she intended, then returned to her moody study of the passenger's side window.

Sal drifted into silence. Guy seemed to only have two modes, eating and talking. At the moment, both were annoying the snot out of her.

She saw a girl exit the establishment, big blond hair, shockingly short skirt, sky-high heels. She had her arm hooked around the elbow of a man three times her age, with the requisite mustache and comb-over. Sonny Bono for the new millennium. The girl was giggling and cracking her gum as they sashayed away.

Guy like that you'd think could put out for a hotel room. Instead, he'd probably demand a blow job in the front seat of his Porsche, fulfilling many fantasies at once.

She'd once given Mac a hand job while they'd been driving down the interstate at night. He'd almost careened off the road and killed them – not quite how it played out in the *Cosmo* cover stories. Once they'd made it home, however, things had gone much better.

That had been in the early days, of course. When they'd both been young and flush with new love and not afraid to be reckless.

Did you ever get those days back? Or was this just it? They would hammer away at each other, finding fresh faults and old annoyances to govern their week to week. Until she gave up, or Mac gave up, and they joined the national statistics.

Her mother had never forgiven her father. Bethie had fallen in love with Quincy, married him, and borne his children. And still he hadn't come home at night. She had never, ever gotten over the slight. And he had never, ever stopped feeling guilty.

How could death be more important than your family?

'What ya thinkin'?' Sal ventured.

Kimberly tore her glance away from the window.

'I'm thinking about fetal development,' she announced crisply. 'I'm thinking that babies react to loud noises at eighteen weeks in the womb, but the inner, outer, and middle ears aren't fully developed until twenty-six weeks. So at twenty-two weeks, just what level of hearing are we talking? The womb is a noisy place, heart beating, blood swishing, food digesting. Maybe the baby can't hear at all. Or maybe she heard everything. Or maybe she just heard the loud parts, the really bad parts. Is that worse? I don't know.'

'Your baby can hear us?' Sal was staring at her belly in fascination. 'You mean, like right now, he, she, it is eavesdropping on everything we say?'

'I don't know. That's what I'm trying to figure out.'

'Wow,' he said. 'That is so cool.'

His words surprised her. 'You mean it?'

'Sure. I mean, think about it. On a good day, I can maybe

start my lawn mower. While you're sitting over there growing life, an honest-to-goodness little person who's gonna say Mama, Dada, and maybe grow up to one day, I don't know, design a better lawn mower. Do you think, when it moves again, that I could touch it? Just once.'

She had to think about it. 'Well, you did buy me pudding.'

'Amazing,' Sal said again, and seemed to mean it.

'You should get a dog, Sal.'

'Nah, I'm allergic.'

'What about a bonsai? There's an agent in our office—'

But before she could continue, the landscape finally changed. Sal saw it, too.

'Target, three o'clock,' he announced.

'Showtime.' Then they were out of the car, homing in on Delilah Rose.

Moment Delilah caught sight of them, she tried to bolt. Sal caught her by the arm, spinning her back around. Kimberly blocked the girl's path to the street. Realizing she was trapped, Delilah went on the defensive.

'I can't be seen with you. For God's sake, go away!'

'You seem a little edgy, Delilah. Come on, surely since the formation of the new Sandy Springs PD, it's not unusual for a prostitute to be questioned by law enforcement.'

'Fuck the police. Fuck other girls' opinions. It's Dinchara I worry about. He thinks I'm squealing, I'll be dead by morning.'

'All right then.' Sal gestured expansively to his unmarked sedan. 'Step into my office. We'll cruise around the block; no one will be the wiser.'

'Please. That thing screams narc.'

'Then we'll take a walk.' Kimberly already had her arm looped snugly through Delilah's. She pulled forward, forcing the stumbling girl to follow. 'Gotta be a family-friendly establishment somewhere,' Kimberly said. 'I doubt

Mr. Dinchara spends a lot of time in those kinds of joints. It'll be like hiding in plain sight, plus we can all enjoy a healthy dinner peppered with your witty repartee.'

'I hate you,' Delilah muttered darkly, but fell into step. 'You're ruining my life.'

'See, the free exchange of ideas has already begun. Can you really walk in those boots? Damn, you're tall.'

Sal and Kimberly kept Delilah wedged between them, rapidly moving her down one block and over three. In the urban mix that marked this section of town, a brightly colored Italian restaurant was only a hop, skip, and a jump away. They dragged her inside, plopped her in a booth surrounded by families of four and passed out menus. Sal announced he was starved and picked out lasagna. Kimberly went with the bottomless soup and salad. Delilah cursed and grumbled, and then, when she finally realized someone else was paying, ordered fettuccini alfredo and the grilled chicken.

Sal and Kimberly let dinner come first. They heaped hot pasta and steaming soup on their starved informant, counting on comfort food to do their work for them. Any advantage helped.

'Do I get reimbursed for lost wages?' Delilah wanted to know, glancing at her watch halfway through the meal.

'No, but you can take home the doggie bag,' Kimberly assured her.

The hooker rolled her eyes. 'What am I gonna do? Shove leftover chicken into my push-up bra while I work the rest of the night?'

'I bet some guys would pay extra for that,' Sal said seriously.

Delilah scowled at him. 'You're the creep who tried to talk to me the first time. I don't like you.' She looked at Kimberly. 'Make him go away.'

'Tried,' Kimberly said. 'He's got the personality of Velcro. Might as well get used to him.'

'Hey, I don't have to get used to annoy—'

Kimberly interrupted the girl's latest tirade by reaching over, grabbing the girl's wrist, and slamming it down into her plate of fettuccini. 'Shut up and listen. You wanted to deal information. Well, here we are. So stop wasting our fucking time and talk.'

Delilah regarded her more warily. 'You kiss your mother with that mouth?'

'My mother's dead, thanks for asking.'

The girl's gaze finally fell. Kimberly withdrew her hand. She watched steadily as Delilah picked up a napkin, dabbed at the splashed white sauce. Sal was doing his part by disappearing into the eggplant-colored booth. They might make it as a team yet.

'Why are you calling me, Delilah?'

The girl looked confused. 'Call you? I haven't called you. I haven't even seen Spideyman since we last talked, and I don't have anything new to report.'

'Who'd you tell about our meeting?'

'Tell? Are you fucking nuts? World I live in, snitches have a short life span. Not something to be bragging about.'

Kimberly appraised her, trying to decide if the girl was telling the truth. Delilah was wearing her dirty-blond hair pulled back in a ponytail. It emphasized the dark blue tattoo of a spider creeping above her shoulders, legs clutching her neck, fangs reaching for the curve of her left ear.

'Did he suggest the tattoo, Delilah? Maybe pay you to do it? Couple of hundred dollars, a thousand? What does it cost to scar a girl's neck?'

Delilah's gaze skittered away, letting Kimberly know she was onto something.

'How long have you known him?'

'Couple of months,' Delilah mumbled, still not making eye contact.

'According to you, Ginny Jones disappeared three months ago, and you both knew Mr. Dinchara prior to that. Makes it longer than a couple of months in my book.'

'Okay, maybe more like six months. Or eight. I don't know. Who's counting?'

'So you knew him prior to becoming pregnant.'

The girl's eyes widened. She went deathly still, gaze fixed on her leftover pasta, arms straight at her sides.

'Delilah?'

'Dinchara is *not* the father of my baby,' the girl expelled in a rush. 'I had a boyfriend. Someone I loved, all right? Someone who I thought loved me. So just fuck off. Don't make this about my baby.'

'Then what's this about? You've known Dinchara for nearly a year. Why rat on him now?'

'I told you why. He did something to Ginny—'

'What about Bonita Breen? Or Mary Back or Etta Mae Reynolds? Any of those names ring a bell?' Sal spoke up now, drawing Delilah's attention. He had moved over, wedging her into the corner, letting her feel how hemmed in she was, how few options she had left.

'What? Who?'

'Or Nicole Evans, Beth Hunnicutt, Cyndie Rodriguez? Roommates, associates, partners in crime?'

Delilah frowned at him, looking distracted, frazzled. 'Cyndie's gone. Has been for months. What's this got to do with Cyndie?'

'Where'd she go?'

'I don't know. Where does anyone go? Away from here.'

'You knew her well?'

'Only well enough to trip over her every other week. That girl liked to party, know what I mean?'

'Drugs?'

'Please, she'd snort anything from superglue to cocaine. Guess you could call her an equal opportunity loser.'

Delilah's righteousness had squared her shoulders again, brought the defiance back to her eyes.

'When was the last time you saw her?'

'Hell if I know. Cyndie was one of those girls who was just . . . *around*. You'd see her here or there. Not like we were pen pals or anything.'

'You know her roommates?'

Delilah frowned. 'Wait a minute. Two girls, right? One a brunette, the other a really badly dyed blonde? Yeah, now that you mention it, I saw her with a couple of girls from time to time. Once, they were lifting her sorry ass off the floor, dragging her toward the door. Guess they might have been her roomies.'

'Seen them around lately?'

'Nah, not really.'

'That happen a lot? Girls appearing and disappearing?'

'Happens all the time. Girls think they'll try on the life, make a quick buck or two. But then it sucks 'em in and burns 'em out. Then they're gone.'

'Where do they go?' Kimberly asked.

'Work the loop,' Delilah said with a shrug. 'If you're not making it here, you head east to Miami, or west to Texas. Everyone's got a story of a friend who lives here or there, making a thousand bucks a night. So off the girls go, to do the same old thing in a different city, as if they'll suddenly strike it rich. Kind of funny, if you think about it. All us working girls are actually optimists at heart.'

'Do any of them ever come back?' Sal wanted to know.

'Sometimes. I don't know. Maybe a year or two later. Unless they get into drugs,' she said matter-of-factly. 'Then they're just plain fried.'

'Cyndie, Beth, Nicole. What about them?'

Another negligent shrug. 'Haven't seen 'em. Why do you care?'

'Why do you care about Ginny Jones?' Kimberly asked.

'Why do you think she didn't set off to find greener pastures like everyone else?'

'Because she wouldn't go like that,' Delilah said immediately. 'She wouldn't leave without telling me.'

'You were that close?'

'Ginny was nice. No one appreciated that about her. They thought she was freaky. But she had plans, dreams, hopes. She was just . . . lost, you know.'

'Ever talk about her mom?'

Another shrug, but less certain this time. She'd gone back to staring at her pasta, and Kimberly could practically feel the girl picking through her brain, trying to find the least obvious lie.

'I think her mom died,' Delilah said softly.

'She tell you that?' Sal asked.

'She . . . implied it. Said she had no one. That she was all alone.'

'And you, Delilah,' Kimberly asked quietly, 'what brought you here?'

The girl recoiled as if struck. Then her head was up, her eyes flashing hot. 'Wouldn't you like to know? Cops! Never around when you need 'em.'

'If you'd like to report a crime—'

'Fuck you!'

'Delilah—'

'No, I'm done. All right? You guys are no better than anyone else. Just a different pair of johns, ready to use and abuse to get what you want. Then you'll kick me to the curb without even tossing me a ten-spot. Fuck it, all right. Just plain fuck it!'

Delilah darted her gaze between Kimberly and Sal, then, having made her choice, planted two hands on Sal's chest and shoved him aside. Short of physically restraining her, there was nothing he could do to stop her.

She stormed over him, several diners pausing over their meals long enough to gawk at the flash of bare legs.

The restaurant manager hurried over, giving them nervous glances.

'Check, please,' Kimberly said.

Manager scurried away. Sal collected himself.

'She's a little hot-tempered,' Sal said.

Kimberly was already slapping money on the table, then heaving out of the booth.

'Come on, Sal. Little Miss Muffet is scared. Let's see where she runs.'

SEVENTEEN

Deliah Rose moved fast for a pregnant girl in four-inch heels. Despite her claims of returning to work, she bypassed five clubs, weaving her way in and out of the long blocks with the practice of a woman who knew her way around.

Huffing and puffing behind her, Kimberly and Sal were forced to hold back, blending into the crowds of young people swelling the doorway of each establishment, then fighting their way free only to latch onto the fringes of the next party strolling up the block. Inevitably, the group would veer off from Delilah's route, leaving the investigators exposed and vulnerable until the next foursome came along.

Delilah had her head down, hands clutching her ragged blue coat closed. She alternated between a near sprint and sudden dead halts, where she glanced every which way with the heightened paranoia of a woman living on the edge.

She went up one side of the block, made a hard right, only to come back down the other side. To flush out quarry? Throw the diligent off her tracks? Kimberly was beginning to get dizzy with the effort of keeping up while simultaneously keeping out of sight, when suddenly,

Delilah homed in on a banged-up Mazda wedged between two four-wheel-drive trucks.

The girl fished underneath the Mazda, finally pulling out a magnetic case bearing keys, and Kimberly felt her heart sink.

'Damn, she has a car.'

'I thought the police picked her up the first time at the MARTA station.'

'Well, apparently that taught her a lesson, because now she's driving.'

Delilah had the door open, was sliding behind the wheel.

'Now what?' Kimberly muttered, holding her left side, which had begun to cramp from the exertion.

'Look,' Sal said rapidly, glancing at her rounded belly. 'You go back for my car. I'll stick with her. These city blocks with a light on every corner . . . Hell, you can pretty much walk 'em as fast as you can drive 'em. With any luck, I can keep her in sight until you can rendezvous with the vehicle.'

He tossed her the keys just as Delilah pulled out. Sal scrambled to follow, dashing for the intersection. Kimberly headed back as quickly as she could, gasping in spite of herself and hoping she didn't throw up.

Mac was right, dammit. In another month, it would be all she could do to waddle down the hall.

Now she pressed her hand against her side and promised Baby McCormack a pony if she'd just hang in there five more minutes. Baby McCormack kicked her, so apparently the child already had Mac's sense of humor.

She made it to Sal's car. Did not throw up. Slid into the driver's seat, then floundered with the ignition, the seat belt, the unfamiliar setup. She was still shaky and panting, not at all like her normal cool, calm self. Pulling out, she cut off another vehicle and earned a blare from a horn and a loud *screw you!*

She careened north, driving with one hand, working her

cell phone with the other. Sal gave her an intersection, but when she peeled over to pick him up, Delilah was no longer in sight.

'Where?' Kimberly started.

'Just headed for the highway,' Sal gasped. 'North. Quick. Find the gas.'

She found the gas and Sal went flying back into the passenger seat. He grabbed his seat belt and they resumed the hunt.

Hitting the GA 400, Kimberly shot into the middle lane and floored it. Sal glued his eyes to the right, Kimberly to the left.

Which is why they almost ran over Delilah's blue Mazda coming up the middle. At the last minute Kimberly saw her, hit the brakes, and dropped way back. She ducked into the right-hand lane, whipping into the exit lane like the normal run-of-the-mill asshole who didn't know where she was going. At the last minute, she jerked back into northbound traffic but with two other cars between them and Delilah's vehicle.

'Where do you think she's going?' Sal wanted to know.

'No idea. Did you ever get her address from Sandy Springs PD?'

'Yeah. Apartment complex, but when I rang the unit number, the fat Hispanic guy who answered the door had never heard of anyone named Delilah Rose. I'm gonna go out on a limb, and say the hooker lied.'

'What about her prints?'

'Nothing in AFIS.'

'Huh,' Kimberly grunted. 'In other words, we still don't know jackshit about her. Clever girl.'

Sal held up his notepad. 'Ahh, but now I can run her plates.'

'Good work, Sal. Good work.'

Delilah had her turn signal on. Whatever else Kimberly thought of Delilah, she was a conscientious driver. Didn't speed, followed the rules. Made it very easy to follow her. It helped that Kimberly knew GA 400 like the back of her hand. Atlanta, Sandy Springs, Roswell, and Alpharetta all formed a line heading up the central thoroughfare. There were times Kimberly felt she spent her entire day driving up and down the 400. Her and the rest of Atlanta.

Delilah exited and a minute later Kimberly followed suit.

The little blue Mazda headed through an office park, into a residential area. It all looked vaguely familiar to Kimberly, but she couldn't place it. The road was wide, double lanes separated by a divider. Delilah stayed to the right. So did Kimberly.

Traffic was thinning out now, the hour nearing midnight. Half a dozen cars became four, then three, then finally just Sal and Kimberly, twenty yards behind Delilah.

'Shit,' Sal murmured.

'Shhh,' Kimberly told him. 'It's dark. She can only see our headlights. As long as we don't do anything stupid, we should be able to get away with it.'

Delilah was slowing down. Kimberly dropped back, too. She was looking out her window, frowning. She would swear she should know where she was. The line of overgrown bushes, the skeletal trees.

And then all of a sudden, she knew. She was coming at it from the opposite direction, but there was no doubt in her mind.

Just as Delilah Rose made the hard turn onto the dirt road where Tommy Mark Evans had died.

Kimberly drove past the lane, then killed her lights and pulled over. 'Get out of the car,' she whispered urgently. 'Time to walk.'

Sal had his glove compartment opened, was rifling through the depths until he found a flashlight. 'We can't take the car?'

'It's a dirt road. No traffic. No way she won't notice us. But I think it's the end of the line for her as well. Only thing down this country lane is a crime scene.'

Sal's eyes widened as he connected the dots. 'This is the road where Tommy Mark Evans was shot? But why would Delilah . . .'

'Yeah. Exactly. Why would Delilah? If we move fast enough, hopefully we'll find out.'

They both tucked their flashlights into their sleeves, pointing them straight down, where a narrow beam of light could discreetly illuminate the ground without giving away their position. Sal had already started running. Kimberly rubbed her side and grimly followed suit.

The road was deeply rutted, washed out in places from the deluge of rain they'd had in the fall, dotted with small rocks and clumps of dirt. They had to weave their way around, trying to move silent and sure even as Sal twisted his ankle and Kimberly tripped over a downed tree limb.

Kimberly could see a faint glow straight ahead. Headlights from a running car. One car, two cars, she couldn't be sure. It occurred to her that Delilah might be meeting someone at this spot, and the most likely person would be the subject who had shot Tommy Mark Evans. If that was the case, they should assume the UNSUB was armed and dangerous, the type of person who wouldn't take the unexpected arrival of two special agents particularly well.

What had she told Mac just last night? She wasn't throwing herself into any shoot-outs, she had voluntarily removed herself from serving high-risk warrants. He should trust her to keep herself safe as she'd done for the past four years.

It came to her, the way the truth liked to come to people when it was ill-timed and unappreciated: She shouldn't be doing this. She was an ass.

Her footsteps faltered but it was already too late.

Sal was flying down the dirt road, trusting her to have his back.

Kimberly pulled out her gun and prayed for the best.

Fifty yards. Forty. Thirty. This close it became apparent it was only one car, twin headlights forming a singular spotlight on the white cross, much as Kimberly's car had done last night.

Slowing to a half-jog, flashlights off, they slid along the edge of the road, moving nearly shoulder to shoulder so they could communicate by touch, feel.

Twenty yards. Ten.

Delilah Rose finally came into view, her back illuminated by the headlights. She was standing in front of the cross. Her hands appeared to be clutched in front of her. Her shoulders were heaving.

Sal's touch on Kimberly's arm. Pointing to the other side of the road. She nodded, then dashed across the open road to the relative cover of the bush-shrouded side. Keeping even with Sal as they homed in, closer, closer. Two bird dogs on the scent.

At the last minute, Kimberly looked up. Nothing.

Gazed side to side. All was clear.

A last glance behind her.

The road formed a long black tunnel of night, swallowing up civilization, a lonely place to die.

Sal counted down on his fingers. Five, four, three, two, one.

He stepped into the puddle of light, gun still down at his side, but finger on the trigger.

Delilah gasped, turned. Her hands flew to her tear-stained face.

'Delilah,' Sal said evenly.

The girl started crying. And in those heartfelt sobs, Kimberly finally understood.

'Hey, Sal,' she said. 'Meet Ginny Jones.'

'You don't understand,' the girl was saying. 'You can't call me by that name. I'm Delilah Rose. It's the only reason I'm still alive.'

Sal and Kimberly had loaded Delilah back into her car, this time with Kimberly at the wheel. They had returned to the main road, where Sal picked up his vehicle, then continued on to a late-night pharmacy where they could easily blend in with other parked cars. Now they had Delilah sitting in the backseat of Sal's Crown Vic, while both of them homed in on her from the front. The cramped quarters were even tighter than the usual interrogation room, and much more effective.

'Why'd you tell us Ginny Jones was missing?' Kimberly asked the girl. 'If we're not supposed to know that name, why bring it to our attention?'

Delilah/Ginny wouldn't look at Kimberly. She was staring down at her lap, twisting the hem of her jacket over and over again.

'I'm the only one left alive,' she whispered. 'One by one, bit by bit . . .' Her head finally came up. 'I wasn't lying before. I do want better for my baby. I want this . . . I *need* this to end. I thought, if I could just get someone to pay attention. To care about us. I'm just so tired.'

'What is this?' Sal pressed gently. 'Start at the beginning, Delilah. Tell us what happened, and maybe we can help.'

'It's my fault,' the girl rambled. 'He pulled over. I accepted the ride. I had no idea. Some guys get violent, you know. Gotta slap a girl around to get their rocks off. But this guy . . . He doesn't want to hit a girl. He wants to own her. Destroy her. And then he kills her. That's what makes him happy. Breaking you.'

Sal and Kimberly exchanged glances. Sal got his mini-recorder going. Kimberly took the lead.

'When did you accept his ride?'

'Lifetime ago,' Delilah replied dully.

'Winter, spring, summer, fall?'

'Winter. February. My mom had locked me out, least I thought so, and I was cold. He appeared in his fancy SUV. I thought I'd gotten lucky.'

'What year, Delilah?'

The girl frowned, seemed to have to think about it. 'Long time. One, two . . . two years ago. Before graduation. I was going to go to beauty school. Everyone thought I was a loser, but I had plans. I was gonna be a hairstylist.'

'So it's February 2006,' Kimberly supplied. 'It's late at night . . .'

'After eleven.'

'You're . . .'

'Couple blocks from my house. Walking. On the main road, you know.'

'Your mother locked you out?'

The girl's lips twisted. 'I was with Tommy. Missed curfew. The jackass.' Her mouth trembled, she looked as if she was going to cry again, but caught herself, pulled it together. 'Mom said if I messed up again, she was gonna teach me a lesson. I got home, things were locked up tight. I thought she'd finally gone and done it. So I hit the road.'

'So you're walking, it's cold, and a vehicle appears. What kind of vehicle?'

'I already told you. A black Toyota FourRunner with silver trim. Limited Edition.'

'And the driver?'

'Dinchara, like I said. Red hat, Eddie Bauer clothes, fancy SUV. Why does everyone assume that just because I'm a hooker, I can't tell the truth?'

Kimberly decided to ignore for a moment that, in fact, Ginny had lied several times. 'So you first met him two years ago?'

'Yeah.'

'When he picked you up.'

'Yeah.'

'What happened next, Ginny?'

The girl's eyes glazed over. She shivered, looking at pictures only she could see. 'He played a tape.'

'A tape?'

'Yeah, in his car. It was a recording . . . of my mom, dying. He made me listen to it again and again. Her screaming and screaming and screaming. And giving him my name. Goddamn bitch. Right up until the bitter end, she couldn't do nothin' right. Goddamn, pathetic, miserable, sorry bitch.'

Ginny sniffled, rubbing her nose with the back of her hand. She curved her other hand around her belly, rubbing her thumb absently over her unborn child. Making silent promises to her baby? Wondering if she could do any better than her own mother had?

'What happened to your mother, Ginny?'

The girl frowned at Kimberly. 'He killed her, I told you that.'

'Did you see anything? Where he did it? What about her body?'

'No, I just heard the tape. Trust me, that was enough.'

'And then?'

'Then he smiled. He said, 'Your turn's next.' He said, 'Welcome to the collection.' '

'What'd you do, Ginny?'

'I bargained, that's what I did,' the girl said hotly. 'I talked my sorry ass off. Promised him the best goddamn blow job of his life. But that made him laugh. ' 'Course you're gonna do that, Ginny,' he said. 'You're gonna make all my dreams come true. Then I'm gonna carve your skin from your scrawny white neck and feed you to my pets.'

'He brought out this knife like I'd never seen before. Long and thin and silver. A filleting knife he called it. And then, God help, I did do everything he asked of me, while he sliced up my arms and legs, all these bloody little cuts all over the place that *hurt*. Damn, they hurt. Then he pulled out a jar.

'Inside was a long-legged black spider with bright red markings. "Black widow," he told me. "Venom is fifteen times more powerful than rattlesnake venom. Bite itself doesn't hurt. In fact, some people don't feel a thing. At first. Then you get this sharp pain in your belly, I'm talking solid, double-you-right-over stomach cramps. And you start to sweat at the same time your mouth goes completely dry. Your eyes swell shut. The soles of your feet start to burn, your muscles catch on fire."

'"You spend days in agony. Hunched over, convulsing, vomiting, praying for death. There is an antivenin, but that's assuming I have a change of heart and take you to the hospital, and what are the odds of that?" He grinned at me. "Normally, the female black widow indulges her violent instincts by eating her mate. But I've discovered that the smell of blood gets her quite excited. Why don't we find out?"

'He started unscrewing the cap and I . . . I begged. I'd do anything he wanted. Anything at all. And then I realized, I was dead. Because my mother had said all those same things and look at what he'd done to her.

'Just as he removed the cap, it came to me. Begging was what turned him on. More I screamed, more I sealed my fate. So I shut up. And when that black widow came creeping out the jar one leg at a time, I took her right into my palm and let her sit. I talked to her. I thought of her as a pet and you know what . . . It worked. She crawled up my arms and touched my lips with her legs. She was gentle, you know. Almost curious.'

Ginny touched her mouth with her own fingers as if in memory.

'Then, real coolly, I lifted her off and replaced her back in her jar. And I looked the man in the eye and I said, 'She's beautiful. Show me another.'

'He flipped me on my back and fucked the living daylights out of me. So goddamn hard I thought he'd break my ribs. Then, when he was done, he sat back in the driver's seat, lit up a cigarette, and I knew I'd survive. I just had to learn to really like spiders.

'We struck a deal. I'd hook for a living. He'd take fifty percent of the money. I'd keep my mouth shut. He'd let me live.' Ginny's mouth twisted in a sour smile. 'And that's how it's been. Once a month, he shows up. Quick fuck, pay up, and we're done for another month.'

'He's your pimp?' Kimberly asked incredulously.

Ginny gave her a look. 'Pimps provide protection services. Dinchara doesn't protect. Some guy beats the shit out of me, stiffs me on the money, what does Dinchara care? He's more like an enforcer, shaking me down once a month. So that no matter how hard I work, I'll never get ahead. No matter what I do, I'll never escape. He kept his first promise, right? I'm a specimen in his collection. My terrarium is a little larger than most, but it's a cage just the same, and he and I both know I'm not getting out.'

'Anyone ever witness one of these transactions? You paying him?' Sal wanted to know.

' 'Course not! He's not an idiot.'

'Anyone see the two of you together?'

Ginny shrugged. 'He comes into the clubs, that's how he finds me. Just like any customer. People have seen him, but I doubt too many have *seen* him, if you know what I mean.'

'He have other girls?' Kimberly asked evenly.

Ginny hesitated, her gaze averted again. 'I'm not sure.'

'Not sure, or won't tell? Come on, Ginny. We've come this far. In for a penny, in for a pound.'

'Hey, remember the terms of the deal. Living means keeping your mouth shut.'

'Too late. You already started talking. Now it's in your own best interest to give us enough to help.'

141

'Girls don't talk! They just . . . disappear.' Ginny suddenly looked up. 'How come the police don't know? How can you not figure out what's going on out there? Every month, another girl vanishes. And no one says boo! It's like we really are nothing but insects, and he can devour as many of us as he wants, and no one gives a damn. A million flies die, and a million more are born the next day. You should know these things. You should *care* about us!'

'How many girls?' Sal pressed.

'A lot!'

'Can you give me names? Dates? I need specifics.'

'Then ask around! I'm not doing your fucking job for you. I'm already risking my neck!'

'What happens to the girls?' Kimberly quizzed, voice rising from the other side, keeping Ginny off balance.

'I don't know.'

'He picks them up in his SUV?'

'I would guess.'

'Takes them home?'

'I don't know. I've never been to his house. All our transactions take place in his FourRunner. I already know too much as it is.'

'But the bodies, Ginny,' Kimberly kept on her. 'If all these girls are being picked off by one man as you claim, what happens to their remains?'

'I don't know!' Ginny cried again, but her gaze was sliding away. 'Isn't that your job? Why am I supposed to know everything?'

'Forget it,' Kimberly declared, sitting back, crossing her arms over her chest. 'You're right. You don't know squat. Let's send her back, Sal. She's worthless. We'll drive her back to the club, drop her off in front. Maybe if she's lucky, no one will notice.'

'You wouldn't!'

'I mean, she's not even that good a liar.'

'Hey!' Now Ginny's eyes were red-hot. 'I'm plenty good enough. I'm still alive, aren't I?'

Kimberly suddenly jerked forward into the girl's face, forcing her to fall back. 'Is that what this is, Ginny? A con? In your own words, you're nothing but a player, looking for a way out. Why should we believe you? Missing girls? Spiders? Please, this is more Stephen King than true crime. What's with you, anyway? You keep calling me and calling me, and yet you refuse to tell me anything useful.'

'Calling you?' Ginny shook her head again. 'I already told you. I haven't seen Dinchara since we last spoke. I haven't had any reason to call you.'

'Come on, dialing me up, making me listen to that audio recording of your mother—'

'You heard the tape?' The girl seemed genuinely surprised, then perked up. 'So you know, then! You know I'm not making this up! He really is killing people. You heard the tape, you can arrest him!'

'Who'd you give my number to, Ginny?'

'I didn't, I swear! I'd be killed for just having a fed's business card on me. Like hell I'm broadcasting the info.'

'Then who called me?'

'I don't know!'

'Yes, you do!'

'No, I fucking don't!'

'Yes, you fucking do!'

Kimberly sat back. Both she and Ginny were breathing hard. She slanted a frustrated glance at Sal. He took over the reins.

'Ginny,' he said, 'what happened to Tommy?'

The girl folded. Her shoulders slumped, her tough veneer collapsed.

'I happened to Tommy,' she said wearily. 'Everyone has to give a name. *He* demands it. It has to be the name of someone you love. He'd already got my mom, remember? Tommy was all I had left.'

'Did you see Dinchara shoot Tommy?'

'No. But I know he did it. Minute I saw the story on the news. What else could've happened?'

'Tommy into drugs?' Sal asked it evenly.

Ginny scowled at him. 'Tommy? No way. He was Mr. Squeaky Clean. Hell, he even thought he loved me. Dumb stupid jerk.' Her hand was fiddling at her neck, where once upon a time, she might have worn a ring, dangling on a chain.

'Is that why you gave me the class ring?' Kimberly spoke up. 'To lead me to Tommy?'

'You said you needed evidence. Well, there you have it. Tommy's murder is unsolved. Plus you heard my mother's tape. Now, throw Dinchara's ass in jail.'

'Nothing would make us happier,' Sal said. 'All we need is his name.'

Ginny gave him a look. 'You think *I* know his name? Why the hell would he be so stupid as to tell me something like that? You're not getting it. *He* has the control. *He* has the power. I'm just a bug he hasn't gotten around to killin' yet.'

Kimberly sat back, pursed her lips. She regarded Ginny for a long moment, wondering if just by staring she could catch a glimpse of what was really going on under the surface. On the one hand, Ginny had made the first contact with the police, and claimed to want justice. On the other hand, she never really told them much. By her own admission, she was brave enough to let a black widow waltz up her arm, but not courageous enough to bolt the minute Dinchara let her go. She was savvy enough to have survived a serial killer for the past two years, but she'd never managed to notice his license plate or any identifying characteristics.

She was more hostile than helpful. A bigger liar than an informant. A manipulator more than an ally.

And yet, as the saying went, she was the best they had.

'So,' Kimberly stated. 'Guy killed your mother, your boyfriend, and maybe a couple of your friends. Seems like you'd want to get even. Have a little justice, set yourself free.'

'Of course I do—'

'Unless, of course, you plan on paying him half your income forever. How's that gonna work once the baby is born, anyway? Think he'll babysit? Volunteer to watch the kid so you can go out and hustle?'

'Hey, I am never letting him near my child!'

'And he'll quietly accept that?'

Ginny looked like she might finally cry.

'Seems to me,' Kimberly continued, 'best option is definitely to throw his sorry ass in jail.'

'That's what I've been saying!'

'But you know, without a name, license plate, personal information . . .'

She let her voice drift. Ginny didn't rush to fill in the blanks. So Kimberly went with plan B. She shrugged. 'Well, there is one last option. I mean, if you're serious about catching this guy.'

Ginny perked up. 'What? How? Just tell me what I gotta do.'

'We'll wire you up. You arrange a meeting with Dinchara, and we'll use his own statements to nail him to the wall.'

EIGHTEEN

I saw my brother today.

He was at the movie theater, three rows ahead of me, arm around a pretty girl with straight blond hair that hung like a silk curtain down her back. I was eating popcorn, but the minute I spotted him, I started to cough, then had to duck down quickly when he looked back in annoyance at whoever was making such a racket.

I stayed for a while on my hands and knees on the sticky theater floor. I didn't know what to do, couldn't figure out how to react.

So after a bit, I decided to do what I did best — nothing at all.

I returned to my seat. I put my popcorn on my lap. And I watched the slasher film, one chainsaw after another. They didn't get any of the details right. Hollywood doesn't know jackshit about real blood.

The blond girl liked my brother. Every time the movie soundtrack grew ominous, she'd snuggle against him, her head tucked against his shoulder. Except soon she didn't bother to lift her head anymore. Just kept it there, against his chest, while his hand curled tighter around her and they both giggled at something that had nothing to do with the bloodbath on the screen.

She had a nice giggle, bubbly fresh, like a summer's day.

In my mind, I gave her that name. My older brother was dating a girl named Summer. I bet they walked under moonlit skies, went necking in the back of my parents' borrowed car, attended the prom with her perky little breasts covered in a giant corsage.

It wasn't fair, I thought sullenly. It wasn't fair that I had died and he still got to live.

I ate more popcorn, drank thirty-two ounces of Coke, and brooded through the end of the film.

Lights came on. My brother and his girlfriend finally rose. He had a letterman's jacket — of course he had a letterman's jacket. He draped it over Summer's shoulders and she giggled again, clutching the front with her hands, curling it around her.

My brother had inherited my father's wiry build. Not tall, but solid. I was guessing he'd lettered in baseball, maybe the star pitcher with the clean-cut jaw, short-cropped dark hair. Then he smiled again, a dimple appearing in his left cheek, and in an instant, I remembered exactly what my mother looked like, and the pain of seeing her face after all these years drove me to my knees.

I gasped, but didn't make a sound. I tried to breathe, but no air would reach my lungs.

So I folded over, quiet, limp, a puddle of dark trench coat on a stained floor.

I watched my brother's feet head up the aisle. I heard his baritone ask Summer what time she needed to be home.

'I still have an hour,' she replied.

'Perfect,' my brother said. 'I know where we can go.'

I followed my brother. It wasn't so hard. He drove a truck now, a giant, extended cab four-wheel-drive vehicle that probably belonged to our father. A bumper sticker declared 'Alpharetta Raiders.'

My family had moved. It made sense. I had moved at least two dozen times. Why shouldn't they?

He turned down a dirt road. I recognized it as a lovers' lane I'd heard other kids talk about. Not that I knew a whole lot, never being allowed to go to school and all that. No letterman's jacket for me. No prom, no pretty blond girlfriend. Nope, I was just the crazy loner who turned up in his Army surplus gear at various rec centers, pale face, shaggy hair. The local freak show. Every town had one.

And for no good reason, I wondered about Christmas. Did my family still hang my stocking up on the mantel, the one with the patched-up toe and my name scrawled across the top in silver glitter? Did they set a place at the table, wrap a gift just in case?

If they had moved, that meant I didn't have a room anymore. What had happened to my stuff? My books, my clothes, my toys? Boxed up, given to Goodwill? Maybe my brother had a two-room suite now. One room to sleep, another room to sprawl.

Probably had his own futon, TV, entertainment system. Had friends over, including giggly blond cheerleaders like Summer. I wondered if he was popular, if the kids at school admired him, the boy who had survived the Burgerman.

Or maybe he was the tragic hero. Lost his brother when he was young, but just look at him now.

And just when I was working up a good head of steam, ready to hate him, out necking with perky little Summer, I thought of my mother again and the pain returned like a knife thrust beneath my ribs.

I wondered if he made my parents proud. I wondered if looking at him helped my mother sleep at night.

I pulled over on the dirt road, jumped out of my little rust bucket and made it behind a tree just before my bladder burst. I pissed thirty-two ounces of Coke and then some. I pissed for goddamn near forever, and when I came back out, my brother's truck had appeared on the dirt road.

There was no time for me to retreat. I could only hope he wouldn't notice me.

No such luck. The truck slowed. The driver's side window came down. My own brother glared at me.

'Hey, aren't you the same creep from the movie theater? What the hell are you doing? Are you following us?'

I didn't say a word.

His frown deepened, he looked on the verge of climbing out. Then I heard the girl's voice from inside the cab. 'Come on, babe. Don't do this. He isn't worth it. Besides, I have curfew.'

'Yeah,' my brother said reluctantly. 'Yeah, guess you're right.'

I saw his hand move on the steering column, putting the truck in gear. And suddenly I was sprinting toward the truck, my long black trench coat flapping, my steel-toed boots eating up the dirt. I had a tree limb in my hands. I don't know how it got there.

'Hey,' I yelled at the top of my lungs. 'HEY!'

'What the fuck—'

'Don't let the Burgerman get you!'

And then I was pounding on the truck door. Hit it hard enough the tree branch shattered. The girl screamed. My brother ducked, covering his head with his hands. I went to town, working on the headlights, the front grill, smashing, smashing, smashing with the short, splintered tree limb, and kicking out with my boots and yelling at the top of my lungs.

And there were tears on my cheeks and snot pouring from my nose and I couldn't stop. I couldn't stop. Because I loved my brother so damn much that I hated him. I loved him for being alive. I hated him for not being me. I loved him for having such a pretty little girlfriend. I hated him for having my mother's dimple. I loved him because he escaped. And I hated him because I wasn't his brother anymore and that's the thing in the world I most wanted to be.

So I beat up his truck. I smashed the living daylights out

of glass and steel until I heard the engine gun and had only a second to leap away.

My brother tore down the dirt road, away from the crazy boy wielding a tree limb.

My brother drove away from me.

NINETEEN

'Among the remarkable phenomena occurring in spiders ranks the peculiar behavior associated with mating. These courtship maneuvers are usually started by the male and continued by him, though in some cases the female may also take part after she has reached a certain pitch of excitement.'

FROM *How to Know the Spiders*, THIRD EDITION,

BY B. J. KASTON, 1978

Kimberly got home late. House was dark, except for the usual light in the hallway, and the small pool of illumination on the kitchen desk where Mac had piled her mail and phone messages. No happy face tonight. Instead, the top sticky note displayed a crude drawing of branching lines ending in small ovals. It took her a moment, then she got it: an olive branch.

The picture made her smile even as she felt a sting of tears.

Her husband was such a better person than she was. How had she gotten so lucky?

She should go to him. Tell him she was sorry and ask for his forgiveness. Then again, was it really appropriate to apologize for pursuing a case she had no intention of giving up?

She paced the kitchen, keyed up in that way she always got when starting a new investigation, brain churning, adrenaline pumping. Delilah Rose equaled Ginny Jones. And Ginny Jones equaled . . . ? Victim, accomplice, something worse?

She opened the refrigerator, reached for a beer. Caught herself, sighed, and put it back.

Into the living room now, staring at the darkened shadows of the leather couch, Mac's recliner, their way-too-big TV. When she was a little girl, she used to practice creeping through the house at night. Not Mandy. No, her older sister was scared of the dark, slept in a room with two nightlights and a lamp blazing at all times. But Kimberly saw nighttime as an adventure. Could she tiptoe from her bedroom on the second story, all the way down to the front door of their four-bedroom Colonial without making a sound?

She would imagine she was stalking bad men. Or, she was outsmarting an intruder who had already entered her house. Nighttime brought monsters and for as long as Kimberly could remember, she wanted to fight them.

Most of the time, her insomniac father caught her in the act.

'Kimberly,' he would say, 'what are you doing out of bed?'

And she, embarrassed about being caught, and not wanting to admit to her Super Cop father that she was stalking shadows, would say, 'I just wanted a drink of water.'

He would watch her for a while. Silence had always been her father's best weapon and he had wielded it masterfully. Eventually, he would go into the kitchen and return with a glass of water.

'Third step from the top,' he informed her. 'It squeaks.'

And the next night, she would get a little farther into the shadows.

After her father moved out, she roamed the house at will. Her mother slept soundly, and until she was fourteen and discovered boys, Mandy had no use for midnight excursions. Just Kimberly would make the rounds, night after night. Keeping her mother and sister safe. Because Super Cop was gone now and she was all the protection against monsters her family had left.

Until the day she went off to college, and Mandy and her mother had been murdered.

Fuck it. Kimberly went to the bedroom.

Mac appeared to be sleeping, one arm flung up over his head, the other curved over his stomach.

She left him alone. Crossed into the bathroom, where she brushed her teeth, scrubbed her face, combed out her hair. She shed her clothes, found her pajamas, opening lots of drawers and the closet doors along the way. Back to the kitchen for a glass of water, setting it down firmly on the nightstand.

Tossing back the covers. Jumping into bed.

Mac grunted.

'Oh,' she declared brightly. 'You're awake!'

Mac peeled open one eye, then covered it again with his arm.

She thumped his shoulder lightly. 'Faker.'

'Am not.'

'Pulleeeze. I've seen this act before.'

He didn't protest anymore, but opened both eyes. For a moment, they regarded each other warily.

'I liked your drawing,' she said softly.

'I'm not a very good artist.'

'Good enough.'

'I don't like it when we fight,' he said abruptly.

'Me, neither.'

'And I don't like worrying about you. And I don't like waking up some mornings, realizing we're about to be parents and we've never even had a puppy. How do we know if we can feed this thing, or bathe it, or keep it alive? You know what I realized for the first time yesterday?'

She shook her head.

'We don't have a ficus tree. Kimberly, how are we going to be good parents, when our current lifestyle doesn't even allow for plants?'

'I guess we won't feed the baby Miracle-Gro.'

He sat up, the covers falling to his waist. With his dark hair sleep-rumpled, his lean face intent, he looked sexy, serious, the man she fell in love with all those years ago. The man who had proposed to her, buck naked, the night before she was to make a ransom drop and the situation was dangerous enough they both knew she wouldn't wear the ring.

He had let her go the next morning, to do what she needed to do, and she had loved him for that.

She reached over now, touched his face gently. 'I saw Delilah Rose,' she said, because there was no other way to do it. 'It turns out she's actually Ginny Jones, kidnapped, she claims, two years ago, and forced into a life of prostitution to stay alive. She alleges her kidnapper killed her mother and is systematically picking off other hookers one by one. She provided no details, physical description, or corroborative information, but Sal believes he has enough to pursue a case. And I'm going to help him. At least until we get enough to put together a full task force.'

'You won't quit even then,' Mac said.

'I don't know. Once the baby comes, I'll have to.'

'You'll work it from your hospital bed, that's what you'll do.'

Her hand fell away. She studied the sheets. 'You're right,' she said shortly. 'I'm not a quitter. Not in my marriage, and not in my job.'

He didn't say anything right away. She sensed she should look at him, but couldn't bring herself to do it. She had no problem chasing down an informant on a secluded road late at night, or looking for a hunter's severed head. But here, in her own house, sitting cross-legged in bed next to her husband, feeling the tension between them, she was afraid.

'Kimberly,' Mac said quietly, 'I've been offered a promotion. Special agent in charge of the Regional Drug Enforcement Office in Savannah.'

She glanced at him, dumbfounded. 'But Savannah . . .'
Savannah was way to the southeast, on the South Carolina
border, closer to Hilton Head than Atlanta. The city was
large enough to command a respectable GBI presence. A
solid RDEO, an excellent promotion. And much too far
away to work while living in Roswell.

'Aren't you going to say congratulations?'

'Congratulations,' she said dutifully.

He wasn't fooled. 'I didn't say anything right away
because I didn't know what to say. But I've been asking
around. It's a great assignment. It would mean a lot for
my career.'

She couldn't speak anymore. She went back to studying
the linen.

Beside her, Mac sighed. 'You're not the only one who
loves your job, Kimberly,' he said finally. 'And you're not the
only one who's good at it. It just so happens that in the past
twelve months, I've helped uncover one of the largest meth
labs in the state, plus broken up an entire network of
dealers. I am making a difference, too, and I like it.'

'I know.'

'The FBI has some regional offices. They're small, but
maybe Savannah could use an extra agent. We could rent a
house in the area, try things out. Last time we visited, we
both remarked on how charming the place was. Close to
the beaches, Hilton Head. It wouldn't be a bad place to
raise a child.'

She didn't say anything.

'Or,' he forged ahead, 'maybe, with the baby coming,
now would be a good opportunity to take some time off,
maybe a leave of absence. See what we think.'

'I'd stay home, you would work?'

'If you haven't tried it, Kimberly, how do you know you
won't like it?'

She needed to find her voice. She couldn't. She felt as
if the wind had been knocked out of her. One day, they'd

been sailing along and now . . . Now everything was up for grabs. His job, her job, the baby. She couldn't find an anchor.

'Did you give an answer?' she heard herself whisper.

'You know I wouldn't do that without talking to you first.'

'And this is our official conversation?'

'I guess so.'

She nodded, picked up the edge of the sheet, twisted it. 'Do I have to answer tonight?' she asked.

'No. But probably I need to give them an answer within a week.'

'All right.'

'All right we can move?' he asked hopefully, but she could tell by his gentle voice that he was teasing.

'All right, we can talk about it for another week.'

'Okay.' His voice grew serious again. 'But you know, Kimberly, for us to talk, you're going to have to actually spend some time at home.'

'Sure,' she said, but they could both tell her heart wasn't in it.

He sighed again, leaned over, turned out the light.

They hunkered down into bed, her body spooned into his, his hand on her stomach. The happy couple, the two about to become three. A joyous event in the lives of two people who loved each other.

She remained wide-eyed long after her husband had returned to sleep.

One a.m., she crawled back out of bed, into the kitchen. She dialed the number from memory, but got voice mail. She left a message she wasn't sure she'd ever left in her life.

'Dad,' she said. 'I need help.'

TWENTY

'The spider is well adapted to living indoors with humans.'
FROM *Brown Recluse Spider*, BY MICHAEL F. POTTER,
URBAN ENTOMOLOGIST, UNIVERSITY OF
KENTUCKY COLLEGE OF AGRICULTURE

Rita was awake. Did that save her life in the end? She would never know.

It was dark out. New moon, so perfect there wasn't even enough light to form shadows across the far wall. Damn nights were long enough without even a light show for entertainment.

And then she heard it. Scuffling in her yard, followed by the creak of her back door opening.

'Joseph,' she whispered, flat on her back in her old double bed, gnarled hands clutching the edge of the covers. 'That you, Joseph?'

But of course it wasn't Joseph. Since when did ghosts make a sound?

She worked on her breathing, slow and steady, as she heard more noise downstairs. The sucking pop of the refrigerator door opening. The whine of an old drawer grudgingly giving way. And footsteps. Lots of footsteps, light and quick, crossing the kitchen, heading up the stairs.

Breathing again, slow and steady. By gawd, she would not be scared in her own home. By gawd, she would not be spooked from her own bed.

And then the boy appeared at the foot of her bed. He looked her straight in the eye, both hands tucked behind his back.

She returned his look just as steadily, her right hand creeping beneath the sheet.

'Scott,' she said evenly. 'Thought we talked about this.'

The boy said nothing.

'Rules are rules, son. A proper guest knocks on the door. A proper guest waits to be invited. A proper guest does *not* sneak into an old lady's home in the middle of the night, scaring her nearly half to death!'

The boy still didn't say a word.

Rita sat up. She knew she must look a sight. Thin gray hair sticking out like twigs, wool cap askew on the top of her head. She wore her customary green plaid flannel and yellow-stained long johns. She dressed for warmth and comfort, not to entertain impertinent young men.

The boy still didn't move or speak. So she kept her gaze upon him. She let him know she wasn't as frail as she looked.

'Show me your hands, Scott.'

Nothing.

'Boy, I'm only going to ask you one more time. *Show me your hands!*'

For the first time, he trembled. Once, twice, three times. Then abruptly, he jerked his hands out from behind his back. He showed her his palms, and declared in a voice nearly shrill with panic, 'I just need a place to stay. One night. I won't be a problem. I swear!'

Rita took advantage of his uncertainty, throwing back the covers and swinging her legs out of bed. Her bones ached when she stood, but she felt better. Stronger. In control.

'Where do you live, Scott?'

He thinned his lips mutinously.

'Do you have parents I should call? Someone who worries about you?'

'I could sleep right here,' he whispered. 'On the floor. I don't need much. Honest.'

'Nonsense, child. No guest of mine is sleeping on the floor. You fixin' to spend the night, we might as well do it right. Come on, I'll take you to Joseph's room.'

She set off in her shuffling gait, passing by the foot of the bed, brushing the boy's shoulder. He fell back, assuming the submissive. Encouraged, she led him down the hall, to her brother's room, where dusty football trophies still lined one dresser, and the quilt had been hand-sewn by her grandmother from pieces of their baby blankets. As the oldest son, Joseph had been given the quilt to pass along to his children one day. Instead, he had perished in the same war that had cost Rita her husband. Stepped on a land mine in France. There hadn't been enough body parts left for a proper funeral. Her parents had buried his dog tags, her father retreating to Joseph's room, where he had stayed for months on end.

Her sister Beatrice should've taken the quilt, but it had remained in Joseph's room, where from time to time, each of them would visit, trying to say goodbye to Joseph in his or her own way.

Rita drew back the old quilt now. She smoothed back the flannel sheets, cold and musty from disuse. She drew the young boy forward and helped him onto the bed.

He was passive now, nearly limp to the touch, his slight frame collapsing into the bed. She brushed a lock of dark hair from his forehead, and he flinched.

'Rita,' he whispered. 'I'm tired.'

And the way he said the word, she understood. He wasn't tired, he was *tired,* a condition of the mind as well as the body. A state of the soul.

She pulled the covers up, tucking them beneath his chin. 'Stay as long as you need, child,' she said and meant it.

Then she shuffled back into her bedroom, where she felt along the far wall until she found the kitchen knife the boy had let drop to the floor. She picked it up, and placed it in the nightstand beside her.

Then she reached beneath the covers, finding her father's old Colt .45. She'd cleaned it yesterday; armed it last night. A beautiful piece of machinery, old, but still capable of getting the job done.

Now she clutched it in her hand as she made her way painfully down the stairs, left hand gripping the railing tight.

In the kitchen, the unlocked back door banged lightly in the wind. She opened it wide, peering into her backyard, cursing once more the lack of moon. She saw shadows above and below. Not a wink of light from a neighbor's house, nor the glowing eyes of a tomcat.

So she shut her eyes and focused on the feel of the night instead. She and her brothers used to do this when they were young. Camp out in the backyard, pretending they were in the wilds of the Amazon. *Don't look with your eyes,* their father would tell them in his hushed baritone. *Look with your mind, seek with your hearts.*

It always made her wonder if Joseph should've shut his eyes that night he'd gone on patrol. Maybe, if he hadn't been looking, maybe, if he'd been *feelin'*, that land mine never would've gotten him.

And then she did sense it. Strong. Cold. Powerful enough to make her recoil.

Something was out there in the night. Hungry. Hunting. Hating.

Rita scrambled back inside her kitchen. Got the door shut, found the bolt lock. But for the first time in ages, she was aware of just how rickety her old house had become. Back door with a big glass window perfect for shattering and a brittle wood frame easy enough to pry apart with a crowbar.

I'll huff and I'll puff and I'll blow your house down. . . .

She was trembling now, tasting the fear like bile in the back of her throat. The gun felt too heavy in her hand, her arm too weak. She could barely walk half the time, how was she supposed to lift this sucker, let alone take aim. . . .

Then, in the next instant, her own cowardliness shamed her. She was not a fool. She was a survivor, last of her family line. This was her home. By God, she would take a stand.

She went from room to room. Checking all nooks and crannies, inspecting all locks. Perhaps in the morning, when she was fresher, she could rearrange some of the furniture. And she had some wood outside. She could hack it into sticks, use them to reinforce the windows.

And bells. From the Christmas decorations. Hang 'em here and there as her very own security system.

Yes, sirree, she had some tricks up her sleeve yet.

That made her feel better, so she shuffled to the stairs, starting the laborious process of pulling herself back up.

When she finally made it to her bed, she collapsed on top of the covers and slept like the dead. First few hours of sleep she'd had in weeks.

When she woke up, her bedroom door was open, and her own gun was placed neatly on the pillow beside her.

The boy was gone.

She wondered if she would see him again.

TWENTY-ONE

'Recluse spiders are six-eyed; their legs do not extend sideways. They weave a sheet of sticky silk in which they entangle insects.'

FROM *Spiders and Their Kin*, BY HERBERT W. AND LORNA R. LEVI,

A GOLDEN GUIDE FROM ST. MARTIN'S PRESS, 2002

Henrietta wasn't doing well. Last night, he had squashed a cricket between his finger and thumb, exposing its internal organs, then placed it in the dark shelter of the ICU next to Henrietta's fangs. He had checked first thing this morning. The mashed insect remained in plain sight. Henrietta herself had retreated an inch, laborious progress given her mangled legs.

He reminded himself that older tarantulas often went weeks without eating after molting. Once, he'd heard a story of a tarantula that had gone an entire year without food and still recovered.

Starvation was not the danger. Dehydration was.

He would help her. They had come this far together. He would see her to the bitter end.

He didn't turn on the light. Instead, he moved around the darkened master bath with the practice of a man used to adjusting his eyesight to the gloom. He'd already brought up a saucer from the kitchen, sterilized in boiling water. Now he filled it with a few drops of water, then propped up an edge on two cotton balls, tilting the saucer enough to pool the water at one end while forming a slight incline. Perfect.

Now the tricky part. Contrary to what people thought, spiders were notoriously fragile. Even the most impressive-looking tarantula was really a relatively small, poor-sighted creature of limited speed. They were easily crushed if improperly handled. Let alone the dangers inherent in molting, pesticides, parasites, and spider-eating wasps. No wonder tarantulas preferred to live in small, dark places all alone.

But Henrietta couldn't hide anymore. She needed water.

Reaching into the container, he cupped his hand over her body as if she were an egg, careful not to squeeze too hard in order to protect his skin from the discomfort of the urticating bristles. His fingers enclosed the legs on one side of her body, while his thumb covered the legs on the other side and his index finger came down and over the top of the chelicerae. In one smooth motion, he turned his hand palm up, with Henrietta nestled lightly inside.

He swung her over to the prepared water dish, where he positioned her with her chelicerae and fangs immersed in the water and the rest of her body uphill. He let go, studying her closely to ensure she didn't slide down into the shallow pool and drown.

After a few minutes, when she remained firmly in place, he rocked back on his heels with a satisfied nod and glanced at his watch. Forty-five minutes ought to do it. Then he'd move her back to the ICU with a freshly disemboweled cricket. Hopefully, that would do the trick.

Now he had other pets to tend.

The master bedroom was large. Two sides of huge bay windows, a charmingly vaulted ceiling. Once upon a time, this would have been the sunny crown jewel of the expansive summer home. Covered farmer's porch that wrapped around two sides. A front parlor with stained glass. Three chimneys, six bedrooms, a sunroom.

Time had faded the heavily flowered wallpaper just as years of neglect had led to peeling paint, broken boards, sagging foundation. In the downstairs, certain windows wouldn't close. Other doors wouldn't open.

The entire house tilted to the right, giving the place a drunken feel.

And yet, it was perfect. Filled with nooks and crannies, twisting staircases, old cupboards, exposed rafters. When the man had first seen the abandoned property, the ceiling of the entire master bedroom had been a tangle of cobwebs. In the course of his walk-through, not one but two spiders had dropped from the rafters onto the shoulder of the startled real estate agent. She had screamed both times. And he had known instantly he would take it.

He had divided his collection among the rooms upstairs. Tarantulas in the master bedroom, recluses in the adjoining nursery, combfooted spiders down the hall. They lived in terrariums or cobweb frames, cleaned once a month and refilled with adequate water. Room-darkening shades kept the sun at bay. Humidifiers kept the spaces at proper levels of moisture. In some of the rooms, he had brought in soil to cover the floors. Good old-fashioned dirt, filled with leaves and detritus and night crawlers. The earthen layer helped insulate the drafty floors and provide a whiff of death and decay. Ambience for arachnids.

The man himself hated dirt. The smell of it. The feel of it sliding between his fingers, sifting between his toes. He might say he was afraid of it, except he did not allow himself to feel fear. Instead, he surrounded himself with the very substance whose smell sometimes roiled his stomach and sent him to the bad place in his mind.

He respected these spiders. He studied them, nurtured them, used them to find the spider in himself.

In return, his collection provided him with sanctuary. A place where he came to brood when the bad spells hit and everyone knew better than to make eye contact. He would lie on the dirt-covered floor, remembering all the things he wanted to forget until his rage bubbled to the surface. Then he would strip off his clothes and open the tops of the fish-tank terrariums, watching colonies of brown recluses pour out. He would dare them to do their worst. He would beg them to do their worst.

But spiders remained shy creatures at heart. The brown recluses might walk across his feet, climb up his hairy legs, explore the veins on his arm. But mostly, they disappeared into the cracks and crevices of the old house, until he was forced to put out glue sheets to capture them.

The glue sheets killed them, of course. Because that's what he did best – destroy, even the things he loved.

He started with the tarantulas now, moving methodically from rectangular glass enclosure to rectangular glass enclosure, lined up neatly on the metal shelves along the walls. Each terrarium was labeled with the species of spider and an index card where he recorded the day's feeding. A new captive might eat a dozen crickets a week, while the average was six to eight crickets a month. Before and after molting, some tarantulas wouldn't eat anything at all.

There was also the matter of variety. Some tarantulas ate only crickets and mealworms. The larger species, however, preferred baby mice and rats, dead but at room temperature (he bought them frozen and ran them under warm tap water; he had learned the hard way never to nuke a dead mouse; it had taken him forever to get the smell out of the kitchen). When he had first started out, he had caught insects in the garden – grasshoppers, cicadas, cockroaches, moths, caterpillars, earthworms. Wild insects, however, were an unsafe food choice – they could be contaminated with pesticides, inadvertently poisoning his pets. Now he bought most of his food from online pet stores, dividing his purchases among several different establishments so as not to call attention to himself.

His collection contained over one hundred and twenty specimens now, not counting the brown recluses whose delicate brown bodies probably numbered close to a thousand. He had spiders he'd caught in the garden, spiders he'd purchased abroad, spiders he'd bred himself, and, of course, a nursery filled with young spiderlings.

And like any proper enthusiast, he was still adding to the collection.

He was at the last terrarium. Even in the half-dark, he could feel the eyes watching him, feral, calculating, predatory.

It made him smile.

Theraphosa blondi. The world's largest spider, with a leg span in excess of ten inches. He had imported this male just last week from South America. The tarantula had arrived, rearing back on its hind legs and hissing loud enough to be heard across the room. With extremely large fangs and a body covered in irritating bristles, it was a lean, mean fighting machine, known to take on anything from rodents to small birds.

The majority of tarantulas were gentle giants. The *T. blondi*, on the other hand, was famous for its bad attitude, with a bite capable of costing the unwary collector a finger, or even a hand.

He could feel the spider watching him late at night. Had watched it in turn as it roamed its new home, delicately tapping on the glass as if testing for possible weaknesses. He had the impression of a wild, churning intelligence. The spider was studying, waiting, plotting.

If the man presented the opportunity, the tarantula would strike.

The man bent over now, studying the dark mottled spider, crouched in the far corner of its cage.

'Hey,' the man said. 'Want a mouse?'

He dangled the dead white mouse, waited to see what the spider would do. A few legs arched out, tested the air.

'Here's the deal,' the man said. 'Behave, get breakfast. Attack, and starve. Got it?'

He waited a heartbeat more. When the tarantula did not rush the glass, or rear up in a hostile display, the man straightened, put his hand on the top of the weighted mesh-screen lid and readied himself.

One, two, three. He popped up the corner, dropped the mouse, and watched as ten inches of tarantula sprang from the corner and caught the corpse midair. Both dead mouse and spider landed with a thud, the mottled dark body already wrapped fiercely around its new treasure. Then the tarantula's head came up, fangs exposed . . .

The man dropped the top more hastily than he intended, falling back.

He caught himself at the last minute, steadying his pulse, eyeing the *T. blondi* with fresh respect.

He rapped a knuckle against the glass.

'Welcome to the collection,' he said, then, feeling that he'd had the last word on the subject, sauntered downstairs.

Boy was in the living room, playing video games. Boy was always holding a remote, eyes glazed over, sullen look on his face. Teenagers.

The man watched him from the doorway, contemplating.

Time was winding down now. A week, maybe more. It surprised him to feel a rush of nostalgia, a teacher for a student, a father for a son.

He walked in the room, shut off the TV. Boy opened his mouth to protest, then thought better of it. The boy hunkered down, waiting.

'Can't you say good morning?' the man demanded, standing next to the sofa.

'Good morning.'

'Hell, think a few manners wouldn't hurt. Haven't I taught you anything?'

Boy looked up now, eyes hot, sulky. 'I said good morning!'

'Yeah, but we both know you didn't mean it.' The man backed off, making some calculations of his own. 'You heard from her?' he asked abruptly.

Boy looked away. 'Not yet.'

'Think she'll do it?'

Boy shrugged.

'That's about right,' the man agreed. 'Nothin' good ever came from trusting a woman. So, you gettin' excited, boy? Come on, we're talking graduation! That doesn't happen every day.'

Boy shrugged again. The man wasn't fooled.

He grinned, but it wasn't a pleasant look on his face. 'Tell me the truth, son. You think she loves you, don't you? You and Ginny, sitting in a tree, k-i-s-s-i-n-g. Gonna get married? Raise the baby? Live in a house with a white picket fence?' Man waved his hand. 'Pretend none of this ever happened?'

Boy said nothing.

'I'll tell you, son, I'll tell you exactly what's gonna happen. You're gonna graduate, I'm gonna offer you a big hunk-o-cash, and you're gonna want to throw it in my face. But you'll swallow your pride. You'll take my money. You'll tell yourself you're gonna pay it back later. When you're what? Gainfully employed as a male hooker, a pimp, a drug runner? 'Cause, you know, elementary-school dropouts don't exactly go to college, or qualify as electricians, or auto mechanics.

'But you haven't figured that out yet. You think freedom is only days away and anything's gotta be better than this.

'Yeah, I give you two months, tops. Then you'll be living on the street, giving blow jobs for five dollars a pop to dirty old men, or shooting anything you can find into your veins. And you'll start to wonder. Was it really so bad here? Big ol' house. Free food. Video games. Cable TV.

'I treated you right, boy. You'll find out soon enough. I treated you good.'

The man headed toward the kitchen. Time for breakfast, then he needed to sit his sorry ass down in front of the computer. Cash reserves were getting low. Had to do some work.

At the last moment, however, the boy spoke up.

'How much?' the boy asked from the sofa, clearing his throat. 'How much cash?'

'Why? Why do you care? You gotta graduate first.'

'I want to know,' the boy said. He had that look about him again, eyes flat, watchful. Like the *T. blondi* upstairs. The boy was growing up. He was also now one inch taller than the man and they both knew it. 'I want to know,' the boy said, 'exactly how much my life is worth.'

The man considered the matter. He turned on his heel, returning to the sofa, and was rewarded by watching the boy brace himself, as if preparing for a blow. But the man didn't strike out. Instead, he leaned down. He said the words almost tenderly, whispering them next to the boy's ear. 'Dipshit, you ain't worth the broken condom your parents used the night you were conceived. But I'll take pity on you. I'll give you a hundred bucks. Ten dollars for each year of service. Be grateful.'

Boy looked at him. 'I want ten thousand.'

'Honey, you weren't that good a fuck.'

'I want ten thousand,' the boy insisted again, and the very emptiness of his eyes spooked the man a little, tingled the fine hairs on the back of his neck, though he was careful not to show it.

He regarded the boy thoughtfully. 'Ten grand? You're serious?'

'I *deserve* it.'

The man laughed abruptly, ruffling the boy's hair. 'You want some extra money, son? Then you'd better earn it. Let me tell you about this new spider I got upstairs . . .'

TWENTY-TWO

*'The brown recluse hunts at night seeking insect prey, either
alive or dead.'*

FROM *Brown Recluse Spider*, BY MICHAEL F. POTTER,
URBAN ENTOMOLOGIST, UNIVERSITY OF
KENTUCKY COLLEGE OF AGRICULTURE

'There are thirty-five thousand known species of spiders
in the world,' Sal was saying. 'According to what I read,
experts believe that's only one-fifth of the total. Better
yet, they are the most popular 'nontraditional' pet in
the United States. Jeez, and I thought all the freaks
collected pythons.'

'Pythons grow too big,' Kimberly informed him. 'Wind
up released in the Florida Everglades, where they're
devouring everything that moves. I don't think the
alligators are very happy about it.'

Sal and Kimberly were sitting inside the cargo area of a
white van, vaguely disguised to appear like a utility vehicle,
while actually belonging to GBI's tech department. It was
night four of operation Fly Trap. Ginny was somewhere
inside the Foxy Lady, wired up and waiting to see if
Dinchara would show. Sal and Kimberly were holding
down the fort in the tech van, floor littered with empty
coffee cups (Sal) and water bottles (Kimberly). Assisting
them was an audio technician, Greg Moffatt, and an
undercover female special agent, Jackie Sparks. Moffatt sat
way in the back, watching a glowing panel of audio bars
while mumbling a litany of technical jargon only he could
understand. Sparks, playing the role of a girl who just

wanted to have fun, was somewhere in the club, keeping tabs on Ginny.

Ginny knew about Moffatt, but not about Sparks. Just because Ginny was risking her life by wearing a wire, after all, was no reason to tell her everything. They'd gone over the audio setup. They'd devised a cover story. They'd turned her loose.

Ginny's assignment: Get Dinchara to admit shooting Tommy Mark Evans, or tie him to any of the six girls from the collection of driver's licenses. That would provide the corroboration Sal needed to formally assemble a task force to pursue Dinchara in earnest.

Four nights later, however, Dinchara remained a no-show, which was starting to make the team anxious. Sal had had to practically beg, borrow, and steal to get this level of GBI resource. In another night, two if the operation didn't deliver results, that would be that.

'Turns out,' Sal continued, headset connecting him to Ginny held against his left ear, tiny black earpiece connecting him to Special Agent Sparks in his right, 'spider collecting isn't as small a niche market as I thought. There are hundreds of Internet dealers offering everything from a spiderling for a few bucks to an adult female *Brachypelma baumgarteni* for eight hundred dollars.'

'*Eight hundred dollars?*' Kimberly asked incredulously.

'Yeah. Females are expensive. They live two to three times as long as the males, plus can be used for breeding. Which was the other education I received – you have no idea how many articles exist on how to sex a tarantula.'

Kimberly stared at him.

'It's a big deal,' he assured her. 'How'd you like to fork out the extra money for a female, only to get sent a male by mistake?'

'I can honestly say I hope never to have that problem.'

'Then there are the various spider societies,' he continued. 'Plus ArachnoCon, the annual gathering of arachnid enthusiasts. I mean, do a Google search for 'tarantula' and what *doesn't* come up? Spiders are everywhere.'

'No kidding.'

'I also turned up allusions to illegal imports of spiders,' Sal supplied briskly. 'The really exotic specimens aren't widely available for enthusiasts, and some guys – or gals – don't like to wait. Hey, as long as a Colombian is importing drugs why not also throw in a *Xenesthis immanis* as well and make a quick extra grand?'

'A xenthis whatis?'

'*Xenesthis immanis*. It's a kind of tarantula, has purple markings at the leg joints, ending in silver tips. Gotta say, online photo looked very pretty. Not that I'm in the market. Point is, that particular species isn't available due to the current ban on Colombian imports. So the rabid collector might resort to a backdoor deal instead. Spider gets shipped to Mexico, from Mexico to Texas, from Texas to rabid collector, with lots of palms greased in between. Happens more often than you think.'

'Given that I haven't thought about it at all,' Kimberly muttered, 'that's probably true.'

'It gives us another angle,' Sal stated. 'Say Dinchara shows up and we get enough on tape to have probable cause for a warrant. Well, unless he leaves his bloody gloves out in the open, chances are we aren't making an arrest that afternoon. On the other hand, the Department of Wildlife or the USDA or whoever the hell it is that has jurisdiction over creepy crawlies might be able to hold him on charges of illegal arachnid import. And that gives us more time and excuses to dig into his affairs.'

'Nice thinking,' Kimberly said, impressed.

'Well, that is plan B,' Sal replied modestly. 'Originally, I was thinking we could use the spider angle to track him down, but once I realized a third of Atlanta has an arachnid fetish, I had to change gears.'

'I wonder about the tattoos,' Kimberly murmured. 'That's an impressive tat climbing up Ginny's neck. What do you want to bet Dinchara took her to the tattoo parlor himself, a place he knew because he had work done there as well?'

'We should photograph her neck,' Sal agreed. 'Get the picture into circulation; see if someone recognizes the artist. Oh, what I'd give to have a real task force at my disposal.'

'You mean, with officers other than our current overworked duo, one of whom may have to abandon the investigation in order to give birth?'

'It's a complication.'

'Story of my life,' Kimberly said drily. 'Complicated.'

She sighed, staring out the front windshield of the van. She didn't want to think about her personal life. The tenuous détente that marked her day-to-day interactions with Mac. That fact that they had one week to figure out the rest of their lives, and here they were, day four and she was once again working late.

Mac didn't ask her anymore. Didn't pry. He just waited, and she found his silence more unnerving than his sales pitch.

He should take the supervisory position in Savannah. It would be stupid not to. He was right; their lives were changing. Might as well focus on his career because one way or another, hers was slipping into low gear. What the hell. She would stay at home. Nurse the baby. Watch Oprah. Read self-help books.

Except that didn't sound like her. She was selfish, emotionally stunted, and obsessed with work. And, in her own way, she was happy.

'We got conversation.' Moffatt, the technician, spoke up.

Sal and Kimberly snapped to attention, obediently tuning in to their headphones. So far, Ginny had been propositioned about half a dozen times. If they'd been working a prostitution sting, they would've done good business.

This, however, appeared more serious.

'*We need to talk*,' Ginny was saying in an urgent voice. The hooker sounded strung out, anxious.

'*Why aren't you working?*' a man was asking. '*Get out there and shake that moneymaker, honey.*'

'*First, we need to talk*,' Ginny tried again.

Sal lifted the black handheld radio from his lap, broadcasting to Special Agent Sparks: 'We need a visual: unidentified male, currently speaking with Miss Jones.'

'Roger that' came the crackling reply, then a short pause as Sparks made her way through the club.

'*I want a blood test*,' Ginny was saying, voice more strident. '*I've been reading about tattoos and the risk of hepatitis.*' This had been Kimberly's idea. '*How do I know I don't have anything? What about my baby? What if it gets sick, too? You need to help me.*'

'I have a visual,' Special Agents Sparks reported in a low murmur. 'I see a white male, approximately mid thirties, five foot ten, one hundred sixty, one hundred seventy pounds. Wearing dark brown workman's boots, blue denim, and long-sleeved green shirt, rolled up to the forearms. Has a worn red baseball cap pulled down low over his face, obscuring his features.'

'*What the fuck?*' the man was grumbling harshly. '*You called me down here for a blood test? What'd I look like to you, an HMO?*'

'*I need money—*'

'*Then get back to work!*'

'*I can't work*,' Ginny whined. '*I'm tired all the time, guys don't want me. Creeps 'em out, you know, a pregnant hooker.*'

'*Shoulda thought of that four months ago. You wanna eat, I suggest you find a bleeding heart who pays extra for a hard-luck fuck.*'

Kimberly heard the swish of denim. The man turning to leave? Then, a quick slap as Ginny grabbed the man's arm.

'*I wanna negotiate,*' the girl said desperately. '*Hear me out. I got something to say.*'

Kimberly and Sal exchanged glances.

'*What do you mean negotiate?*' the man asked suspiciously.

'*Not here,*' Ginny said. '*Privately.*'

'Ah shit,' Sal said.

'She's going AWOL,' Kimberly seconded. Ginny was under strict orders to remain in public view. They should've known better.

'Jackie . . .' Sal rumbled into the radio.

'I'm on it,' the special agent replied.

'*Don't fuck with me,*' the man was saying now, voice ominous.

'*I just wanna talk. All right? We'll go to your car. Fool around. It'll be like old times.*'

The man didn't reply. Kimberly had a mental image of Ginny pulling him through the churning crowds.

'Subject approaching the front doors,' Special Agent Sparks intoned over the radio. 'Exiting in three, two, one . . .'

The front doors opened. Ginny stumbled out first, looking shaky and agitated. She wore the customary micro mini, but a longer top to help conceal the hardware they'd tucked inside her push-up bra. She fiddled with the bra now, jiggling the cups a little, and a rush of static flooded the headphones.

'Tell me she didn't just—' Sal started, but then audio returned. He breathed a sigh of relief, but Kimberly didn't think they were out of the woods yet.

A man had appeared behind Ginny. Trim, wiry build. Brown hair, tanned forearms. Jeans and shirt were nicer than she expected. Less chicken farmer, more Eddie Bauer. The brim of a faded red baseball cap was pulled low over his face, leaving behind the impression of a hat, instead of a person. Now you see him, now you don't.

The man headed down the street, Ginny no longer talking but hanging on to his arm. A moment later, the front door opened and Sparks appeared, making a show of lighting up a cigarette, then strolling off in the same direction as the happy couple, cigarette dangling from her fingertips.

Sal and Kimberly exchanged another glance.

'What the hell is Ginny doing?' Sal whispered in agitation.

'I don't know.'

'We're FUBAR.'

'Wanna tell Sparks to abort?'

'Nah,' Sal said nervously. 'Not yet.'

They went back to their headsets, listening for Ginny in one ear and Special Agent Sparks in the other.

From the left, the sound of a car door opening, slamming shut. *Ginny's high-pitched giggle. 'So you really are happy to see me . . .'*

From the right, Sparks's clipped tones. 'Subject and Miss Jones have entered a black Toyota FourRunner with silver trim. Vehicle coated with mud; can't read license plate.'

'We can have him picked up on a minor infraction,' Sal whispered.

'Shhhh.' Kimberly held a finger to her lips.

'So what's it gonna be, big boy,' Ginny was saying. *'Suck or fuck?'*

'Talk, you little bitch. I didn't come all the way down here to get played by some hooker. Asking me to pay for a goddamn blood test. What the hell is wrong with you?'

'It wasn't my idea,' Ginny said hastily. *'I mean, I couldn't think of any other way to get your attention.'*

Long pause.

'Ginny, you'd better start talking, or so help me God, you won't be worrying about hepatitis no more.'

'They're asking about me.'

'Who?'

'Special agents. From the GBI. They claim that working girls are disappearing. They wanna know what's going on. They keep asking for Ginny Jones.'

'What'd you tell 'em?'

'Nothin'! I mean, girls head to Texas all the time, right? I said maybe they should try there.'

'Other names they mentioned?' the man pressed.

'Dunno.'

He slapped her. The sharp crack of the blow caught Kimberly off guard, made her flinch.

'Don't lie to me.'

'I didn't—'

Another *thwack* of skin connecting with skin. Sal's knuckles had gone white on the headphones. His face was grim.

'DON'T LIE TO ME!'

'I don't remember! I'm sorry, they were talking, there were so many names and I was trying to be quiet, not call attention. No, don't hit me, I'm not lying, I swear, I swear, I swear, I swear.'

Another blow. More screaming.

'Abort,' Kimberly said, looking at Sal, the lines etching his face. 'She's done. We gotta get her out.'

But Sal shook his head. 'No, he's just messing with her. He's not serious yet. That's what's so crappy about it. He doesn't even mean it yet.'

And maybe Sal was right, because the other end of the headphones finally grew quiet.

'You got thirty seconds, girl. What the hell do you really want?'

The silence again, long and taut. Then Ginny exclaimed in a rush: 'I want to see my mother, okay? I just wanna . . . see her.'

'What?'

'Holy mother of God,' Sal intoned.

'She's going for it,' Kimberly agreed, and found herself on the edge of her seat. Ginny had given up trying to get Dinchara to mention the names of the missing girls. She was attempting to tie him to her mother's murder instead. Kimberly was torn between wanting to hear what Ginny was going to say next, and wanting to bolt down the street straight to the mud-covered SUV, because this wasn't going to end well.

'*I remember the tape,*' Ginny was whispering. '*I know she's gone . . . what you did to her. I tried to tell myself it doesn't matter. It's not like she ever cared about me.*'

'*You implying I did something wrong, Ginny Jones?*' the man asked coldly.

'*I'm just saying. . . .*'

'*You, the high-school dropout, ran away from home to sell your ass for twenty-five bucks a pop, four months knocked up?*'

'*Stop it. . . .*'

'*I mean, if I were a cop, I'd say you look pretty good for it. Small-town girl nobody ever liked. Killed your mom to get away, killed your rivals in order to compete. Do we got lethal injection in Georgia? I don't remember, but seems to me it wouldn't be that hard for a jury to send white trash like you off to where you belong – inside stone walls, baby taken away, strapped to a gurney, needle entering the vein . . .*'

'*I hate you,*' Ginny whispered. '*Why are you like this? You're so mean.*'

'*Why are you such a loser, Ginny? Why do you sell your body, get yourself knocked up? Hell, seems to me you're the one with all the problems. I'm certainly not dialing you up to piss and moan all night.*'

'*You're a monster.*'

'*Nah, I'm the man in charge. And you'd better start remembering that. Now get the fuck out, and don't bother*' me again. It's the cops' job to ask questions. It's your job to shut the fuck up. Got it?'

'I want to see her.'

'Girl, weren't you just listening—'

'She was my mom! And now I'm gonna be a mom. And it . . . It just doesn't feel right, ending like this. I wanna talk to her again. Tell her 'bout the baby. Make peace. Say goodbye.'

'What are you, fuckin' crazy?'

'She's somewhere, right? I mean, you buried her or dumped her or burned her or did whatever it is you do to the bodies. But she's somewhere. A grave. If you could just tell me where, so I could go to her . . . I won't touch anything. I just wanna talk.'

'Jackie . . .' Sal whispered nervously.

'Are you wearing a wire?' Dinchara's voice suddenly boomed.

'Wh-wh-what? Don't be crazy—'

'Are you setting me up? Are you setting me up?'

A hastily indrawn breath, Ginny's sharp, short cry.

'Jackie!' Sal, over the radio, demanding now.

Kimberly, rising out of her seat, trying to figure out what to do.

'Where the hell is it! Tell me! NOW!'

'Stop it! Stop it! You're hurting me! Let go of my arm. I just wanna talk to my mom. Haven't you ever been around a pregnant woman before? It's hormonal. Honest!'

'Where is it, where is it, where is it? Fuck, fuck, fuck . . .'

'Stop, stop, stop! It hurts. Oh God, let go—'

Kimberly leapt for the door of the van, hand on the door, preparing to slide it open. Just as Ginny started to scream in her ear again, high-pitched and thin, a sudden pounding sound came from the other side of her brain.

'Hey.' Special Agent Sparks's giddy voice broadcast through the madness. 'Sounds like a party. Can anyone join in?' Another high-pitched giggle, the crack of chewing gum. 'Hey, mister, nice wheels. You like to go fourwheelin'? How about takin' me for a ride?'

'Holy mother of God.' Sal looked like he was having a heart attack. He was doubled over in his seat, both hands on his head.

Kimberly wavered next to the door, equally transfixed.

Sparks babbled away: *'I mean check this out. I haven't seen mud like this since I rode my daddy's John Deere across the chicken farm.'*

'Get out.' Dinchara spoke up tersely. 'Private party.'

'Now, now, now, mister. It's a slow night. Can't blame a girl for trying, 'specially with a fine-looking man. Been a while since I've seen a full set of teeth, know what I mean. Hey, honey, are you pregnant?'

'I'm tired,' Ginny intoned. *'I think I'd like to go now.'*

'Oh, honey, you'd better. Working while you're pregnant? That's no way to live.'

'Ah fuck it,' Dinchara said. *'I'm tired, too.'*

'Now, now, no need to be like that. I mean, if you really wanna rumble, big fella—'

Door creaking open. Sounds of a minor scuffle. Ginny's startled exclamation. The man's low curse. *'Get the fuck off me!'*

'Hey, now, big daddy—'

'I am not your fuckin' daddy. Get out of my truck!'

'Okay, okay, no need to get testy. I'm just a sucker for leather seats. Reminds me of the pigs on my daddy's farm—'

'GET OUT!'

'I'm going, I'm going, don't get your panties in a wad. Men. Give 'em fancy wheels and they think they rule the world.'

Footsteps now. A vehicle door slamming shut. An engine roaring to life.

Sparks, back in the earpiece, her voice clear and concise. *'Suspect has pulled out, heading north—'*

Her tone got them both moving again. Sal grabbed the

radio, describing the vehicle and requesting a traffic stop. Kimberly opened the van's door, preparing for Ginny and Sparks to scramble in.

She spotted Sparks half a block away, running up the street, pulling Ginny behind her. Ginny's right cheek bore the red imprint of the man's hand. Her nose was running, her lashes clumped with tears.

'Who the hell is this?' she screeched immediately upon spotting Kimberly. 'Did you send someone to spy on me?'

'More like backup,' Kimberly said briskly.

She helped them both climb in, glancing left, then right. So far, so good. She slid the door shut behind, while Sparks unhanded her charge, then held out her other arm in triumph.

'Brought you a present,' the special agent declared. 'Look what fell out of the truck amid all the confusion: I got the man's boot!'

TWENTY-THREE

'For most species . . . a husband's place is 'in the digestive tract of his wife.' '

FROM 'SPIDER WOMAN,' BY BURKHARD BILGER,
New Yorker, MARCH 5, 2007

Kimberly drove home all jazzed up. Three a.m., GA 400 was finally empty and she zipped along, humming under her breath, tapping her fingers on the wheel and wishing she drove a Porsche. This was the kind of night it would be great to open the sucker up and watch the speedometer soar.

Instead, she kept her Passat station wagon safely under sixty-five, but that didn't stop her mind from racing.

Sal would be requesting the creation of a multijurisdictional task force first thing in the morning. Dinchara hadn't magically confessed to abducting and murdering any of the prostitutes on Sal's list, but he hadn't sounded or acted like an innocent man, either. They were onto something, and tonight's recording would back them up.

Unfortunately, uniformed patrols never came across Dinchara's vehicle for the requested traffic stop. That didn't surprise Kimberly overly much. For all of Dinchara's lowbrow speech, she had an impression of a cold, calculating intelligence. Even on home turf, he'd kept his hat pulled low and obscured his license plate with mud. She had a feeling he'd taken additional precautions with his exit from Sandy Springs.

182

They still had a BOLO out, however, so hopefully sometime over the next few days someone would spot the vehicle. Plus Sal was going to have Special Agent Sparks and Ginny sit down with a sketch artist and put together a composite drawing they could get into circulation.

By this time next week, hopefully, they'd know Dinchara's name and vitals. And then the real fun would begin.

She hummed again, 'Tainted Love,' and tapped her fingers to the beat.

It occurred to her that she was looking forward to going home. That she wanted to pull into her driveway, bound into her house. She wanted, more than anything in the world, to see her own husband.

That was it. Enough of this nonsense. Minute she got home, she was waking up Mac. They would hash this thing out once and for all. He could move to Savannah on a trial basis, they could find a house somewhere in between, she could explore her options at one of the Bureau's regional offices. There was a way, there was always a way. They just needed to talk.

Then, she was jumping his bones, because there was nothing like a successful night's work to make one horny.

Kimberly finally pulled into her driveway. Mac's truck was gone. Instead, she walked into her living room to discover her father and his wife, Rainie. Quincy sat in the recliner, flipping through the paper. Rainie was curled up on a corner of the sofa, staring at some syndicated sitcom but clearly half asleep. Both roused when she entered the room.

'What the hell are you doing here?' Kimberly blurted out.

'Thought we were overdue for a visit,' her father said simply. Quincy always had been impossible to rattle.

And then Kimberly remembered – the last fight with Mac, her late-night phone message. All at once she blushed, feeling needy and overexposed. She should've called her father right back, told him to ignore her plea, she was just having a moment. She should've . . . done something.

'Working?' asked Rainie, barely suppressing a yawn. 'Anything interesting?'

'No. Well, maybe. What time did you arrive? Have you had anything to eat? Did Mac show you your room? I'm so sorry to keep you up so late.'

'We're on Oregon time,' her unflappable father assured her, still sitting in the chair, still holding the newspaper. 'It's not so late.'

Rainie gave him a look, muffled another yawn, then said, 'We got in shortly after ten. Mac was home, but got called. I'll confess, we ate all the leftover pizza—'

'We?' Quincy interjected.

'All right, *I* ate all the pizza. The Jolly Green Giant over here' – she pointed a thumb at Quincy – 'made a salad.'

'We have vegetables?' Kimberly asked in surprise.

'Iceberg lettuce, red onions, and tomatoes,' her father supplied, 'which I would assume are condiments in this house, but can be turned into a garden salad if one desires.'

'Huh,' Kimberly said.

Rainie finally broke the ice by crossing the room and giving Kimberly a welcoming hug.

'How are you feeling?' Rainie asked.

'Good. Good. All good.'

'The baby?'

'Healthy, growing, kicking.'

'You can feel it move?' Rainie's voice picked up, sounded momentarily wistful. Late in life, Kimberly's stepmom had decided she wanted children. She and Quincy had looked into adoption, but it hadn't gone as planned. They never talked about it, but Kimberly was relatively sure those doors were closed to Rainie now, and the only children in her life were the ones she assisted as an advocate for abused children.

Did Kimberly's pregnancy make her jealous, awaken old hurts, fresh regrets? Rainie was a former law enforcement officer, well-practiced in schooling her features and holding her tongue. Whatever she was feeling on the inside, it was doubtful it would ever show.

'Wanna touch it?' Kimberly asked.

'Yes.'

She took Rainie's hand, moved it to her left side, just around the curve. Baby McCormack, engaged in her nightly aerobics, did not disappoint.

'Boy or girl?' Rainie asked. 'What do you think?'

Quincy had gotten off the recliner and was standing next to his wife. He'd never ask, so Kimberly took his hand and pressed it against her side. The baby kicked again. Her father flinched, jerked his hand away. Then he smiled.

'Boy!' he said immediately. He placed his hand back, palm flat against her side.

'I would guess boy as well,' Rainie was saying. 'Girls are supposed to steal their mother's beauty; you still look plenty beautiful to me.'

Kimberly nearly blushed. 'All right, all right. Give the beautiful mother some air. And a glass of water.'

She headed for the kitchen, fetching a glass of water for herself, a second for Rainie. Quincy was a dedicated coffee drinker, so even though it was three in the morning, she brewed him a pot. They all moved to the kitchen table, a touching family scene except that not one of them had thought to turn on the overhead light. That alone said something about their chosen professions.

'Mac say anything before he bolted?' Kimberly quizzed now.

'Not to wait up.'

Kimberly grunted, chewed on her lower lip, trying to think what might be going on. She didn't know what Mac was working on these days. They'd talked about her cases, but not his.

'And your night?' her father asked.

'Stakeout,' she supplied. 'Guy didn't magically confess, but he did beat the shit out of our informant, which seems to indicate we're on the right track.'

Quincy raised a brow in interest. 'What kind of case?'

'Serial murder. Prostitutes have been disappearing, including six girls whose driver's licenses were left on the windshield of a special agent's car. We think this guy might be good for it.' Kimberly chewed her lower lip again. 'Problem is, we haven't turned up any of the remains. Given the lifestyle, the defense can assert the girls simply moved on. Makes for a very messy case. Though, you know, if we could get the tape admissible, that might work.'

'The tape?' Rainie spoke up.

'Audio recording of one of the missing women being killed. Or at least, it sure as hell sounds like she's being murdered. Get this – the subject makes each victim choose the next victim. In this case, the woman, Veronica Jones, gave up the name of her daughter, Ginny Jones, who is now our informant.'

Rainie stated the obvious. 'But he didn't kill Ginny Jones.'

'According to her, she talked him out of it. The subject has a thing for spiders. So does Ginny. Given their mutual interest, he let her live – if you call working as a prostitute for the rest of your life, while handing over fifty percent of your earnings, living.'

'He remains in control,' Quincy said.

'Exactly. This dude has a thing for control.'

'Can I hear the tape?' Quincy asked.

'It's at the office. I can get it tomorrow.'

'How did he ask the woman to choose the next victim?'

'Torture. He said he would end it when she gave him the name of someone she loved.'

Quincy had that look. 'Did the victim comply immediately?'

'Actually, she tried to give him a fake name. But when he pressed her, why that name, how did that person matter, she fell apart. You can hear her stress, her disorientation from the pain. It's difficult to think under those circumstances, let alone lie.'

'So she gave up her own daughter. That would seem to imply all the victims share some kind of connection for him.'

'We're working on it. Actually, a GBI special agent is working on it. Sal already knows three of the prostitutes were roommates; they disappeared one by one. But certainly, we lack major pieces of the puzzle. There are probably some girls on our list of missing persons who did move to Texas, and others who have also disappeared but we haven't heard about yet.'

'All from one concentrated geographic area?' Rainie spoke up. 'What's the prostitution scene like in Georgia?'

'Vast and varied. There's the streetwalkers in the red light districts such as Fulton Industrial Boulevard – mostly African American, mostly into drugs. Then you got the massage parlors in places like Sandy Springs – mostly Asian, mostly sex slaves. Then there's the club scene, which has a bit of everything, white, Hispanic, black, Asian, drugs, nondrugs. And finally, we got the usual sort of activity around the Air Force base in Marietta – local girls offering a few extra services while tending tables.

'Georgia's a big state; lots of geographic and socioeconomic diversity. If our subject is hopscotching his way through the underground scene, it'll take a lot of conversations with various agencies to connect those dots, which is one of the reasons he's been able to stay under the radar for so long.'

'What else do you know of the UNSUB?' Quincy again.

'Well, having seen him for the first time tonight . . . Mid thirties.'

'Seasoned. Capable of moving about, taking his time, stalking his target.'

'To judge by the tape, I'd say Veronica Jones was not his first victim. He's had time to refine his methods. Physically, he's white, five nine or five ten, maybe hundred and seventy pounds. Not big, but lean, wiry. And outdoorsy – hiking boots, jeans, the SUV.'

'Hunter?'

'In this state, a strong possibility.'

'Loner.'

'Interestingly enough, we don't think so. The GBI special agent involved has received two envelopes on the windshield of his car. Both contained driver's licenses from missing hookers. Given that no note or further means of communication were attempted, Sal thinks the packages may have come from someone close to the killer, and not from the killer himself.'

Quincy arched a brow, considering the matter. 'Fair enough. Most killers, if they're going to make contact, will engage in some petty taunting while they're at it.'

'Exactly. Unfortunately, the envelopes yielded no physical evidence. So we still need to identify and track the killer on our own. Once we know who he is, however, we may be able to identify a spouse or family member who can be of some help to us.'

'Socioeconomics?' Quincy moved along.

'Can't figure him out. Talks white trash, but can also sound very crisp when he wants. And the SUV is nice – a Limited Edition Toyota FourRunner. Clothes as well; he looks casual with the jeans, the flannel shirt, but they're nice jeans, nice flannel. Maybe once a redneck, but now a yuppie.'

'He's upwardly mobile. Likes material possessions,' Rainie filled in.

'I think so.'

'It's going to come down to the money.' Rainie was looking at Quincy. 'A seasoned killer like that, ten-plus victims. The amount of time and energy he's putting into it now. Preparing the kill kit, trolling for victims, covering his tracks, hiding the bodies. It's a full-time job, especially if he stalks them for a while, too.'

'Has to,' Quincy spoke up. 'If he's letting Victim A choose Victim B, then he'll have to do a lot of reconnaissance about Victim B before he can move.'

'So he's busy,' Rainie continued. 'Working hard at this. Which means he's probably not gainfully employed anymore and having to turn to other means to fund his lifestyle.'

'Such as pimping prostitutes,' Kimberly murmured drily.

'Yes. Or fraud, burglary, drugs. There was this case a while back of a guy who was arrested by the Treasury Department for forging checks. When they went through the man's storage unit, they found boxes and boxes of photos of bound and gagged women being sexually assaulted. Turned out, the guy was a classic sexual-sadist predator who'd operated for years up and down the eastern seaboard, abducting, raping, and killing women. Forging checks was simply how he covered his costs.

'Have you heard of an organization called NecroSearch International?' Quincy asked.

Kimberly shook her head.

'They're often referred to as the Pig People. It's a nonprofit organization, comprised mostly of retired scientists and cops. I've been thinking about joining.'

'Oh boy,' Rainie said drolly.

But Kimberly was regarding her father with interest. 'What do they do?'

'Find bodies. They're most famous for burying pigs in order to research techniques for locating clandestine graves. They're also the ones who located Michele Wallace's body in Colorado, nearly twenty years after she first disappeared.'

'Michele Wallace?' Kimberly repeated, doing a quick

mental search but coming up empty. 'Sorry, don't know the case.'

'That's because you're too young. 1974. Wallace was twenty-five years old, living in Gunnison, Colorado. An experienced hiker, she set out for a weekend in Schofield Park with her German shepherd. Returning to her vehicle, she encountered two men having car troubles and offered them a ride. She was never seen alive again.

'According to one of the men, Chuck Matthews, Wallace dropped him off in town, then continued on with his friend, Roy Melanson. Not long after that, Roy Melanson was arrested on an outstanding warrant. In his possessions, the police recovered Wallace's license, camping equipment, even the pack for her dog. The more they dug into Melanson's background, the more worried the police became. Melanson was wanted for questioning in three separate rape cases, plus a murder in Texas.

'The police began applying pressure, while launching a massive search for Wallace's body in Schofield Park. And you know what happened?'

'What?'

'Nothing. Police couldn't find any evidence of foul play, so they couldn't put together a case. Melanson claimed Wallace gave him everything as a gift. Who could contradict? Melanson was eventually found guilty on fraud charges for cashing stolen checks, served thirteen years, then walked. Michele Wallace's mother, on the other hand, committed suicide, leaving behind a note that if her daughter's remains were ever found, to please bury them next to her.'

'Oh God.'

'In 1979, another hiker in Schofield Park came across a pile of hair in the middle of the hiking trail, still attached to a scalp and fashioned into two perfect braids – just like Michele Wallace wore. The police put the hair in storage and that was that. Until 1990.

'A new detective, Kathy Young, contacted NecroSearch International about the case. NecroSearch brought in a botanist, a forensic anthropologist, an archaeologist, as well as other experts. The botanist studied the plant matter found in the braids and, based on the ratio of the various types of needles and tree bark, determined there were only a few places in the entire park where that same ratio of tree species could be found. The scientists homed in on those areas and after a few days of grueling, methodical sweeps, they found Wallace's skull. In September 1993, Roy Melanson was finally found guilty of Wallace's death. And April '94, Michele Wallace's remains were finally laid to rest next to her mother's.'

'Oh jeez,' Kimberly murmured, momentarily looking away. The story had choked her up. She hated that.

'Point is,' her father continued, 'bodies matter. If your theory is right, there are at least half a dozen remains hidden somewhere. If traditional policing can't get the job done, maybe the right expert can.'

She thought about it. 'We do have a new lead. A special agent recovered a muddy hiking boot from the UNSUB's vehicle. I was thinking of contacting one of my buddies from the USGS. See about getting some soil samples analyzed, that sort of thing.'

'Test it for lime!' Quincy stated immediately.

'I know.'

'And get a botanist. Ravines have a tendency to be dense with ferns . . . Perhaps an entomologist or arachnologist, as well. You mentioned spiders . . .'

'I know, Dad.' She sounded impatient.

Quincy smiled. 'Am I lecturing again?'

She caught herself. 'No. You're offering help, and God knows, with this case, we could use help. It's just . . . late.'

'Of course. The baby. You should sleep.'

'Yeah, I should.' But no one was moving from the table. Kimberly sipped more water. Wondered about spiders and soil and where the twists and turns of a case could lead a person. Like the last time she worked with the U.S. Geological Survey team, leaping across rattlesnake-infested rock piles, spelunking into a polluted cave, dashing through a burning swamp. Life when she had been younger, quicker, and responsible for only her own welfare.

'How long are you staying?' she finally thought to ask.

Her father and Rainie exchanged a glance. 'We left it open-ended,' Rainie replied lightly. 'We've never spent much time in Georgia. We thought it might be fun to see the sights.'

Kimberly eyed them skeptically. 'And your own cases?'

'The joys of being a self-employed consultant,' her father assured her. 'You can always bring the work with you.'

'Because he still can't leave it at home!' Rainie quipped.

Kimberly nodded. She finished her water. So had Rainie.

'I'll take you to your room,' she said, picking up everyone's glasses, herding them down the hall.

Rainie went into the guest room first, in her own discreet way giving Kimberly and her father a moment alone.

Kimberly never knew what to say. Her father excelled at silence, but too often, she merely felt choked by all the words wanting to burst out of her throat. She wanted to ask him if he was happy. She wanted to ask him if a lifetime of dedication to his craft had been worth all that he'd lost along the way.

She wanted to ask him about her mother, and what it had been like when they had been a young couple expecting their first child. She wanted to ask him everything, so she asked him nothing at all.

Her father leaned forward and kissed her on the cheek.

For a moment, they both stood like that, eyes closed, foreheads touching.

'Thank you for coming,' Kimberly whispered.

And her father said, 'Anytime.'

TWENTY-FOUR

'When food is short and spiderlings are hungry, they may even eat each other.'

FROM *Spiders and Their Kin*,

BY HERBERT W. AND LORNA R. LEVI,

A GOLDEN GUIDE FROM ST. MARTIN'S PRESS, 2002

The boy was back. He returned one bright afternoon, obediently knocking on her back door, so she put him to work splitting firewood. He labored for over an hour, long enough to shed his shirt, revealing his scrawny chest, painfully bony ribs. Afterward, she made him a cheese omelet, with four thick pieces of toast and two glasses of milk. He ate it all, sopping his toast along the plate to get the last of the omelet grease, then licking each finger.

They moved on to inside chores. She showed him how to jam kindling into the window frames as extra security. Then sent him to the basement for her box of Christmas ornaments. He returned with the box in both arms and a fat brown house spider on his shoulder. When she tried to swish the spider off him, he got offended and insisted on sitting in her kitchen, playing with the thing as if it were a pet.

'Spiders won't hurt you,' he told her. 'Spiders kill insects, not people. 'Sides, spiders are really cool. Have you ever tasted a spiderweb?'

She left him with his pet and tied Christmas bells around the handles of her front and back doors, the poor woman's home security system. She had a few final chores to do, but first, she needed to run two errands.

'Well, child, are you coming or not?'

He scrambled to his feet. 'Where are we going?'

'Hardware store.'

She struggled into her coat, her hat, her gloves. The boy only had on a thin shirt, so she sent him upstairs to Joseph's room. He returned with a flannel top that fell almost to his ankles. She dug through the entryway closet until she found one of her mother's old navy blue coats. That fit him better than her brother's gear.

They hit the driveway, the boy stopping expectantly next to the garage.

'Don't be foolish, child. God gave us legs for a reason.'

'God gave us cars for a reason, too,' the boy retorted, which made her cackle in surprise.

'Sold the car nearly ten years ago,' she informed him. 'At my age, I have a hard enough time walkin' a straight line, let alone drivin' one.'

She headed down the hill, the boy falling in step beside her. She was too slow for him, so after a bit, he scampered forward and to the side, advancing, then retreating, in that puppylike way young boys had. He kicked at slush piles, jumped into puddles. Coated his borrowed clothes in muck.

It didn't bother her. A fine young boy like him should be playing and jumping and getting covered in muck.

He should not, however, be spending his time with an old woman.

It took her nearly an hour before she arrived at the local hardware store. The boy walked in with her, but once inside, she lost track of him, having to concentrate. She needed chain locks. Three of them. Something sturdy that wouldn't snap.

The price of steel locks made her blink, her hands trembling on her purse.

In the end, she bought only two and it was painful at that.

She discovered the boy outside the store when she was done, waiting for her.

'Now what?'

'Groceries. Young man, you can eat.'

She hobbled off for the convenience store. The boy bounded along beside her.

Mel was at the register. Looked up at her entry, raising his hand in greeting. His face stilled when he saw the boy, his hand dropping to his side, but he didn't say anything. He appeared alert, however, watchful.

'I want Froot Loops,' the boy said.

'Too expensive.'

'Please, please, please.'

'Child, I buy food, not puffs of sugar. You want Froot Loops, buy 'em yourself.'

The boy wandered off to eye the candy bars. Rita stared at eggs and wondered when the whole world had gotten so expensive. She had twelve dollars left. Had to last her at least a week. But the boy obviously needed to eat more.

She would start making more omelets, beating water with the eggs to stretch the supply. She could make her own pasta, too, used to all the time. Big egg noodles tossed with the canned tomatoes in her basement would make a fine meal.

She wished she could buy orange juice, the boy could use the vitamins and it tasted so nice and tart on the tongue. In the end, she settled for powdered milk, which would probably make the boy fuss, though after all these years, it was fine enough for her.

Sausage was out of the question, bacon, too. She found the expired bread, and some mealy apples in the bargain bin. She'd mash the apples into sauce, toast the bread. Thinking along those lines, she found some half-priced beef and moldy carrots and onions, perfect for a stew.

Still, it broke her heart to count out each precious penny, and get only two bags in return. She eyed Mel expectantly, waiting for him to go into the back and complete their little routine.

Instead, he was eyeing the boy, who was still in front of the candy bars.

'Friend of yours?' he asked Rita stiffly.

'Helped me split some wood.'

That took some of the starch out of Mel's spine. Now, he merely appeared uncomfortable. 'I wouldn't give him inside chores,' he muttered under his breath, but still loud enough she was sure the sharp-eared boy had heard.

'Mind your business, Mel. I'll mind mine.' She took the two bags, struggling a bit to get them down from the counter, and Mel had the good grace to suddenly flush.

'Sorry, Rita, let me help you—'

But she no longer felt like dealing with the likes of him. She made her own way to the door. 'Child,' she called, because she didn't like saying the name Scott, didn't think it fit him any more than her brother's old shirt. 'We're done now.'

The boy dutifully came to her, following her out the door. He had his hands in his pockets. She had to clear her throat three times before he took the hint and grabbed one of the bags. Then, once more in silence, they trudged up the road.

A quarter way up, Rita had to stop to catch her breath. Her stomach growled, protesting its light breakfast, as she'd fed her toast to the boy. At her age, she was shrinking year by year anyway. The boy needed the calories in order to grow.

She looked up to find the boy eating a Kit Kat.

'Want one?' he asked politely, right before she grabbed him by the ear.

'Child, where did you get that candy?'

'Ow!'

'Answer me, boy! Did you pay for that chocolate? Go up to the cashier, count out some money when I wasn't looking?'

'I . . . I . . .'

'You stole it, didn't you!'

'I was just trying to help! You have hardly any money and he has that big store filled with so much food. What's one little candy bar anyway? He won't even notice!'

'Show me your pockets.'

She let go of his ear long enough to force him to turn out his pockets. He had two candy bars, a bag of peanuts, and three Slim Jims. She shook her head in disgust.

'Well, there is only one thing left to do.' She picked up the groceries and started marching back down the hill.

'Where are you going?' The boy scrambled to keep up. When Rita was angry, she had some life left in her yet, and she was sorely angry right now.

'I'm fixin' to take you back to the store, young man. Where you're gonna give *everything* back to Mel. And then you're gonna sweep out his storeroom as an apology.'

The boy stopped walking. '*Why?* You need food. I was helping you. See, I'm useful. You don't like Slim Jims? Show me what you want. I'll get it next time. Though you'll have to keep buying eggs. They're too big to steal.'

She stopped walking, just so she could glare at him. 'Stealing is wrong.'

'I've seen your cupboards. They're empty. I can help.'

'The good Lord helps those who help themselves.'

'Yes, exactly!' His eyes lit up. She realized she might not have picked the best proverb.

'Child! Enriching yourself at the expense of others is a sin. I am poor. My cupboards are bare. But I am strong and clever. I will prevail, without resorting to a life of crime. Now march!'

She kicked at his leg, prodding him into moving. He scowled at her, but scuttled forward, looking more perplexed than angry. At the bottom of the hill, however, he balked, refusing to enter the store.

She took everything from him, went inside herself, and laid it on the counter.

'My apologies,' she informed Mel. 'It won't happen again.'

'He's trouble,' Mel murmured, arms crossed over his chest.

Rita regarded him haughtily. 'He said he was only trying to help.' She gave him one last glare then shuffled her way out of the convenience store with as much dignity as a half-crippled old woman could manage.

The boy had retreated across the street. He followed her back up the hill, looking more and more subdued. They were just approaching her house when he finally burst.

'That was stupid! *You* are stupid! That was my candy. I *earned* it. You had no right to give it back.'

'Rules matter.'

'No, no, they don't. You don't know anything!' Then he took her precious grocery bag and slammed it to the ground. She heard the eggs break, saw the yellow yolks begin to ooze inside the bag.

'Of all the darn fool things to do, child. Now we'll both be hungry.'

'Good. Good, good, good!' the boy roared. He pulled back his arm. She thought he would hit her, punch her across the face. But at the last minute, he dropped his arm, turned, and fled.

She watched him go, his thin legs pounding, as he headed up the next rolling hill, toward the dilapidated Victorian. She wanted to be angry with the boy; mostly, she wondered what awaited him there.

Another minute passed. Then she laboriously bent over, retrieving the bag, cradling it carefully in her hands. She made it into the kitchen, where bit by bit, using a rubber scraper, she coaxed the runny yolks into a glass bowl.

She did the only thing she knew how to do, saving what could be saved.

TWENTY-FIVE

Burgerman is up to something.

I can feel him studying me when he thinks I won't notice.
I'll be watching TV and he'll come in, standing in the
doorway, staring, staring, staring. Then he'll reach down,
scratch his balls, and disappear.

Burgerman spends a lot of time alone these days. Out
and about, locked in his room. Sometimes, I can feel the
darkness of his moods. Sometimes, I can match 'em with
my own. We are like father and son, mutually
contemptuous.

He doesn't touch me anymore; I'm too old. I can't fetch
like I used to, either. A pale-faced teenager is automatically
suspect on most playgrounds. People think I might be
trouble, maybe a drug dealer or petty gangster. Little do
they suspect.

I'm still small. Burgerman doesn't feed me much, a last-
ditch effort to stave off puberty, I guess. After all, there's
still the money from the movies, but even that's not what it
used to be. In the world of porn, the big money is in kids,
not gaunt, scrawny-chested teenagers.

Lately, he's started talking about graduation. 'Son, there
comes a time in everyone's life when you gotta start lookin'
ahead. You're growin' up, boy. Gettin ready to graduate.'

I don't know what graduation means. Certainly no cap and gown ceremony, or one-way ticket to college. What does he think I'll do? Go to trade school, get a job? Move into a trailer park with all the other perverts? Only one thing I know how to do. What's the graduation ceremony like for that?

I know lately, when I come home, my hand stills after I put the key in the lock. I wonder when I turn it, if it'll still work. And if my key does turn, I wonder when I push the door open, if the Burgerman will still be there.

Because I'm starting to get the picture, you see. Life has to have value. And I outgrew my value about two years ago. Now I'm like that old nag in the barn, can't run, can't breed, but costs a fortune in room and board. You know, the horse that's ultimately sent to the glue factory.

Burgerman probably hopes I'll run away. I've thought about it, believe me. But after all these years, I don't know where I would go or what I would do. This is the only life I know; Burgerman the only family I have left.

Maybe he'll dump me and disappear.

There are, of course, other possibilities.

Burgerman came into my room last night, stood at the foot of my bed. Staring, staring, staring.

I kept my breathing steady, but watched him beneath the narrow slits of my eyes. I wondered if he had a knife, a gun. I wondered what I would do if he attacked.

Burgerman is talking of graduation.

I must remain alert.

TWENTY-SIX

*'A stinging sensation is usually followed by intense pain. The
tissue affected locally by the venom is killed and gradually
sloughs away, exposing the underlying muscles.'*

FROM *Biology of the Brown Recluse Spider*, BY JULIA MAXINE HITE,
WILLIAM J. GLADNEY, J. L. LANCASTER, JR., AND W. H. WHITCOMB,
DEPARTMENT OF ENTOMOLOGY, DIVISION OF AGRICULTURE,
UNIVERSITY OF ARKANSAS, FAYETTEVILLE, MAY 1966

Harold loved the boot.

'Holy crap! Do you know what this is?' he exclaimed.
'Wow, a Limmer boot. Where did you get this? Do you
know what this means?'

Kimberly didn't know what a Limmer boot was, or what
having one meant. That's why she'd asked Harold to journey
down from the high ground of Counterterrorism to VC's
tiny, third-floor sanctuary. The CT agents hated to travel.
After all, they had an entire floor complete with half a dozen
TVs blaring Fox News. In contrast, Violent Crimes had . . .
cardboard boxes, some maps, a couple rolls of yellow crime
scene tape strewn around for general aesthetics.

Fortunately, Harold had been intrigued by her request
for help. He was a geek. It was one of the things Kimberly
liked best about him.

Kimberly had commandeered an unused desk by a bank
of windows. There, she had laid out the dark brown hiking
boot on top of a sheet of butcher paper. To the side, she
had spread her kit of stainless steel instruments: metal file,
tweezers, scraper, a host of different-size metal picks. Sure,
she could've gone with the Popsicle sticks favored by so
many evidence technicians, but that wouldn't have looked
nearly as cool.

She'd completed an initial examination of the boot, noting size, color, brand name, tread pattern, and surface markings. She'd recorded that the boot was a men's size 10, with a badly scuffed inner heel and big toe. It appeared to be made from an all-leather upper, with a rubber sole. Shoelace was brown, threaded with dark green. She snapped a dozen photographs to record its initial state.

Then she'd started the process of chipping off caked mud, plant materials, and other debris from the bottom of the boot. Select samples were captured in glass vials to be sent to the FBI lab. The rest of the detritus would remain captured in the butcher paper, as it was folded up, slid inside a larger brown paper evidence bag, and stored in the evidence vault for future consideration. Finally, she would cast the boot's tread pattern in tinted dental stone for possible match later with any impressions recovered from a crime scene.

The life of an evidence collector was all about painstaking methodology and practiced patience. You sorted, studied, and saved, all in the name of someday. Except Kimberly didn't feel like waiting these days. She wanted answers now. Harold, former naturalist and U.S. Forestry Service employee, seemed her best bet.

'A Limmer boot is special?' she ventured, straightening up with a metal pick still clutched in her right hand.

'Sure. Limmers are a high-end hiker's boot, made by a family-owned shop in New Hampshire. You're not talking something you pick up at your nearest Wal-Mart. This is an enthusiast's boot. A serious hiker for sure.'

This got Kimberly's attention. 'High-end? What does that mean? Limited quantities? Highly traceable?'

'Well,' Harold drawled now, taking the pick from her and starting to poke at the boot himself. 'Back in my day, Limmers were custom fit. But if memory serves, they contracted with an outside company to manufacture a small line of ready-to-wear hiking boots. So I guess the real question is, what kind of boot do we have here? Handmade custom fit or mass-produced ready-to-wear?'

He snapped on a pair of latex gloves, hefting up the boot and rolling it between his hands. 'Feel the weight of this sucker. That's a good two pounds, easy. Full-length nylon shank, double-layer midsole, Vibram outsole. Nice.'

'If these boots are so special, why haven't I ever heard of them? I'm a hiker.'

Harold gave her a look. 'When's the last time you did the AT?'

'AT?' she muttered, thinking hard. 'Appalachian Trail? Ummm, it's on my list.'

'Yeah, you're a day hiker. These are boots for the pros.'

Kimberly murmured something low and disparaging under her breath, but couldn't refute his point.

'So I could contact Limmer and they might be able to tell me who purchased this boot?'

'It's possible. Especially if it was a custom job. May I?'

Harold still had the metal pick, waving it at the rubber insole. Kimberly shrugged and let him have at it. She'd been studying the boot for an hour now. All she had to show for it was a headache.

She wandered off for a glass of water. When she returned, Harold had pulled over a chair and was getting into it.

'Lotta minerals,' he reported, sifting through the crumbling bits of dried mud. 'Quartz, feldspar, even some amethyst. Do you have a flashlight?'

Kimberly retrieved her field kit from beneath her desk, pulling out a flashlight.

'Magnifying glass,' Harold chirped.

She produced a magnifying glass.

'Glass of water.'

She rolled her eyes, but obediently fetched water.

Harold didn't drink the water, but used an eyedropper to squeeze several drops into a glass vial, then added a clump of mud, then more water. He turned the mud into silt, swirling it around within the vial, before starting the painstaking process of pouring out the silt into a second glass tube.

'Look at this, all these tiny reflective particles?' He held up the first glass vial, now devoid of brackish water. 'You're talking a soil very high in metals and minerals. Got a microscope?'

Kimberly arched a brow. 'Harold, we're evidence collectors, not evidence analyzers. No one has a microscope.'

'I do,' Harold said.

'What?'

'Well, you never know,' he stated defensively. 'Sometimes, life simply calls for a microscope.'

Kimberly couldn't think of a single thing to say to that. She sent him upstairs for his microscope. When he returned, they rinsed the mineral sample a second time and prepared a slide. After all, sometimes life does call for a microscope.

'Gold,' Harold murmured at last. 'Mostly feldspar and quartz. But also a trace amount of gold.'

'Really?'

'Sure. After all, the first gold rush in America happened right here in Georgia. 1829.' Harold straightened up from the microscope, returning to the boot and scraping off more debris. 'In the Chattahoochee National Forest. Where'd you think the expression 'There's gold in them thar hills' came from?'

'Hadn't given the matter any thought.'

'You should visit Dahlonega sometime. Check out the museum, tour the old mines. There's even a hotel that has its own gold mine in the basement.'

'I thought Dahlonega was wine country.'

'Gold for the new generation,' Harold assured her. 'Now this is interesting. Take a look at this.'

Kimberly obediently leaned closer. Harold had picked out several green scraps of plant matter from the mud-caked boot. Now he mounted the first object on a slide and slid it under his microscope.

'What is it?' Kimberly prodded.

'Looks like crushed leaf of a mountain laurel.' Harold made some adjustments, then slid out the first slide and replaced it with a second. 'And this here looks like white pine. Also got some dried oak leaves, bits of beech. Yeah, I'd say your subject's been in the Chattahoochee National Forest, without a doubt. Someplace with a lot of broadleaf hardwoods and evergreen conifers. Look, there's even some hemlock. Hmmm . . .'

'Would that be a good place to hide bodies?'

'The Chattahoochee National Forest?' Harold asked, still hunched over the microscope.

'Yeah. We think this subject may have kidnapped and killed ten women. It'd be a lot easier, however, if we could locate a body. Maybe the Chattahoochee would be the place to start.' Not to mention that by virtue of being a national forest, the Chattahoochee fell under FBI jurisdiction.

'If you're gonna hike through the Chattahoochee National Forest,' Harold commented absently, 'I'd order a pair of Limmers first.' He finished at the microscope, returned to the boot.

'Why?'

'The forest contains over seven hundred and fifty thousand acres.'

'*What?*'

'Told you we had good hiking in this state.'

'Ah damn.'

'Wait. I got another present for you. Tweezers.'

Kimberly rifled her instrument kit, found the tweezers. 'More gold?' she asked hopefully. 'How about the driver's license from one of the victims?'

'Better.'

'Better?'

'Yeah. Check it out. I got a spider casting.'

Kimberly managed to reach Sal by phone shortly after three p.m. She'd eaten four puddings and a buttermilk biscuit for lunch and was feeling the sugar rush.

'So I talked to a guy at Limmer Boot,' she reported in one quick burst. 'If we can get him the boot, he'd be happy to examine it for us. Sounds to him like it's one of their standard mountaineering boots. They're sold by a variety of dealers now, with men's size ten being the most common size, so that's the bad news. But if it was a custom fit – he won't know until he sees it – he might be able to track down the name.'

Sal didn't sound nearly as impressed as he should be: 'Dinchara bought a boot in New Hampshire?'

'Maybe. Or by mail order. Point is, this is a pretty serious hiking boot, generally purchased by pretty serious hikers. Harold's convinced Dinchara's been stomping around the Chattahoochee National Forest, which finally limits our search area from the entire state of Georgia to a mere seven hundred and fifty thousand acres.'

Sal grunted.

'Okay,' Kimberly tried again. 'What did you do today?'

'Had my ass handed to me by my supe.'

'Uh-oh.'

'Klein rejected my request to form a task force. He doesn't believe we've adequately provided evidence of foul play.'

'But the driver's licenses of missing women left on your car. The recording of Veronica Jones's murder—'

'Unsubstantiated.'

'Dinchara's conversation with Ginny. Hell, Dinchara's treatment of Ginny—'

'She's welcome to press charges.'

'Ah crap,' Kimberly said, feeling deflated now, too. 'What exactly does he want from us?'

'A body. A corroborating witness. More substantiation that the women really are missing, and not just relocated.'

'But that's why we need the task force. So we can do the legwork to get the substantiation. Or, here's a thought, find a body.'

'I know.'

'And in the meantime, Ginny Jones is hanging out there, alone and unprotected, after ruffling Dinchara's feathers.'

'I know.'

She scowled, chewed her lower lip. 'Some days, this job really sucks.'

'I know.'

They sat in silence for a moment, then Sal said, out of nowhere, 'My dad used to do that – slap my mother around. It wasn't too bad, until my brother disappeared. Then my father started to drink heavily. He'd beat the shit out of my mother, and she'd just take it. Like everything lousy in life really was her fault.'

Kimberly didn't know what to say.

'I hated it then, and I hate it now. Goddamn, I just want to arrest the son of a bitch.'

'Sal—'

'Never mind. I'm just having a bad day. Nothing I won't get over. So.' He cleared his throat. 'I located Ginny's real address, using the info from her vehicle registration. Jackie agreed to monitor Ginny tonight. I'll take tomorrow night, see what happens.'

Sal paused expectantly, waiting for her to offer to take night three. Kimberly tapped one finger on her desk, thinking guiltily of Mac, wanting her to return home to discuss major life changes. Then there was the matter of her father and Rainie, who'd flown in all the way from Oregon.

'You know,' Sal prodded more forcefully, 'Dinchara's

pretty riled up. A guy like that, once he decides he's got a liability, isn't exactly going to send Ginny on a trip to Disney World. We're the ones who wired her up. To walk away now . . .'

'I have to look at my calendar,' Kimberly said.

'Well, well, well, if you gotta wash your hair—'

'Don't be an ass.'

'I'm just saying—'

'I know, I know. Dinchara's mad, Ginny's vulnerable. Things are happening fast. Why do you think I spent the whole afternoon hunched over a filthy hiking boot? We're going to pull it together. After all, we've already struck gold. Oh, and found a spider casting.'

'A spider what?'

'Exactly.'

Next phone call was from Mac.

'Dinner?' she tried. 'I promised Rainie chicken-fried steak with gravy. Rainie's buying the groceries. Dad's picking up the Lipitor.'

'Can't. Gotta work late.'

'But you love chicken-fried steak.'

'Then save me a plate,' he said, already sounding irritated. Kimberly took that as a hint and shut up. Mac stopped talking, too; the silence stretching long.

'Rough case?' she finally ventured.

'You know how it is.'

'Guess I do.'

'Don't wait up.'

'Guess I won't.'

'We can't keep doing this, you know,' he said abruptly. 'You're working late, I'm working late. We pass each other in the night, with barely a peck on the cheek. What kind of way is this to live?'

'Our way,' she said softly.

'Something's gotta give.'

'I'm ready to talk when you are.'

'Oh sure, now that you're no longer busy.'

The open hostility in his voice shocked her. She clammed up again, feeling she'd waded into a minefield, not sure how to proceed.

'Ah fuck it,' Mac said. 'I'm tired, that's all.' Then he hung up on her.

When her cell phone rang again, she picked it up without thinking. She thought it might be Sal, reporting more news. She hoped it might be Mac, offering an apology.

Instead, she got silence.

And then she knew.

She sat back in her chair, already digging around in her jacket, trying to find her mini-recorder.

'Why don't you care?' the voice asked, high-pitched, tinny. This time around, she thought she could catch a faint distortion, a hint of electronics.

'I'm listening,' she said, fumbling the recorder, finally getting it on top of her desk, switching it on.

'I thought you would care,' the voice echoed petulantly, ping-ponging through the earpiece, '. . . do something.'

'Let's meet,' she said evenly. 'Talk in person. I want to help.'

'It's not my fault. "Step into my parlor," said the spider to the fly. And they do, they do.'

'Tell me your name. I need an address, a phone number. I'll list you as a confidential informant. No one will know but us.'

But the caller wasn't listening to her. His voice had grown to a higher-pitched whine, sounding angry. 'Why didn't you try harder? You forgot about us. You abandoned us to his web. Now it's your turn. He's gonna get you. But I don't care. I *refuse* to care. It's not my fault.'

'Veronica Jones,' she said crisply. 'The other women . . . I know what he did, but I need proof. What does he do with them? Where does he hide their bodies? If you help me find them, I can make this stop.'

But the voice didn't respond. She heard silence, followed by a crackle of interference. Then, when she had almost given up: 'I'm gonna graduate.'

She hesitated, then took a gamble: 'You mean like Tommy Mark Evans?'

'That was not my fault!' the voice cried. 'You don't know what it's like. Once his mind's made up there's *nothing* you can do.'

'Then meet with me. Explain it to me. Help me help you.'

'No. Too late. You had your chance. Now it's my turn, and I'm gonna graduate.'

'I don't know what that means.'

'All I have to do is kill you.'

'Pardon?'

The caller was agitated now. 'Someone loved me once. A long time ago. I wish I could remember her face. But she's gone now. This is all I have left. I want to survive. I want to graduate. I *will* kill you.'

'Let me help you!'

'Say goodbye,' the voice whispered, then the caller was gone.

Night was falling by the time Kimberly checked out for the day, taking the elevator down to the lobby, walking out to the parking garage. Temperature hovered around the high forties, cool enough to make her hunch her shoulders inside her camel-colored coat, scarf wrapped tight around her neck.

The sprawling office park was quiet as she followed the sidewalk along the embankment, shallow stream to her right, parking garage to her left. She had one hand in her pocket, curled around her car fob, largest key tucked between two fingers like a shank.

The wind whispered over the slight hill, stirring the

hair at the nape of her neck, tickling the upturned collar of her coat.

She turned to study the emptiness behind her, picked up her step.

The shadows grew longer, chasing her into the parking garage toward the crouched form of her station wagon. She didn't relax until she had checked the full interior, including the backseats and cargo space. Even then, sliding behind the wheel, closing the door, hitting all the locks, she could feel her hands tremble as Baby McCormack gave a fluttering little kick to her side.

'It's okay, baby,' she whispered. 'You're safe, everything's all right.'

But she wasn't sure who she was trying to convince anymore, her baby or herself.

TWENTY-SEVEN

'Time spent in the company of spiders can cure anyone of his sentimentality about nature.'

FROM 'SPIDER WOMAN,'
BY BURKHARD BILGER,
New Yorker, MARCH 5, 2007

Dinner was a somber affair. Kimberly over-cooked the meat, burned the gravy, and remembered why she stuck to takeout. Her father and Rainie tried to be kind about it. They praised the microwaved green beans and moved bites of chicken-fried steak around their plates in an appearance of eating.

If they were curious about Mac's absence, they didn't say anything and Kimberly didn't feel like talking about it. What was there to say, anyway? He was working late. Happened all the time.

'We went to the aquarium today.' Rainie spoke up in a determined voice. 'What an amazing place. I particularly enjoyed petting the stingrays.'

'Uh-huh,' Kimberly said.

'Quincy, what about you? What did you enjoy most?'

Kimberly's father blinked, a deer caught in headlights. 'Ummm, the beluga whales.'

'Yes, they were also beautiful. And very playful. I had no idea!'

'Uh-huh,' Kimberly said again.

'So I'm thinking tomorrow we'll visit the Coke museum. I never realized an entire state could worship soda pop until we arrived here. What do you think, Quincy?'

'Sounds like a plan.' He had picked up his wife's forced enthusiasm.

Kimberly set down her fork. 'Dad, what was Mom like when she was pregnant?'

That brought the conversation up short.

'What?' her father asked.

'Did she have morning sickness, blotchy skin, mood swings? Or was she one of those radiant pregnant women, all aglow with maternal anticipation? Maybe she knit booties, stenciled nursery walls, made list after list of potential baby names . . .'

'Your mother? Knitting?'

'Was she *happy*? Did you guys have Amanda's birth all planned out? Mom would stay home, you would take a leave of absence. You'd decorate the nursery together, take turns rocking your bundle of joy.'

'Kimberly, in all honesty, that was over thirty years ago—'

'Well, you must remember something! Anything! Come on, Dad. I'd ask Mom directly, except, you know, she's dead!'

Quincy fell silent. Kimberly blinked her eyes, ashamed by her own outburst, the emotion that had risen out of nowhere and now clogged her throat. She should apologize. Say something. But she couldn't, because if she opened her mouth, she was going to burst into tears.

Her father drew in a breath. 'I'm sorry, Kimberly,' he said quietly. 'I know you have questions. And I would like to answer them, I would. But to tell you the truth, I don't remember much about Mandy's birth, or even your own. I think when your mother was pregnant with Amanda, I was working a string of bank robberies in the Midwest. Four men in an unmarked white cargo van. They liked to pistol-whip the tellers, even when the women were cooperating with their demands. I remember interviewing eyewitness after eyewitness, trying to get a feel for how the team operated. And I remember walking into the ninth bank and discovering that, this time, they had shot the teller between the eyes. Heather Norris was her name. Nineteen-year-old single mother. She had just started at the bank in order to earn enough money to go to college. Those were the things that made an impression on me. As for your mother and what she was going through . . .'

'She hated you,' Kimberly said quietly.

'Eventually, yes. And I would say, not without cause.'

'Did you hate her?'

'Never.'

'What about Mandy and me? Two more females interfering with your precious work?'

'You and Amanda are two of the best things that ever happened to me.' She saw him squeeze Rainie's hand. It didn't improve her mood.

'Oh sure, you say that now. But at the time, when you were working one hundred cases a year of murdered kids and mutilated women, each of them needing your complete focus, and there we were, demanding that you come home for dinner, attend the school play, watch our talent show. How could you not get frustrated? How could you *not* grow impatient with all our petty demands?'

'They were never petty.'

'But they were. They can be. How do you manage it all? How do you find enough time and energy? Enough love? How can you be all things to all people?'

Her father was silent for a moment. 'Did you know your mother had a job before you girls were born?' he asked abruptly.

'She did?'

'Yes. She worked at an art gallery. Your mother had a master's in fine art. She hoped to be a curator of a museum someday. That was her dream.'

'Then she got pregnant.'

'Things were different back then, Kimberly. Your mother and I had always assumed she would stay home with our children. It never occurred to us to do anything different. Though maybe, in hindsight, we should have.'

'Why do you say that?'

Her father shrugged, obviously choosing his next words with care. 'Your mother was a bright, creative woman. While she loved you and your sister, life as a stay-at-home mom . . . It was hard for her. Not as fulfilling as she had hoped. And then, with me gone all the time . . . I think it was easier sometimes to blame me for her dissatisfaction. I loved my job. And she . . . didn't.'

'Would you have let her go back to work?'

'I don't know. She never asked. And I was never home long enough to realize how unhappy she was. Until, of course, it was too late.'

'I don't know how to do this,' Kimberly whispered, her hand curling over her belly. 'I thought I did, but here I am, five months pregnant, and suddenly, I don't understand anything anymore. How to be a wife, an agent, let alone a mom. I haven't even had the baby yet, and I'm already terrible at this!'

'I wish there was something I could tell you, Kimberly. But life isn't a one-size-fits-all model. These are the questions you should be asking. These are the concerns you and Mac will get to address. All I can say is that as a parent, I think I made every mistake a father could make, and I still wound up with a positively wonderful daughter.'

Kimberly shook her head. She knew he meant the words kindly. She wanted to accept them gracefully. But all she could wonder is if Mandy would say the same, and thoughts of her sister, dead by the age of twenty-three, simply broke her heart all over again.

Kimberly waited until bedtime to bring up the phone call. Five months ago, she would've mentioned a death threat to Mac. They both would've scoffed at it, having received their fair share. Now she didn't think she could talk about it with Mac, so she told her father instead.

He approached it with his usual practicality. 'What do you know about the caller?'

'Nothing.'

'Nonsense. Try harder. You've spoken to the person three times. Plenty of opportunities to learn.'

She remembered now: Her father was a hard-ass. 'Umm, the caller has access to a computer and a credit card and is knowledgeable enough about the Internet to use call spoofing.'

'Okay.'

'Caller knows the FBI's general information number; not that hard because it's also in the phone book. But,' she considered now, 'caller also knows my cell phone number, which is harder to get.'

'What else?'

'Caller sounds like a male, but that could be the result of voice distortion. I have the impression, however, that the caller is younger. Some of the expressions used, the general moodiness and anger. I'd guess adolescent.'

'Excellent.'

'There's a slight regional accent, so I'd say he's a local. Calls have happened during the evening, small hours of the morning, and now daytime. So someone with a flexible job or schedule, or perhaps no job at all.'

'Goes along with your theory of an adolescent.'

'Yes.'

'Motive? Why is the caller reaching out? Why you?'

She had to think about it. 'At first, when the caller shared the Veronica Jones tape, I thought it was to help. A person, possibly a victim him- or herself, was trying to bring attention to what had happened so that Dinchara would be punished. The second call also sounded like a warning. Someone still trying to help. Also, we know someone close to Dinchara is delivering envelopes bearing the missing girls' driver's licenses, potential 'trophies.' It's possible the caller is the one who made the deliveries, a first attempt at outreach that, unfortunately, didn't get the job done.'

'And today's call?'

'Angry,' she said without hesitation. 'The caller was pissed off. Like I'd personally failed him. Maybe because he's made the effort but I haven't magically come through with an arrest? I'm not sure. But tonight the tone had changed. I'm no longer his ally. I've become his target.'

Quincy's face held a ghost of a smile. 'That does sound like an adolescent.'

'Exactly!'

He paused thoughtfully. 'Is it possible that your caller is still in contact with your UNSUB? Perhaps the UNSUB himself changed the dynamics of the relationship. You said the caller wants to 'graduate.' And to do that, he/she claims he has to kill you.'

'Yes.'

'Perhaps because it is the UNSUB's bidding? Which brings us to the next logical question: Why you? Is it because the caller was told specifically to kill Special Agent Kimberly Quincy? Or that he/she was told to kill a law enforcement officer? Or a woman?'

'Me specifically,' Kimberly replied slowly. 'From the very beginning, the caller has known I was involved with the Dinchara case. So I don't think he chose me at random. It's because of my involvement in the case. That's what put me on his or her radar screen.'

'Likely suspects?' her father quizzed.

'Ginny Jones. Knows my cell phone number, has met with me regarding the case, and knows what happened to both her mother and Tommy Mark Evans. And,' she added thoughtfully, 'she has a good reason to be angry with me, considering what happened between her and Dinchara last night. Whatever problems Ginny hoped to solve by contacting law enforcement, I don't think it's worked out the way she planned.'

'But?'

Kimberly shrugged. 'But why mess around with call spoofing? We've already met face-to-face. There's nothing in the phone calls she couldn't have told me in person.'

'Shy?'

'Don't think so.'

'Scared?'

'I think it's a bigger risk to be following up by phone, versus telling me everything when we're in person. Then again, girl like her . . . Who the hell knows?'

'Do you think the caller was serious?' Quincy asked her quietly. 'Do you feel your life is in jeopardy?'

She chewed her lower lip, unsure of how to answer. 'It's spooky to be threatened.'

'But do you feel your life is in jeopardy?'

'I'm not sure. There's a big difference between preying on prostitutes and gunning for a fed. Then again, there's gamesmanship here. Ginny . . . the caller . . . I feel like a pawn being moved around a board for reasons I can't see. And that, more than anything, makes me nervous. Even if I'm not the main target, I could still wind up collateral damage.'

'You've filed a report with your supervisor?'

'Left him a memo with a copy of the tape tonight.'

'What do you think he'll recommend?'

'I'm hoping like hell he'll finally agree to form a task force,' she declared drily. 'One thing the caller did drop was that he or she knows something about Tommy Mark Evans. And there's an unsolved homicide, where, heavens to Betsy, we have a body. Maybe that will finally get the wheels churning, because God knows poor Ginny nearly got her face caved in for nothing. And I am pissed off about it!'

'That's my girl,' Quincy told her.

That, more than anything, finally made her smile.

'I think Sal's onto something,' she said seriously. 'I

think Dinchara has been preying on prostitutes. Ginny escaped. She was the lucky one. Now we need to do something about the other girls. I want to find them. I want to bring them home. And then, I want to nail Spideyman to the wall.'

'Given what you learned with the boot,' her father said, 'I'd head to the woods. Bring some cadaver dogs.'

'Sure, seven hundred and fifty thousand acres. Couple of dogs will blow through that in a day.'

'You get your sarcasm from your mother's side.'

'Don't you wish. But hey, Harold has an old friend who is an arachnologist. He's arranged for us to meet with her first thing in the morning. Normally I wouldn't place a lot of weight on the analysis of molted spider skin, but given Dinchara's predilections . . .'

'Can I attend?'

'Ah, Dad, and miss Coca-Cola World?'

Her father said seriously: 'Please, I'm begging you.'

She stayed up after Rainie and Quincy retired, watching late-night TV in bed while waiting for Mac. At one a.m., she couldn't take it anymore. She rubbed her lower back, regarded her slightly swollen feet, decided she had grown bigger since just yesterday and it was definitely time to sleep.

'Sweet dreams, Baby McCormack,' she whispered to her belly, turning off the light, dragging the covers up.

Sleep was not kind to her. She found herself running through a bloody house, which she dimly recognized from crime scene photos of her mother's murder. She was desperate to find Bethie. She had to see her mother. There was so much she needed to say.

Except then she heard the wail of a baby and she knew it wasn't her mother she had lost. She was racing to find her baby. Following the cries through the house. Following the blood trail.

Then, a ghostly white bassinet finally appearing in front of her . . .

'Shhhh,' Mac's voice told her. 'Shhh, you're all right, Kimberly. It's just a bad dream. It's okay, sweetheart. I got you.'

She clung to him. Felt his arms go around her, tucking her against the solid warmth of his chest. Except she couldn't stop shaking. Couldn't stop trembling. Even in her husband's arms, she didn't feel safe.

The phone rang. Once, twice.

The third time, she finally managed to pull herself to the surface. The clock glowed five a.m. Mac was sleeping with his back to her. Her cell phone chimed again next to the bed. He stirred groggily as she snatched it up.

She checked the display screen, then put it to her ear.

'Don't you ever sleep, Sal?'

'She's gone,' he said flatly. 'Jackie could never track her down last night. We finally stopped by first thing this morning. Apartment's packed up and cleared out. Ginny Jones has disappeared.'

TWENTY-EIGHT

'Just as birds can be identified by their singing, so spiders can
be sorted by their methods of killing.'

FROM 'SPIDER WOMAN,'
BY BURKHARD BILGER,
New Yorker, MARCH 5, 2007

'There are two kinds of poisonous spiders in the United
States,' USDA arachnologist Carrie Crawford-Hale was
explaining. 'First is the Lactrodectus mactans or black
widow, known for the bright red markings on her
abdomen. Only the females bite, generally only when
harassed. The second poisonous spider is the Loxosceles
reclusa, or brown recluse, known for the violin-shaped
marking on its back. Both males and females are
equally toxic. Fortunately, they're very shy, sedentary
spiders who prefer to stay tucked behind woodpiles
rather than intermingle with humans. Even then,
there's at least a dozen bites reported a year, some with
serious consequences.'

'Define serious,' Sal spoke up. He stood close to the door
and about as far away from Crawford-Hale and her
microscope as he could get. A mounted scorpion was to his
right; some kind of giant black beetle with enormous claws
directly above his head. The GBI special agent looked tired,
haggard, and nervous as hell.

In contrast, Kimberly was trying to figure out if it was
polite to ask if she could peer through the microscope.
She'd never seen molted spider skin at 10x magnification
before. According to Harold, it was pretty cool.

Unfortunately, Crawford-Hale's office was roughly the size of a janitor's closet, already overflowing with equipment, filing cabinets, and jarred and mounted specimens. Harold and her family had had to wait outside. Shame, because Quincy probably would enjoy what the arachnologist had to say.

'The venom of the *Loxosceles reclusa* contains an enzyme that necrotizes the flesh of the victim.' Crawford-Hale adjusted the microscope as she shifted from right to left. 'To protect against the venom, the body walls off the arteries around the bite. The skin, starved of blood, begins to die, turning black and sloughing off. I've seen pictures of open wounds anywhere from the size of a quarter to a half dollar. In some cases, it's a small reaction that clears up in weeks. Other times, an entire limb might swell up and it can take months, even a year, to fully recover. The variation seems to have to do more with the response from the victim's own immune system than from the potency of the particular spider. Basically, some people are more sensitive than others.'

Sal appeared horrified. He'd already eaten this morning, judging by the smudge of ketchup on his dark gray lapel and the pervasive odor of hash browns coming from his suit. At the moment, however, it looked like breakfast wasn't agreeing with him.

He shifted farther away from Crawford-Hale, shaking out both arms as if feeling something crawling up his skin. 'How do you know how sensitive you are?'

'First time you get bit, you learn.' Crawford-Hale straightened up at the microscope. 'I'm ninety percent certain this is a *Loxosceles reclusa*. You can still make out the upside-down violin shadowing the carapace; then there's the light brown color, the thin, almost delicate body. A more definitive diagnostic feature is the eyes – brown recluses have a semicircular arrangement of six eyes in three groups of two, while most other spiders have eight eyes. I can't make out that level of detail from this molting, but I'm still relatively confident in my classification.'

'Aren't brown recluses common in Georgia?' Kimberly asked with a frown.

'Absolutely. The southern states, Kansas, Missouri, Oklahoma – we're lousy with brown recluses. I got a case three months ago where a family reported an infestation. I collected three hundred specimens in the first three hours. Interestingly enough, no one in the family was ever bitten. Spiders really aren't interested in taking on creatures that can squish them with one move of their big toe.

'Of course, then there's Southern California, which is grappling with the *Loxosceles laeta,* a species of recluse that came from Chile, Peru, and Argentina. If the venom of the *reclusa* is a cup of tea, then the venom of the *laeta* is a double shot of espresso.'

'Another reason not to live in California,' Sal murmured. He'd finally spotted the scorpion mounted beside him. He turned to give it his back, only to discover the next mounted specimen – a cockroach of truly incredible size – staring at him nose to nose.

'I don't get it.' Kimberly was still puzzling it out. 'Why would a spider enthusiast collect a specimen as common as the brown recluse, especially given that it's venomous and thus difficult to manage?'

'Oh, I wouldn't say brown recluses are difficult to manage,' Crawford-Hale corrected immediately. 'They're some of the only spiders that can be raised communally. And there's not an aggressive instinct among them. Provide a terrarium with plenty of dark places to hide – leaves, stones, tree bark – drop in a few crickets every week, and they'd probably live quite contentedly.'

'So . . . spider enthusiasts do collect them?'

The arachnologist considered the matter. 'Have you ever heard of the Spider Pharm?'

'Umm, no.'

'It's a facility out in Arizona where they raise spiders to milk for venom—'

'They what?' Sal interrupted, horrified look back on his face.

'Milk them for venom,' Crawford-Hale supplied. 'Think about it: The venom from a single spider can contain nearly two hundred compounds, including substances that can dissolve flesh and short-circuit the nervous system. How great would it be to be able to analyze and duplicate some of these compounds for the pharmaceutical industry? It's cutting-edge science.'

'They *milk* the spiders?' Sal asked again.

'They have a special machine,' Crawford-Hale stated breezily. 'I haven't gotten to do it myself, but apparently they use tweezers wired with an electrical stimulator. A very low dose of electrical shock is transmitted to the spider, which makes its venom gland contract. A droplet forms on the spider's fang which is caught in a glass tube. Doesn't hurt the spider, but does generate lots of venom for study. Now, at a place like the Spider Pharm, believe me, they collect, breed, and house plenty of *Loxosceles reclusa*.'

'What about a more general enthusiast?' Kimberly asked. 'We believe the subject has several tarantula specimens and at least one black widow.'

Crawford-Hale shrugged. 'Honestly, collectors are collectors. I went to school with a guy who found a black widow outside the dorms, so he caught it and turned it into a pet. Then, to feed the black widow, he started raising crickets. Next thing he knew, the black widow died and he was the owner of two hundred crickets. So now he farms crickets for various pet stores. Maybe you and I wouldn't do such a thing, but it works for him.'

'How would a collector get a brown recluse?' Kimberly pressed. 'Is that a specimen he would buy online, like the tarantulas, or maybe a specialized market?'

'Around here?' The arachnologist arched a brow. 'He could

probably just go down to his basement. Or his woodpile. Or check under rocks when hiking in the woods—'

'Hiking?'

'Sure, the brown recluses live outside year round in Georgia.'

'As in the Chattahoochee National Forest?'

'I'm sure you can find them there.'

Kimberly sighed, worried her lower lip. She turned to Sal. 'So the spider casting might not have anything to do with his collection at all. Might just be another bit of debris that became stuck to his boot when hiking around the Chattahoochee.'

'He could've picked up the spider casting from hiking in the woods,' Crawford-Hale said. She added thoughtfully, 'One thing, though: Brown recluses are notoriously shy. They retreat to dark, hidden places at the best of times, let alone when they are molting, which is a time of extreme stress for a spider. Chances are, your suspect didn't come across this casting walking along a main trail. Much more likely he was bushwhacking, someplace remote, without a lot of people.'

'Someplace you'd hide a body,' Kimberly muttered.

'That would be your expertise, not mine,' the arachnologist said. 'Anything else I can do for you?'

Kimberly had to think about it. The conversation had not been as illuminating as she had hoped. Judging by the look on Sal's face, he felt the same.

She couldn't come up with any more questions. Instead, she stuck out her hand, thanking Crawford-Hale for her time. Sal followed suit.

'If we ever encounter a real-live brown recluse,' he asked at the last minute, 'what should we do?'

'Hold very still.'

Sal shook his head. 'Man, how can you do this, analyze eight-legged insects day in and day out? I'd have the creepy crawlies all of the time.'

'Oh, spiders aren't insects,' Crawford-Hale corrected him. 'Insects have six legs. Spiders have eight. Spiders *eat* insects. It's a big difference.'

Not to Sal. 'I don't like spiders,' he stated flatly as he and Kimberly exited the office, then journeyed down the basement corridor, awash in buzzing fluorescent lights.

'Look on the bright side: At least they're smaller than rattlesnakes.'

'Rattlesnakes? What were you doing with rattlesnakes?'

'Playing hopscotch,' she informed him. 'Trust me, it didn't work.'

They made it to the end, climbing up the stairs, then finally pushing through the glass door into the blinding sunlight. Harold, Quincy, and Rainie were waiting patiently in the parking lot, Harold's lanky frame folded cross-legged on the hood of Kimberly's car, Quincy and Rainie standing beside him.

'Good news?' Harold spoke up hopefully.

Kimberly shrugged. 'The casting belongs to a brown recluse, which around here isn't much different than finding a ladybug. Whoop-de-doo.'

Her father arched a brow.

'It's a technical term,' she assured him.

'What are you going to do?' he asked quietly.

Kimberly looked at Sal. 'Still no sign of Ginny Jones?' she asked.

He checked his cell phone for messages. 'Nope.'

Kimberly had gone straight to Ginny's address after receiving Sal's call. She concurred with his initial assessment: no evidence of breaking and entering, no sign of a violent struggle. The tiny apartment appeared to have been quickly and crudely packed up, dusty imprints indicating where precious items once had been, everything else left behind.

In the bedroom, half under the bed, Kimberly had found a copy of *Good Housekeeping's Guide to Pregnancy*. One more little detail to torture her late at night.

A BOLO had been issued for Ginny and her vehicle, while pictures of her and Dinchara were being circulated among the uniformed officers. Eight hours later and still counting, it was a waiting game.

'And still no task force,' Kimberly supplied with a sigh, before adding drily, 'Though my supe is encouraging us to cooperate with Alpharetta on the matter of Tommy Mark Evans's murder.'

'Have you spoken to the lead investigator?' Quincy spoke up.

'Not yet. Been kind of busy, in case you haven't noticed.'

'It would be interesting to know if they recovered any shoe impressions from the crime scene,' Quincy commented.

'Oh, to be so lucky,' she agreed.

'And in the meanwhile?' her father prodded.

Kimberly shrugged, regarding Sal again with his rumpled suit and sallow, sleep-deprived features. If he found this killer, would that allow him to finally forgive himself for standing by helplessly while his father beat his mother? And if she helped him, would that make it easier for her to visit Arlington and place flowers on her mother's and sister's graves?

They were both chasing the impossible. And even knowing it, they couldn't stop.

'We have another lead,' she said.

'What?'

'The gold on Dinchara's boot. According to Harold, it probably came from the Dahlonega area. We could take a little field trip, circulate our composite sketch of Mr. Dinchara. If he's an avid hiker who spends a lot of time in that area, maybe someone will recognize him.'

Sal brightened immediately. 'Let's do it!'

And her father said, without missing a beat, 'Naturally, we'll join you.'

TWENTY-NINE

'Indoors, these spiders are commonly found in houses and associated outbuildings, boiler houses, schools, churches, stores, hotels and other such buildings.'

FROM *Biology of the Brown Recluse Spider* BY JULIA MAXINE HITE,

WILLIAM J. GLADNEY, J. L. LANCASTER, JR., AND W. H. WHITCOMB,

DEPARTMENT OF ENTOMOLOGY, DIVISION OF AGRICULTURE,

UNIVERSITY OF ARKANSAS, FAYETTEVILLE, MAY 1966

Dahlone fell under the jurisdiction of the Lumpkin County Sheriff's Department. Unfortunately, the sheriff was out for a week on a D.A.R.E. training seminar. Instead, Sal managed to line up a four o'clock appointment with Sheriff Boyd Duffy of neighboring Union County.

Harold had to bow out. He already had an afternoon meeting with a couple of bankers helping him trace terrorist money online. His parting advice: 'Visit the U.S. Forestry Service fish hatcheries by Suches. Those guys know *everything.*'

That left Sal, Kimberly, Quincy, and Rainie. With Dahlonega an hour's ride north on the GA 400, they decided to shoot straight up and back. It would mean a late night, but they'd all worked later.

They formed a small caravan: Sal and Kimberly in the lead car, Rainie and Quincy bringing up the rear. Sal's mood hadn't improved since their meeting with the arachnologist. He drove with his swarthy face set in a perpetual scowl, preoccupied with thoughts he apparently didn't feel like sharing.

Kimberly worked her cell phone. She called Mac first, but he didn't answer. She left him a message, hoping she didn't sound as defiant as she felt. She debated touching base with her supe, but decided less was more. No one really cared what she did for one afternoon, as long as she got the paperwork processed and kept her assigned cases moving ahead.

Which she would do. Later tonight. First thing in the morning. Absolutely.

Next, she tried the lead investigator for Alpharetta, Marilyn Watson. Watson picked up, just in time for Kimberly to lose the signal. She tried again, with mixed results.

'No latent prints . . . air . . . ber. Projectile . . . impressions.' Watson reported when Kimberly asked what evidence had been recovered at the Tommy Mark Evans homicide.

'Wait, you got a shoe print?'

'Tire tread . . . sions.'

'You got tire tread impressions? Do you know what kind of vehicle?'

More static. Fuzz. Then dead silence.

Kimberly glanced at her cell phone. Signal strength had dropped. Sure enough, she heard three beeps, then the call was gone.

She scowled while eyeing the digital display, waiting for signal strength. No such luck.

'She said they got tire tread impressions,' Kimberly reported at last. 'Still not sure about shoe print or not, and it sounded like they did recover a projectile. Or maybe not. It was that kind of conversation.'

'What kind of vehicle?'

'Didn't get that far. But assuming they cast the impression, we should be able to examine it ourselves. If I ever get a signal back, I'll see if she can e-mail the digital photos. I have some contacts that should be able to tell us fairly quickly if the tire is feasible for a Toyota FourRunner.'

Sal finally looked at her. His eyes were dark, brooding. They called to her in a way even she understood wasn't healthy.

'You ever do anything other than work?' he asked.

'Never.'

He grunted, eyes returning to the road. 'Me, neither.'

She smiled, but it was sadder than she intended.

She gazed out the window, watching the concrete jungle of greater Atlanta give way to flat brown fields. They came to a light, headed north onto Highway 60 and began to climb. The countryside gave way to startling ravines and towering hillsides, all choked with thick green kudzu vines. They passed luxury condos, a pristine golf course, exotic water features.

Kimberly started to connect some dots. If the past thirty minutes had involved hardscrabble chicken farms and trailer parks, then this section of northern Georgia was about money. Lots of it. Harold had been right – there was gold in them thar hills.

'We're supposed to meet Sheriff Duffy at the Olde Town Grill in the center of Dahlonega,' Sal spoke up.

'You got an address?'

'You've never been to Dahlonega, have you?'

She shook her head.

'Trust me, no address is required.'

She figured out what he meant fifteen minutes later, when they blew by a McDonald's, passed through an intersection, and entered a picture-perfect postcard of nineteenth-century American architecture. Bare broadleaf trees soaring in the middle of a charming public square, dominated by a two-hundred-year-old brick courthouse, now serving as the Dahlonega Gold Museum. Quaint storefronts bore signs declaring general store, gift shop, antiques, homemade fudge. Tourists meandered down quaint red-bricked sidewalks.

'I think we just entered a time warp,' Kimberly said.

'Something like that.' Sal looped around the town square, giving her the nickel tour. The flower beds were decorated with winter greens and interspersed with items such as a stagecoach wheel, or horse drinking trough, or bleached steer's skull. It was like visiting a movie set of the Old West, except she was still in Georgia, the state she knew best for its stifling hot summers and fresh peaches.

'In late September, early October,' Sal was explaining, 'this place is lousy with leaf peepers. Can't get a parking space to save your life. You and your husband should check it out sometime. I mean, if you're into that sort of thing.'

Sal's voice had taken on an edge. It was enough to make her say, 'Absolutely. Romantic getaway, cute bed-and-breakfast, tour of the wineries. Mac would love it.'

Sal didn't speak again, which was just as well.

He found parking in front of a giant wooden stamp wheel that, according to the plaque, had once been used to help extract gold ore. They waited for Rainie and Quincy to park, then followed the tiny arrow to the Olde Town Grill.

Sheriff Boyd Duffy was already there, occupying half of a corner booth. He was a big bear of a man with piercing black eyes and salt-and-pepper hair. Kimberly was guessing former football player, avid hunter. Probably scared the shit out of the local kids. Good for him.

He was also black, which made him a bit of an anomaly for this part of Georgia.

Upon spotting them, he called out in a booming voice, 'Special Agent Martignetti!' He heaved his large body from the booth with surprising agility. 'And Special Agent Quincy, I presume.' He took her hand, shaking it without crushing it, further moving him up in her esteem. 'Please, call me Duff. Like the beer from *The Simpsons* cartoon. Yeah, it's a long story. Welcome, welcome. Northern Georgia's a fair sight prettier than that smoggy ol' city. You're in for a treat.'

More handshakes for Rainie and Quincy, then he gestured to a larger table where they could all have a seat. Another wave of his giant arm, and a blonde with bouffant hair appeared, bearing menus and mason jars of sweetened tea. 'Food here is excellent,' Duff extolled. 'Fried chicken will blow your mind. Then there are the homemade cinnamon rolls and the biscuits and gravy. I recommend one of everything, but then, for a fella like me, that's 'bout what it takes.'

Kimberly couldn't pass up a cinnamon roll. Neither could Rainie. Quincy, predictably, ordered black coffee. Sal, at least, made the sheriff proud by going with the fried chicken. A little more small talk, and they got down to business.

'So now four busy folks like you didn't head all the way up to the Blue Ridge Mountains just to take in our sights. What can I do for you?'

Sal took the lead: 'We're pursuing a person of interest in the disappearance of approximately ten prostitutes. We have reason to believe that the subject, an avid outdoorsman, might be familiar with this area, so we came to take a look.'

Duff raised a brow. He was no dumb bunny. 'In other words, you think he dumped the bodies somewhere in these hills.'

'It's a possibility.'

The big man sighed, folded his hands on the table. 'All right. So who's your person of interest?'

'We don't have a name yet, just a picture.' Sal opened up his dark green binder, took out a copy of the composite sketch prepared by Special Agent Sparks and Ginny Jones, and handed it over to the sheriff. 'I have extras if you need them,' he offered. 'We'd like to get this circulating to as many law enforcement agents as possible.'

'Hold on, hold on. One thing at a time.' The sheriff was fumbling around with his breast pocket. He finally extracted a pair of black-framed reading glasses and perched them on the edge of his nose. He regarded the sketch, grunting softly to himself.

The waitress arrived bearing platters of food. Duff raised his arms, still holding the sketch, and the waitress slid a platter of turkey and gravy in front of him.

'Got any pictures of him without that cap?' the sheriff wanted to know.

Sal shook his head.

Duff regarded the sketch a moment longer, then set it aside, picked up his knife and fork, and cut neatly into his meal.

'Well,' he said brusquely. 'First things first. I don't recognize the fella; then again, you white guys all look alike to me.'

Sal appeared startled. Duff shot him a grin. 'That was a joke, son. When you're peeling a sixteen-year-old you've known all of his life off the pavement after he decided to go Evel Knievel with his new motorcycle, you gotta learn to laugh a little. You big-city boys investigate strangers. I handle my own neighbors, day in and day out. If your *subject*, as you called him, lived around here, I'd probably know him, even with that stupid cap.'

'So he's not local.'

'Probably not full time,' Duff said. 'Then again, we got tens of thousands of tourists each year, not to mention the summer people, the day hikers, the weekend hunters. Mountains are a four-season resort and we got the traffic to prove it. Now, you tell me a few things, and we'll see if we can't whittle this down. Where were these prostitutes last seen alive?'

'Mostly around the greater Atlanta area. Sandy Springs in particular. The club scene, not streetwalkers.'

'So your subject is working the metro-Atlanta area. Why'd you come here?'

'According to one witness, he's an outdoorsman. We

also recovered a hiking boot from the subject's vehicle that contained plant material consistent with the Chattahoochee National Forest—'

'Couple of acres,' Duff interrupted.

'The sole of the boot contained traces of gold. That got us thinking Dahlonega.'

Duff nodded his head, chewing thoughtfully. 'Been to the gold museum yet?'

'No, sir.'

'Should. It was on those front steps that Dr. Stephenson, assayer at the mint, tried to stop all the Georgia miners from bolting to California for the 1849 gold rush by saying, 'Thar's gold in them thar hills,' pointing of course to the Blue Ridge Mountains. See, even back then folks were being encouraged to work and buy local.'

No one had any comment on that, so Duff returned to the matter at hand:

'Well, let's start with your subject. Let's assume for a moment that he is a hiker or hunter or whatnot, and like most of 'em in the state, he spends his weekends up here. Guy like that needs to eat, sleep, buy supplies. Looking at Lumpkin County, biggest town is Dahlonega. And around here, people are gonna eat at the Olde Town Grill, the Smith House, Wylie's Restaurant, couple of other places. For lodging you got the major chains – Days Inn, Econo Lodge, Holiday Inn, Super Eight. Also, the Smith House again, which is right around the corner. It's got good food, reasonably priced rooms, and better yet for your purposes, a gold mine on the premises. You can wave your picture in front of the staff there, see if they can tell you anything.

'For supplies, there's the general store, but that's really for tourists. Most folks go to Wal-Mart. Given the crowds they see, not sure if the cashiers will be able to help you. If this guy is as serious a woodsman as you think, I'd head fifteen miles north of here to Suches, which is my neck of the woods.'

'Suches?' Kimberly interrupted.

'Valley Above the Clouds,' Duff assured her. 'You haven't seen pretty till you've been to Suches. Now, Suches is blink-and-you'll-miss-it tiny. But given its access to the Appalachian Trail, couple of camping grounds, and the lake, it sees some traffic. You're talking hikers, hunters, campers, four-wheelers, fishermen, bikers—'

'Bikers?' Rainie asked. 'You mean like cyclists?'

'Motorcyclists. They cover the road like tar every summer. Now, if your guy is a hiker, chances are he's stayed in Suches. Meaning he's eaten at either T.W.O. or Lenny's, and he's purchased supplies at Dale's. I'd start by taking your sketch to those three places. Face it, town that small, there's no place to hide.'

Sal was taking copious notes. Now he looked up. 'But by your own admission, Dahlonega and Suches are very busy places—'

'Sixty thousand tourists each year.'

Sal nodded grimly. 'Well, see now, that's a problem. Whole point is that this guy has been dumping bodies for over a year without anyone noticing. Given all the hikers, hunters, fishermen, *motorcyclists*, how would such a thing be possible? Forget the gold. There are tourists in them thar hills, and they photograph everything.'

Duff flashed a smile. He finished up his turkey, going to work on the mountain of mashed potatoes, before speaking again. 'If your guy is dumping bodies, it's not off a major hiking trail – you're right, no way someone *wouldn't* have run into him by now.' He held up a hand, starting to count off fingers. 'That rules out Woody Gap, Springer Gap, the AT, the Benton MacKaye Trail, Slaughter Gap Trail—'

'Slaughter Gap Trail?' Rainie spoke up.

'Provides access to Blood Mountain—'

'Blood Mountain?' Rainie looked at Kimberly and Sal. 'Personally, if I were looking for bodies, I'd start with

Slaughter Gap Trail and Blood Mountain. But that's just me.'

Duff grinned again. 'As I was saying, Slaughter Gap Trail and Blood Mountain are pretty popular these days, making them *not* the best choice' – he gave Rainie an apologetic smile – 'for hiding bodies. However, then we have the U.S. Forestry Service roads, many of them hard to find, easy to get lost, and almost always remote, crisscrossing all over the damn place.'

'The fish hatchery!' Kimberly remembered.

Duff nodded approvingly. 'That's right. We got the fish hatchery located off of USFS Sixty-nine. Then there's USFS Forty-two, also known as Cooper Gap Road. But see, by USFS standards those two roads are like superhighways. It's the dozens of other muddy, unmarked, nearly impassible roads that make life interesting. They're used just enough that if a four-wheel-drive vehicle was spotted parked overnight, no one would question it. And yet, the roads and trails are also remote enough, you can go for miles without ever seeing another soul. For your guy, they'd be perfect.'

'How many of these roads are we talking?' Sal asked.

Duff shrugged. 'Hell if I know. I've lived in these mountains my entire life and I doubt even I know all of 'em. What you need is a decent USFS map. And probably a USGS map, as well, because those government types don't always talk.'

'That would be the other option,' Kimberly said immediately. 'The U.S. Forestry Service and Geological Survey teams. You're right, they're the ones traipsing all over these mountains, collecting samples, building databases. I worked with a team out of Virginia once. They spend more time in the backwoods than any hiker out there. If we could get them our composite sketch, plus a description of the suspect's vehicle, they might know something.'

'I got some friends there I can call,' Duff offered. 'They are the eyes and ears of the mountains, so to speak.'

'So,' Sal murmured between pursed lips. 'We can distribute our flyer to some of the local establishments, see if we get any hits. Then strike up a dialogue with the USFS and USGS folks.'

'You know, between Sheriff Wyatt and myself, we got quite a crew. Most of our deputies would be happy to assist with something other than the normal naughty tourist or punch-drunk high schooler. Wyatt'll be back by the end of the week. I'll debrief him, then we'll both take a crack at it.'

'I don't want the subject spooked,' Sal stated. 'Priority at this point is to find the girls and/or their remains. Then we go after Dinchara.'

'Dinachara?' Duff frowned. 'Thought you said you didn't have a name.'

'It's an alias. An anagram for arachnid.'

'Say what?'

'You know, arachnid, as in spiders.'

'I know arachnid, son. I'm just not sure what a grown man is doing naming himself after a bug.'

'Catching prey,' Kimberly said quietly. 'Except for one. Sal, tell him about Ginny Jones.'

It was after six by the time they left Duff. Most of the stores were closed, but they managed to find Wylie's Restaurant and show off the sketch. No one recognized the drawing, but the manager promised to keep her eye out. Sal handed her his card, then they were on their way.

Next up was the Smith House, once a grand private residence, now a recently renovated hotel, country store, and restaurant. The lobby smelled like buttermilk biscuits and candied yams. That was enough for Kimberly.

'Dinnertime!' she declared.

Rainie and Quincy were game. Sal, who'd already dined on fried chicken, merely shrugged. 'I can always eat.'

Food was served family style. They paid a flat fee to the girl working the cash register in the lobby. She gave them tickets to take downstairs to the dining hall, where they would be served all the fried chicken, baked ham, roast beef, dumplings, okra, steamed vegetables, and homemade rolls they could stand. No alcohol, but unlimited iced tea and lemonade.

At the bottom of the stairs, they discovered the entranceway to a twenty-foot mining shaft. All Kimberly could see was a deep black hole, barricaded with Plexiglas. Didn't seem that exciting, but Quincy and Rainie lingered long enough to watch the video documenting its discovery.

A red-cheeked waitress found Kimberly and Sal two seats next to a family of six. They met Grandma and Grandpa, Mom and Dad, and four-year-old twin boys. The twins ran laps around the table, while the very tired mother shot Kimberly a wan smile and said, 'Hope you don't mind.'

'Not a problem,' Kimberly assured, and then patted her own stomach.

The woman's eyes widened. 'Oh, is it your first?'

'Yep.'

'You and your husband must be very excited.' She shot Sal a smile.

He froze with his hand on the bowl of peas. 'What?'

'I'm very happy,' Kimberly told the woman. 'At least at the moment.'

The woman laughed. 'Yes, ma'am, that's the way it is. Is it a girl or boy? Do you know?'

'No, we want to be surprised.'

'So did we,' the woman said. 'And boy, were we. If I could offer one bit of advice?'

'Yes?'

'Don't have twins.'

Rainie and Quincy arrived and made their introductions. Rainie dug into the fried okra with gusto.

Quincy picked his way delicately through the steamed vegetables and baked ham.

The smell of meat didn't bother Kimberly as much as it had yesterday. Another phase ending? A new phase beginning? Life, even prenatal life, didn't stand still. She nibbled on some ham, okra, catfish. She started to feel that warm, contented glow that came from a good meal, a productive day, the companionship of family and friends.

She'd forgotten about the sketch until the waitress returned with refills of iced tea.

'Oh, is he a friend of yours as well?' the waitress asked, gesturing at Kimberly's open bag.

'Who?'

'The man in that picture. We used to see him in here all the time. With his boy, of course. Those teenagers, my Lord, they can eat.'

Sal stopped chewing. He held a drumstick suspended between his greasy hands, staring at the sketch, the woman, the sketch again.

Kimberly recovered first. 'You know him?'

'I recognize him. In the fall he came in quite often. About yay-high, right? Not real big, but strong looking. Has some muscle to him. And always wearing that cap, even when at the table.' The waitress shook her head. 'I tell you, in my day, my grandmother would've tanned my hide for less.'

'His name?'

'Oh um . . .' She bit her lower lip, cradling the pitcher of iced tea on her hip, thinking. 'Bobby? Bob? Rob? Ron? Richard? You know, I can't remember now. I'm not sure he said.'

'What about the boy?' Kimberly pressed.

'Skinny white thing. Sixteen, seventeen years old. All arms and legs, but no meat on his bones. You know how teenage boys look – like they've never been fed. He's a quiet one. Sat, ate, barely said a word.'

'And the boy's name?'

Again the waitress shook her head. 'You know, some folks come here because they're feeling social, they like to introduce themselves and strike up a friendly conversation. Others . . . hey, they just come for the okra. Who are we to judge?'

'Do you remember how the man paid?' Rainie spoke up, following the conversation intently.

'Sorry, ma'am, that would've been taken care of upstairs.'

'But if he paid with a credit card . . .' Kimberly murmured, following Rainie's train of thought.

'We need to speak to the manager,' Sal announced.

The other family was aflutter now. 'Is everything all right? Who is this fellow? Anything we should know?'

All eyes were on Sal. Even the twins had stopped running. 'Routine investigation,' he assured them brusquely, then he had his arm on Kimberly's shoulder, pulling her up.

She didn't need any encouragement. They made a beeline for the manager's office.

Turned out going through all the credit card receipts would take some time. They needed to provide more specifics. Date, time, amount? The waitress was summoned to see if she could recall an exact date. She thought the man and his son had come in half a dozen times between September and November. With a bit of prodding, she narrowed one of the visits to sometime over the Columbus Day weekend. The amount would be for two people, late in the evening, the waitress believed. She had been surprised the boy was allowed out at that hour.

Credit card receipts were not computerized. Instead, the manager pulled open a file drawer, organized by month. Turned out the Smith House was a popular choice for lodging and meals. Particularly Columbus Day weekend.

Kimberly returned to the dining hall to find her father and Rainie and deliver the happy news.

'Manager needs some time to sort the records, so guess what, folks? We're spending the night!'

THIRTY

Burgerman made his move.

I woke up last night to the sound of muffled screams. It went on all night. Burgerman always rode his new toys long and hard, until they broke. Just like me.

In the morning, I knew the drill. Got up, went into the kitchen, ate breakfast. Pretended it was the most natural thing in the world to see a naked seven-year-old boy sitting at the beat-up table, stupefied, in front of an overflowing bowl of cereal. Boy didn't say anything. Just stared at his Froot Loops as they slowly turned dark red, green, and blue.

I didn't make eye contact. Didn't want the boy to think I had anything to do with anything.

Burgerman was still in the bedroom. Probably recovering from the night's exertions. I noticed the phone had disappeared and the door had gained a new bolt lock up high, beyond the new toy's reach. My pulse quickened slightly. I wondered if the Burgerman remembered the phone in my room. I wondered if he had snuck in in the middle of the night and stolen it.

I did my best to nonchalantly stroll back to my bedroom. Phone was still there. I decided not to take any chances, and I removed it myself, hiding it up in my closet.

Like hell I was losing privileges just because Burgerman couldn't control his appetites.

Back in the kitchen, I poured another bowl of cereal and sat munching in the silence. My presence must have galvanized the boy, because he slowly picked up his spoon and slurped up some soggy cereal. I wondered if he would keep it down. Some did. Some didn't.

He'd be gone in a day or two, once the Burgerman had had his fill. Did he kill them, turn 'em loose? I didn't know. I didn't care. I couldn't remember anymore what year I had been born, my exact birth date. But I must have been a teenager, because the only emotion I could muster anymore was contempt. For Burgerman, the kid, myself.

And then, for no good reason, I thought of the very first boy. All those years ago. The one I'd thought I could help. I wondered if they ever found his body, or if he remained, rotting alone under the azalea bush.

The thought made me angry. I grabbed my cereal bowl, slammed it into the sink. The sound made the new toy flinch.

Burgerman walked into the room.

He'd put on pants, but not a shirt. The years hadn't been kind to him. His beard held more gray than black, his frame had grown slack from too much beer and greasy food, the skin hanging from his thin chest and scrawny arms. He looked exactly like he was, an aging, white-trash son of a bitch, one foot in the grave and still mean as a rattlesnake.

I hated him all over again.

He looked at me. Then put a hand on the new boy's shoulder. At the first contact, the boy flinched, then froze, sitting motionless while tears welled up in his eyes.

Suddenly, the Burgerman beamed at me. 'Son,' he announced triumphantly. 'Meet Boy. He's your new replacement.'

And I knew, in that moment, that the Burgerman must die.

I *waited until the Burgerman retired to his bedroom, dragging Boy behind him. Then I disappeared into my own room, stocked such as it was with a dumpy twin mattress, milk crate clothing bins, and a tiny black-and-white TV I'd salvaged from the neighbor's trash and repaired myself.*

My room stank. The sheets, bedding, dirty clothes. Everything held the rank, sweaty odor of unwashed skin, too-long nights. The whole dingy apartment smelled this way. Milk soured in the fridge. Dirty dishes overflowed the sink. Cockroaches scuttled across the stove.

It pissed me off all over again. The rancid stench of my own life. The endless, gray nothingness that marked my existence. Because the Burgerman had chosen me and after that I'd never had a chance.

Now there wouldn't even be graduation. Oh no, the Burgerman had a new plaything now. A toy he planned on keeping. Meaning my days were numbered.

And for no good reason, the sting of Burgerman's rejection hurt me more than his affection ever had.

I was stupid. I was weak. I was nothing.

The Burgerman had killed me. I just didn't know how to die.

The screaming again. The poor stupid boy shrieking as if that would make a difference.

I crawled into the middle of the bed, pulling the blankets over my head and covering my ears with my hands. I went to sleep.

When I woke up later, it was dark. I lay on my mattress for a long time, watching the way the streetlight filtered through my blinds, creating slashes of light against the far wall.

Then I got up, went to the closet, and fetched the telephone.

Back to my mattress, I lifted the corner and retrieved a

*phone book I'd smuggled inside the apartment when the
Burgerman wasn't looking.*

*When I finally found the number, my hands were
shaking and my mouth had gone dry.*

*I didn't let myself pause, didn't let myself think
too much.*

Plug in the phone. Dial the digits.

*At the first pickup, 'Help me,' I whispered, 'Please help
me.'*

Then I hung up the phone and cried.

THIRTY-ONE

'Spiders are experts in the art of poisoning. A spider releases venom through fangs that look like curved claws beneath its eyes.'

FROM *Freaky Facts About Spiders*,

BY CHRISTINE MORLEY, 2007

'What happened to your parents?' the boy asked. He sat on the front porch with her, drinking a glass of powdered lemonade. He'd been working most of the morning, since he'd appeared shortly after six a.m. She'd let him in without comment, feeding him breakfast, making light conversation.

He didn't bring up their last encounter and neither did she. She'd done the same thing with Mel when the older man had rung her doorbell yesterday afternoon, bearing a box filled with freshground sausage, eggs, and orange juice. He'd handed it over without a word. She had accepted it with a single nod of acknowledgment. Then he'd gone his way and she'd gone hers.

Sometimes, things were easier that way.

She noticed the boy moved stiffly as he'd helped her roll up rugs and drag them outside for a good beating. His ribs seemed to bother him, and from time to time, she caught him rubbing his backside. She didn't ask, he didn't tell. They had a theme to their gray, chilly day. And now this.

'My parents died,' Rita said presently. 'Long time ago.'

'How'd they die?'

She shrugged. 'Old age. Everyone dies in the end.'

'You're old,' the boy said.

She cackled. 'Think I'm gonna keel over, child? Leave you without a breakfast companion? Don't worry. World's not done with me yet.'

The boy was regarding her seriously, however.

'I had parents,' he said abruptly.

She stopped laughing, smoothing out Joseph's old green plaid flannel shirt, the hem of which fell nearly to her knees. 'I see.'

'They died, too.'

'I'm sorry to hear that.'

'I don't know how,' he continued relentlessly, his voice growing thicker. 'I had them, then one day they were gone. Just like that. My sister, too. She was little. Always gettin' into my stuff, wantin' to play with me. I'd be mean to her. Tell her we were playing hide-and-seek, but once she hid, I wouldn't look for her. I'd go play all by myself. Then she'd cry and I'd call her a baby and my mom'd get mad at me.'

'I had an older brother like that myself.'

'He was naughty? Then the family sent him away to live with the other naughty boys?'

'We all loved him.' She said it matter-of-factly. 'Then he went off and got himself killed in the war. Brothers and sisters fight, child. But they still love.'

'I once gave my little sister a teddy bear I got for my birthday,' the boy whispered. 'I knew it would make her happy.'

'Did it?'

'I think so. Sometimes . . . sometimes, it's hard to remember. I try to picture them, but it gets jumbled in my mind. Like my favorite flavor of ice cream. I think it's chocolate, but it's been so long . . . Maybe it's vanilla. Or strawberry. Can someone take your favorite flavor from you? I get confused. . . .'

'What happened to your sister, child?'

He shrugged. 'She's dead, I guess. They're all dead. That's what he says.'

They were on treacherous ground now. Rita could feel it, even if she didn't understand it. When she'd first met the boy, she'd assumed he came from an 'unfortunate' home situation. Those were the words the social workers always used in her day. *This child comes from an unfortunate home situation.*

Lately, however, Rita had begun to wonder. She tried to pick her next words with care.

'When your parents were alive, child, did you live around here?'

He frowned at her. 'Where is here?'

'Dahlonega. The Blue Ridge Mountains of Georgia. Is this where you were born?'

He was quiet for so long, she wasn't sure he was going to answer. But then, slowly, he shook his head. 'Macon. Macon Bacon, that's what my father always said, when we were driving up the highway. 'Macon Bacon, Georgia, where it's all about the chickens!' And he'd laugh. He liked bacon, too. And scrambled eggs in the morning. Do you think that's what killed him? Eating eggs and bacon?'

The boy's eyes were guileless. The expression made him appear smaller, more vulnerable. Rita wondered again if she was doing the right thing. Then she spotted her brother Joseph, racing along the front yard, leaping up to snag the lowest branch of the old oak tree, swinging himself up just as he used to do when they were kids.

Joseph spent the afterlife forever young. She wondered if that was because he died young, or if it was a choice each spirit was allowed to make. She was tired, she thought. Tired of the ache in her joints, the way the chill of a winter morning bit so deep into her wrinkled flesh. Not much time left, she figured. All the more reason to spend it wisely.

'When your parents died,' she asked, 'did you have any other family?'

The boy studied her curiously, seeming almost perplexed.

'Did a social worker visit you?' Rita forged ahead. 'Explain to you about foster parents and your new home?'

'What are foster parents?' the boy asked.

Rita stilled in the rocker, then forced herself to move again. Her mind was racing. If the boy wasn't living with his parents, other relatives, or foster parents . . . She wished that she got out more, knew her neighbors. She'd dearly like to ask someone what they knew about the house on the hill, the man who lived there, when they had first started noticing the boy. Because they were beyond an unfortunate home situation now, she was certain of it. She was journeying instead into something darker, more sinister.

'Who lives with you, child?' she asked quietly.

The boy shook his head.

'It's okay to tell me. I'm an old lady, you know. We're the best at keeping secrets.'

The boy wouldn't look at her. His gaze fell to the floor. 'I don't think I should be talking anymore,' he whispered.

'Tell me your name, child.'

The boy shook his head.

'How about your birthday?'

'I don't have one. There's only homecoming day, the day you belong to him.'

'Are there others?' she insisted. 'Children, adults, pets? Tell me about them. I won't judge.'

The boy studied his empty lemonade glass, then the shape of the porch banisters. Rita rocked back and forth in her chair, watching the dark clouds pile up on the horizon, feeling the electric pulse of the impending storm. She wanted to push harder, but she didn't. Children talked when they felt like talking. You had to have the patience to let them come to you.

'He's going to kill you,' the boy said.

She waved her hand. 'Nonsense. I'll die when I'm good and ready to, and not a minute sooner.'

'You don't know what he's like. He gets what he wants. He *always* gets what he wants.'

The first gust of wind hit, laced with rain, tasting like distant pines. Rita heard the boom of thunder, followed shortly by the crack of lightning. The storm would be a good one. The kind to rattle a house down to its very foundation.

The boy stood. 'I gotta go—'

'Nonsense. You'll stay the night.'

'The rain is coming,' the boy insisted. 'I gotta get back.'

'You'll stay the night.'

'Rita—'

'*Sit down!*'

The boy paled at her firm tone. He sank down into his chair, wary now, skittish.

'If you will not talk to me,' Rita said curtly, rocking furiously in her little wooden chair, 'that is your business. But you'll not be returning to the house on the hill. I couldn't in good conscience send you back, and that is my business.'

'He'll be angry. You don't want him angry.'

'Pish posh. At my age, what's some man gonna do that isn't already about to happen? If he gets angry, he can visit me himself. Because I have a few things to say!'

She finished brashly, rising out of her rocker, stomping her foot. Neither she nor the boy were fooled, however. Rita didn't know the man, but she already understood: If Scott's 'guardian' appeared on her front porch, it wouldn't be to talk.

'Rita—'

'Shall I call the police, child?'

'*No!*'

The boy spoke instantly, in wild-eyed panic. Enough to let her know that the moment she picked up the phone, the child would bolt.

'Then it's settled,' she declared. 'You'll stay. We'll make

stew. Have hot cups of cocoa. We'll hunker down inside and watch the world go to holy hell. It's the best way to spend a stormy night.'

The boy looked at her, his eyes wide, filled with something she hadn't seen before. Fear, hope, longing. He opened his mouth. She thought he'd argue. Or maybe, leap from the porch and dash up the hill.

But then he closed his mouth. He squared his shoulders. Not happy, she noticed, not relieved, but a soldier resigned to war.

Rita guided the boy inside, shutting the old door behind them. He headed for the kitchen, while she paused in the foyer to work the locks. First fat drops of rain hit her driveway. She fastened the newly installed chain lock, pretending she didn't notice the darkness gathering outside her window or the lights glowing in the old Victorian up the hill.

THIRTY-TWO

'During daylight hours, brown recluse spiders typically retreat to dark, secluded areas.'

FROM *Brown Recluse Spider*, BY MICHAEL F. POTTER,
URBAN ENTOMOLOGIST, UNIVERSITY OF
KENTUCKY COLLEGE OF AGRICULTURE

Kimberly woke up to a string of bad news. The manager at the Smith House had come up with forty-five possible credit card receipts. A lightning storm was forecast by mid-afternoon. Her supervisor wanted to know why she hadn't attended yesterday afternoon's meeting for Violent Crimes.

And Mac hadn't returned her call.

She took them in stride as best she could. All receipts would be photocopied for her and Sal to divide and conquer upon their return. Given the approaching storm, they would leave for Suches immediately. She put in a message with her supervisor that she was following up on a major lead.

And she put Mac out of her mind. At least, the best she could.

They all climbed into Sal's car and headed for Suches.

Highway 60 took its own sweet time. It looped through an endless series of S-curves, climbing higher and higher. They passed a gold mine, a bunch of boiled-peanut stands, various log cabins for rent. To the right, the Blue Ridge Mountains soared up as a dense wall of green underbrush and gray boulders. To the left, a deceptively thin wall of towering trees gave way to sudden views of a plunging valley that spread beyond the line of sight.

The first heavy drops of rain splattered the windshield just as they burst from a dark tunnel of trees into a gently unfolding valley. The land went from thick underbrush to painstakingly cleared fields, framed with white painted fences and dotted with red farmhouses. If Dahlonega was tucked up in the mountains, then Suches was a remote northern outpost. Handful of farms. Requisite double-wides. Too many boarded-up buildings.

Kimberly tried not to blink so she wouldn't miss it.

Too late.

'That says T.W.O.,' Rainie just got out, finger pointing, as Sal blew by on Highway 60.

'Wait, there's Dale's,' Kimberly echoed as Sal swung his head left and totally missed the convenience store on the right.

He scowled, tapped his brakes, fishtailed on the rain-slicked road, and finally did the sensible thing and slowed down. They came to a stone schoolhouse – *Smallest public school in Georgia!* Kimberly read on the sign – and Sal turned around.

They hit Dale's first, pulling up outside the gas pumps, then making a dash for the glass doors through the pelting rain.

Inside, Kimberly registered three things at once: a blast of warmth, the smell of homemade chili, and an entire display of bright orange hunting gear. Dale's, apparently, did carry a little of everything.

'Is that chili I smell?' Sal was already inquiring at the counter. 'Well, as long as we're here . . .'

The back part of Dale's included a couple of tables. They had a seat and an older gentleman wandered over to assist. Not Dale, they learned, but Ron. Dale was out.

He didn't explain, and judging by the reserved look on his face, Kimberly guessed Ron had already pegged them as outsiders and not in the need to know. He took their order, brought their food, then returned to meticulously wiping down tables.

Sal waited until halfway through his chili to get into it. Ron was cleaning the table beside them when Sal brought out the sketch and said, in the nonchalant voice favored by detectives and TV actors, 'Say, do you happen to know this fellow here?'

Ron wasn't fooled. He looked from the sketch to Sal and back to the sketch. Then he shrugged and returned to spritzing tables.

'He's a person of interest,' Sal said with more emphasis.

Ron paused, thought about it, went back to wiping.

'You might have seen him with a teenage boy,' Kimberly spoke up. 'Maybe they live around here.'

'Boys,' Ron corrected. 'I've seen him with two boys. One older. One younger. They're not much for talking.'

Sal set down his spoon. 'Do you know their names?'

'No, sir.'

'Are they local?'

'Nah, not locals. But they come up a fair amount, 'specially last fall. Must've seen 'em half a dozen times. The man mostly. The boys waited in the truck. Except one time – the younger one had to use the john, so the older one brought him in. Looked like trouble to me, those three, but they just did their business and cleared on out. Who am I to judge?'

They'd all stopped eating and stared at Ron, who was still tending to his duties.

'Can you describe the older boy?' Kimberly pressed.

Ron shrugged. 'Dunno. Teenage boy, seventeen, eighteen years old. White. Maybe five ten or so. Scrawny thing. Wore Army cargo pants about two sizes too big, the way boys do nowadays. Kept his hands in his pockets, walking all slouched over. Like I said, didn't talk much. Just came in, delivered the younger boy, waited, then left.'

'And the younger boy?'

Another shrug. 'Eight or nine. Shorter brown hair. He was bundled up with a heavy sweatshirt and orange hunting vest. On the small side would be my guess, but hard to tell with all those clothes on. The man had on a nice pair of hiking boots, but the kids were just wearing tennis shoes. I remember thinking at the time it'd be a miracle if they didn't twist an ankle. But you know, good boots are expensive and with kids growing so fast ... Dunno. Up here, some kids come walking in wearing more than I make in a week's pay, all geared up for their annual hiking weekend. Takes all kinds, I guess.'

'What did the man say when he came in?' Sal spoke up urgently. 'Did he buy anything?'

Ron stopped wiping long enough to search his memory. 'Bottle of water. Candy bar. Oh, and some crickets. We have 'em for the fishermen and that got him all excited, so he bought a container. Don't think he was fishing, though, he was dressed all wrong.'

'He ask about any particular hiking trails, mention where he'd been, anything like that?'

Ron shrugged again. 'Not that I remember.'

'Did anyone else see him and the boys?'

'Oh, all sorts. Fall's busy around here. Not like at the moment.' Now he sounded almost apologetic.

'How did he pay?' Rainie asked.

Ron pursed his lips. 'I'd guess cash, only 'cause it wasn't that big a purchase.'

'Did you happen to notice his vehicle?' Kimberly's turn.

'No, ma'am. Little too busy in the fall for car shopping.'

'Did the man interact with the boys?' Quincy asked. 'Say anything to them when they entered the store?'

'Mmmmm, not much. The boys came in.' Ron paused, seemed to be picking his way through his memory. 'The older one looked at the man, said, 'The kid's gotta pee, whatta you want me to do about it?' then led the kid to the john. Man didn't say anything, just looked annoyed. He'd probably told the boys to stay in the car. You know how kids are.'

'He didn't use a name?' Quincy pressed. 'The older boy called the younger boy 'kid'?'

'Yes, sir, that's how I remember it.'

'Seems to imply they aren't brothers,' Quincy murmured. 'The teenager's distancing himself from the younger one. Objectifying him. Interesting.'

'Do you remember which direction they were coming from when they turned in here?' Rainie asked. 'From the north or south?'

'No, ma'am.'

'And was it a particular time of day? You saw them in the morning, afternoon . . . ?'

'Afternoon, ma'am, but only because that's my shift.'

Rainie nodded, pursed her lips. They all three looked at Sal again.

'Anyone else you can think of who might be able to shed more light on this man and the two boys?' Sal pressed. 'It's important that we learn his name. He's wanted for questioning regarding a very serious matter.'

Ron, however, shook his head.

'Like I said, they're not local. We just saw 'em a lot in the fall. Maybe as late as early December. Can't really remember now, to tell you the truth. You might want to try out T.W.O. Even the tourists gotta eat and since he never bought much here . . .'

'Okay, we'll do that.' Sal fished out a card, handed it over. 'If you think of anything, or see him or the boys again, give me a call. And I'd appreciate it if you didn't broadcast this conversation too widely. We want to find the man, not spook him.'

Ron had finally registered the state police shield on Sal's card. His eyes widened a notch. He stuck the card in his front pocket, using two fingers to pat it into place.

'Is it drugs, sir? Used to be all you could get in these mountains was moonshine. Now everything's meth, meth, meth. Ruining our county it is.'

'He's trouble,' Sal said simply. 'If you see him again, don't say a word to him. Just get me on the phone and we'll take care of the rest.'

They finished their lunch. Kimberly found a six-pack of pudding. Rainie armed herself with a Snickers. Quincy topped off his coffee. They hit the road.

The manager at T.W.O. didn't recognize the drawing, or remember a man in a baseball cap with two boys. Two Wheels Only specialized in the biker set, which was not to say they didn't have some other business, but it was smaller. He'd keep his eyes open.

The rain was coming down in sheets now. They splashed their way through the muddy parking lot before piling into Sal's car. With the bustling metropolis of Suches exhausted, they had no choice but to turn back toward Dahlonega.

They drove in silence, windshield wipers on high, car buffeted by the wind.

Kimberly kept her eyes on the woods. At the towering trees, the nearly impenetrable underbrush. She wondered where Ginny Jones was right now, if the girl had holed up someplace safe and warm, where she could feel the new life growing inside her. Or if even now she was racing panicked down a back alley, danger looming behind her.

'Wait!' Kimberly cried.

Sal hit the brakes too hard. The car careened dangerously close to the center line.

'What the hell—' Sal started.

'Back up, back up. That was a logging road. Let's take it.'

Sal had the car at a complete stop now. He looked at her as if she were nuts. 'In case you haven't noticed, it's pouring out.'

'I know, I know. Just a quick detour. What else do we have going on?'

'Something better than getting stuck in the mud.'

'He drove these roads, Sal. If he drove these roads, we can damn well give them a try. Come on, we won't go too far.'

'We're in Suches,' Sal muttered. 'Apparently, that's far enough.'

He gave her another look, but when Rainie or Quincy didn't raise any protest, he put the car in gear, backed up along the empty ribbon of road, and hung a sharp right.

The Forestry Service road started out paved, which surprised Kimberly. She had been expecting something more rustic. She was also caught off guard by the number of residential homes, perched on various hillsides, peering out from thick groves of mountain laurel. But a mile down, the pavement turned to gravel and the forest seemed to win the war against civilization. They looped around, slowly descending into a gully, the rain creating a thick, muddy stream that raced alongside them.

They came to a turnabout. Kimberly had Sal stop. And then, before he could react, she'd popped open her door and stepped into the deluge. She was vaguely aware of him protesting. Of other car doors opening. Of Rainie and Quincy joining her in the madness.

She didn't look at them. Didn't say a word. She didn't need to. They lived in the same world she did, where monsters were real, and good people got hurt, and you could spend your days feeling overwhelmed, or you could do your best to do something about it. It seemed for as long as she could remember, she and her father had hunted the specter of death. It was probably some of the only moments either one of them truly felt alive.

And then she thought, vague again, in the back of her mind where it couldn't hurt her as much, that Mac should be here. It had always been her, Mac, Rainie, and Quincy. She missed Mac.

'He's wrong,' she whispered softly, looking around at

the soaring bare-branched trees above, the dense grove of green underbrush below.

'Who?' Sal demanded. He stood in front of her, rain pouring down his nose, plastering his dark hair to his face. He looked intent, angry in a way that should have scared her, except she understood that kind of rage, how it felt when you were trying so hard, only to realize that your best wouldn't get the job done.

'Ron. Dinchara and the boys are local. They have to be. Ron said it himself: They don't buy much, so they must already be well supplied.'

'Kimberly, it's wet, it's cold, I'm soaked to the goddamn bone. Whatever voodoo you're pretending to do, stop yanking my chain.'

'It's a matter of logistics,' she stated firmly, studying the thin vein of gravel road, the tall, skeletal trees, the thick clumps of underbrush that surrounded them. The rain had molded her hair to her skull, was rapidly soaking her shirt. She didn't care. The rain didn't matter. The mud didn't matter. It was all about the woods.

'Killing someone is easy,' she supplied. 'Disposing of the body, however, is hard. Ninety-five percent of the time, that's where killers mess up. Now, we're chasing a guy who has done this not once, but possibly a dozen times. What does that mean? He's very good at logistics.'

She had made it to the edge of the woods, where ferns grew high enough to brush her leg mid thigh. She ticked off on her finger: 'One, where to dispose of the bodies?'

'The woods,' Sal filled in, less angry now, more curious.

'Okay, so two, how to transport the bodies?'

'His truck, SUV. Plenty of room in the back.'

'Until you get here,' Kimberly countered, gesturing to the green and brown mudbath around them. 'Then what?'

Sal nodded, seeming to get into the spirit of things, even as his gray suit turned black and the rain ran in rivulets down his neck. 'It's late at night, or an early hour of the morning – a time where he can reduce the risk of being seen. He needs a remote area, so he picks a Forestry Service road, drives for a ways. Then he pulls over, gets the body out of the back of his vehicle . . . dumps it down a ravine?'

'Forestry Service ranger would spot it,' Quincy spoke up immediately. He stood off to the side, where he could hear everything while still having the space to formulate his own thoughts. He was good at this game; one of the best. 'From the road, you would see trampled bushes, even broken branches. A ranger would get curious about deer, bear, bobcat, whatever, and investigate. One or two times, maybe the UNSUB could get away with it. But a dozen times later . . . Someone would spot the disturbance and find the body. Especially given the amount of traffic on the roads and in the woods during peak seasons.'

'So he carries it away from the road,' Sal stated.

'Body's heavy,' Kimberly supplied. 'A grown woman is a good hundred-plus pounds of deadweight. Even in a fireman's hold, that's tough.'

'He walks downhill?' Sal guessed.

Again Quincy shook his head. 'Anything disposed of below can be seen from above, especially in the winter when the leaves are off the trees. This is a popular destination for hunting, hiking, camping, fishing. That's lots of people trampling through these woods, even in supposedly remote locations. Safest choice is high ground. Above the trails, where others don't tread.'

Sal looked at the three of them. 'I don't get it.'

'He has help,' Kimberly said softly. 'The older boy would be my guess. Whether he's involved in the killing or not, I'm not sure. We didn't hear anyone else on the tape. But at the very least, the teenager helps dispose of the bodies. One man walking alone on the trails late at night is suspicious. A father and son on the other hand . . .'

'They're out camping,' Sal filled in.

'Explains the large pack they're carrying, or perhaps pulling on a trundle behind them.'

'Shit,' Sal said tiredly and put his hand over his eyes.

'It would take them hours,' Rainie spoke up, peering into the woods with a keen look on her face. 'They'd need tools – rope, burlap, shovel, pick. Then food, water, first-aid kit, compass, the basics. Kimberly's right; to do what they need to do, Dinchara's well stocked. Meaning if he's not buying locally, he has a place all set up.'

'The younger boy,' Kimberly murmured.

'Exactly,' Rainie said, following her train of thought. 'The waitress at the Smith House hadn't seen him, which implies he's left behind. Maybe he's too young yet, would slow them down. So they leave the younger boy someplace, then Dinchara and the older boy head off to complete their nightly chores.'

'He's gotta have a home nearby. It's the only thing that makes sense. Maybe the girls are even alive when they're brought up here. Imagine one of those little cabins we drove by, all alone in the woods. Even if a girl screamed all night, or happened to get away, who would hear her, where would she go? A cabin solves so many problems.'

'We can check tax records,' Sal spoke up. 'Anyone who purchased homes around Dahlonega or Suches in the past five years. Cross-reference those names with the receipts from the Smith House for Columbus Day weekend.'

'And chase employment,' Quincy prodded. 'If they're up here enough, Dinchara's going to need money. At least in my day, fifty percent of a single prostitute's earnings wasn't that much. So he either has a string of girls you haven't learned about yet, or another source of income. Given what we know about him, he would make an excellent wilderness guide or—'

They all got it at the same time, 'Forestry Service employee!'

'Would give him all the knowledge and access he needs

of the back roads of the Blue Ridge Mountains. Even a built-in excuse if he ever did get caught. Not to mention he'd know when others were due to conduct surveys in areas where he'd disposed of bodies, allowing him to either move the corpse or perhaps redirect the survey.'

'Ah crap, I am never going hiking again,' Sal said tiredly.

'We should visit the fish hatchery tomorrow,' Kimberly said.

'Yeah, got that.'

'Get some property records from the town, find out who we can meet from the Chattahoochee National Forest.'

'Yep, yep, yep.'

Rainie was still walking around the muddy turnoff point. 'You know what I find surprising?' she asked now.

They all turned toward her.

'It's February. The leaves are off the trees and you still can't see more than three feet ahead. I mean, look at these mountain laurels—they're the size of small homes. Then there's the grasses, the downed logs, the copses of white pine. In any other woods, you'd be able to peer through the trees for twenty, thirty yards. But not here. Hell, I grew up in the woods and even I'm creeped out.'

'On that note,' Sal muttered, yanking at his rain-soaked collar, 'can we please get back in the car?'

'Okay,' Kimberly agreed, 'but next stop is Wal-Mart. In case you haven't noticed, we're all soaked to the bone. What are we supposed to wear tomorrow to the fish hatchery?'

'We're spending another night?' Sal grumbled.

'You got anyplace better to be?'

They went to Wal-Mart.

THIRTY-THREE

*'To compensate for their weaknesses, spiders have evolved an
array of weapons, tactics, and freakish mutations that bring
to mind a tiny band of supervillains.'*

FROM 'SPIDER WOMAN,'

BY BURKHARD BILGER,

New Yorker, MARCH 5, 2007

Mac called her shortly after dinner. Kimberly had just
returned to her room at the Smith House, thinking for once
that elastic waistbands were the best invention of the
modern world. She had devoured nearly an entire fried
chicken, a pound of okra, and two servings of cheesecake
and yet her pants felt expansive, even roomy, as Baby
McCormack engaged in her nightly game of kick
Mommy's spleen.

Rainie and Quincy had already retired for the night, but
Kimberly was keyed up, agitated in the way that came right
before a case blew open and she could finally see the
answer that had been waiting for her all along. Her hotel
room was good-sized, tucked under the eaves of the old
building to form a long L, perfect for restless pacing. She
went from the king-size bed to the desk to the bed and back
again, her hands rubbing the sides of her swollen belly, her
thoughts churning over and over. If Sandy Springs was
Dinchara's hunting grounds, then Dahlonega was his lair.
Any day now, they would search the right records,
interview the right person, and the last piece of the puzzle
would click into place. They would find Ginny Jones, the
missing girls, Dinchara himself. They would—

Cell phone rang, displaying Mac's number. Immediately,

she stopped pacing, her stomach cramping nervously. That pissed her off enough to swipe up the phone and declare loudly, 'Kimberly.'

Static, three clicks, an echoey buzz. 'It's . . . me.'

'Hi, honey,' she said with more force than was necessary.

'Where . . . are you?'

'Dahlonega still. Have a few last visits to make first thing in the morning.'

'. . . weather?'

'Raining cats and dogs. You?'

'. . . gotta go out . . . special assignment . . . back . . . tomorrow morning.'

'What's that? Reception sucks. Can you try a different spot?'

She thought she heard crunching feet. More sounds in the background, like men shouting orders. Then she put it together. The late hours, his special assignment. Mac and the narcotics squad were about to deploy, most likely to raid a suspected drug house or meth lab. And he was calling now because that's what spouses did right before donning their flak vests and heading out. They made that last call home, buttoning up their personal life. Just in case.

The baby fluttered against the palm of her hand, and Kimberly sat down on the edge of the bed.

'Where?' she whispered.

'Can't . . . talk. Later . . . in the morning.'

'Is SWAT coming?'

'Full . . . deployment.'

'Mac . . .' She should say something. Anything. But for the life of her, she couldn't figure out what. And all at once, she was aware of the distance that still loomed between them. The unanswered questions, the unbroken silences.

She wished she were home. It didn't seem right to do this over the phone. They should be in their house, where she could hold him tight enough that he could feel the baby kick. Where he could whisper in her ear that he loved her and she could feel the tickle of his breath upon her skin as she spread her fingers over the beating of his heart. Life can change in an instant. A loved one could walk out the door and never come home again. She knew these things. She visited the tombstones twice a year to make sure she never forgot.

'Be careful,' she whispered.

'Al . . . ays.'

'You'll call?'

'Try . . . to . . . home?'

'Tomorrow afternoon maybe. We need to visit the fish hatchery, trace some records.'

'. . . feeling?'

'Baby's happy. I can feel her stronger now, moving around more. Oh, she's a carnivore. I'm finally allowed to eat meat.'

His chuckle faded in and out over the spotty connection. It brought him closer to her, so that she could picture the crinkles that appeared at the corner of his eyes, the half curve of his smile.

'I love you,' she said.

'. . . love you, too.'

Then the phone beeped and the call was dropped. She didn't try to reconnect. Mac needed to do what he needed to do. And she . . .

She sat alone in her hotel room, wondering why, if she loved her husband so much, he felt so far away. At what point did distance go from being a marital phase to a new state of the universe? And what was a stubborn, hardheaded person like herself supposed to do about it?

Baby McCormack quivered. Kimberly rubbed her belly, listening to the wind outside howl across the parking lot, rattle the windows.

She put on her coat and headed out.

She found Sal sitting on the covered porch, tucked away from the wind, watching the wind swirl sheets of rain around the streetlights. Kimberly took a seat without asking, telling herself she had not sought out Sal on purpose. That was not why she left her room. This was not what it was about.

For his part, Sal didn't seem to be in the mood for talking. He simply watched the storm, his face set in the dark, brooding look she recognized from before. His thoughts had taken him to an unhappy place. She wondered how long he'd been there.

'You ate chicken,' he said presently. 'Thought the baby didn't like meat.'

Kimberly shrugged. 'Baby changed her mind. More evidence it's a female.'

He finally turned to look at her, his gaze dropping to her rounded belly.

'Are you nervous?'

'Yeah.'

'Gonna work after the baby's born?'

'That's the plan.'

He regarded her more curiously. 'Do you think it will change you? I mean, first time you're called out for a homicide involving children, or a child abduction case, or the sex slave rings, or arson, or any of the other shit out there in the world that touches young lives and breaks them. Won't that be tough?'

'There, but for the grace of God, go I,' she murmured.

'Not good enough,' he said flatly. 'You're ERT, right? You get to recover the body. Then what, go home to little Janey and pretend you can wash the smell off your hands, let alone erase the image from your mind?'

'It's what I do now.'

'No little Janey.'

'Theoretically, little Janey is a bundle of joy. Why should a good thing make the rest of the world harder to bear?'

He scowled at her, clearly not expecting that argument. After a moment, when he couldn't come up with a retort, he went back to watching it storm. And after another moment, she reached over, picked up his hand, and placed it on her stomach just in time for Baby McCormack to give a little *thump*.

Sal jerked back his hand, sat up straight. 'Holy crap!'

'Pretty strong, huh?' Kimberly said.

'What is she, Mia Hamm?'

'Maybe.' Kimberly shrugged. 'Dunno. She can be anything she wants. I think that's the point. You ever hear of the banality of evil, Sal?'

'Banality of evil?'

'Yeah. A psychologist did an experiment once. Took a group of clean-cut young men, all known for their high moral standards, and had them form a mock prison. Some became inmates, some became prison guards. They tried to make it as lifelike as possible, had the 'guards' arrest the 'prisoners' during class, that sort of thing. The experiment was supposed to last a few weeks. If memory serves, the professor had to pull the plug after just three days because the pseudo inmates started suffering nervous breakdowns due to the very real abuse they were experiencing at the hands of the pseudo guards, including being stripped, debased, and sexually abused. All this by young men who'd never done so much as shoplift. Basically, even good people do really bad things if they think no one cares. The banality of evil.'

Sal grunted. 'You're talking about the Nazis.'

'I'm talking about human nature. That everyone has inside him- or herself the capacity for evil. Some people will never act on it, others will definitely act on it, and still others will act on it only if the right circumstances present themselves. They'll make it twenty, thirty, forty years being a fine, upstanding citizen. But then the forty-first year . . .'

'How is that an encouraging thought?'

She shrugged. 'Who said I was being encouraging? It's a fact of life. And just because I'm about to become a mother, doesn't mean I'm suddenly going to stick my head in the sand. The world is a hard place. People suck. Monsters do live under the bed – or, frankly, in Daddy's room down the hall. But you know what?'

'If I kill myself now, it won't hurt as much later?'

'There's a corollary to the banality of evil, and that's the banality of heroism.'

Sal groaned. 'Please tell me you're not talking Superman.'

'Actually, I'm talking the opposite of Superman. I'm talking about the Everyday Average Joe that one day, when the right circumstances present themselves, suddenly saves the day. The stranger on the subway platform who jumps down to assist the fallen commuter. The woman shopping in the store who not only notices the sad little girl, but calls the police. For every act of cruelty, there is an equal and opposing act of courage. That's human nature, too.'

'Your mother and sister are murdered,' Sal said softly, 'so you save the rest of the world?'

'I don't need you to tell me my story, Sal. I know who I am.'

Sal flushed. His gaze returned to the storm, but his hands were fidgeting on his lap.

'I'm not quitting, Mac. It's not what I do.'

'You just called me Mac.'

'I did not—' But then she caught herself, realized she had, and it was her turn to flush. She didn't know what she was doing anymore. She should return to her room. She should do something.

But she remained where she was, sitting next to Sal, watching his hands fidget, feeling the darkness wash off him in waves.

And it occurred to her for the first time – the banality of evil. Was that what she was doing here? Waiting for the right circumstances to present themselves so she could do what she knew she shouldn't do? Touch Sal's face? Turn him toward her? Find his lips with her own because something in him called out to something in her? The hurt, or maybe it was the rage. The need, the deep, endless need because something had gone wrong long ago and there was nothing that could be done about it now but nurse the wound.

She wanted him. Or at least was drawn to him. It startled her. Scared her. She thought of another psychology paper she had analyzed in college. That most people didn't require the cruelty of strangers to screw up their lives; most people were perfectly capable of doing it themselves.

Sal had turned. He was studying her, his eyes unreadable in the dark. She could feel his hunger, taut, restrained.

And then the lightning cracked, illuminating the small alcove with a flashing wink before casting them back into shadow. She saw his face, stark with physical need. And she heard her husband's voice, telling her he would be home in the morning. The thunder boomed. Sal leaned forward. She tilted her head up.

'I'm sorry,' Kimberly whispered.

She got up, clenched her hands into fists, and quickly walked away.

Her room was dark when she opened the door. She fumbled for the light switch, flipped it, but nothing happened. She entered, closing the door behind her, starting to tremble now with the aftermath of what she'd nearly done, feeling supremely rattled. She was not that kind of woman. She did not do those kinds of things.

Goddammit, when had she become such a basket case?

She made her way to the bed, reaching for the bedside lamp when she suddenly heard a warning hiss and realized she was no longer alone.

Something significant, black, skittered across her bed. She reached instinctively for her shoulder holster, then remembered that she'd disarmed for dinner. She grabbed the lamp, throwing it at the racing form as she fell back, hitting the wall. She slid along its length until she banged into the desk at the opposite end of the room. Her fingers found the desk light, scrambling for the switch, while across the room, she once again heard the primitive hiss.

She snapped on the lamp in time to register two things at once: The world's largest, scariest damn spider was reared back on its hind legs on her bedside pillow, waving its fangs. And a teenage boy sat calmly beside it, holding a gun.

'Who the fuck are you?' Kimberly exploded. Belatedly, she glanced at her field kit where she'd stashed her Glock .40. Eight steps away max. But she'd lose another minute unzipping the bag, reaching in, retrieving her semiautomatic . . .

Her gaze ping-ponged to the door instead. Ten steps away max, but then twisting the knob, yanking it open, getting all the way clear . . .

She returned her attention to the boy. He sat calmly, gun level, hands steady, still not saying a word.

She tried an experimental step forward. Moment she moved, the oversize tarantula reared back and hissed again. She stopped; it dropped back on all eight legs, waiting.

'Who are you?' she tried again, eyes on the spider, but head angled toward the boy. 'What do you want?'

'His name is Diablo,' the boy supplied conversationally. 'He's a *Theraphosa blondi* – a species of tarantula from South America. Most tarantulas don't have enough venom to harm humans. Their bites feel like nothing more than a bee sting. Not Diablo. He's capable of ripping off your fingers, tearing the flesh from your hands. He hasn't had dinner yet, and as you can tell, he's a little pissed off about it.'

Kimberly's hands dropped in front of her rounded belly. Field kit, she thought again. Quick dash, unzip the bag, reach inside for her weapon . . . No dice. Kid could pull the trigger of his gun in a split second. And the spider . . . She didn't want to think about it.

'You're the caller,' she ventured. 'The one who had me listen to Veronica Jones's tape.'

'I tried,' the boy said flatly. 'I gave you a chance. You failed.'

'I'm here now. We can talk.'

The boy merely waved his gun. 'I didn't come to talk, lady. I came to graduate.'

Kimberly contemplated the door this time. If she could just inch to the side, get close enough . . .

'Does Dinchara know you've escaped?'

'Escaped? Lady, who the hell do you think sent me?'

She faltered, tried again: 'He knows we're here?'

'Everyone knows. You and your friends paradin' all over town, flashing pictures. It was always only a matter of time. But that's all right. Your visit simplifies things. Now I don't have to hunt. We can cut straight to the main event.'

'Is that what *you* want? I know what's going on. What he makes you do. It doesn't have to be like that.' She inched forward half a step. The boy and tarantula didn't react. She went for another step. 'Dinchara picks up the prostitutes, doesn't he? He brings them home, does terrible things to them. And you hear it, don't you? Maybe you're even in the room. Forced to listen and watch, but there's nothing you can do. Then it's over and he makes you clean up the mess. Plastic, paper, does he put anything down or does he prefer to make you do all the work?'

The boy was staring at her with a fascinated look. She'd gotten it right, or at least close enough. She was talking to him about all the things he was never allowed to mention, and that had him hooked.

'He drains the blood,' the boy murmured. 'In a tub. Less mess, less weight, makes it easier for later.'

'He wraps them up, or do you do that?'

'Both. Body's hard to manage, it takes two.'

'What does he prefer? Old bed linens, garbage bags, burlap? Or has he experimented around with it? The choices are endless.'

'Nylon. From the Army surplus store. Cheap, efficient. He likes things like that.'

'You help him carry the bodies to the truck.' She made it another inch.

The boy shrugged. 'You do what you need to do. That's how the game works. You make him happy and then he doesn't hurt you so much.'

'How long have you been with him?'

'Too long to do anything differently now.'

'Is he your father?'

'My parents are dead.'

'He's your guardian?'

'He's the Burgerman,' the boy said mournfully, spider sitting beside him. 'Grinding the naughty boys into dust.'

'It's not your fault,' Kimberly said. She'd made it a foot closer to her field kit, her fingers wiggling impatiently at her side. 'You're obviously assisting him only under duress. Work with me now and I can make this stop. I can help you.'

But the boy's face abruptly shut down. His mood shifted and it wasn't in her favor. 'I am making this stop,' the boy stated, raising the gun. 'He's already found a replacement. Time for me to go.'

'The younger boy. Did he kidnap him, too?'

'Stay still. I know what you're doing. Just stop it, all right. Don't move!'

'What's your name? Tell me your name. Let me help you.'

'You don't get it. I don't have a name. He took it. He takes *everything*!' The boy's voice was rising now, getting agitated. She forced herself to still, remain calm. The spider was playing with the base of the fallen lamp, allowing her to home in on the twitchy teen.

'What about Ginny Jones?' she asked, taking a shot in

the dark, because both the boy and Ginny knew Dinchara, so it was reasonable to assume they also knew each other.

The boy blinked, appearing uncertain for the first time. 'What about Ginny?'

Kimberly drew a deep breath, took another gamble: 'What about Ginny's baby? Aren't you the father? Don't you want a life with her someday?'

'That's what she says.'

'Have you heard from her? Is she okay—'

'She's outside. Waiting in the car to drive me away.'

'What?'

The boy burst out in a rush: 'She chose you, you know. Read you took on some other killer guy, thought you might be able to work some magic. I told her she was crazy. All these years later, like some chick with a badge is really gonna make a difference. Guess it doesn't matter anymore. You failed, so here I am. Me and my little friend, just like Al Pacino said. Ready to get the job done.'

'Please, Dinchara will never let either of you go. You help him dispose of the bodies. Ginny earns him cash. Why would he ever let you graduate?'

'He's got a replacement—'

'A young kid! Too small to help haul a body.'

'We put them on litters. Drag 'em up. Boy'll get tough soon enough.'

'All the way up Cooper Gap?' she asked incredulously.

The boy took the bait. 'Cooper Gap? What the fuck are you talking about? We got our own network, above Blood Mountain and all the skippy little Cub Scouts. Dump a hooker, watch a little boy pee. Makes for a great day with the Burgerman.'

'It's not your fault,' Kimberly said softly, urgently, three feet forward now, so close to her field kit, so damn close . . . 'Surely you understand, it's not your fault—'

'*I just want to fucking graduate!*' the boy screamed, suddenly sitting up. The commotion startled the tarantula.

It reared, fangs arching. The boy turned, pointed his gun, and pulled the trigger.

The tarantula and the lamp exploded on the bed. Kimberly sprang forward, feeling bits of ceramic sting like shrapnel slicing into her skin. She made it three more steps, then the boy screeched: 'DON'T MOVE!'

She was at her field bag, fingers on the zipper. But she forced her hands down, forced herself to take a deep breath, regard the boy calmly. He was bleeding, too, across his nose, on his cheek, his chin, his neck.

'Let me get you a towel—' she started.

'He did terrible things to me,' the boy said dully. 'You have no idea. And then I did terrible things because I didn't know what else to do. And it's been so long now . . . I don't even . . . I had parents once. At least I think I did . . . I am tired. I'm just . . . so tired.'

'Talk to me. Help me understand.'

'Ginny wants us to get married,' he said as if she'd never spoken. 'She wants us to go away, have our baby, be a family. I don't know what a family is.'

'We can make this happen. It's not too late—'

'Do I get a job? Wear a tie? I never finished fourth grade. What kind of job does that get you? I know how to fuck, kidnap little kids, and kill hookers. Where's that needed in the workforce? Find me that want ad—'

'You're young, there's still time—'

'She doesn't know what I did. That's all. She thinks Dinchara did it, but no, that would be too easy. He handed the gun to me. *'Pull the trigger, boy. Don't be an asshole. You know she'd run back to him if she could. Pull the goddamn trigger.'* So I did and then he was dead and it's only a matter of time before she figures it out or Dinchara tells her just for kicks.'

'You shot Tommy Mark Evans.'

'I had to. You don't understand. Practice, you see. So I could graduate. So I could finally be free.'

Blood had pooled on the gashes on his face. Now it began to slowly trickle down, like a trail of tears, as he raised the gun again, took careful aim.

Kimberly's hand flew to her duffel bag, fingernails scrabbling frantically against the nylon surface. Goddammit, why'd she have to zip the bag? She was never gonna make it. The gun leveling, pointing . . .

She grabbed the bag, held it in front of her swollen belly, as if that would make a difference . . .

'I can't be a daddy,' the boy whispered. 'I can't be around little kids. All I know how to do is destroy them.'

And then, in the next heartbeat, the gun turned, found his temple. Her voice, starting to scream. *'Nooooooo!'*

'Don't let your baby ever meet someone like me. Don't ever let it fall into the hands of the Burgerman.'

The boy pulled the trigger.

The shot deafened her. Or maybe it was her own desperate wail, trying to call it back, as the far side of the boy's skull opened up, blew against the wall, rained gray matter across the bedside table.

She was still screaming when her father forced open the door, when Rainie and Sal bolted into the room, when the boy's body finally fell with a silent thud against the carpet and she could see one sightless eye, staring at her accusingly, and she still didn't know his name.

THIRTY-FOUR

The woman who used to be my mother was waiting where she said she'd be. She sat at a little wrought-iron table, outside a busy coffee shop. She had one leg crossed over the other, her hands clasped nervously on her knee.

I watched her from across the street, hidden in the shadows of a doorway. I kept telling myself to step forward. But my legs didn't want to move yet. I stood, I watched, I felt something heavy and hard grow in my chest.

First time I called, she hung up on me. Second time, she accused me of playing a cruel prank. Then she'd started to cry and that upset me so much I hung up on her.

Third time, I composed myself better. I kept it simple. I had information on her missing son. I wanted to meet with her. I thought I could be of help.

I don't know why I put it like that. Why I didn't just say I was her little boy. I'd been snatched out of my own bed when I'd been too young to save myself. I'd spent the past ten years surviving unspeakable horrors. But I was old now. The Burgerman didn't want me anymore. Maybe I could return home. Maybe I could go back to being her little boy.

I wanted to tell her these things. I wanted to see the smile I remembered from my sixth-birthday party, when she led me to the garage where there was a brand-new Huffy bike topped by a big red bow. I wanted to watch her flip back her long dark hair the way she did when she leaned down to help me with my homework. I wanted to snuggle up with her on the sofa, my head against her shoulder as we watched Knight Rider *on TV.*

I wanted to be nine years old again. But I wasn't.

I caught my reflection in the glass of the store window. My sunken eyes, hollowed-out cheekbones, overgrown shaggy hair. I looked like a hoodlum, the kind of kid shadowed by security officers at the mall, the kind of kid other parents didn't trust hanging out with their son. I didn't see my mother's features imprinted onto my own; I saw the Burgerman.

Across the street, my mom was fidgeting restlessly, twisting a ring on her right hand over and over again. She kept glancing over her left shoulder as if waiting for me to appear.

All at once I got it. She wasn't looking for me. She was checking in with someone else.

I followed her line of sight, and finally made out the uniformed officer, standing just around the corner from the coffee shop. He turned to frown at my mom, as if to warn her to settle down, and I saw his face.

I sucked in my breath.

These are the things that no one tells you, that you must experience in order to learn:

You never can go home again. A boy raised by wolves will someday only have wolf left inside him.

And a mother's love can burn.

I arrived back at the apartment at 3:05 p.m. I remember because when I walked through the door, the first thing that I noticed was the clock hanging on the far wall. It read 3:05 and that struck me as funny. Such a normal time. Such a normal day. Such a normal afternoon.

For such an abnormality.

I didn't take off my coat. I didn't kick off my shoes. I had never crossed the street to my mother. Instead, I had headed to a pet store five blocks away. Now, I had a brown paper bag in one hand, a brand-new Louisville Slugger in the other. I left the apartment door wide open and strode straight into the Burgerman's bedroom.

He slept on his back, one hand on his doughy stomach, the other hand flung above his head. He was naked, the sheet tangled low around his waist. At the far edge of the bed, the boy was curled up, also naked, no covers, shivering in his sleep.

I slapped his shoulder hard. His eyes popped open.

'Get out,' I ordered harshly.

The boy eyed me blankly. I leaned down until we were nearly nose-to-nose. 'Get your scrawny ass out of this fuckin' bed,' I told him, 'or I will cave in your fuckin' skull.'

The boy scrambled out of bed and hightailed it out of the room. Did he leave the apartment? Run for the neighbors? Yell for the police?

I didn't care. Not about him, the police, the neighbors. I came here with one thing to do, and by God, I was getting it done.

I opened the brown paper bag, took out the box. I'd wanted a pit bull or maybe a python. With thirty bucks, however, this was the best I could do. I remembered what the kid at the pet store had told me — spiders made great pets, actually hated to bite. In fact, they only attacked if you really pissed 'em off.

So I opened the box and tossed the huge black spider smack-dab in the middle of Burgerman's chest. Then I reached down and pinched one of the spider's legs — hard — to make sure the female was good and pissed off.

The tarantula promptly sank her fangs into Burgerman's hairy chest. And he bolted awake with a roar.

The next few moments happened in a blur: Burgerman, looking down, seeing the huge black tarantula dangling from his chest. Screaming harder, plucking at its bristled body, then shrieking louder when the tiny barbs covering its legs needled his fingertips.

Me, hefting back the baseball bat.

Burgerman, looking up, yelling, 'Get it off, boy! Holy mother of God, get it off get it off get it OFF!'

Me, swinging the Louisville Slugger, connecting nice and solid with Burgerman's nose.

There was a cracking sound. The spray of blood. A deep oomph as Burgerman whomped backward onto the mattress, one hand now clutching his shattered nose, the other hand still groping blindly at the spider.

'Aaargh!' Burgerman yelled, something wet and slurpy gargling in the back of his throat.

The Burgerman ripped the tarantula out of his chest. I had an image of a hairy black spider, suspended midair, giant flap of skin still dangling from its fangs, blood pooling in the hole left behind. Burgerman dropped the spider, started to rise up with another enraged roar.

So I hit him. Right kneecap. A crack. A scream. Left kneecap. A fresh crack. A fresh scream.

'Boy, boy, boy, what're the fuck're you doin', boy? Don'tcha know I'm gonna kill you, boy? Boy, boy, boy . . .'

I thought, coolly, with composure I never knew I had, that the Burgerman was a first-class whiner.

He was on his side. Fingers clawing at the stained sheet, trying to find traction. If he could just pull himself up, he'd come after me. I could see it in his eyes. Even now, about to meet his Maker, the Burgerman was not thinking about repenting. He just wanted to kill somebody.

I wondered if that's what I looked like. And instead of feeling ashamed, for the first time in my life, I felt strong. Powerful. In control.

I wound up the bat and hit him. Again. In the face this time. Connecting with his jaw, hearing his teeth shatter, then aiming for his cheekbone. I stood over that mattress, and I swung my bat until my arms ached and I gradually became aware that Burgerman didn't make any sound anymore and the only noise I heard was the wet smack, smack of my baseball bat connecting with his caved-in skull and the moisture running down my cheeks wasn't tears at all, but Burgerman's blood and brains, dripping off the bat, into my hair, down onto my clothes.

I think I started laughing then. It was hard to be sure. I just knew I couldn't stop swinging that bat because at any time, the Burgerman's eyes would pop back open and he'd rise out of the bed and get me again. That's the way it worked in the movies. No matter what you did, the monster always rose from the dead.

Eventually, however, my shoulders gave out. The bat came down and no matter how much I wanted, I couldn't raise it again. I sank down on the carpet, panting hard, sweat-soaked, gore-spattered, my bloody hands cradling my bloody head.

I waited for a while, I don't know why. For the neighbors to knock on the door. For the cops to come pounding up the steps. For the new boy to return and see that I'd finally done it: The Burgerman was dead.

After a time, when nothing happened, I walked to the bathroom, trailing the bat behind me. I noticed idly that the boy had closed the front door behind him; maybe that's why the neighbors never came, or maybe it was because the Burgerman had a knack for choosing apartments where the neighbors didn't care.

Once in the bathroom, I turned on the water, climbing in fully clothed, trying to rinse off the worst of the gore. But not letting go of the bat. Just in case, you know. Just in case.

In my bedroom now, shedding my wet clothes into one bloody pile. Pulling out my second pair of jeans, an old T-shirt, sweatshirt, the few articles of clothing I had left.

At the last minute, I got smart. Found a duffel bag in Burgerman's closet, went to the front hallway, and loaded up on cash and porno tapes. Given that I starred in most of the home movies, I figured they were the least I deserved.

I tried to think of what else to take with me; there was so little of value in this place. Burgerman spent money on booze, drugs, and whores. He'd never even bought me a goddamn video game.

The rage hit me all over again, and for an insane moment I wanted to go back into the bedroom and resume whacking him with the baseball bat. I had to catch myself, focus. The other boy was long gone. No doubt already spilling his guts to the police.

I had to get out of here.

At the last second, as I headed for the door, I caught a faint blur of movement out of the corner of my eye. I stumbled over my feet, groping blindly for the baseball bat, pivoting toward Burgerman's bedroom.

I'd just raised the bat over my head, when I realized that wasn't Burgerman's foot moving under the sheet. Instead, the white folds parted and a hairy black spider emerged.

The tarantula lived, working her way carefully around the bloody sheets.

After another brief hesitation, I found the pet store box, scooped her inside, and slid her into my duffel bag.

I'd never had a pet before.

I thought I'd name her Henrietta.

THIRTY-FIVE

'Spiders may feed on other spiders, and because of this tendency to cannibalism a social or communal life is hardly to be expected.'

FROM *How To Know the Spiders*, THIRD EDITION,
BY B. D. KASTON, 1978

She wanted to call Mac. It was her knee-jerk reaction, born of terror and the resulting aftermath. But of course, he was out in the field now, doing the job he loved and beyond her reach just as she was so often beyond his.

So Kimberly huddled on the floor of her hotel room, arms wrapped protectively around her unborn child, aware of the blood on her cheek, and the fact she shouldn't wash up until the crime scene photographer had documented her face. She'd already contacted her supervisor who in turn would raise the local sheriff as a courtesy call. Sheriff Wyatt would be leaving his D.A.R.E. training. Sheriff Duffy would be roused out of bed. And with their blessing, her own ERT would probably be activated to process the scene.

So many wheels in motion. The law enforcement machinery grinding into gear. She knew it. She understood it. She lived it.

She squeezed her eyes shut and felt nearly dumbstruck with exhaustion.

'Water?' Sal asked. He took a seat beside her, careful not to touch. Quincy and Rainie were outside the room, standing in the hallway with the wide-eyed hotel manager, discussing something in low tones they obviously didn't want her to hear.

'You okay?' Sal asked.

She nodded.

'The baby?'

She nodded again, best she could do. Her belly felt fine, no cramping, no nausea. Mostly she felt jittery with the adrenaline dump, while her arms stung from a myriad of tiny cuts. Nothing a Band-Aid couldn't cover. She was fine, absolutely, positively fine, except for the fact that she would never be fine again.

The boy's body still lay slumped on the floor. A cursory attempt at finding a pulse had confirmed that he was dead. They had not bothered to call 911 or raise an EMT; this stage of the game was all about protecting the crime scene.

Which included the blood in her hair, the gore on her cheek, the rich, coppery smell she could not get out of her nostrils.

The boy's voice, trying to explain to her that he was tired, so very tired.

It was the senselessness that was hardest to take. That a life could be born into this world and, through no fault of its own, never stand a chance. Kimberly pressed the heels of her hands against her eye sockets, not wanting to see what she saw, not wanting to know what she knew.

'He confirmed that Dinchara murdered the missing prostitutes,' she whispered finally, taking the glass of water from Sal, watching it tremble in her hand. She didn't want to drink. She forced herself to take little sips of water anyway, because she couldn't risk dehydration while pregnant.

Sal's turn for silence.

'The boy also shot and killed Tommy Mark Evans, acting under Dinchara's directions. It was considered his practice run, for his 'graduation.' There's another boy as well, younger. The teen referred to him as his 'replacement.' '

'Where?'

'Somewhere close. According to the boy, Dinchara knows we're here asking questions. Maybe we even walked right by him, I don't know. But he's local. Definitely local.'

'What else?'

She closed her eyes tiredly, resting the glass of water against her forehead. When she opened them again, she saw she had smeared blood on the curve of the glass and the sight of it, dark, fleshy, made her stomach roil dangerously. She fought to hold it together.

'He helped dispose of the bodies. They pulled them by litters up Blood Mountain. But not the primary trail – Dinchara has his own. Someplace above the main traffic flow where they could look down at the activity below. That should help narrow our search.'

'Okay.'

She turned to him finally, her agitation starting to slip through the cracks, ruining her attempt at composure. 'Okay? I just watched a teenage boy blow out his brains, and all you can say is okay? Dinchara kidnapped this child. He raped him, he corrupted him, he turned him into an accomplice until the boy would rather die than risk a future with his own child. Nothing about that is *okay*!'

Sal looked at her strangely. 'Kimberly, it isn't your fault—'

'What isn't my fault? That a child was kidnapped? That nobody ever rescued him? That Dinchara used him as a tool for murder over a dozen times and no one ever noticed? We're the cops, Sal. If it's not our fault, whose fault is it?'

'The kid shot Tommy Mark Evans—'

'Because he had no choice!'

'He could've just as easily shot you.'

'You know what? *That doesn't make me feel any better!*'

And then, through her own rising hysteria, remembering suddenly: 'Shit! Ginny Jones. She's waiting for him in the parking lot. Quick, before she hears the sirens, we gotta find Ginny Jones!'

Quincy and Rainie were unarmed civilians. They were not the type, however, to let such details stop them. Quincy took the lead with Rainie following him swiftly and quietly over the dark, rain-slicked asphalt.

The worst of the thunder and lightning seemed to have passed, leaving behind merely the pouring rain and howling wind. It was difficult to hear. Even more difficult to see. For Quincy, the conditions brought to mind another time, not so long ago, when he and his future son-in-law, Mac, had slipped and slid their way through the Tillamook County Fairgrounds in a desperate bid to get a glimpse of the man who was holding Rainie for ransom.

That day had not gone as planned. And this moment?

The streetlamps reflected off each car's water-beaded windshield, distorting the view, making it difficult for them to peer in while not so hard for a driver to see out. It occurred to Quincy that they were going about this all wrong. They didn't need to inspect each vehicle's interior; they simply needed to examine each exhaust pipe.

Bank Robbery 101: The getaway car was already fired up and ready to go.

He motioned for Rainie to take the right side of the parking lot, closest to the street. He worked to the left, running in a half-crouch down the line of vehicles. Then, straight ahead, right by the exit for the side street, a small economy car with its engine running.

He caught Rainie's attention with a wave of his hand. She started over and he realized at the last moment that they had a problem after all. Ginny Jones was armed with a car at the very least, and perhaps a gun as well. All they had was their charm and wit.

Quincy went with plan B. He picked up a large rock, placed it in his fist, and wrapped the whole affair with his coat. Four strides later, he suddenly loomed in the driver's side window. Ginny Jones opened her eyes in alarm. He slammed his covered knuckles through the window, shattering the glass and yanking the keys from the ignition.

The girl screamed.

He popped open the door and gave her his best predatory smile.

'Bad news,' he said, 'my daughter's still alive and you're coming with me.'

Ginny Jones screamed again.

'Please,' Rainie said, materializing at his side. 'As if either of us care.'

They dragged Ginny from the car into the storming night, just as the first police cruisers roared into view.

Rainie and Quincy made it up the stairs with Ginny. They turned the corner. Kimberly caught sight of them and launched herself up off the floor.

'Kimberly, no!' Quincy got out, then Kimberly's shoulder was driving into Ginny's chest and the two women went down in a tangle, Ginny yelling something incoherent while Kimberly screamed at the top of her lungs: 'You played Russian roulette with my baby. You lying bitch! *How dare you risk my baby!*'

Rainie tried to grab one of them, Quincy the other.

Both of the women were moving too fast, Ginny smacking Kimberly across the face, Kimberly getting a grip on the girl's hair.

'*Where's the boy? I'm not asking you again. Where does Dinchara keep the* second *boy!*'

While Ginny wailed, '*Where is he, where is he, where is he? What did you do with Aaron?*'

'*You had no right to risk my life! I was trying to help, all you ever had to do was tell me the truth!*'

'*Aaron, Aaron, Aaron!*'

Sal finally waded into the fray. He got Kimberly under the armpits and dragged her off Ginny's flailing body just in time to whisper in her ear, 'Enough already! You're putting on a show!'

Kimberly finally stopped struggling long enough to look up. Two of Sheriff Wyatt's deputies stood in the hallway, eyes wide, hands on their holstered firearms. They looked from Ginny to Kimberly to Rainie, Quincy, and Sal.

'Special Agent Sal Martignetti,' Sal supplied crisply, using one hand to flash his creds while his other hand maintained a tight grip on Kimberly's arm. She fisted her hands, still overloaded on adrenaline. She tried to rein it in. Didn't work. She wanted to scream. To scream and scream and scream. Then she wanted to curl up in a ball and cry in her husband's arms.

Rainie and Quincy introduced themselves, then Ginny Jones. The tension was starting to wind down, the deputies' hands moving away from their holstered weapons, everyone taking a deep breath.

'Ma'am,' the older deputy said slowly as he appraised the scene, and in particular, Kimberly's blood-spattered hair. 'Are you hurt? Do you need medical attention?'

'No.' Kimberly's gaze returned to Ginny, who was finally getting to her feet with Rainie's assistance. The girl scowled back at her, chin up, shoulders thrown back defiantly.

'*Bitch,*' the girl mouthed.

That was it. Kimberly dabbed a smear of blood from her cheek. Then she reached over and very deliberately wiped the gore on Ginny's exposed collarbone.

'Hey, what the fuck—'

'That's from Aaron,' Kimberly said. 'Guess what? He didn't graduate.'

Ginny screamed in rage, launched herself at Kimberly, and they went down again, this time with the two deputies joining Quincy, Rainie, and Sal in trying to figure out what to do.

Thirty minutes later, Ginny and Kimberly sat at opposite ends of a table in the empty dining room in the basement of the Smith House. Sheriff Duffy had arrived to supervise the party until Sheriff Wyatt returned. The majority of the deputies were upstairs, cordoning off the scene in preparation for the evidence recovery team. Quincy and Rainie sat on either side of Kimberly. Sal sat beside Ginny.

Kimberly thought they were like boxers in the corners of the ring. Which made Duff, seated in the middle, the referee.

'Why don't we start with the preliminaries and work our way from there, shall we?' Duff suggested in his deep, grumbling baritone. 'Everyone has water. Now we'll all play nice together.'

He turned to Ginny Jones and indicated the tape recorder he had sitting in front of him. 'State your name and the date for the record, please.'

Ginny glared at him, and for a minute, Kimberly thought she might be justified to go across the table for some more whoop-ass, but then Ginny's shoulders sagged, and the last of the fight seemed to leave the girl.

'Ginny,' she whispered. 'Virginia Jones.'

Duff got the full names and badge numbers from the law enforcement officers in attendance. He also noted date and location. Then he read Ginny her rights, as well as having her sign the waiver. Finally they got into it.

Yes, Virginia had driven Aaron Johnson to the Smith House tonight. Yes, she knew he was armed and intended to possibly shoot federal agent Kimberly Quincy.

Except Aaron Johnson wasn't his real name, but an alias manufactured by a second unknown subject so he'd have something to call the boy in public. The second subject, known as Dinchara, was the one who supplied the 9-mm and identified FBI Special Agent Kimberly Quincy as the target. In return for shooting Special Agent Quincy, Aaron had been promised his freedom – that basically, Dinchara, who had kidnapped Aaron Johnson more than a decade ago, would finally let the boy go. Dinchara referred to the event as graduation, and Aaron Johnson had wanted to graduate.

'And your role in this?' Duff pressed the girl.

She shrugged. 'Just drive.' She had her hand folded on her barely rounded tummy. 'We're gonna have a baby, Aaron and me. That's why he needed to graduate. So we could be together.'

Her gaze shot to Kimberly, some of the earlier heat returning. 'What did you do to him? He was just a kid. He didn't know any better. How could you shoot a boy?'

Kimberly thinned her lips and clammed up. Ginny didn't know yet what had happened in the hotel room and law enforcement types weren't much for sharing.

'You set me up,' Kimberly stated. 'Aaron needed a target for his 'graduation' and you chose me. Why?'

'I did not—'

'*He told me all about it!* Now start talking, or your baby's gonna be born in a prison hospital and yanked away from you at the moment of birth. I can get you whole articles on what it's like for pregnant inmates. Going into labor with their wrists and ankles shackled to the table, nothing but broodmares, birthing a baby for someone else to raise. You want to know the details, see what awaits you—'

'Dinchara made me do it! Don't you remember? He's only happy if he can kill someone you love. Except Aaron didn't have any family left. Dinchara was the one who took him away. So who was left for him to love?'

Ginny's eyes skittered away at the last line and, in that instant, Kimberly got it. She sat back, stunned, and felt the first of the outrage leave her body.

'You,' she breathed. 'You were the logical target. And both of you understood that, didn't you? That Dinchara would ask Aaron to kill *you*. Unless you found someone else.'

'It had to be a good target,' Ginny said, not looking at

289

any of them anymore. 'Someone important, but threatening to Dinchara as well, so he'd take an interest. I read an article on the Eco-Killer, what you did. I showed it to Dinchara and . . .' She shrugged. 'He liked you. A good-looking female who kicked ass. He thought it was pretty funny. And then I knew it would work.'

'Why didn't you say something?' Kimberly asked tiredly. 'We could've helped you, set up a whole operation. You just needed to tell us what was going on.'

'Like my mom begged for help? Or Tommy?' Ginny's lips curved in a smile at Kimberly's shocked expression. 'Of course Dinchara told me what Aaron did. It was too perfect for him not to share. How Aaron stood there with the gun shaking in his hands. How Tommy begged. Called him sir, offered him his truck, his money, even a blow job. And you can hear Dinchara in the background, this whispering little ghoul, 'Shoot him, shoot him, shoot him, pull the fucking trigger, you pantywaist. Shoot him, shoot him, shoot him . . .' Until Aaron pulls the trigger.

'I still hear it, sometimes late at night. My mom screaming, Tommy begging. And Dinchara, chortling away. So really, how are you gonna help me, Little Miss FBI? How can *anyone* help me?'

Ginny stopped talking. Her hands were still on her stomach, caressing the little round bulge now, trying to soothe.

'Aaron was the one who called me, wasn't he?' Kimberly asked. 'You gave him my cell phone number, he called me to bait the trap.'

'He gave you information,' Ginny countered. 'All you had to do was find Dinchara, and none of this woulda happened.'

'And the packets of driver's licenses, left on Special Agent Martignetti's windshield?'

Ginny shrugged. 'Don't ask me. I was just doing what I was told.'

'*You* delivered them?' Sal interrupted. 'But why? Ordered by whom?'

Ginny gave him a funny look. 'By Dinchara, of course. Who the hell do you think's running this show?'

Kimberly shared Sal's confusion. 'Dinchara *wanted* the IDs delivered to the GBI?'

'He wanted them delivered to Special Agent Martignetti. Showed me a picture of him and everything.'

'Why?'

'*Why?* Why not? Haven't you guys been paying attention? You don't ask Dinchara any questions. Not if you plan to live. He told me what to do. I did it. End of story.'

Kimberly frowned, not liking this bit of news.

Duff cleared his throat. 'Ma'am, this Mr. Dinchara, he got a real name, a physical address? That's the kind of information we need.'

'I don't know.'

'Liar,' Kimberly said immediately.

'Hey, I already said—'

'Liar!' Kimberly slapped a photo on the table. They'd taken it from Ginny's purse an hour earlier. The tattered black-and-white showed Ginny and Aaron, foreheads touching, laughing about something only they understood. Now the close-up caused both Ginny and Sal to do a double take. 'Afternoons together at the mall. PDAs, photo ops. Obviously you developed a relationship with Aaron. Only way that happened is if Dinchara introduced you two.'

'He brought Aaron on one of his trips to Sandy Springs—'

'What, and graciously paid for Aaron to make whoopee?'

'And *filmed* us having sex. That's what he does. Makes porn, then sells it on the Internet. You know the perv that sends out spam asking if you want to see pictures of a thirteen-year-old having sex with a goat? That's Dinchara.'

'So he has a studio—'

'Backseat of a car—'

'Bullshit. Not for an operation that involved. He's got a studio, in a house, where he's taken you and you've been with Aaron.'

'I was blindfolded!' the girl cried. 'He never let me see. You don't know what he's like—'

'Bullshit! We know exactly what he's like. I got files of just his kind stacked all over my desk. Now stop stalling and tell us what we need to know.'

But Ginny wasn't having it. She leaned over the table, wild-eyed. 'No, really, you haven't met his kind. I didn't realize it, either. Not until he took off his hat. He doesn't just like spiders. He thinks he *is* one. Honest to God, he has eyes tattooed all over his forehead.'

It took another two hours. Ginny denied knowing about the second boy. She insisted Dinchara always kept her blindfolded. She'd never met Aaron on her own, she didn't know nothing about anything.

One a.m. Two a.m. Kimberly's team had arrived. Rachel Childs led the work in the hotel room. Kimberly disappeared long enough to give a statement, have her hands swabbed for GSR, have her face photographed. When Harold was done with the photos, she asked him to accompany her back down to the basement dining room with the camera.

Ginny still sat at the end of the table, pale, hands shaking from exhaustion. Sal had moved to the far wall, his arms crossed over his chest, his features shut down, impossible to read. Rainie had disappeared, probably back to her room to sleep. Only Quincy and Duff seemed to still be hanging in there.

Kimberly placed the digital camera in front of Ginny. She started with the first close-up of Aaron Johnson, revealing his shattered skull. She went through all one hundred and fifty-two photos.

'This is what Dinchara did,' Kimberly stated calmly. *Click, click, click.* 'He twisted Aaron.' *Click, click, click.* 'Corrupted him.' *Click, click, click.* 'Destroyed him.

'Aaron killed himself because he thought if he stayed alive, he would harm your child. Isn't that what Dinchara taught him? You must destroy the thing you love. And he loved you, Ginny. With this bullet, fired into his brain, he sent you his love the only way he knew how.

'So what's it going to be? Are you going to let Dinchara get away with this?'

'I hate you.'

'Going to write off one more loss? Going to try to return to a world where a man like Dinchara roams free – and knows all about your baby? What's it gonna be?'

'He's going to kill you. Once he hears about Aaron, it's only a matter of time.'

'What's it gonna be, Ginny?'

'He'll go after me, too, if I help you. He'll know. He knows everything.'

'So what's it gonna be?'

Ginny Jones hugged her belly. She started to cry. Then she gave up the address.

Sal pushed away from the wall. 'All right,' he said. 'I'm calling SWAT.'

THIRTY-SIX

'Spiders tend to be solitary hunters ...'

FROM 'SPIDER WOMAN,' BY BURKHARD BILGER,
New Yorker, MARCH 5, 2007

Henrietta was dead. He found her on her back inside the ICU, mangled legs curled up tight against her abdomen. He prodded her with his finger, the way a child poked a lifeless pet long after the moment had passed. Henrietta didn't move. He tried one more time. Wasn't ever going to move again.

He sat back in the darkened bathroom and for a moment he couldn't breathe.

Was this what grief felt like? A hard, tight feeling in the chest, a shortness of breath, an overwhelming desire to scream? He pressed the heels of his hands against his eye sockets. It didn't give him any relief. He could feel the pressure building, building, building.

And for no good reason, he thought of that toddler, the one the Burgerman had forced him to bury under the azalea bushes. His throat burned and his shoulders shook and he hated everything about it, the force of his grief, the ugly sound of his sobs, the impotence of his own pathetic tears.

The police had never recovered the boy's body. The man knew because he searched the Internet from time to time. That boy remained lost, just as he himself was lost and Aaron and the new boy Scott, and approximately tens of thousands of other children each year.

His brother had been right, so many naughty boys for the Burgerman to grind into dust.

That's what he'd been doing for decades now. Grinding, grinding, grinding. Devouring lives by the dozen, from the innocent to the not-so-innocent. It hardly mattered to him. He took, because destroying others was the only time he wasn't afraid.

The end was coming. He could feel it now. The police scanner had been humming for the past three hours with word on a shooting at the historic Smith House. The dead was not a federal agent, but an unidentified boy. Aaron had failed. The agent had gotten him first, or who knows what. It hardly mattered. Henrietta was dead, Aaron was dead, and the younger boy had disappeared into the house lower on the hill. All that was left was Ginny, and she was nothing but a lying slut.

If the police found her first, she would give him up. Betrayal was what women did best.

He had to think, form a plan, but first, of course, he needed to tend to Henrietta.

Three-oh-five a.m. He happened to glance at the time, and the moment he noted the hour, it came to him. He knew exactly what needed to happen.

He laid out Henrietta in the middle of his bed. Then he crossed to his shelves, where the rest of his collection rested in row upon row of glass terrariums. He started on the left side and worked his way to the right, removing each lid. Then on to the nursery, the brown recluses' room, the spinners' room. Slowly, methodically, he set each and every spider free.

Then, out in the garage, he gathered half a dozen cans of gasoline.

He started with the computer, as that had the most evidence against him. Then into the living room, saturating the sofa cushions, the curtains, the cheap particleboard bookcases. Then into the boys' room, moving from there up the stairs into his inner sanctum. He soaked the mattress bearing Henrietta's body, a funeral pyre for a great warrior. Then headed back to the garage for the final two cans.

He heard sirens in the distance. More patrol officers heading to the Smith House. Or coming for him?

He'd already spent ten long years in the cruelest goddamn prison on earth. Like hell he was going back.

They should've found him, he thought with a fresh burst of outrage, uncapping the gas can, pouring, pouring, pouring. The stupid police should've trailed the Burgerman, burst into that first hotel room, and carried him valiantly away. But no, they never came. Not once in ten years. Not even at the bitter end.

They had failed him. They had let him become what he had become.

And now he would show them. He would show them everything the Burgerman had taught him how to do.

Last gasoline can was empty. He threw it into the guest bedroom in disgust, droplets spraying onto his hand and filling his nose with an acrid odor. He could hear the sirens again, gaining in intensity.

Not much time left.

At the top of the landing, he had to dance over four hairy forms, the first of the tarantulas escaping from their terrariums, trying to get the lay of the land. He took the stairs two at a time. At the bottom, he found two more of his pets, already locked in a savage embrace, fangs trying to rip through hard exoskeletons, legs grappling with each other's heads. First taste of freedom and the territorial cannibals had already started to fight.

Girls, he wanted to tell them, *you ain't seen nothin' yet.*

But no time for talking. He jerked open the hall closet, where he kept the gun safe. A swirl of the dial, flick of the wrist. He popped open the vault and regarded his arsenal.

Sirens, cresting over the hill.

Nine millimeter, Glock .40, shotgun, .22 rifle. Boxes and boxes of ammo. He stuffed everything into his rifle bag, hands shaking, spilling out some of the shells.

Tires, screeching out front.

'*Fuck it!*' The man grabbed his bag and bolted for the back patio.

At the last moment, he remembered, fishing the Zippo lighter from his pants pocket, and letting it rip.

The first spray of fire leapt through the kitchen, singeing the hair on the back of his hands, making the droplets of gasoline on his own flesh start to burn. He swatted at his left hand impatiently, watching as the fire burst down the hall and made a mad dash for the stairs.

And maybe it was just his imagination, but he thought he heard the first spider start to scream.

Destroying the thing he loved. Doing what he did best.

Except there was one more person who owed him. A love that had never died, even after all these years. Aaron had failed. The Burgerman would not.

He hefted the dark green bag over his shoulder and slipped out the back door, as a white police van roared into his driveway, as the downstairs window blew out with the force of the flames, and as his entire collection started to burn.

Rita was awake and looking out her window when the first siren split the air. She didn't react to the sound, but stayed in bed, watching as a bright orange ball rose above the trees.

She understood immediately where the fire was coming from, the old Victorian up the hill.

And it didn't surprise her one whit when the boy suddenly appeared in her doorway, hands behind his back.

She didn't talk, just threw back the covers, got out her gun.

'Child, you have something to do with this?'

'No, ma'am.'

'Been here all night?'

'Yes, ma'am.'

'All right. He's coming then. We'd better tend to the doors and windows.'

The boy drew out a knife.

THIRTY-SEVEN

'. . . spiders kill at an astonishing pace. One Dutch researcher estimates that there are some five trillion spiders in the Netherlands alone, each of which consumes about a tenth of a gram of meat a day. Were their victims people instead of insects, they would need only three days to eat all sixteen and a half million Dutchmen.'

FROM 'SPIDER WOMAN,'
BY BURKHARD BILGER, *New Yorker*, MARCH 5, 2007

By the time Kimberly and Sal arrived, the house at the address provided by Ginny was engulfed in flames. The fire department had deployed, stubbornly working their hoses, but Kimberly and Sal could tell it was a lost cause.

They stood at the perimeter, watching orange flames light up the night sky while feeling the heat of the blaze against their cheeks. Neighbors clustered around them, belting their bathrobes against the drizzling rain as they gathered in the street to watch the show.

'Pity,' an older woman commented, gray hair neatly arranged in row after row of pin curls, 'used to be such a pretty house in its day.'

'You know the owner?' Sal asked sharply, he and Kimberly moving closer.

But the woman shook her head. 'Used to, long time ago. But the house sold two, maybe three years ago. Rarely saw the new owner. He certainly didn't take an interest in caring for the house or garden, I can tell you that.' She gave a disapproving sniff.

'You said he,' Kimberly pressed.

The woman shrugged. 'That's all I ever saw – younger guy climbing in and out of his black SUV. Always wearing a baseball cap, even in the dead of winter. Struck me as an odd sort. He definitely wasn't friendly.'

'He wasn't,' another man chimed in, standing a few feet away in a blue flannel robe. 'My wife brought over a plate of brownies to welcome him to the neighborhood. Through the side window, she could see him standing in the entryway, after she rang the doorbell. But he didn't open the door. Finally, she just set down the brownies and left. Definitely an odd duck.'

'Ever see a boy?' Sal asked.

Man frowned. 'Eighteen, nineteen years old? He rarely left the house. I figured he was the son.'

'There's a younger boy, too.' The first woman spoke up authoritatively. 'At least lately, I've been seeing one out in the yard. Don't know if he's just visiting or not.'

Sal and Kimberly exchanged glances. 'And tonight?'

'Didn't see a thing,' the woman provided. 'Least not till I heard the sirens and realized there was a fire.'

They turned to the man. He shrugged apologetically. Apparently, the neighbors on this street actually slept. Which was more than Sal or Kimberly could say for their evening.

They rounded up the first responder, a young deputy who didn't have much to add. He'd heard Dispatch ordering all units to the address in pursuit of an unidentified suspect. When he'd arrived, the first red coils of fire already glowed in the front windows. Next thing he knew, the windows blew out and the house was one giant fireball. He put in a call to the fire department and that was that.

They tried the fire chief, a portly man with a graying mustache and a weathered complexion.

'Definitely an accelerant,' he boomed. 'No way a structure would've lit up this fast in these wet conditions without a little help. From the smell, I'd guess gasoline, but we gotta get Mike in before we'll know more.'

Mike turned out to be the county arson specialist. He'd been called, but couldn't begin his walk-through until the fire was extinguished and the building cooled and secured. Probably late morning at the earliest, if not midafternoon.

In other words, nothing to report, nothing to do. Get some sleep, the fire chief advised them. He'd let them know when it was their turn to play.

Kimberly thought that was pretty funny. As if she'd ever sleep again. Just the thought of it made her giggle in a way that wasn't entirely sane. And she could feel the heat again, smell the astringent odors of burning insulation, melting electrical wires, sprayed gasoline.

She wondered about the younger child. If somewhere in that burning structure, a small body was already curling up in a pugilist's stance. She had failed one boy this evening. And his younger counterpart? The so-called *replacement*?

The fire punched its first hole through the roof, discovering a fresh supply of oxygen and exploding with an ear-cracking roar. There was a warning groan from the old structure. A yell to fall back from the fire crew.

Then, with a tremendous, creaking sigh, the old house twisted, seeming to hang in midair one last moment. Then it collapsed. Red embers spewed into the darkness. Fresh flames skyrocketed into the overcast night. The neighbors gasped. The fire crew surged forward with renewed determination.

Sal led Kimberly back to his car. They drove wordlessly to the hotel, where Rainie and Quincy slept, where Kimberly's ERT team worked, and where the remains of a lone boy were finally being loaded up by the EMT. Ginny Jones had already been taken away to the county lockup. One ordeal ending, the next just beginning.

Sal led Kimberly to his room.

'He knows,' Kimberly murmured. 'Dinchara knows that Aaron failed. That's why he lit the fire. Because he knew we were coming and wanted to cover his tracks.'

Sal drew back the bedcovers, sat her on the edge of the bed, then carefully laid her down and tucked her in.

'We need to do something,' Kimberly continued relentlessly. 'What if he decides the younger boy is a liability? Or what if he decides to come after us? We need a plan.'

Sal picked up a pillow, placed it on the floor.

'He's coming, Sal. I can feel it. He's going to do something awful.'

'Sleep,' Sal told her. He lay down on the floor, no blankets, just the pillow.

Kimberly stared at him in amazement. Then, much to her own surprise, she closed her eyes and the world mercifully disappeared.

'Here's the deal,' Sheriff Duffy explained shortly after eleven a.m. He'd convened the first task force meeting in the basement of the Smith House. Everyone was in attendance, including Kimberly's evidence response team and a bunch of local deputies who'd already been up all night. Coffee flowed fast and furious, followed by platters of buttermilk biscuits and homemade sausage. As task force meetings went, the food was superb.

'There are two major trails leading up Blood Mountain.' Sheriff Duffy had a large USGS map spread out on the first table. Now he stabbed the first thickly drawn line with his dark finger. 'There's the Woody Gap trail off of Highway Sixty. Or, you can take Highway One-eighty to Lake Winfield Scott and head up Slaughter Gap to Blood Mountain. Slaughter Gap is shorter and steeper; might be an issue if you're lugging a body and supplies. Both hikes are pretty damn popular, however. I sure as hell can't figure how two men could drag dead bodies up time after time without someone noticing something.'

'They didn't follow a major trail.' Kimberly spoke up tiredly. She sat beside her father and Rainie at a second

302

table, cradling a mug of steaming coffee between her hands. Her cell phone was clipped to her waist, still stubbornly silent though she'd already left multiple messages for Mac.

She'd slept for three hours, showered for thirty minutes. She was as close to human as she was going to get.

Sal sat all the way across the room from her. If her father or Rainie thought anything was odd about that, or wondered where she had spent the night, they hadn't said anything yet.

Kimberly continued now. 'The boy, Aaron, said they had their own trail. One above the major trails where they could look down at other hikers. Cub Scouts,' she added belatedly. 'He said Dinchara liked to watch the 'skippy little Cub Scouts.' '

Duff arched a brow. 'Last I knew, scout troops hiked either trail. So we're still looking for a trailhead next to either Woody Gap on Highway Sixty or Slaughter Gap on One-eighty.'

'Or around the other side entirely,' Harold interjected, his lanky frame bent over the map. He drew several lines with his finger. 'Look, you could access, here, here, or here. By the time you crest the summit, you're looking down on either trail. And any of these options would be safer than trying to hike up parallel to a major trail, plus over here in particular, you have a nice smooth ascent. That's what I'd look at. You know, if I were to haul bodies up a mountain.'

He glanced up in time to catch them all watching him curiously. 'Well, I *am* a hiker.'

'I think the problem,' Rachel Childs started to say from her position beside Harold, 'is that there are too many options for accessing the summit. You're talking a good eight miles just to get from the trailhead of Woody Gap to the summit of Blood Mountain. Then there's the Slaughter Gap side, the connection with the AT, and miscellaneous other ascents. From an ERT perspective, it's a huge search area in very difficult terrain and in very difficult conditions.'

She gestured absently toward the outside, where the rain fell in a steady drizzle.

'True, true,' Duff conceded. 'But if they were carrying bodies up the trail on litters, they must have trod a pretty decent path. We're not talking bushwhacking our way up a mountain. More like searching the bottom perimeter for the proper opening—'

'Easier said than done given the dense underbrush,' Rainie cut in.

'It will be accessible.' Quincy spoke up abruptly. 'Given what we know about the UNSUB, his skill as an outdoorsman, his aptitude for secrecy, it's quite possible that he's covered or disguised the entranceway to the trail. But the UNSUB is obviously quite familiar with this area and Blood Mountain. And the dumping grounds in particular are even more special to him, something geographic profilers refer to as a 'totem place.' It's where he can relive his fantasies, as well as alleviate his anxieties. It's the one place he feels powerful and in control. Naturally, he will want to reconnect with that feeling as much as possible by returning to the totem place.'

'So,' Rachel Childs quizzed drily, 'if we just whisper *Abracadabra,* the secret passageway will magically open up and show us the way up the mountain? Either way, we gotta find the opening to the trail. And to do that, we're gonna need help.'

'You mean the National Guard?' Duff scowled.

'No, I mean trained search experts. Presumably with dogs.'

Duff's eyes widened. 'You think cadaver dogs could catch a scent? I haven't worked with 'em much myself, but like you said, it's a good eight miles from trailhead to summit. Can a dog really catch the whiff of a decaying corpse eight miles away?'

Rachel pursed her lips. 'I don't know. I'm not a dog handler. Special Agent Quincy said the subject reported dragging the bodies up the mountain on a litter. That should leave a scent trail.'

But Harold, their resident expert on everything, was shaking his head. 'Dogs work off of scent. The human body is constantly shedding skin rafts and bacteria, creating an odor we never notice but is discernible to dogs' keen sense of smell. In the case of cadaver dogs, the scent is from decomp and starts off strong, but fades as more organic matter disappears. If these dumping grounds are too old, and too far away, there might not be enough scent for the dogs to home in on.'

'I once worked with a pair of dogs that hit on fully skeletalized bones in a dry creek bed,' Rachel countered. 'There wasn't any decaying matter left at that point, either, and they still found the bones.'

'Was the dry creek bed your target area?'

'Yes—'

'Well, there you go. The dogs were working a limited target area, which enabled them to home in on a fainter odor. But in your own words, we're not a small geographical search area. We got a whole friggin' mountain.'

'Search dogs,' Kimberly interrupted quietly. 'Forget a cadaver dog. What we need are search dogs.'

Her two teammates stopped squabbling long enough to study her.

'Why search dogs?' Rachel spoke up first. 'I thought we were looking for the bodies. At the magic totem place.'

'Who were carried up the mountain by two men, one of whom's clothing we now possess.'

Harold got it first. 'Get the socks from the boy's body,' he filled in excitedly. 'Give 'em to the dogs—'

'And tell the dogs to look for the boy. With any luck, they'll pick up his trail and follow it straight up to the dumping grounds,' Kimberly finished for him, taking another sip of scalding coffee. Her father had finally relaxed beside her, a tacit sign of approval.

'God knows the last time the men headed up the mountain,' Duff spoke up, 'I thought, for trailing dogs to work, they had to be on track within hours.'

'Not bloodhounds!' Harold supplied cheerfully. 'They can follow a scent that is weeks old, especially in these kinds of cool conditions. Sure, Labs make better cadaver dogs, but still nothing like a pair of bluetick hounds for tracking the escaped felon. Find us a pair of bloodhounds, and we have a chance.'

Everyone stared at the local cop.

'Bloodhounds? In Georgia?' Duff smiled. 'Let me make a call.'

The bloodhounds were named LuLu and Fancy, and they were handled by an old-timer who called himself Skeeter. Skeeter wore faded blue overalls and wasn't much of a people person. He spoke to Sheriff Duffy in a series of shoulder shrugs and head bobs. He didn't speak to the rest of them at all.

At Harold's insistence, they started at Highway 180, following a ridgeline Harold had picked up from the elevation map and considered the best hiking option. Despite some mutterings about 'totems,' the team had taken to heart Quincy's assertion that the subject would favor a trail that was accessible and manageable. Even killers were practical.

LuLu and Fancy started working the underbrush with Skeeter, while a German shepherd named Danielle was sent over to the Woody Gap trail with her handler. Another search team was on its way from Atlanta and would be ready to go after lunch, picking up at Lake Winfield Scott.

With LuLu and Fancy on the job, there was nothing for the rest of the task force members to do but stand around, watching the rain drip off the brim of their caps.

Kimberly wandered over to where Rachel and Harold were hanging out under the relative cover of a large fir tree, each wearing a bright yellow rain slicker. The rest of the team was parked along the road in a short train of cars, led by one very big white crime scene trailer. The trailer was their basic model, stocked with a large canopy, evidence bags and tags, surveying equipment, protective eye gear, all-weather gear, generator, tarps, and rolls of butcher paper. Already, Kimberly could tell Rachel wished she'd brought the Green Gator all-terrain vehicles for roaring over Blood Mountain. The life of an ERT leader: so many toys, so little time.

Rachel had just lifted a hand in greeting when the cell phone finally rang at Kimberly's waist. She checked the digital display, keeping her features calm while giving Rachel an apologetic shrug and heading for a quieter spot on the other side of a tree. She had to push back the hood of her raincoat to place the phone against her ear. It took her trembling fingers two tries to get it right.

'Hey,' she said into the phone, voice slightly breathless, pulse accelerated.

'Hey yourself,' Mac replied.

'Your night?'

'Bagged eight dealers, seized couple hundred pounds of cocaine. You know, the usual.'

She smiled, pinching the bridge of her nose against the pressure building behind her eyeballs. 'When'd you wrap up?'

'Two hours ago.'

'You must be tired.'

'Sleeping sounds like a terrific idea. But I wanted to call you first. You know, listen to my wife's lovely voice.'

His voice sounded edgy to her. Angry, tired, hurt? She didn't know anymore and the silence dragged on until she knew he was feeling it, too, the distance that hadn't seemed like such a big deal at first, but had now grown large enough to frighten.

'Your night?' he asked finally, his voice somber, and not at all like himself.

'There was . . . an incident.'

'Kimberly?'

'I'm okay. But the informant, the one who's been calling me. He showed up at the hotel where we were staying and shot himself.'

'Kimberly?'

'He confirmed that Dinchara has been kidnapping and killing prostitutes. The boy helped dispose of the bodies. He was one of Dinchara's victims, too, kidnapped when he was just a child. He didn't . . . He couldn't . . . He shot himself. He placed the gun on the side of his temple and blew out his brains. All over my hotel room.'

'Are you okay?' Mac asked softly.

And she surprised them both by saying, 'No. I'm not okay. I'm angry. I'm furious. I want to scream, but what's the use? I'm too late. We're all too late. This boy needed us ten years ago. We failed him. We failed Ginny Jones, we failed Tommy Mark Evans. This case is nothing but a long trail of heartaches that never should've happened. And now I'm standing at the base of something called Blood Mountain, where if I get really lucky, we'll find even more bodies dumped by the son of a bitch who started it all. I can't believe I'm going to have a baby in a world where child sex slave rings are growing larger not smaller. Where children are snatched out of their beds, or hotel rooms, or family vacations in state parks. If law enforcement is a war, then we're losing it, and I'm just . . . pissed off.'

'I'll drive up,' Mac said.

'Dammit, no. You've been up all night. Get some sleep.'

'Are you by Woody Gap trail or over by the lake?'

'You know Blood Mountain?' she asked, startled.

'I grew up here, remember?'

'Mac . . . You really should sleep.'

'Just give me two hours. What can go wrong in two hours? I love you, Kimberly, and I'll see you soon.'

The call ended. Kimberly stood behind the tree, trying to figure out if she was nervous or relieved, frightened or confused. Mostly she was aware of her pulse, still pounding too hard at the base of her neck. And rain, dripping off the tree branches, onto the top of her head and down the back of her neck, until it felt to her as if the woods were crying, and she wasn't the kind of person for such foolish notions.

So she touched her stomach instead. Gently, tentatively.

'Hello, baby,' she whispered. And a moment later, 'I'm sorry,' though she wasn't entirely sure what she was apologizing for.

Out of the corner of her eye she caught her father standing next to the road, trying to get her attention. She sighed, walking toward him.

'Have you spoken to Ginny Jones this morning?' her father wanted to know.

She shook her head, eyeing him curiously as Rainie crossed the road to where they stood.

'I have a question,' Quincy said. 'Something I'd like to ask her. It might help shed light on some things.'

Kimberly shrugged. Bloodhounds were working, the rest of them just standing around. It's not like they had anything better to do.

'All right, let's give her a call.' Kimberly dialed the county sheriff's department, putting her cell phone on speaker and holding it between herself, Quincy, and Rainie, as they huddled close.

When the phone picked up, she gave her name and requested to speak with the officer in charge of booking Ginny Jones. It took a few minutes, then a harried deputy came on the line.

'What'dya want?' he asked.

'FBI Special Agent Kimberly Quincy. I'm following up

on a recent arrest, Virginia Jones. I was wondering when she was scheduled to be arraigned—'

'Already happened.'

'Excuse me?' Her startled gaze flew to her father and Rainie, who appeared equally surprised.

'Arraignment was at nine-thirty a.m. We took her over, bail was set, and she was released at ten-fifteen—'

'*Excuse me?*' Rainie and Quincy blinked at her angry exclamation, while at the end of the line, the deputy paused.

'Well, the bail was set at ten grand,' the deputy started.

'For *accessory in the attempted murder of a federal agent?*'

'Well, the subject in question killed himself, not you, so that seemed to take the heart out of the DA's argument.'

'Ginny had no way of knowing that's what Aaron would choose to do.'

'I'm just telling you what the judge said. Bail was set at ten grand. The bond was paid—'

'By whom?'

'Umm . . .' They heard the *thunk* of a phone being set down, then a voice calling to the back of a room. 'Hey, Rick. You know who posted bail for the Jones girl? Was it a local bondsman, family? Huh. Okay.' The deputy returned. 'Not a bondsman. Some local. Had a cashier's check for ten grand. Rick assumes he knew the girl because she hugged him in the parking lot.'

Kimberly closed her eyes. 'Tell me he wasn't wearing a baseball cap.'

'Hey, Rick . . .' A moment later. 'Yep, a red baseball cap.'

'*Fuck!*' And in that moment, she got it. And she didn't know whether to laugh or to cry, so she slammed her phone shut and kicked a clump of grass instead. '*How could we have been so stupid? Goddammit, she played us like violins!*'

Her father and Rainie were looking at her wide-eyed, so she spelled it out for them, still kicking at the grass, feeling almost crazy with rage. '*You must kill the one you love*. Those are the rules. *You must kill the one you love*. Aaron Johnson died. What does that really mean?'

Quincy got it first. 'She graduated. Ginny Jones set Aaron up so she could graduate.'

'Yep, and we're the morons who let her get away. Dinchara posted her bail and picked her up. She was spotted hugging him in the parking lot. They're out, they're together, and we're screwed.'

'You don't believe . . .' Rainie started.

But their conversation was suddenly interrupted by the loud baying of a hound dog, followed by an excited shout. The three looked up to see a surge of humanity running forward, followed by more excited exclamations. The dogs had picked up the scent, pulling Skeeter and the rest of the team into the woods.

THIRTY-EIGHT

*'The jumping spider has huge eyes that detect even tiny
movements of passing insects. First, it creeps up on its prey.
Then it jumps, opening its jaws mid-flight to deliver a lethal
bite when it lands on its victim.'*

FROM *Freaky Facts About Spiders*,
BY CHRISTINE MORLEY, 2007

They hiked for hours, Lulu and Fancy straining their leads
in their eagerness to follow the scent. Harold walked beside
Skeeter, easily covering the steep, uneven trail as it wound
around tree stumps, rocky outcroppings, and washed-out
gullies. Periodically, he'd stop and tie an orange surveyor's
ribbon around a tree, marking the trail for his slower, more
human, counterparts. Rachel had also assigned Harold
camera duty, assuming he'd get to the site before everyone
else and could get to work documenting the scene.

Several ERT members stayed behind to man the van, in
touch by radio. Should need for additional supplies arise,
Rachel could call in her order, with an agent following the
orange ties up the mountain. Per protocol, everyone wore
flak jackets and carried first-aid kits as well as personal
firearms. Safety was always a primary concern, even when
pursuing dead bodies.

Kimberly fell back sooner than she would've liked. Her
mind was willing. Her body had other ideas. She could
feel a pulling sensation where the top of her thighs met
her steadily increasing abdomen. The tight stretch of
tendons and ligaments already struggling to adjust to one
demand on the body, without the additional pressure of
sprinting up a mountain. Quincy and Rainie walked

beside her. Kimberly presumed Sal was farther ahead, up with the action.

'Need to rest?' her father asked presently.

'Fine.'

'I need to rest,' Rainie announced.

'Oh, shut up. I'm pregnant, not stupid.'

Rainie grinned, and they kept moving, though it was possible that Kimberly's pace had slowed another notch. She could hear the dogs in the distance, an occasional murmur of voices. Otherwise, the woods had folded around them, a damp, green canopy that smelled of moldy leaves and decaying logs. This high up, the trail formed a series of narrow switchbacks, with dense root systems forming crude stair steps beneath their feet. The grade was steep, the footing slow going. They were all panting hard from the exertion.

'Mac call?' her father asked.

Kimberly nodded, not having enough air for speech.

'How was his evening?' Quincy continued.

'Successful drug bust.' She paused. 'He's . . . happy.'

'You tell him what happened?' her father asked mildly.

'He's driving here now,' Kimberly managed to gasp, which was answer enough.

'You said Dinchara posted Ginny's bail money?' Quincy started. 'Any idea why?'

'Maybe they're heading out of town,' Rainie ventured. She paused at the top of a switchback, reaching for water. Kimberly took advantage of the rest to draw in some deep lungfuls of air.

'He needs her,' Kimberly said at last. 'Otherwise, why would he risk showing up at the county courthouse after burning down his house? Why surrender ten grand? He bailed her out because he has a plan. I'll be damned, however, if I know what it is.'

'You think she's his accomplice?' Quincy asked.

'I don't know,' Kimberly said. 'I mean, to hear Ginny

talk, Dinchara picked her up and forced her into a life of prostitution. She's the victim. And yet . . . She lived on her own in Sandy Springs. Think of the options for running away. Instead, she sticks around for two years, even after she knows he killed her mother and engineered Tommy Mark Evans's death. The girl is smart enough to target an FBI agent, but not clever enough to run when she had the chance? I don't buy it. Whatever's going on, she's not doing it just because Dinchara told her to. She likes it. The danger, the manipulation, the violence. That girl is seriously warped.'

'Stockholm syndrome,' Quincy said quietly.

'More warped than that,' Kimberly said flatly.

'You don't like her.'

'She did try to arrange for me to die.'

'But you don't blame the boy Aaron, who held the gun.'

Kimberly shifted impatiently, angrier at this line of questioning than she knew she should be. 'Hey, from the sound of things, he had to live with Dinchara. He was taken younger, endured more.'

'But if he was taken later, endured less? What exactly is the line that separates victim from not victimized enough?'

'Well, that's the million-dollar question, isn't it?' Kimberly gave her father a look, to let him know the discussion was done. He could debate semantics all he wanted. In her mind Aaron and Ginny were not the same and that was all there was to it.

They got moving again. The sound of the dogs grew louder. They finally crested a small hill to discover the rest of the team gathered at the edge of a clearing. The dogs were working the perimeter, snuffling at bushes, backtracking, pushing ahead, backtracking. Skeeter followed patiently behind, matching them step for step as the dogs yanked his arm front and back, side to side.

'They lost the trail,' Harold reported, coming to stand beside them. 'See, the dogs can pick it up right about there,

314

but then they lose it again, hence all the forward and back, forward and back.'

Rachel was looking around the clearing with an expression Kimberly knew well.

'You think this is it,' Kimberly said, a statement, not a question.

'Got the right feel. What'd you think?'

Kimberly inspected the area. They were probably two-thirds of the way up the mountain, in a twenty-by-forty-foot clearing formed in part by a rocky ledge. The back half appeared meadowlike, a grassy field sheltered by a yawning canopy of evergreens. Toward the front, a massive rock jutted out to form a sitting area. On a clear day, the boulders probably offered a decent view, maybe even one that included skippy little Cub Scouts. All in all, a nice place to grab a bite of lunch.

Or dig a shallow grave.

'You bring the surveying equipment?' Kimberly asked Rachel.

'As if I would ever forget. Harold?'

Harold dutifully turned around, revealing a backpack with long orange rods strapped to one side. He handed over his pack, then went to discuss the matter with Skeeter and Sheriff Duffy. Kimberly started laying out supplies as Rainie and Quincy looked on with interest.

'Ever participate in an outdoor recovery?' Kimberly asked them.

They shook their heads. Quincy's role as a profiler would've had him entering the picture after the fact. Rainie might have had a chance as a small-town deputy, but apparently had managed to miss that piece of luck. Kimberly, on the other hand, assisted with at least half a dozen of these exercises a year. Like all her teammates, she'd spent a week training at the outdoor recovery school at the Forensic Anthropology Center at the University of Tennessee, better known as the Body Farm.

'Here's the drill,' she explained, picking up the first slender rod and holding it up for display. 'We're going to stand shoulder to shoulder, forming a line that stretches from one side of this clearing to the other. We'll all advance one step, probe the ground, wait for our neighbors to do the same, then advance again as a single unit. If you feel, say, a soft pocket of earth, where the soil has obviously been disturbed, or, perhaps a hard item worth further exploration, you'll flag that spot.

'When the line search is done, we'll grid and map the entire area. Then a second team will follow up on the flags, working grid by grid to process the site.'

'How do you follow up on a flag?' Rainie wanted to know.

'You get down on your stomach and dig with a trowel. Each scoop of dirt is placed in a bucket, each filled bucket is carried to a nearby spot, where it will be dumped in a mesh sifter and processed by another team. Their job will be to look for fine bone fragments, projectiles, teeth, etc. It's amazing how tiny some human bones are, particularly the ones in the fingers. If you're not sifting, you can pass 'em right by.'

Rainie had a slightly horrified look on her face. 'We're going to sift every bucket of dirt we dig up?'

'That's protocol.'

Rainie looked around at the clearing. 'We're going to be here for days.'

'Possible,' Kimberly concurred. She shrugged. 'Depends how many areas we flag. Clandestine graves inevitably appear as a series of depressions and mounds next to each other. The mound is from the dirt the killer removed to dig the grave; the depression from the grave itself as the body decomposes, causing the fill material to sink. You want to steer away from the base of big trees – the roots make it too hard to dig, even for a homicidal maniac. Finally, you want to keep your eye out for lots of weeds, which seed nicely in the loose soil of freshly turned earth. The tricky part is that old tree falls create the same pattern of mounds and depressions. Rule of thumb is "trowel it and see."'

'Why on your stomach?' Quincy wanted to know. 'That sounds awkward. Why not just dig with a spade until you hit something?'

'Because most clandestine graves are shallow. If the body is fully skeletonized, you can do real damage nicking it with a spade. Body recovery follows the same protocol of an archaeological dig – meaning we want to disturb the skeleton the least amount possible while excavating the soil all around it. You'll see us using brushes, all the stuff from the History Channel. And before we ever move a bone, we'll document the hell out of the skeleton in situ, photographing, mapping, graphing. You have to, because there's no way to remove a skeleton as a whole. Instead, when we're finally ready, we'll bag it bone by bone to be reassembled later by a forensic anthropologist.'

'You have a lot more patience than I do,' Rainie said.

'Not really.'

Harold was back with Sheriff Duffy and Sal in tow. 'Skeeter says his dogs need a break. He's not sure if they've lost the scent, or they're just getting fatigued, but either way, now would be a good time to rest. He'll take them off for a bit and we can get going on searching the clearing.'

Duff cleared his throat. 'All right, I'll assemble my men. You'll tell us what to do?'

'Absolutely.'

Duff headed over to his deputies, who were shaking out their rain gear and downing bottles of water. In five minutes, he had the group assembled and Rachel gave them the official rundown on how to probe for clandestine graves. Then Harold lined them up, the inexperienced volunteers sandwiched between the pros from the ERT. Sal ended up standing beside Kimberly, neither of them speaking, as they prepared for the first step forward.

The storm had finally passed, the rocks steaming up as the afternoon sun broke through the dark clouds. Beneath her rain poncho, Kimberly shifted restlessly, feeling the building heat, the sweaty discomfort of fabric that didn't breathe. She couldn't bring herself to look at Sal and was aware of him returning the favor.

She should say something, break the ice before Mac showed up, took one look at the both of them, and assumed the worst.

Second step. Third. Fourth. Somewhere down the line one of the deputies made an excited exclamation and Harold helped him stick in a yellow flag. Mostly, however, the officers exchanged concerned frowns. Did I just feel a dead body? What did a dead body feel like anyway? Until you'd been through the drill a few times, it was hard to know.

Kimberly found a loose pocket. Flagged it. Beside her, Sal cursed under his breath.

'What?' she asked.

'I don't know. It's . . . something. But maybe it's a rock something or a root something or a clump of dirt. It's hard, but too small to be a bone.'

'Bones can be quite small,' she supplied mildly. 'If you're not sure, flag it. Better safe than sorry.'

'I don't know how you can do this for a living,' Sal muttered, flagging the site.

'Because every now and then, we find the smoking gun. Or the body of the missing girl whose parents have had to wait four years for the funeral. Or maybe, just a gold wedding band. It doesn't sound like much, but when your loved one was on the plane that hit the Pentagon, a wedding band is all that's left. And you'll take it. You'll take anything to hold on tight and help you grieve.'

Sal opened his mouth, looked like he might say something, but then another shout went out, calling for a yellow flag. The line ordered up, and on Harold's count, took the next step forward, moving quicker now as everyone got the hang of it.

By the time they crossed the clearing, three dozen yellow flags protruded like dandelions in the meadow. Kimberly didn't like it. The spacing wasn't right. The flags were too haphazard, too random. Given the size of a shallow grave, there should be clusters of flags where multiple steps or multiple people encountered an object. There wasn't.

Kimberly could tell from ten feet back that Rachel shared her opinion. The redhead had both hands on her hips and was scowling.

'What do you want to do?' Harold was asking.

'Grid it, of course,' Rachel snapped. 'Don't have a choice really. When in doubt, trowel it out.' She ran a hand through her hair. 'We have both too many flags and not enough. Dammit.'

'We could bring up a cadaver dog,' Kimberly suggested. 'See if one hits.'

'We could've used cadaver dogs?' Sal spoke up.

'Gotta probe it first,' Rachel commented absently, chewing her lower lip. 'The probing releases the decomp gases. You allow thirty, forty minutes for everything to ripen and settle, then bring in the cadaver dog. Works like a charm.'

'It took us four hours to get up that trail,' Sal pointed out. 'No way we're gonna get a dog in the next thirty minutes. What about the bloodhounds?'

'The team is a search team, already working a scent. This'll just confuse them.' Harold spoke up. He was regarding Rachel. 'We could split the crew,' he suggested. 'Leave half of us here to start working these flags, send the other half with LuLu and Fancy, assuming they catch the scent again. Might as well check out the summit. Least then we'll have a better idea for where to start tomorrow.'

'Mountain's only so big,' Kimberly commented. 'If it's not here, it's close.'

Rachel nodded absently. 'Yeah, okay. Find Skeeter, see what he has to say about his dogs. We'll break the team in half. The tired ones' – her gaze flickered to Kimberly – 'will stay here. The maniacs' – her gaze flickered to Harold – 'can continue on to the summit, look for a better site.'

Kimberly was not amused to be lumped in with the less fit members of her team. Then again, her belly ached and she was starving. Harold went to find Skeeter. Sal announced to the group in general that now would be a good time to eat.

He followed Kimberly over to where Rainie and Quincy had taken up position on a fallen log. Quincy was munching on granola. Rainie had king-size Reese's Peanut Butter Cups. Kimberly sat next to Rainie.

'Peanut butter cup?' Rainie asked.

'Absolutely. Pudding?'

'Don't mind if I do.'

Sal had a ham sandwich, which was quickly ruled too boring by the women. They sat in comfortable silence, shedding their raincoats and munching on their snacks until Sal looked over at Kimberly, did a little double take, and went pale.

'Don't move,' he whispered.

'What?' Kimberly asked in surprise, immediately starting to move.

'DON'T MOVE!'

This time, she stilled, starting to look at Sal in alarm. 'What?' she whispered.

'Rainie,' he ordered softly, 'you're closer. There, on her shoulder, do you see it?'

'It's a spider.' Rainie spoke up, then frowned. 'Why are we this excited about a little brown spider?'

'Oh no,' Kimberly looked at Sal with dread. 'A brown recluse?'

He nodded.

'I thought they were shy,' she said weakly, very conscious now of the exposed skin on her neck, the scoop collar of her shirt, the salty sweat drying at the base of her throat.

'Maybe they like peanut butter cups.' Sal had put down his sandwich. He stood, took a step closer, eyes on her left shoulder. 'I'm going to try to do this quickly.'

'Is it on my shirt?'

'Not quite.'

She closed her eyes. 'You have to be committed, Sal. Once you move, just get the damn thing off. If you hesitate . . . the spider will panic and bite.'

'I know, I know.'

Rainie and Quincy had gotten to their feet, clearly very concerned. Then Rainie glanced over at Quincy, yelled, 'Shit,' and slapped his collarbone. He was still looking confused when Rainie went after his shoulder and the top of his thigh.

'One, two, three,' Sal counted quickly, and smacked Kimberly's shoulder. The minute he did, she leapt from the log, whirling around.

'Holy crap,' Sal cried out and whacked her back three times.

'What is it? What is it?'

'Spiders. There are . . . spiders. Everywhere.'

The four fell back from the log. And now Kimberly could just make them out, thin, delicate brown bodies running across the crumbling bark, looking desperately for a place to hide.

Rainie was dancing around, trying to check her front, her back, her sides, while Quincy ordered her to stay still so he could help out. Then Sal was spinning in little circles, checking his shoes and socks, the bare skin of his calves.

Kimberly watched them all, looking from the people to the spider-covered log to the people again. Crawford-Hale had told them that brown recluses were shy. She had said it would be uncommon to encounter them, and yet here was an entire infestation.

At the end of a trail that had been hiked by Dinchara and his captive. In a clearing that would be perfect for disposing bodies, except none of the flags made sense.

And in that moment, it came to her. What she had been told in the beginning. What she should have remembered from the start.

Kimberly stepped closer to the log.

And looked up.

THIRTY-NINE

*My first few weeks of freedom, I didn't know what to do.
I moved into a Best Western hotel, flush with cash, eager to
live the high life. I bought my first video game, and spent
ninety-six hours staring at the screen until my eyes grew
bloodshot and I passed out from the force of my headache.*

*I walked the five miles back to the store to buy a new
game, and while I was there, fell in love with a Huffy bike.
So I bought that, too, and new clothes and clean
underwear. And that made me feel so good, I bought
Henrietta her very own glass terrarium with colored
pebbles and a shallow drinking bowl. I set her up on top of
the TV, where she could watch me play video games all
night long, my hands jittery from lack of sleep, my skin
growing more and more pasty white.*

*Couldn't rest, couldn't relax, couldn't stop staring at the
door. Waiting for the knock to come. Waiting for the door
to swing open and reveal the Burgerman, looming in the
hallway with his bloody, caved-in skull.*

*'Boy,' he shouted in my dreams. 'Did you really think
you could kill a monster like me?' And then he'd laugh and
laugh and laugh until I woke up drenched in cold sweat,
screaming, absurdly, for my mother.*

I played a lot of video games those first few weeks.

By week three, the manager was watching me every time I appeared for free breakfast bagels. One morning, he asked me if he could see ID. I panicked, stuttering like an idiot, then pulled it together long enough to tell him I had to get it from my room.

I ran all the way to the store for three heavy-duty duffel bags. Back in the hotel room, I packed up everything, including Henrietta. Minute it was dark, we were outta there. Fuckin' manager.

I found a youth hostel, figured I'd be less conspicuous surrounded by other lone teens. The place wasn't much. Spartan room, no community TV. First night, someone stole my bike. Second night, someone stole my video console.

Henrietta and I took off again. Running from place to place, little sleep, little food, little time to rest. Have to keep moving. Burgerman is coming.

I'd wanted a better life. Thought I'd live in a clean apartment in a nice section of town. I'd thought, having finally slayed the dragon, that I could be normal again.

I ended up right back on the same streets Burgerman had used as his hunting grounds, smoking crack cocaine and doing my best never to come back down to earth.

Then the money ran out. I crashed. Woke up in a pool of vomit, everything stolen but the bag Henrietta lived in.

And it occurred to me for the first time that the Burgerman really was gone. No more running back to a seedy apartment. No more demanding ten bucks because I'd earned it. No more Hostess Twinkies magically appearing in the cupboards.

The Burgerman was dead and I was alone.

I cried like an idiot for hours. Blubbered inconsolably, curled up next to a Dumpster, terrified of my aloneness, hating the uselessness of my tears. I took Henrietta out of the duffel bag and placed her on my bare collarbone. Begged her to bite me, to put me out of my misery. Begged her to do her worst.

She just sat there, stroking my neck with one hairy leg, until finally I calmed, shuddered, and fell asleep. When I woke again, Henrietta was sitting three inches from me, devouring a cockroach. I watched her for a bit, admiring her dainty precision as she ripped off the roach's head, sucked out the juicy insides, started mashing the entire carcass into a buggy pulp.

Another cockroach went scampering by. I grabbed its fat body between my forefinger and thumb and popped it into my mouth. First bite, a terrible warm, salty liquid gushed over my tongue. I spit the bug out, gagging, swiping at my lips with the back of my hand. I'd leave roaches to Henrietta. I wanted a Twinkie.

Except I didn't have any money, a street address, or valid photo ID. I'd gone from being the Burgerman's plaything to a homeless punk. So I did the logical thing. I propositioned the next six men that happened by. Soon enough I had room money for the night.

Was this all there was for me? Endless days of dropping my pants for fat, hairy men who could only get it up by screwing kids? Maybe on a good day getting a free joint or acid hit to make it all less real, more manageable?

Henrietta was the one who lived in the cage, yet I was the one who couldn't get free.

And then I remembered — I still had Burgerman's movies, tucked safely and securely beneath Henrietta's watchful eyes in that last duffel bag. Hours and hours of videotape. These men loved that kind of shit.

I sold the first tape for fifty bucks. Guy liked it so much, he was back in four hours, offering me a thousand dollars for the whole lot, his eyes overbright, the saliva pooling over his lower lip. In that moment, I knew I was onto something. I sold him one more tape for five hundred, then marched down to the nearest electronic store to invest in my newfound business.

Store manager was very helpful, especially once he

realized they were 'home movies.' Suddenly, he had a back room he needed to show me. Except this time, he was the one on his knees and I was the one with the power. I liked it. I really, really liked it.

Bob taught me things. How to edit, slice and dice, and scramble three hours of video into eight different home videos, all available to resell. He bought me my first computer. He introduced me in the right chat rooms, where online users identified as Fuckemdead and Justwantpussy educated me in the finer points of setting up my new home-based business – kiddie porn.

I learned how to tap the larger international market, where commercial websites such as mine could store valuable images on a variety of servers, making it difficult to trace. Or, as law enforcement officials grew smarter, how to break a single image into component parts, with each fragment hidden in a different corner of the world. The digital age, making life easier all the time.

Child porn is a spectrum. The low-end 'cheap users' will settle for a sexed-up photo of a young child fully clothed, but perhaps provocatively posed. Then there's the hardcore addicts. The serious buyers. They want the kids under the age of twelve, female, and screaming.

Like all businesses, porn follows the money. There are over ten thousand websites out there. And ninety-one percent of them feature prepubescent kids, screaming.

Bob, it turned out, liked that. And when he found out nothing could shock me, Bob was a very happy guy. Happy enough that he started to really piss me off.

So one day, I went to his apartment and beat him to death with a Louisville Slugger. I don't know why I did it. Maybe because it was spring, and everywhere I went I could smell freshly turned earth. Or maybe because it had rained the night before and that made me want to kill someone.

I took his computer and recording equipment, plus the

fake ID he'd graciously supplied. Henrietta and I once more hit the road.

We wandered. I was older now, less conspicuous. I bought a car, found a cheap apartment, one where the neighbors never noticed anything. I spent my days on the Internet, surfing chat rooms, YouTube, MySpace. I learned there are a lot of lonely kids out there who think I honestly want to be their friend. And I learned there are a lot of parents out there even more naive than my own.

I slept an hour or two at a time during the day, then prowled the Internet at night. I made a lot of money and used it to stock up on tequila, so when the bad spells hit, and the darkness descended for days at a time, and all I could hear was kids screaming, or the Burgerman grunting, or the scrape of a shovel carving out hard-packed earth, I could pour tequila down my throat a bottle at a time. I offered the worms to Henrietta, but she wouldn't eat them.

One night, half a bottle into it, trying to explain to Henrietta how much I needed to sleep, I was hit by a great idea. Henrietta had been there. Henrietta had helped kill the Burgerman. And Henrietta slept all the time. Why? Because she had eight eyes, she could see in all directions.

So I marched down to the nearest tattoo parlor, Henrietta sitting on my shoulder, playing with my hair. I told the guy exactly what I wanted. And when he blanched and tried to talk me out of it, I plopped down five thousand dollars in cash and took a seat, bottle of tequila still in hand. I screamed for the next five hours, till he got the job done. It hurt like a son of a bitch for another month, my forehead swollen and hot to the touch.

First day the swelling went down, I slept for four consecutive hours. I told Henrietta she was brilliant. And I knew at that moment, I was going to survive. I was going to win. Henrietta had saved me.

Then one day I saw him. He was playing basketball in the park. Undersized, but wiry. The scrawny little kid who's learned to compensate for his lack of height by moving fast. He went for a layup, and I caught the movement out of the corner of my eye. For a moment, I had a sense of déjà vu so strong I couldn't breathe.

The boy looked exactly like me. Twenty years ago. When I had had a name. When I had had a family. When I had had a future.

And I knew what I must do.

You think you're safe. You think you're middle-class, suburban, the right car, the nice home. You think bad things happen to other people – maybe the poor schmucks in trailer parks where the ratio of kids to registered sex offenders can be as low as four to one.

But not to you, never to you. You're too good for this.

Do you own a computer? Because if you do, I am in your child's bedroom.

Do you have an online personal profile? Because if you do, I know your child's name, pet, and favorite hobbies.

Do you have a webcam? Because if you do, I'm right now convincing your child to take off his or her shirt in return for fifty bucks. Just a shirt. What can it hurt? Come on, it's fifty bucks.

Listen to me. I am the Burgerman.

And I'm coming for you.

FORTY

'The Portia spider is a real cannibal. It creeps into another spider's web and tugs on the silk. The web owner crawls toward the intruder, thinking it has trapped an insect. Then the Portia spider attacks, kills and eats the surprised web spider.'

FROM *Freaky Facts About Spiders*,
BY CHRISTINE MORLEY, 2007

Kimberly didn't see anything at first. Then the wind blew and she caught the shape, swaying gently fifteen feet above her head, almost like a pinecone, except the size was much too large.

'Rachel! Harold!' she cried out excitedly. 'Everyone, look up! The bodies are in the trees! They're *hanging* from the tree limbs.'

She was vaguely aware of other people, leaping to their feet with startled exclamations, and stumbling back to regard the branches overhead. Mostly she kept her eyes on a long, oblong shape swathed in a mottled green and brown fabric. Now she could make out the narrow tip of bound feet, moving up to the wider expanse of shoulders, the rounded shape of a head. It looked like an Egyptian mummy, wrapped in cloth and rope, then suspended for all eternity.

The wind blew again, the long, narrow form rocking with an eerie quiet that prickled the skin of her forearms.

'What the hell,' Sal whispered beside her. Behind them came another shout, then another, as others started to spot the macabre forms dangling above their heads.

'He thinks he's a spider, remember?' Kimberly murmured. 'So he's wrapped them in a cocoon, suspended them from his web. My God, no wonder no one ever found them. Whoever thinks to look up?'

'Silk,' Quincy supplied behind them. 'Old Army parachutes, that would be my guess. Silk because it's fitting, Army camouflage because it blends better with the trees.'

'Nylon,' Kimberly stated. 'Aaron told me. It's a practical concern – silk is fragile, yielding to total decay in under thirty-five months. Same with wool. Cotton does slightly better, making it to forty-eight months, while nylon shows no sign of deterioration even after four years. It's the toughest fabric around.'

Her father was regarding her with a small smile. 'I stand corrected. Nice work, Agent.'

'Well, don't get all mushy on me yet. I still have no idea how we're going to get the corpses down.'

Harold had returned to the center of the clearing. Rachel, too. Kimberly and Sal went to meet them, huddling for a powwow, while the deputies and ERT members continued to search the branches overhead.

'We're up to ten bodies and counting,' Harold exclaimed. 'I'm sticking a yellow flag at the base of every tree, on the side where the body is hung.'

'We'll need the Total Station,' Rachel declared, chewing her lower lip as she worked through the logistics of their next moves. 'Only way to graph a crime scene that's literally in midair. I'll call down, have Jorge and Louise bring it up. We'll need a survey marker, however, as our reference point. Harold?'

'I can check the USGS map in my pack. Otherwise, the command post can access the website for the nearest marker. I'm sure it's somewhere fairly accessible; the USGS folks don't like traipsing through the underbrush any more than the rest of us.'

'Okay. We'll bring up the Total Station, shoot the reference point, then start by graphing the site as a whole, before diagramming each body as a mini scene. Speaking of which, we'll need rolls of butcher paper, body bags, evidence bags for the rope, and litters to get the bodies off the mountain. We should also put a call in to the ME's office, so they can arrange transport. Let's see, that leaves us with . . . generator, floodlights. . . . Can I get a Green Gator up that trail we just hiked?'

'No,' Harold said.

'Different path?'

'No.'

'Shit.' Rachel went back to chewing her bottom lip. 'I'm activating two more teams. If hiking's the only way we're gonna get this done, we need more legs—'

'Hey, hey, HEY!' came a fresh cry from deep in the woods. 'I got movement. I swear to God – this one's *alive*.'

'Holy crap!' Rachel said, then they all started to run.

'We need a ladder,' one of the deputies was declaring.

'No, wait, I can shoot it down,' declared another.

Rachel muscled her way between the two uniforms, standing staunchly beneath a thick fir tree. 'Back away. Bodies are my business.'

The deputies backed away.

Rachel stood with her hands on her hips, studying the wrapped shape overhead. Kimberly spotted the activity the same time her team leader did. A bulge down low. Then a faint ripple up high.

It sent a fresh chill up her neck and she could tell from the uneasy look on Rachel's face that the team leader didn't think the body was alive, either.

'Harold?' Rachel asked quietly.

'I don't know,' Harold said, his voice as subdued as Kimberly had ever heard it.

'We have to check,' Rachel murmured. 'Just in case. You

never know.' But she didn't sound happy about it. She sounded deeply concerned.

The team leader took a deep breath. 'All right, we lay down tarp, right over here.' She delineated an area with her finger, roughly below the dangling cocoon. 'We'll need to lower the form onto the tarp, then we can safely unwrap it. Harold?'

He had wandered over to the trunk of the tree, which he was now skimming with his fingers. 'See these holes? At regular intervals? I'm thinking the subject has spiked shoes, maybe like the kind worn by utility workers to climb telephone poles. He used them to ascend the tree to throw the rope over the higher branches. Then he could return below and pull on the end of the rope. Would take a fair amount of muscle, but then again, there might be some kind of pulley system at the top. Or, he had help. Or both.'

'Can you tell what kind of rope?' Rachel wanted to know.

'Let's find out.' Harold dug out a pair of binoculars and started to adjust them. 'Looks like . . . nylon. Holy crap! The whole thing's dancing now. Rachel, I don't think . . .'

'I know, I know. But we gotta be sure, Harold. It's the only way.'

Harold took a steadying breath. 'I'll climb up.' He tested a few branches with his hand. 'I think I can get high enough that I can lean out and cut the rope without disturbing the knot.'

'And then the poor soul can crash to the ground?' Rachel inquired.

'Oh, oh yeah. Hmmm. I'll climb up,' Harold said again, 'get closer to the rope and see what our options are.'

'Okay, you do that.'

Harold donned a pair of heavy-duty leather gloves and started to climb, working his way gingerly from branch to branch.

Sal moved over to where Kimberly was taking in the action. 'How do you get a body out of a tree?' he asked.

'I have no idea,' she murmured. 'Never came up at Body Recovery School.'

'That body's not alive, is it?'

'I doubt it.'

'Then what's making it move?'

'We'll find out soon enough.'

Harold was ten feet up, dangling out on a limb now, edging closer to the body. The tree branch dipped down precariously. Harold whistled nervously.

'I found the end of the rope,' he called out. 'He has kind of . . . an elaborate system here. From what I can tell, the rope loops around a variety of branches, almost like a pulley system. I think if I partially cut the rope here, then climb up to the highest branch and yank hard, I might gain enough rope to lower the body to the ground. At least, fairly close.'

'How close?' Rachel demanded.

'I don't fucking know,' Harold called out in exasperation, which raised Rachel's and Kimberly's eyebrows as they'd never heard Harold swear before. He seemed to catch himself, soldier on. 'We could try a ladder,' he started to say, then, 'ah jeez.'

The body was moving again. The nylon bulging around the crisscross pattern of the rope wrapped around the mummified form. It didn't look like arms and legs struggling to get free. It looked . . . alien. A separate life-form, rippling beneath the surface.

'Rachel?' Harold called down in a strained voice.

'All right. Do what you think is best. But save the knot.'

'No shit, Sherlock,' Harold muttered, earning more raised brows.

There was the sawing sound of Harold working on the rope. Then a deep, concerned sigh before Harold resumed his climb up to the higher point of the subject's pulley system.

This limb was noticeably thinner than the lower branch, and as Harold once again eased out on his stomach, the branch began to dip. Then several things happened at once.

The rope snapped at the half-sawed cut, whipping up the tree with a scissoring slice. Harold yelped, grabbed for the nylon line with his gloved hands, and the whole body careened down five feet before yanking to a halt.

'Holy mother of . . .' Harold exclaimed. 'I can't . . . It's gonna . . . *Shit!*'

He lost the end, and the body crashed down another five feet before the rope tangled and the body lurched to a halt. Harold wasted no time, sliding down the tree trunk in a shower of green needles. He reached the lower branches, shimmied straight out, and grabbed the rope again.

'Incoming!' He untangled the line. The body dropped, two deputies rushing to grab the form and lower it gently onto the waiting tarp.

This close it was easy to discern the tightly bound shape of a human body, wrapped in a camouflage-patterned fabric, bound with brown rope. The nylon material rippled again, and with a little yelp, one of the officers fell back.

'All right,' Rachel said, taking control of the situation as Harold swung out of the tree and everyone gathered around the twitching form. 'Anyone who is not me drop back. We're gonna do this slow and controlled.' She donned booties, as well as a hairnet, mask, and gloves. The tarp was the crime scene, meant to catch whatever trace evidence fell out from the nylon wrapping. Rachel's job was to limit cross-contamination of the scene.

'I'll do it,' Harold said immediately, reaching for the knife Rachel had in her hands.

'It's okay, Harold. This is why I get the big bucks.'

Despite her brash tone, Rachel approached the form warily. For the first time, Kimberly could catch the smell. Decay, light but pervasive.

Harold hunkered down at the edge of the tarp. Kimberly

moved closer to him. Sal, too. They watched as Rachel gingerly made her way across the blue plastic, eyeing the thick rope that started at the ankles and wound all the way up the body.

She was looking for knots, Kimberly knew. It was always important to preserve knots. Just ask the officers who pursued the BTK killer in Kansas.

Rachel found the first knot at the ankles. She went an inch above it, slid the blade of her knife beneath the rope, and carefully sawed through the tough nylon. It took some time. Then the rope gave, falling away from the feet. Rachel pulled gently, easing the rope from underneath the body, slowly starting to unwind.

The whole form shifted slightly, seemed to sigh. Rachel caught herself, continued on. She was crouched above the head now, the majority of the body directed away from her, allowing for a quicker getaway.

She fished the last of the rope from around the neck. Now Kimberly could see the folds of the nylon fabric, how it wrapped around the form.

'All right,' Rachel said quietly. 'I'm gonna start at the middle. Everyone, look sharp.'

She stood up. Bent over. Grabbed the first seam of fabric at the body's waist, gave it a firm tug.

The form exploded. *Like Jiffy Pop,* Kimberly thought wildly. The unbound material burst open and a flood of spiders poured out, black and brown, big and small, eight-legged shapes scurrying desperately from their nylon prison while Rachel screamed and fell back, and Harold leapt to his feet, shouting, 'Well, look at that!'

Then a rifle boomed from the trees and red bloomed across Harold's shoulder and he exclaimed a second time, 'Well, look at that!'

Harold fell to the ground.

'Take cover!' Rachel cried, already scrambling for the bushes.

As Sal fell on Harold's injured form, Kimberly leapt toward her father and Rainie's side, hunkered behind a larger boulder.

As they all learned what the Burgerman knew how to do best.

FORTY-ONE

'Experiments with the venom of the brown recluse have shown that both sexes are capable of inflicting poisonous bites to mammals.'

FROM B*iology of the Brown Recluse Spider,* BY JULIA MAXINE HITE, WILLIAM J. GLADNEY, J. L. LANCASTER, JR., AND W. H. WHITCOMB, DEPARTMENT OF ENTOMOLOGY, DIVISION OF AGRICULTURE, UNIVERSITY OF ARKANSAS, FAYETTEVILLE, MAY 1966

The rain stopped, the sun breaking through briefly before once more being replaced by the gray pall of dusk. By mutual agreement, Rita and the boy didn't turn on any lights. They maintained their vigil from the relative sanctuary of the shadowed kitchen, supping on cheese and crackers, the occasional sip of orange juice.

Together, they had wrestled an old armoire through the house, propping it against the back door, which Rita perceived as the weakest point in their line of defense. Next, Rita had brought down old linens, holding them in place while the boy tacked them over the lower-level windows. She didn't want the man peering in, watching their movements, planning his attack. And if he did break the glass, she hoped the tangle of old fabric would buy them precious minutes. Three, four? She wasn't sure, and as she and the boy went from room to room, reinforcing and reconfiguring, it occurred to her that their hastily erected defenses, geared at keeping one man out, inevitably trapped both of them in.

She did not tell the boy this. He had his knife strapped to his thigh with a strip of cloth he'd torn off an old pillowcase. She thought he had enough on his mind.

She didn't dial 911, or bother to contact the local sheriff. Mostly because she knew the boy would bolt before talking to men in uniforms. Also, what was there to say? She and the boy were at war. They knew their enemy. They understood the battle that must be fought. But in practical terms, she had nothing to report.

She had never met the man who lived in the old Victorian. She had never spoken with him, never looked him in the eye. She feared now her first glimpse of him would be her last. But she was tough, she had her Colt pistol. She liked to believe that she and the boy would have the last laugh yet.

By five p.m., as the sun sank and the shadows grew long, she yawned conspicuously. It had been a long night, followed by a longer day. She yearned to stretch out on the parlor loveseat, rest her tired bones.

They should sleep in shifts. Isn't that what sentinels were supposed to do? She wished Joseph's ghost could talk, because she'd never been at war before and she could use some advice.

The boy was studying her, waiting to see what she would do next.

She said, 'You should take a nap. Sleep until midnight, then we both must look sharp.'

'I'm fine.'

'Nonsense, child. Even soldiers rest. What're we gonna do tomorrow if neither of us sleep tonight?'

'He'll come.'

'But he's not here yet. So sleep, child. While you can.'

He scowled, but her words must've made some sense, or he was even more tired than she had guessed, for he nodded reluctantly and dragged himself toward the stairs.

'I'll set a timer,' she called out softly behind him. 'Wake you in six hours.'

'Three,' he said stubbornly. 'Then it's your turn.'

'Six. At my age, there is no such thing as sleep.

The body seems to know that eternal rest is coming soon enough.'

The boy didn't argue anymore. She thought his shoulders were more hunched than she remembered, his feet scuffing across the floor like a dead man walking. He expected the worst, she realized. Every night, when he went to bed, he expected not to wake up again.

She wondered how long it had been like that for him. And even if they made it through tonight, what did morning really mean for a boy like him? She thought if he ever chose to talk, he would tell stories not even Joseph could have imagined.

And she wished she were younger, because, Lord help her, she would like to keep this child. She would hold him close, smooth his hair when he woke up screaming in the middle of the night, take his hand on the bad days, when all his memories were dark and he forgot that he was still innocent and loveable and good. That the bad things were not his fault. That there were people in the world, people like her, who were proud to know him.

She had never been much for prayer. In Rita's world, if you wanted something, you set out yourself to get it done. But she prayed now. Because night was falling. Because she loved this child. And because she knew, from the bottom of her heart, that an almost ninety-year-old woman did not stand a chance against someone like the man on the hill.

Fate was coming for her. She prayed to be strong and mostly, to save the boy.

Rita dozed off. She didn't mean to, but she must've, because next thing she knew, the doorbell rang, and she startled upright, almost falling out of her little wooden chair next to the kitchen table.

The doorbell was followed by a light knock, so Rita planted her hands against the table and struggled to her feet. Curiosity, more than anything, led her to the front parlor, Colt tucked in the waistband of Joseph's old pants, hidden by the encompassing shape of his favorite green flannel shirt.

Would the bad man be so audacious as to simply show up and knock? Maybe for all her strategizing, she had missed the most important piece of the puzzle – the boy did not belong to her, and if the man appeared with police officers demanding the boy's return, there was nothing she could do.

She was wrestling with that piece of knowledge when she arrived at the front door, gingerly pulling back one corner of a draped sheet to peer out the side window. Not a hulking, scary man after all. Just the girl from down the street, chomping away on a wad of gum while holding the neighbor's big ol' black tomcat by the scruff of its neck.

Midnight must've done something in the girl's yard. Maybe buried a few presents in the garden, or eaten her favorite chipmunk. Rita didn't see what the girl could complain about, given that she lived in a double-wide and most of her front yard consisted of crabgrass. Rita had never really spoken to the girl, just seen her come and go during the odd hours of the night, probably working at a local bar doing God knows what.

The girl knocked again, looking impatient now, so Rita went to work on the locks.

She'd barely opened the door before the girl thrust the cat at her. The tomcat yowled. The girl shook him impatiently.

'This your cat?'

'That's Midnight. He belongs next door.'

'If he belongs next door, then what the hell was he doing sitting on your patio? Looks to me like he feels mighty comfy here.'

'Midnight's a tomcat. He feels comfortable anywhere.'

The girl scowled as if she didn't believe Rita, taking a step into the house, still wielding the cat.

'I'm telling you now, I've had it to here with this damn

cat. You like him at all, you'd better start keeping him inside, 'cause the next time I catch him digging up my yard, I'm filling his backside with buckshot.'

'For the last time—'

'Rita.'

The voice came from behind her, so quiet she barely heard it. Rita half-turned, saw the boy standing in the doorway. And she could tell from the look on his face that she'd made a mistake, a horrible, horrible mistake.

'Hey, Scott,' the girl said flatly. 'Burgerman says hi.'

The girl flung the tomcat at Rita. Rita fell back, her feet tangling in Joseph's baggy pants. The next instant, she crashed to the ground, her old brittle hip giving with a *crack* as Midnight raked his claws over her forearm, then went springing across the parlor.

'Run,' Rita cried feebly to the boy. 'Run!'

The boy took off. The girl paused long enough to slap Rita across the face and produce a fistful of zip ties.

'I'll deal with him, soon enough.' The girl dispassionately looped one tie around Rita's tiny wrists and yanked it tight. 'That'll keep you busy for a bit, old lady.'

Then the girl slammed the front door shut and set out after the boy.

Rita remained on the floor, the pain in her hip spreading steadily down her body, rooting her in place. She could not move her legs. She could not move her hands. Her first confrontation with evil and she hadn't even made it thirty seconds.

Her eyes stung. She thought she might cry and that bothered her so much, she rolled onto her stomach, gritted her teeth against the dizzying pain, and started to crawl.

'Joseph,' she whispered. 'Be patient for my soul, brother dear. Help me tonight. One last night. Then I will be with you soon enough.'

FORTY-TWO

'Spider evolution, though, has mostly murderous ends.'

FROM 'SPIDER WOMAN,' BY BURKHARD BILGER,

New Yorker, MARCH 5, 2007

Gunfire. Lots of it. In all directions.

The deputies had spooked. Maybe the federal agents, as well. Most had drawn their handguns and were firing wildly into the trees, trying to provide enough cover for Sal to drag Harold out of the clearing, toward the massive boulder that sheltered Kimberly, Rainie, and Quincy.

Rachel Childs was fifteen feet away, hunkered down behind a tree, Glock in one hand, radio in the other. She was screaming at the top of her lungs, 'Officer down, officer down. We are under fire. I repeat, we need immediate backup and medical assistance. I want choppers, SWAT, National Guard, I don't fucking care, just get me armed choppers and a medical evac now, now, *now*. We are on Blood Mountain. Requesting *immediate* assistance.'

Kimberly had her Glock drawn, mentally urging Sal on as she scanned the surrounding woods for sign of the gunman. Sal made it two feet. Three. Another rifle shot cracked in the distance. Sal dropped on top of Harold's body, shielding the fallen agent's face with his arms as bark exploded off the tree beside him.

'There,' Quincy breathed. 'Over there. To the left.'

He pointed with his finger and Kimberly obediently opened fire, allowing Sal to dart up again, grab Harold under the armpits, and heave. He wasn't going to make it. Not one man pulling one hundred and eighty pounds of deadweight across such an expanse. Someone needed to help him.

She tensed her legs immediately, ready to leap out, and then . . .

She stopped.

She wasn't going to go out there. She couldn't go out there.

She was pregnant. She could risk herself, but she had no right to risk her child. Oh God, she was going to become a mom and one of her first acts of motherhood was going to be staying behind this damn boulder, watching as her own teammate was gunned down.

The rifle cracked again, a distant boom with local consequences. Sal dropped. Kimberly opened fire. Her teammates joined in, a last-ditch effort against an enemy they couldn't see.

Beside her, Quincy was breathing hard, one hand on Rainie's shoulder, his other on Kimberly's arm as he scanned the trees with an intent look.

'Kimberly,' he started.

'Go,' she gritted out. 'Help him, dammit. Someone has to help him.'

Quincy dashed out. And Kimberly resumed cover fire, aware of Rainie's taut form beside her and the tears now pouring down both of their cheeks.

Another shot rang out, just as Quincy reached Sal's side. The GBI agent flinched, but did not go down. Quincy grabbed Harold's right arm. Sal grabbed his left. They started to run, Harold's limp body crashing across the bumpy ground.

Just as Kimberly thought they might make it, that heroism would indeed persevere, another shot rang out, and Sal lurched to his left and tumbled down.

Vaguely, she was aware of Sheriff Duffy rising from behind a dead tree fall. Rifle butt against his shoulder, sighting a light that had flashed in the distance, pulling the trigger. The crack of the rifle, the jerk of his solid body, absorbing the recoil.

Then Quincy had dragged Harold to safety, and Rainie had her arm around Sal's shoulders, guiding him behind the rock.

Duff ducked back down.

The forest finally, eerily, fell silent.

Harold's shoulder looked bad. Kimberly ripped open his shirt, trying to clear dirt and debris from the pulpy mess. Harold's pulse was erratic, his eyes rolled back into his head. If he didn't get immediate medical attention, he wasn't going to make it.

Sal propped himself up against the boulder, holding his side. Rainie had tugged away his white dress shirt to reveal a deep furrow along his left rib cage. The wound appeared painful, but on a relative scale, he was in good shape and knew it.

'We need first-aid supplies,' Kimberly murmured. 'Bandages, saline flush, an antiseptic solution. It's all in the packs.'

'Where are the packs?' her father asked promptly.

Kimberly jerked her head toward the other side of the boulder, and her father peered around long enough to wince.

'That's not going to be easy,' he observed. Most of the packs were still in the clearing, a good twenty feet of exposed space away.

'Gotta do something because Harold's going from bad to worse and it's not like an ambulance is gonna come crashing through those woods.'

'I'll do it,' Sal said, already struggling to his feet.

'Oh, shut up and sit down. You've earned enough glory for one afternoon. Time to share the wealth.'

Sal tried to appear offended, but as testimony to his level of pain, stayed seated. 'You're not going to . . .'

'Nope, I'm playing the role of Florence Nightingale. Which means Dad or Rainie can go for the John Wayne number.'

'We'll both go,' Rainie decided. 'With any luck, the guy is indecisive and two targets will slow him down.'

Kimberly arched a brow to show what she thought of that logic, but didn't argue. She rolled up her rain jacket as a pillow and placed it under Harold's feet, then put two fingers in her mouth and whistled. Rachel's head obediently appeared from around the tree. Kimberly communicated their game plan in a series of silent hand motions. Rachel nodded, and bit by bit, the plan was communicated down the line.

When Rachel reappeared, Kimberly counted down from five on one hand. As she folded her fingers into a fist, Quincy and Rainie dashed out and the agents in the forest once again opened fire.

Five, six, seven, eight. Rainie and Quincy arrived at the packs. Grabbed one for each hand. *Ten, eleven, twelve, thirteen.* Scrambled for the safety of the boulder, shoulders hunched, legs bent, trying to form a smaller target.

Fourteen, fifteen, sixteen . . .

Rainie and Quincy careened around the boulder, dropped to the ground, and the woods once again fell silent.

Kimberly resumed breathing just in time to realize that Sal had passed out cold. So she ripped open an antiseptic towelette from the first-aid kit and placed it against his bloody side.

Sal awoke with a scream, and from somewhere far away Kimberly could swear she heard a man laugh.

'I gotta get moving,' Sal was muttering over and over again. 'Gotta get down the mountain. Owe it to my mother . . . Isn't fair.'

Rachel had made it behind the boulder. She had taken

over Harold's care, bathing the agent's wound in saline solution before covering it with sterile gauze. She glanced up now, and frowned at Sal's sweat-slicked face.

'Shock?' she murmured to Kimberly.

'No,' Sal answered the senior team leader, wincing through clenched teeth. 'Just . . . being practical. Losing one son . . . hard enough.'

He had himself to sitting now, back against the boulder, breathing hard.

'Stop moving,' Kimberly barked at him, voice low. 'You're a terrible patient.'

'Think he's . . . still around?'

'Let's put it this way – when the choppers show up with their big guns, I'll feel better about things.'

She kept her tone light, but both she and Rachel exchanged glances. The radio had continued crackling until Rachel had finally turned it down, fearing it would draw the shooter to them. Ten minutes had gone by without fresh activity, but it was hard to know if that was a good sign or not. Had the shooter given up, or was he circling through the woods, due to pop up at any time, right behind them?

Quincy had taken over Kimberly's Glock .40 and between him and Rainie were doing their best to keep watch. But there was no mistaking the vulnerability that came from knowing they were on the shooter's home turf, not their own.

Out on the tarp, the decomposed body had finally stopped moving. Even the spiders had fled and now only the partially mummified corpse remained, a silent reminder of just what Dinchara could do.

Kimberly returned her attention to Sal, bringing a small bottle of water to his lips. He looked worse than she would expect from such a wound, but Rachel was right, that could be the shock of the incident, followed by the adrenaline dump of remaining in perilous circumstances.

'Your mother still alive?' she asked Sal now, wanting to keep him talking while she mopped at his forehead and inspected his side.

'Yes.' She pressed the jagged flesh a little too hard and he sucked in a breath. 'Hey—'

'Sorry, grass. Your father?'

'Don't . . . know.' She removed a fresh piece of dirt, he gritted his teeth. 'She kicked him out . . . years ago. Finally . . . got wise . . . it wasn't her fault.'

'What wasn't her fault?'

'My brother's disappearance.'

'He ran away?'

Sal shook his head. 'Abducted. He was only nine. Too young . . . for life on the street.'

Kimberly regarded him. She had a vague memory of talking to Sal about his family once before. 'Then again,' she countered softly, 'you implied once that your father was pretty quick with his fists . . .'

Sal shook his head again, shifting restlessly as he struggled to ease the pain in his side. 'Got worse . . . afterward. Old man couldn't find his son . . . drank more.'

'Sorry.'

'Yeah, well, these things . . . happen. Been a long time now. You feel the scar . . . don't think about the wound underneath. Then little things will tug it open. Line from a movie. Picture of a boy on an old Huffy bike. That damn photo of Aaron Johnson in Ginny's purse.'

'Why the photo of Aaron Johnson?'

'You kiddin'? The dark hair, pointy face, sunken eyes? Could be a family photo, don't you think?'

Kimberly shrugged. She had never truly contemplated the picture of Aaron Johnson alive. She was too busy seeing him dead on her hotel room floor.

'You wanna hear something funny?' Sal was saying, looking a little better now, some of the color returning to his face. 'My brother's abduction – that's why I became a cop. The lead detective, Ron Mercer, seemed tough, you know? Cool, calm, and collected. Figured if I could be as tough as a cop, bad things wouldn't happen anymore.' He smiled, winced through the pain, and added with an ironic smile, 'Oops.'

Quincy had hunkered down beside them, an intent look on his face. 'Sal, are you sure you don't know what happened to your brother?'

'Thirty years later, yeah, my mom and me are pretty sure we know my brother's fate.'

'No,' said Quincy softly. 'I don't think that you do.'

Then, finally, blessedly, they all heard the wash of rotors beating overhead as the first of the choppers crested Blood Mountain.

Tense moments followed. The SWAT chopper trying to drop down a litter, then several armed guards, from lines overhead. Duff and the rest of them looking sharp as they sought to fend off an attack that could come from any direction.

Then, when it seemed that the shooter had forsaken his hunt, everyone rushing to get Harold onto the litter and off the mountain. Then waiting thirty minutes more for the next chopper, bearing a litter for Sal, who agreed only reluctantly to be strapped in. Kimberly was loaded up with him, an unspoken courtesy to a pregnant agent that left her feeling relieved and guilt-stricken all at once.

Her father and Rainie made the third chopper, as person by person, each federal agent and county law enforcement officer was plucked from the clearing and flown down to the command post.

Kimberly's first sight was Mac, standing on the perimeter, his face pale and concerned. Then, when he caught sight of her, a grin transformed his face, and even thirty yards away, she could feel the impact of that smile straight in her heart.

She looked down once at Sal, still strapped into the litter. He raised his hand in parting.

'Go to him,' he mouthed.

And she did. She ran without hesitation, leaping into her husband's arms, feeling his arms close around her and their baby, and he whispered in her ear that he loved her, and for the moment, at least, it was enough.

Night finally closed around them, and from far away came the sound of sirens as the ambulance whisked Harold away.

Rita made it to the kitchen. She was breathing hard, panting really, like a dog she'd once seen trying to pick itself off the road after being struck by a speeding truck. That animal had made it five feet before dropping dead.

She had to make it four more.

She had a target in mind. The telephone. She could claim a break-in, fire, rape, it didn't matter. If she could just knock the phone down and dial 911 . . . She was an old woman. They would come for her.

And maybe they could save the boy.

No noise above her. Just the occasional creak of an old floorboard, groaning under stealthy footsteps. The girl stalking, Rita figured, the boy tucked away someplace safe. She hoped he'd picked a good spot, one that would buy time.

She made it six painful inches, squirming on her belly, her good leg kicking her awkwardly forward, her injured side useless. She could feel the weight of the Colt digging into her thigh. At the rate she was going, she'd probably shoot herself. But her fingers had long since turned blue, deprived of blood by the girl's efficient bindings. Nothing she could do with the gun now.

So she wriggled, inch by inch, eye on the prize.

She'd just reached the edge of the kitchen counter, phone dangling tantalizing above her. If she could just find a chair, maybe prop herself up on her elbows, then whack at it with her bound hands . . .

'What the hell do you think you're doin'?' the male voice boomed behind her.

Rita startled, turning awkwardly toward the noise. She wanted to believe it was a neighbor coming to help her. She already figured she wasn't gonna get that lucky.

The man stood before her, holding a flashlight. And as he pushed up the brim of his red baseball cap, she spotted his forehead, covered with row after row of glowing yellow eyes.

FORTY-THREE

'Social spiders work together in construction teams to build enormous spider cities. [They] also feed in groups so that they can catch and share a larger prey.'

FROM *Freaky Facts About Spiders*,

BY CHRISTINE MORLEY, 2007

'You were standing next to Harold when the first shot was fired,' Quincy was saying to Sal. 'If Harold hadn't jumped to his feet, the bullet would've hit you, not him.'

Sal was sitting in the back of an ambulance, holding up the hem of his shirt as he grudgingly received treatment from an EMT. He'd already refused a ride to the hospital. Quincy, Rainie, Kimberly, and Mac remained with him, awaiting the EMT's official verdict as the young man inspected the damage.

Sal scowled at the man probing his side with a pair of tweezers. 'Ow!'

'Told ya you should go to the hospital,' the EMT said mildly and went back to work, tweezing fibers from the wound.

'Ginny said Dinchara wanted the envelopes of driver's licenses to be delivered specifically to you. Why you, Sal? Haven't you wondered about that?'

'Missing persons . . . it's my hobby. I already . . . said that.'

Kimberly's turn to frown at the GBI special agent. 'Dinchara targeted you because of your 'hobby'? Now who's being stubborn?'

'Makes about as much sense as leaving his trophies on the windshield of my car. Come on, guy really wants to bait me, there are easier ways to get things done.'

'Expediency isn't what drives serial killers,' Quincy said firmly. 'Their rituals are based on emotional need and are often quite elaborate. In this case, we have a man who in his everyday life feels powerless. His fantasy life, therefore, is all about being in control. He thrives on secrecy and manipulation. He is the spider, weaving a web to catch a prey. An approach like this – inciting your involvement by baiting a trap – would fill his emotional need, his image of himself as a superpredator, even if it is impractical at other levels. If you can understand the emotional drive, then you can catch the killer.'

'*You must kill the one you love*,' Kimberly murmured. She looked at Sal. 'Maybe, all these years later, he still loves you. And maybe, all these years later, he wants to graduate.'

Sal had finally stilled in the back of the ambulance. 'My brother is dead!' he said harshly, but they could tell from his voice that he was no longer sure.

With night blanketing the mountain, Rachel declared the crime scene off limits. They would not approach the summit again until a tactical unit had secured the area and placed snipers for ongoing protection. The team should rest. Rachel was off to the hospital; she'd phone the moment she had news on Harold.

Quincy and Rainie retired to the hotel for another night. Mac and Kimberly offered Sal a ride as he was obviously in no shape to drive. Sal climbed into the back behind Kimberly. He sat in silence, his side covered in white gauze, his bloody shirt untucked at his waist.

Every law enforcement agent in the country had now been notified with the few vital statistics they knew about Dinchara. His actions had earned him immediate placement in the FBI's top ten most wanted list, and even now the powers that be were preparing a press release for the major news networks.

By morning, Dahlonega and the surrounding area would be swarming with every state officer and National Guard unit available. If today had been a horror movie, then tomorrow would be a circus. Times like this, Kimberly simply hoped no one would get hurt.

Personally, Kimberly doubted Dinchara would try to flee the country. She pictured him more as an Eric Rudolph sort – the Olympic Park bomber who had holed up for five years in the Great Smoky Mountains, living on a diet of wild game and acorns. By all accounts, Dinchara had the same outdoor expertise and loner instincts.

Plus, there was still Ginny Jones and the missing boy to consider. Which made her wonder . . .

Her cell phone rang. She glanced at the screen, registered the local number, flipped it open. 'Special Agent Quincy.'

'Deputy Roy here. We spoke earlier regarding the Jones girl.'

'Oh yes. The Jones girl your department managed to release even after she was an accessory in the attempted murder of a federal agent. I remember.'

Roy chuckled. 'Thought you would. Now, technically speaking, it's the judge you should yell at—'

'I mean to get to that the first moment I'm back in town.'

'I'm sure you will. Listen, Rick and I feel real bad about how that all worked out, especially given what happened on Blood Mountain.'

'Especially.'

'So we did some thinking, and it occurred to Rick that he saw Ginny Jones hugging the man standing next to a vehicle. So he went to the courthouse this afternoon and collected the security video of the parking lot.'

'Yes?'

'And sure enough, the man walks away, but you can see

Ginny get into the vehicle. It's a blue Nissan hatchback, with Georgia plates reading . . .'

Kimberly grabbed a pen, frantically writing down the information. 'Nice work, Officers!'

' 'Course we're issuing an APB, as well. But thought you'd like to hear the news directly. We do more than eat fried okra and shoot possums round here, you know.'

'You shoot possums?'

'Never mind.'

'Thank you. I mean that, Officer. Thank you very much.'

Kimberly hung up the phone. She regarded Mac, then Sal in the rearview mirror.

'Hey,' she said. 'I have an idea.'

'We've been operating under the assumption that the younger child didn't accompany Dinchara and Aaron on the hikes, correct?' Kimberly was explaining excitedly, as she directed Mac to Dinchara's old neighborhood. 'Based mostly on the waitress from the Smith House saying that she only ever saw Dinchara with a teenager. Also, a young boy would slow them down when packing supplies up a trail that steep.'

'Okay,' Mac agreed, though it was his first time hearing any of this.

'Well, what if he didn't leave the boy alone? What if Dinchara had a babysitter to watch the kid? Someone he trusted to ensure the kid didn't run away?'

'Like Ginny Jones,' Sal filled in from the back.

'Exactly! And maybe that's why he was willing to spend ten grand springing Ginny from county jail. Because he wanted to come after us – or really, you, Sal – meaning he needed someone to take over childcare.'

'I can follow that logic right up to the moment we turn into his old neighborhood,' Mac murmured, following the direction of Kimberly's pointing finger onto the rolling rural road of said neighborhood.

'All the way up at the top of the hill,' she instructed him. ' 'Bout three miles in, last home on the right.'

'Or look for the big pile of smoking rubble,' Mac filled in drily. 'Which would be my point: You said the home burned to the ground. So the kid can't be there.'

'No, but according to the neighbors, neither was Ginny Jones. None of them reported seeing a girl at the house, but she obviously spent a lot of time with Aaron and Dinchara. Which makes me wonder. What if she has a home locally, too?'

'But she works in Sandy Springs,' Sal protested. 'We saw her apartment.'

'A cheap one-bedroom,' Kimberly granted, 'convenient for the nights she works as a prostitute. But remember what Ginny said – Dinchara's other line of work is Internet porn, and she and Aaron both filmed movies for him. So there must be times she's up here, assisting with that business. So why haven't any of the neighbors seen her? We know she hangs out with Aaron, we believe she babysits the younger kid. She's gotta have her own place. It's the only answer. Someplace close would be my guess. Where Dinchara could keep an eye on her. Such as right there. STOP. Wait. Next driveway, then stop.'

Mac lurched the car forward another two hundred yards, to the next property, then pulled over. 'What are we looking for?'

'Blue Nissan hatchback. Like the one sitting outside that house with the big covered porch. Ladies and gentlemen, I believe we have found Ginny Jones.'

By mutual agreement, Kimberly would wait in the car. Mac and Sal would proceed. She would call for backup. She could tell her very note of cheerful acceptance had Mac suspicious. He kissed her, hard. She grabbed his shoulders and kissed him back.

Sal turned away.

Then Mac and Sal were at the trunk, opening Mac's locker of supplies, including bulletproof vests, a shotgun, extra ammo.

Kimberly got on the radio, advising Dispatch that they had discovered a vehicle that matched an active APB and were now proceeding with caution. Backup requested, please proceed with discretion. No lights, no sirens. With any luck, Mac and Sal could lure Ginny out, and it would all be over before it even started. They'd arrest the girl, save the child. After the day they'd had, they could use a happy ending.

The men drifted down the street and, soon enough, were swallowed by the gloom.

The man flipped Rita onto her back. She cried out as the motion aggravated her hurt hip. For her troubles, he slapped her. He was tough, this one. Better than the girl. He went through the bulky rolls of her clothes, quickly finding the Colt and yanking it from the waist of her pants.

He straightened, his teeth a flash of white against the shadows. 'Arming yourself against me or the boy? Bet you don't know just how much trouble that kid is. Why, the things that boy has already done . . .'

He chuckled to himself, as if privy to a joke she'd never understand. Then he lifted her bodily off the floor and stuffed her roughly into sitting position in one of the kitchen chairs. She bit her lip this time to keep from screaming, but the fresh wave of pain made the world spin. She thought she might black out.

He must've thought she would, too, because he slapped her again, and that jerked her to attention. She thought she saw a faint movement behind him. A shadow flickering along the wall.

Joseph, she prayed in her mind. *Please, Joseph, if there was ever a time to cause a stir . . .*

Except the shadow turned into a solid form. The girl, coming down the stairs, dragging the boy behind her.

' 'Bout time you got here,' the girl said. She shoved the boy forward. He stumbled, then fell at the man's feet. His cheeks were covered with bright red marks, some already dewed with blood.

He had not gone without a fight; the girl's arms bore similar scratches, though she now held his knife in her fist.

'Found him in the attic,' the girl reported. 'Stupid little shit.'

The man reached down, grabbed the boy by the scruff of the neck, and jerked his head back, until the boy was forced to look him in the eye.

'What'd I tell you, boy? No such thing as gettin' away. You belong to me.'

The boy didn't say anything. His face had closed up, shut down. Rita could tell he was sinking somewhere deep inside himself. Saving what little bit of himself he could.

The man seemed to know it, too. 'Well, boy, you know what's gotta happen.'

The boy didn't talk, didn't move.

'You disobeyed me. Now you gotta be punished.'

'Can I do it?' the girl asked immediately.

'Shut the fuck up. Don't you think you've caused me enough headache for one day?'

The girl shut up.

The man was regarding the boy. Rita was waiting for him to do something violent. Strike out with his fist, lash out with his leg. Instead, the man started looking around the room. Then his gaze fell on the Colt pistol, sitting on the kitchen table.

He picked it up. 'Boy,' he said. 'Come here.'

The boy obediently rose to his feet, stepped forward.

The man pointed to Rita, where she sat, bound and pain-crazed on the hard wooden chair.

'You brought this on yourself, boy. I told you there could be no outsiders. I told you what would happen if you ever asked for help. Do you remember what I said?'

357

The boy's gaze dropped down. With a crack, the man open-handed him across the face. 'Look at me when I'm talking to you, boy! Do you remember what I said? DO YOU REMEMBER?'

'Yes, sir,' the boy whispered.

'I didn't lie, boy. I never lie.' Then the man turned and pointed the pistol at Rita's forehead.

'Tell her goodbye.'

'Goodbye,' the boy whispered.

And just as Rita closed her eyes, just as she braced herself for the impact of the bullet shattering her temple, the cracking sound happened again, and she opened her eyes to discover the man had struck the boy, this time so hard the boy had fallen to the floor.

'DO YOU THINK I'D LET YOU GET OFF THAT EASY? DO YOU THINK I'M THAT NICE? OR DO YOU THINK I'M THAT STUPID?'

'No, no, no,' the boy whispered, begged, pleaded.

'GET TO YOUR FEET, BOY.'

The boy rose.

'TAKE THIS PISTOL, BOY.'

The boy obediently reached for the Colt.

'NOW SHOOT THAT BITCH!'

The boy turned and pointed the gun at Rita.

She didn't close her eyes this time. She wanted him to see her face. She wanted him to know that she forgave him.

Behind him, a cupboard door suddenly opened.

The man whirled, looked around. 'Who goes there?'

Joseph, Rita prayed in her mind. *Please, Joseph*.

A drawer rattled, cracked open.

'What the fuck?'

Then the pans were shaking in the cabinet, the teakettle sliding across the stove, the faucet cranking water. The man stood in the middle of the kitchen; he screamed at Rita at the top of his lungs. 'Who the hell is doing that?'

It came to her, maybe just the memory of what the girl

had said, or maybe with Joseph's help. She said, 'The Burgerman says hi.'

The man started to roar.

The boy pulled the trigger.

At the front of the house, Mac and Sal crept up the steps. They approached the door, hunkered low to keep out of sight of the windows. They came up on either side of the glass panes, did a quick inspection, then returned to their positions of backs pressed against the exterior walls.

'Windows are covered,' Mac whispered.

Across from him, Sal nodded. 'Guess Ginny doesn't want her neighbors seeing in.'

Mac leaned forward, tested the knob, found that it turned.

'Open,' he mouthed.

Sal arched a brow at that piece of luck, then shrugged. 'All right, let's do it.'

Mac had just twisted the knob when they heard a booming scream, followed immediately by a gunshot.

Sal had his radio out, rattling off the address. 'Shots fired, shots fired. Requesting immediate backup. All units to assist . . .'

Then he and Mac ducked low and rushed into the parlor. 'This is the police. Drop your weapons!'

Kimberly was just leaning forward to adjust the radio volume when a knock at her window jerked her upright. She was already reaching for her shoulder harness when her eyes registered the curler-capped face outside the car window. It was the neighbor woman from last night, or maybe that was this morning. The one she and Sal had talked to while watching Dinchara's house burn.

Kimberly popped open the door, got out.

'You're the police, right?' the woman was asking, clearly agitated.

'Can I help you?'

'Something's wrong at the house next door. I just happened to look out my bedroom window and notice the light on in the attic. Someone had taped something to one of the windows. It looks like nine-one-one.'

Kimberly jerked her head toward the structure in question. 'You mean that house, where the girl lives?'

The neighbor frowned at her. 'Girl? Rita's no girl. Hell, she's ninety if she's a day. Her family has owned that house for generations.'

Kimberly's turn to be confused. 'I thought you meant the house next door, the one with the big, wraparound covered patio . . .'

'That's the one.'

'No girl lives there?'

'Not that I know of.'

'Does . . . does a girl visit sometimes?'

'No. Least not that I've seen. Though a man showed up about twenty minutes ago. Wearing a red baseball cap.'

The man felt pain first. That surprised him. It had been so long since he had felt anything connected with his own body, he had assumed his nerve endings were done, used up, burnt out. His skin was nothing more than an exoskeleton and he liked it that way.

But his side felt like it had caught on fire. He grabbed at it, startled to feel more pain, then encountered the shocking wetness of his own blood.

He turned to the boy. The kid pulled the trigger again.

This bullet caught him up high, in the shoulder. He twisted back, still standing, and heard another *boom,* felt another searing pain, and then heard another *boom* and another one.

His legs buckled. He slowly sank to the ground, staring at the gray pall of the ceiling. Was it his imagination, or were the shadows moving up there? He thought he saw the Burgerman's face, and he whimpered.

The girl was screaming. Why was the stupid girl screaming if he was the one who'd been shot? He wished she would shut up. He wanted everyone to shut up. The girl, the gun, the terrible violence seeping into his brain.

And then he heard fresh yells, this time deep and authoritative. 'Police, police. Hands up. Drop your weapon.'

The girl was screaming again, the old woman telling the boy, 'Put it down, child. It's okay, just put it down.'

He could feel his blood seeping out of him, into the floor. He could feel himself dying and he ought to know, as he'd seen it enough times. The way that first boy's body had sagged, then collapsed all those years ago. And the girls, one by one, their blood running from their veins down the bathtub drain as he watched excitedly, until the last drop was gone and they became nothing more than limp dolls, and he suddenly went from feeling so powerful to being nothing but an overgrown kid, playing with oversize toys. Until he kidnapped the next one, of course. And the one after that.

The girl had the gun now. He knew because the police were yelling at her, and the old woman was telling the boy to duck, duck, duck. The girl was trouble. He'd always known that. It was why he could never quite bring himself to kill her. Because she was trouble and the thrill was always bigger when he could force her into line.

Maybe she would shoot him, too. She would like that.

He wondered about the baby. His? Aaron's? Another man's? And he thought, in these last few seconds he had left, that he was glad he was dying. Before he ever saw the baby. Before he ruined its life.

Then a window suddenly shattered in the back of the kitchen. From the corner of his eye, he saw the girl turn to counter this fresh attack. A shape flew across the space, caught the girl at the knees, and crashed her to the ground.

A moment later, a bloodstained detective rose from the floor, the Colt in his hand.

'Brother,' the man whispered.

And Sal finally looked him in the eyes.

Kimberly couldn't climb through the window. Instead, she had to wait until Mac moved the armoire and opened the back door. She had raced around the house, seeing the lone beam of flashlight on the kitchen, and had heard enough to understand what was going on. She'd aimed the rock in Ginny's direction and prayed the distraction would be enough for Sal and Mac to seize control.

Now, as Mac flipped on the overhead light, she spied an old woman, hunched, panting in pain, confined to a kitchen chair, while a young boy with a blank expression knelt at her feet. Ginny Jones was on her stomach five feet away, hands cuffed, feet bound.

And Sal was bent over the body of a man sprawled in blood on the floor.

'Vincent,' Sal murmured. 'Vinny.'

He touched the man's face, his fingers so gentle it hurt to watch.

'I'm sorry,' Sal whispered. 'I'm sorry, I'm sorry, I'm sorry.'

'Saw you . . . that day.'

'I'm sorry.'

'Wanted . . . to see Mom. Come . . . home. Saw you.'

'Shhh . . . shhh . . . shhh.'

'Good . . . son. In your uniform. Not me. You were right . . . about the Burgerman . . . Grinding naughty boys to dust.'

'Shhh . . . shhh . . . shhh.'

'Not strong . . . not like you. Hurt. Tired. Very tired.'

'It's all right now. I'm here, Vinny, I'm here.'

'Azalea bush. Must find . . . azalea bush.'

'It's okay. Everything's going to be okay.'

'I wish,' the man gasped. 'I wish.'

The man died. Sal cradled his brother's body in his arms, and wept.

EPILOGUE

It took eight days to remove all the bodies from Blood Mountain. Each corpse was carefully lowered onto a clean sheet, then wrapped up and carted down the mountain in a specially prepared litter. A team of forensic anthropologists came in to handle the load, setting up shop in the county morgue, where they could murmur at the wonderful condition of the mummified remains. Not many bodies were found after long-term exposure hanging in the woods. The potential for case studies was staggering.

Family members of missing girls were notified of the proper process for submitting DNA samples to match against the remains. A database was built. Testing began. People could expect to wait six to nine months for results.

Ginny Jones submitted DNA, claiming to want to identify her mother's remains. Kimberly wasn't sure the girl would. How much had Ginny cared about her mother's death? It certainly hadn't stopped her from forming a twisted alliance with a twisted man.

The state prosecutor charged Ginny with six counts of accessory to felony murder. He contended that Ginny had knowingly lured fellow prostitutes to their death, while also aiding and abetting in the abduction of a seven-year-old boy, Joshua Ferris, aka Scott.

Ginny had countered with the victim card. She had been kidnapped by Dinchara, raped, brutalized, tortured. At a certain point, she had to help him, it was the only way she could survive. Just listen to the tapes, the endless tapes of all that he had done, including to her mother.

Interestingly enough, the only recording that survived was the one Kimberly had made from Aaron's first anonymous phone call. Everything else appeared to have been destroyed in the fire at Dinchara's residence. But the bodies remained, the thin, mummified forms testifying louder than words to just what one man had been able to do.

Sal had taken a leave of absence from work. Kimberly had called him twice. He never returned those calls. She heard through the grapevine that he was spending a great deal of time with his mother. The initial public outcry had been so great, with sensational details of the murder spree screaming across every headline, he and his mother had had to go into seclusion.

According to the rumor mill, Sal had filed papers requiring DNA testing of Ginny's baby. If the child was Dinchara's, Sal and his mother planned on asking for sole custody.

Kimberly wondered if it would be enough for them, or if they would simply lie awake, night after night, waiting for something terrible to happen down the hall.

Life went on. Harold recovered from his wound, returned to work with a medal from the governor and enormous fanfare. When Kimberly's ERT presented him with his very own pair of custom-fit Limmer boots, he blushed like a schoolboy. And Rachel hugged him so hard the betting pool was already taking odds on a wedding date.

While Kimberly grew fat. Enormously, couldn't-see-her-toes fat. True to her prediction, Mac had to tie her shoes for her. Which didn't happen so much anymore, as she was officially on a leave of absence. With two weeks until her due date, she had to set up a nursery in their apartment in Savannah while Mac worked long hours in his new position, trying to get up to speed before the baby was born.

So Kimberly fussed over gingham ruffles and teddy bear stencils and all the stuff a woman like her had once sworn was foolish, but now had become the center of her entire being. She ironed curtains, dusted the ceiling fans, and washed the top of the refrigerator. Then she purchased a medicine cabinet and demanded Mac install it that very night, because there was no way she was giving birth with their minor collection of pharmaceuticals still housed in a baby-accessible bathroom drawer.

Sometimes, when she was not nesting with the frantic compulsiveness of a nine-months-pregnant woman, random thoughts would pop into her head. She might discover a garden spider and spend the next hour thinking of Dinchara, the boy he had once been and the man he had become. And she would remember Aaron and that last look on his face before he pulled the trigger.

Aaron turned out to be Randy Cooper. He had been kidnapped walking home from school in Decatur ten years earlier. His family had claimed his body, his twenty-two-year-old sister, Sarah, now at Harvard Law, returning for the funeral. Sarah had thanked the small gathering of neighbors and law enforcement officers on behalf of her family. They were grateful for the closure the funeral allowed. They understood they were fortunate to have this moment, as so many families didn't. And they would choose today, and all days, to remember Randy as the laughing, happy boy they had known, and not the victim he had become.

Kimberly wondered if Sal was struggling to make the same choice. Each day, every day. How best to know his brother.

Kimberly installed additional locks on every bedroom window. She ordered a home security system complete with a panic alarm. She purchased a video baby monitor so she could see at all times what was happening in her baby's room.

And maybe it was panicky and neurotic. But maybe this was what a woman who worked in crime and had already buried two members of her family needed to do. Mac didn't question her. He let her do what she did, and when she could bring herself to speak, of both her consuming fear and her tentative hope, he made the time to listen.

One week before her due date, Kimberly went into labor. With Mac by her side, and Rainie and Quincy flying in, she gave birth to a little girl, Elizabeth Amanda McCormack.

Three days later, she and Mac brought their little girl home. Mac took a couple of weeks off from work and they happily spent their time changing impossibly small diapers and marveling over ten perfect fingers and ten perfect toes. After much debate, they determined that little Eliza had Mac's dark hair, but Kimberly's pointed face. Obviously she possessed her mother's intelligence, as well as her father's strength. As for the temper tantrums, they both considered the other one guilty of providing that DNA.

Mac returned to work. Kimberly stayed at home and discovered . . . she was okay. Nursing and tending and fussing was not the death sentence she had feared, but rather a new set of challenges to explore. She could handle it for a bit. Six months, she thought. Maybe a year. That sounded about right.

So she took her time. She held her daughter close. She took her for walks to the park. She got up every three hours and rocked her baby girl in the middle of the night.

And during those months, little Eliza snuggled against her breast, Kimberly thought that while life may not be perfect, at least it offered moments that were perfect enough.

'I love you, Eliza,' she promised and smiled as she listened to her infant daughter snore.

Strawberry is my favorite flavor of ice cream.
   My mom told me as she dished it up for me the first

night I came home. I nodded as if I remembered, then ate the whole bowl, wishing it were chocolate.

Life will return to normal. That's what everyone says. I'm lucky. I'm a survivor. Something bad happened, but now, Life Will Return to Normal.

I'm like Pinocchio, waiting to wake up one morning and discover I'm a real boy.

In the meantime, I pretend to sleep on top of my bed, instead of huddled underneath, where I can see people enter my room without anyone seeing me. I pretend I don't notice that my parents never leave me alone with my little sister. I pretend I don't hear my mother crying every night down the hall.

Life Will Return to Normal.

But I don't think I ever will.

Some days, when it's really bad, my dad drives me the two hours to Rita's house. I chop wood, pull weeds, mow her lawn. She can't move too well due to her hip, so she can always use the help. Better yet, she never asks me anything. She gives me chores, barks at me to move. Rita is always Rita and maybe she isn't normal, either, and I like that.

Sometimes, when I'm whacking away at dandelions, I find that I am talking, things are pouring out. So I work harder and talk faster and Rita hands me more lemonade and it's okay when Rita's there. When Rita's there, I feel safe.

Sometimes, my dad returns while I'm still ranting. So he'll chop wood and pull weeds and paint spindles and I daresay Rita has the best-looking house on the block. It's the least she deserves, you know. I wish I could stay with her always.

But sooner or later, gotta go home. Life Will Return to Normal.

I don't sleep. I see things behind my closed eyelids I don't think other boys see. I know things I don't think other boys know. Can't imagine going to school. Can't imagine hanging out with my old friends.

I play dolls with my baby sister. I do whatever she tells me to do. I think of it as practice. Sooner or later, I'll know how to be a six-year-old girl. Seems a lot better idea than being me.

My mom takes me to a therapist. I draw pictures of rainbows and flowers and he gazes at me with deep disappointment. So I draw birdies and kittycats. Goldfish and unicorns. I tell Rita about it later and she laughs, but I can tell she's concerned.

Sometimes, on the really bad days, we simply rock on the front porch and she holds my hand.

'You are strong, child,' she tells me. 'You're tough and smart and capable. Don't let him take that from you. Don't give him that.'

I promise Rita I won't and we both forgive the lie.

Rita lived to be ninety-five years old. She died in January. I came over that Saturday and found her sitting in the front parlor, one arm in her mother's old coat. Joseph was sitting beside her. It was the first time I ever saw him. Moment I opened the door, he looked up at me, smiled, and disappeared.

I didn't cry at the funeral. Rita's was a good death. Peaceful. It gave me my first glimmer of hope. Someday, I want to die like that, sitting on my sofa, just waiting to get out the door.

I like to think Rita is running around with Joseph now, looping around the old apple tree. I like to think she's watching over me.

I didn't make it in public school. I tried to be a real boy, but you know, I'm not. 'Nother kid started picking on me. Called me a faggot. Told everyone I liked sucking dick. Then made slurping sounds every time I walked down the halls.

Kid was big and brawny. I'm too small to take on someone his size and he knew it.

I told my father about it. He raised holy hell. The kid was suspended. That bought me five days of peace from one kid, and a pack of trouble from a whole lot more. Soon the entire school was making sucking sounds every time I entered the cafeteria.

Kids don't like me. I know that. They look at me, they wonder what happened. They wonder if it will happen to them.

I frighten them and no adult is ever gonna change that.

I go to a private school now. Small class size. Lots of authority figures around to keep us all in line. I don't bother to make friends. I just get through the day. That's the one thing I'm good at, getting through.

My sister loves me. She's the only person in the world who hugs me without pausing first, wondering if she should. She throws her arms right around me. 'Joshi,' she'll cry, 'Joshi's home,' and some days, I think I survived everything just to hear her say that.

I get moments. Not a lot of them, but still. There are times it's almost okay to be me. So I cling to that, 'cause I gotta cling to something. I gotta try to be something, or Rita's right: He's won. Even from beyond the grave, he's taken me from me. I won't have that. I won't.

I killed him once. I'll be damned if he doesn't stay dead.

Then one night, I had a revelation. I couldn't sleep. My head was crazy with blood. I hated my clothes, my room, the feel of carpet against my skin. I hated the walls of the house and the window that stared at me like a blind eye.

I hated my mom and my dad, who kept studying me and studying me like at any time now, I oughtta be fixed, when if they'd done their job right I never would've gotten broken.

So I went to the kitchen for matches. Except halfway there, in the middle of the living room, I saw it. The computer.

I remembered things. Things I'd never told the police.

I took a seat.

It didn't take long for me to find them. Or really, to make them think they had found me. I sat at the keyboard *for three hours, walking the walk, talking the talk. I know how these men think.*

At five a.m., I heard my father get up to pee, so I turned off the computer, crept back to my room, and crashed on top of my bed. When I woke up again, I knew what I was going to do.

I took a couple of classes. Did a little research and that took care of the rest.

I go on three nights a week now, always after midnight. And I go hunting.

Special Agent Salvatore Martignetti. He's back with the GBI now, working some drug task force. I can find quotes of him discussing latest arrests, moments of triumph. I can find his picture, dark face, sunken eyes. Sometimes, if the pose is just right, he looks so much like Dinchara, I want to put my fist through the computer screen. But I don't.

Special Agent Kimberly Quincy. She's back to work, though her assignments are harder to track, the FBI being savvier about these things. So I found her daughter instead. Little Eliza Quincy McCormack, enrolled in the local Montessori preschool. The entire school roster is available online. The page is marked parents only, *but it only took me three tries to guess the password – the initials of the head schoolmistress. Amazing how many organizations think they're being 'safe' when really they're just amusing guys like me.*

Ginny Jones. She's at the state prison, serving the last of her twelve-year sentence. Jurors are suckers for young, pregnant victims and only found her guilty on accessory to kidnapping. I don't know where the baby went, but give me some time, I'll figure it out. In the meantime, Ginny's been sleeping with enough prison guards to earn herself computer privileges. So I set myself up as her latest e-mail buddy. She can't wait to meet me one day. Trust me, the feeling's mutual.

I'm patient, careful, observant.

Just a spider on the wall, you know, slowly spinning my web.

After checking on my past associates, I move on to the evening's real event. I hit the sites, the blogs, the chat rooms. I make new 'friends' and I tell these men everything I know how to do. I promise them action. I promise them live footage. All I need is a little info first. And once I have it, I strike.

I empty their bank accounts. I max out their credit cards, then take out new ones in their names. I set up second mortgages on e-banks and issue lines of credit. I become them, cyber identity theft. And I transfer all their money to the Center for Missing and Exploited Children. Thousands of dollars, tens of thousands of dollars, hundreds of thousands of dollars. I take everything; it's the least they deserve.

They could complain, of course. All they'd have to do is turn over their financial records – including their online activities – to their wives, their business partners, the police.

I wonder what it feels like, when they finally realize what's going on. That those credit card charges are not a mistake. That those e-mails from their PayPal accounts warning them of unusual activity aren't phishing. That their checking account really is empty, and that new line of credit, already maxed out.

I wonder what it feels like when they realize there is nothing they can do. That their home is going to be foreclosed on, their brand-new car seized. That their bank accounts are frozen, their credit cards capped, and their online activities . . . hey, nobody's gonna let a broke schmuck download kiddy porn.

I wonder what it feels like when they realize that they are finished, washed up, done. When they realize they are going to live the rest of their lives a specimen in the collection.

ACKNOWLEDGMENTS

It takes a lot of people to write a book. First, there is my cute and adorable daughter. She helped inspire the book, mostly by becoming obsessed with spiders. Her newfound interest was kindled by neighbors Pam and Glenda, who gave her a set of fun-colored spider lights, then stoked by Paul and Lynda, who presented her with a tarantula roughly the size of a terrier. My daughter immediately declared the tarantula to be the mommy spider and set her up in our formal living room.

Once you've started living with a dog-size tarantula, a suspense novel is bound to follow.

Then there is fellow writer Sheila Connolly, who, upon hearing that I was working on a book involving spiders, offered her husband, an entomologist, to assist. Dave Williams is the kind of guy who once kept a black widow as a pet, so he was extraordinarily helpful. He not only sent me photos of brown recluse spider bites, but helped me track down an excellent article on body decomposition in outdoor hanging cases. Not everyone appreciates these things, but I learned a lot. Thanks, Dave!

Then there is my dear friend Don Taylor, who was so taken with my daughter's hobby that he sent her several books on arachnids. We both loved the novels, though after reading Doreen Cronin's *Diary of a Spider*, my daughter is also now into flies and worms. Thanks, Don!

Next up is dear friend Lisa Mac. I was bogged down one night trying to research on the Internet unusual ways to hide bodies (note to readers: search term 'good ways to dispose of bodies' leads to some scary chat rooms). When I called Lisa to let her know I was running late, she literally screeched into the phone, 'Stop, I have the perfect idea. I'll be right there.' You know what, Lisa? You were right.

Then I must thank longtime friend and associate Dr. Greg Moffatt. When I mentioned I needed to come to Georgia to research a novel, he and his family rolled out the welcome mat. Now, most hosts will show you around town, but how many will take you crime-scene shopping on Blood Mountain? Once again, Greg, you went above and beyond the call of duty. Thank you for a wonderful, if slightly different, Georgia tour.

I must also thank Supervisory Special Agent Stephen Emmett of the Atlanta FBI for helping me understand the Atlanta field office; Special Agent Paul Delacourt, who updated me on the post-9/11 bureau, and better yet, mentioned that the ERTs would be a perfect extracurricular for Kimberly; and finally Special Agent Roslyn B. Harris, senior team leader of the Atlanta Division Evidence Response Team, and Supervisory Special Agent Rob Coble who then graciously agreed to answer my multitude of questions regarding ERTs and the use of the Total Station. Of course all mistakes are mine and mine alone.

Forensic anthropologist Lee Jantz, from the University of Tennessee's famed Body Farm, kindly walked me through the basics of an outdoor search and body recovery. Thank you also, Lee, for your research into fabric decomp and other little tidbits that I hope created one really creepy scene. Again, all mistakes – and fictional license! – are mine and mine alone.

Under care and feeding of authors: Thank you to my brilliant editor, Kate Miciak, and the entire Bantam

373

publishing team, who make the real magic happen; to Meg Ruley and the entire Jane Rotrosen Agency team, who understand neurotic authors and, through their hard work, actually allow us to be slightly less neurotic; to Michael Carr, my first reader whose laserlike analytics shredded the original draft, left me cranky beyond words, and, of course, helped create a better novel (in return, I'm taking his wife to a spa and leaving him alone with four kids, hah!); to Kevin Breenky and the other nice folks at Jif for the care packages, kind notes, and shared smiles. To John and Genn from the J-Town Deli, whose daily supply of raspberry yum-yums kept me cranking through the late afternoons; to Larry and Leslie of the Thompson House Eatery, who graciously opened up their home for the book jacket photo shoot and, even better, fed us lunch. And to Brandi and Sarah for all the reasons they know best.

Finally, I owe a huge thanks to my husband. For years, I have praised the rich, chocolaty confections he has showered upon me during the final crush of deadline. This time, my husband went one better: He got me an out-of-the-house office. I told him he was nuts. Work is work, doesn't matter where you do it. I am happy to report that in this case, the office made all the difference. So here you go, love, the three words all husbands would like to see in print: You were right!

(We will now resume our normal operating system.)

I hope Kathy Ransom, winner of the fourth annual Kill a Friend, Maim a Buddy Sweepstakes, enjoys seeing her daughter, Nicole Evans, immortalized as a Lucky Stiff. Likewise, I hope Beth Hunnicutt, winner of the *Oregonian*'s 'Why I Should Be a Corpse in Lisa Gardner's Next Novel,' finds satisfaction in her fictional death, given the genuine trials she's survived in real life. And finally, thank you to Lynn Stoudt, whose generous donation to the Gwinnett County Library entitled her to be a character in this novel (one of my first living entries!).

For those of you wishing you could get in on the action, don't worry: The annual Kill a Friend, Maim a Buddy Sweepstakes kicks off every September at www.lisagardner.com. Check it out and maybe in my next novel, you too can meet a grand end.

In closing, I would like to dedicate this novel to Jackie Sparks and the other staff members of Children Unlimited, Inc. Of all the novels I've written, this book is by far the most violent, and yes, it was difficult to write. I would like to tell you that the Burgerman is fictionalized, that his actions are nothing more than the warped product of my twisted imagination. Sadly, most of the information in those scenes came from true cases. The Burgermans of the world are real, and the damage they do is heartbreaking.

Which is why I am so grateful to the everyday heroes among us. People like Jackie, who, through early intervention services, child advocacy, and other programs, have dedicated their lives to helping kids. They provide the support, nurturing, and therapeutic services necessary for young lives to recover. They provide a voice for children whose fears often can't be spoken.

Thank you, Jackie, for fighting the good fight. And thank you to all the early intervention services providers and child advocates out there, who understand that every child should be able to feel safe, valued, and loved.

Sincerely,
Lisa Gardner

Postscript
January 30, 2008
I started researching *Say Goodbye* in the fall of 2006, completing work on the manuscript in August 2007. Like most authors, I was grateful to finally complete a year-long project, and closed up my files without a backwards glance. Thus, I was dismayed to turn on the news the first week in January 2008 and hear that a young woman,

Meredith Emerson, had gone missing while hiking Blood Mountain. Sadly, her body was discovered days later, a tragic end to a very promising life. I hope readers will understand that the fictional scenes portrayed in *Say Goodbye* were never intended to mimic any real world homicides, or exploit a genuine tragedy. My heart goes out to Meredith Emerson's friends, family and community, now left to pick up the pieces.